No S[illegible]

Of Mine

J.J. CARLIN

Michael Terence
Publishing

First published in paperback by
Michael Terence Publishing in 2019
http://mtp. Agency

ISBN 9781913289034

Dedicated to Linda…

To Margaret.

Love & Fond memories

1

Bran lay back and closed his eyes, a soft gasp escaped his lips as he felt the warm breath move down the taut muscles of his belly; soft wisps of blonde hair touched his skin sending shocks of pleasure to electrify his already heightened senses. He slid his hands across the dark blue satin sheet until he found the soft, warm skin of his lover. Entwining his fingers in the long, silky locks, he groaned softly, moans of pure pleasure escaped his lips as he enjoyed the sensual foreplay of his experienced partner. Bran arched his back as soft fingers gently caressed him, driving his senses to levels beyond pleasure; beyond desire. He gave another shuddering moan as the hot mouth descended, spiralling his inflamed senses almost beyond control!

"For Christ's sake, stop fuckin' about," he gasped.

There was a soft laugh as two strong hands grasped his shoulders and rolled him over, so he was lying face down on the satin sheet. He trembled with anticipation, burrowed his face deep into the blue satin pillow to muffle the cry of pleasure and pain as his lover took him once again. Jason gently kissed Bran's shoulders and brushed the sweat damp hair from the nape of his neck. Bran shivered involuntarily as another thrust of Jason's hips elevated the pleasure of their lovemaking to another level; gradually, Jason's slow rhythmic movements built in intensity, his gasping breath echoed Bran's gasps of pleasure. Their mutual need for release building to a crescendo that exploded with an intensity that left them both spent and exhausted.

Jason lifted the weight of his body from Bran and collapsed, exhausted at the side of his lover.

"God! You're one hell of a bloody good screw!"

Bran rolled onto his back and stretched luxuriously, putting his hands behind his head.

"Wish I had more opportunities to get over here to see you Jay," he said as he rubbed his back sensuously against the satin sheet, enjoying the smooth feel of the silky fabric.

"Not too often," Jason laughed, "I'd be permanently fuckin' knackered!" he propped himself on one elbow and studied the man who shared his bed, "God! He was so bloody good looking."

Six foot two, his muscled body and lean hips were a testament to his regular workouts at the gym. The dark brown smouldering eyes that sparkled when he smiled were edged by long dark lashes and shaded by shapely eyebrows.

The sensual, pouting lips parted to reveal perfect white teeth and the shock of dark brown hair framed the handsome face that had the same natural tan as the rest of his body. The body that Jason knew only too well, the body that was so temptingly good to touch. He leant over and ran his hand gently down Bran's ribs.

Bran smiled and, reaching up, pushed his fingers through the shoulder length honey blonde hair, pulling Jason's head down till their lips met and parted, his tongue explored the sweet recesses of that soft, provocative mouth. The kiss was long and sensual and Jason's hands were gentle as they slid across his shoulders, fingers as light as a whisper as he massaged Bran's neck and slowly pushed through the thick mop of dark hair as he enjoyed the gentle intimacy of his lover's kiss, such a stark contrast to their energetic lovemaking a few moments earlier.

Bran opened his eyes and looked up into the ice blue eyes that gazed down from his lover's face, grinning as he realised that Jason had an erection yet again.

Jason saw the grin and followed Bran's gaze, laughing, he rolled onto his back,

"Bastard!"

"I'm going to have to go, Jason," Bran said reluctantly as he swung his legs over the edge of the bed, "I'm working tonight; the old man will be pissed if I'm late!"

Jason watched as Bran stood and stretched, He looked like a Greek God, standing naked in the soft light. Jason still couldn't believe his luck, finding someone as perfect as Bran from a chance encounter during a taxi journey. He remembered that night vividly, it had been raining, not one of those heavy abrupt downpours that came and went in a few minutes but a soft; misty rain; sticky rain. Rain that hung like a grey curtain and seemed to stretch endlessly across a bleak Liverpool sky.

It was the end of the semester and Jason had needed to move some of his artwork from the university to the flat.

The taxi had seemed expensive, but he didn't want to ruin months of work by allowing it to get wet. He remembered standing at the back door of the University art complex as the hire car pulled up waiting as the electric window slid silently down.

"You the fare for Anncolm Heights?" The soft Irish accent that had floated from the darkness of the taxicab was as smooth as the head on a pint of Guinness and as mysterious and the misty cliffs of Mohr.

"Yeah; can I put these in the boot?" Jason asked, indicating the canvasses stacked just inside the doorway. He had felt a small spark of interest on hearing the sexy Irish accent.

The taxi door opened, and the most gorgeous guy Jason had

ever seen had stepped out. The spark had quickly blossomed into a flame.

Over six feet tall, with a tanned complexion and muscular build, dark brown hair falling in sexy wisps onto his face. It was a handsome face, featuring a strong jawline but with none of the hardness that seemed to mar so many good looks these days. He was wearing black jeans and a black t-shirt; he didn't seem to mind the rain as he walked round to open the boot of the car.

Jason watched appreciatively as the squalls of rain made the T-shirt stick to his body. The water ran in little rivulets down his face and arms. He had so wanted to follow the path of those raindrops with his fingers and brush the wet hair from that sexy face.

Shaking himself slightly, collecting his artwork and covering the canvasses with a sheet of plastic, Jason stacked them carefully in the boot of the taxi.

The driver climbed back into his seat, Jason slid into the back of the cab and closed the door.

"Anncolm Heights?" the driver confirmed.

"Yeah, that's great!" Jason said, glancing at the driver's mirror. His heart skipped a beat as his eyes met two of the most tantalizing, deep brown eyes he had ever seen! Quickly he looked away, not wanting this stranger to see the desire in his eyes. It wasn't a good idea to give Liverpool cabbies 'the eye'

The traffic was quite heavy as the taxi headed into the city. Jason didn't mind the delays as it gave him time to study this Adonis's profile from the safety of the back seat, glancing at the mirror, hose beautiful brooding eyes met his gaze for a moment before Jason quickly looked away.

"Shit! Shit! Shit!" He thought to himself, "I need to get to know him because we are almost back at the flat!"

"Are you an art student then?" The soft, Irish voice snapped him out of his thoughts.

"Yeah, second year," Jason replied as he peeked at the mirror once again. This time, however, he caught and held the gaze of those rich brown eyes for a moment.

"Thought so," the taxi driver said as their eye contact was broken.

The car pulled into the parking area designated for the block of flats. Jason, climbing reluctantly out of the taxi as he dug deep into his pocket asked, "How much?"

The driver got out to open the boot, "four twenty-five," he said as Jason retrieved his paintings.

Balancing the canvasses in his arms, he handed over a grubby five-pound note. he turned reluctantly, heading for the entrance to the flats. "Keep the change," he said.

"Do you want a hand carrying that lot in?" The question stopped him in his tracks. He turned and looked at the taxi driver and smiled, this time the eye contact was not broken.

"That would be great," the reply came quickly, perhaps a little too eagerly, but the cabbie followed, nevertheless. He led the way up to his flat, it was small, but it was warm and clean.

They stacked the pictures in the lounge, "Would you like a coffee?" Jason asked almost afraid to hope that this hunk of a man would want to sit and drink coffee with him!

But the taxi driver, Bran, had stayed for coffee; he called at the flat for coffee quite often until one night, just as he was about to leave, hesitantly he had turned to Jason. "You know, I'd really like to wake up with you in the morning?"

That night Bran didn't go home It had been the first of many such nights, the start of a relationship which had blossomed into the full-blown love affair they enjoyed now!

Jason's eyes followed hungrily as Bran padded barefoot into the bathroom, he heard the sound of running water and smiled to himself, a shower would feel so good right now.

Bran stood under the high-powered jets of hot water; the continental style 'wet room' shower was great, lots' of room to move around.

At six foot two, he found normal sized shower cubicles very restricting. This was great, he could bend and stretch without cracking his head or elbows on the usual Perspex panels, even better; he grinned to himself, "there was room for two in this shower!" He squeezed shower gel onto the net 'scrunchy' and started massaging his chest and legs.

Bran was thinking about the jobs he had to do tonight when he realised that someone else was in the shower, massaging his back. He grinned, enjoying the sensation. The soapy hands massaged his back, his hips, and his buttocks then slipped provocatively between his thighs.

"Bugger off Jason!" he laughed, swiping him with the soap filled scrunchy! "I've got to work tonight!"

"OK! OK!" Jason said grinning and slapping Bran hard on the buttocks, "I know when I'm not wanted! I'll make the coffee!"

Jason Foster was an only son; coming from a somewhat privileged background: His parents were both very successful professionals,

Jason had always been a sensitive and artistic child. His mother, lecturing in fine arts at Bristol University, had encouraged his artistic abilities and his father was a successful pharmacist, whose money had ensured that he made the most of the opportunities available to him.

It had come as something of a shock, when at his seventeenth birthday party, Jason had introduced his parents to his boyfriend, Dominic!

A strikingly handsome youth Jason had always attracted attention from both sexes. Shoulder length honey-blonde hair fell in soft waves around his face, the blonde highlights enhanced by the long hot summers and foreign holidays. Piercing blue eyes shaded by a somewhat brooding expression seemed to change colour with his mood, from sparkling ice blue to a thoughtful aquamarine. His Greek nose and high cheekbones were softened by the sensuous lips that framed his sparkling white smile.

Jason's parents had been approachable and understanding but somewhat concerned that Dominic, at twenty-eight was considerably older than Jason at seventeen. They had been quite relieved when Jason happily agreed to enrol on a fine arts degree course at Liverpool University; at least there he would be surrounded by students of a similar age.

Jason's parents had found and financed the comfortable flat at Anncolm Heights. Arranged for a small allowance to be paid into Jason's bank account, having received an assurance that he would concentrate on his studies and work hard towards his honours degree. Happily, and quite confidently, left their son to get on with his life.

Bran walked into the kitchen, a towel wrapped round his hips, he took the mug Jason offered and sipped appreciatively at the hot coffee. Glancing up at the kitchen clock he swore as it as was almost eight.

"Gotta go, lover," he said, tossing the towel into the washing machine, "I am soooo in the shit!"

He strolled back into the bedroom and retrieved his 'True Religion' designer jeans from the floor. He pulled them on and zipped up the fly, noticing how snugly they sat on his hips. The Armani shirt was draped carelessly over a chair and his black Ferragamo sneakers lay where he had kicked them off earlier.

His wallet, car keys and mobile were on the bedside cabinet. He slipped the wallet into his back pocket and turned on the mobile phone.

Almost immediately the 'new message' alert sounded. Bran read the message; it was from his younger brother Kieran.

'Yr L8 wr t fuk R U?'

Bran flipped the phone closed. There was no point in answering; he would be at the garage in fifteen minutes.

"See you, Jay," he said walking out onto the landing as he made his way down to the ground floor and out into the parking area. The lights of his black Audi TT flashed as he deactivated the alarm.

From the balcony above Jason watched as the car, with its personalised number plate B7RAN, pulled smoothly out into the road.

Bran took a deep breath as he headed towards the docks towards the garage on Allen Street; towards his 'other' life. Just like an actor he mentally prepared himself for the role he was about to play; the role he had become very familiar with; the role he played every day of his life.

Bran knew all the side streets through the city and he soon reached his destination, having avoided the usual backlog of traffic from the tunnel. He turned into the yard behind the

O'Donnell's Taxis office and drove his Audi straight into the huge garage complex.

Pat O'Donnell was talking to two drivers when he saw his son's Audi pull into the garage. He was a stockily built man in his mid-sixties; his heavy build may have given the impression of good living, but Pat O'Donnell was anything but soft. His chunky five-foot-nine frame was solid muscle and despite his age, his responses were still fast as lightning.

He was a man who was used to giving orders and expecting them to be obeyed. His narrow mouth seemed set in a permanent scowl and his nose; slightly enlarged and reddened from alcohol abuse was a little crooked, having been broken many times during boxing matches.

His upbringing had not been an easy one, but he had stood on his own two feet all his life and he expected others to do the same; especially his son's, especially Bran, the eldest son; Brandon Patrick O'Donnell; his firstborn.

Pat had been born in Belfast in the early nineteen forties and had grown up amidst the traumas and upheavals of the 'troubles' in Northern Ireland.

Part of a large Catholic family that had strong political and religious beliefs, Pat had stood alongside his father and brothers at the political rallies that had taken place throughout Northern Ireland.

He had married a good Irish Catholic girl; Cathleen Connor and very quickly started a family with the birth of his son Bran.

A brief involvement with the I R A had been cut short when he signed up as a merchant seaman and for five years, he had sailed on cargo ships between Belfast, Dublin, Liverpool and the Continent.

It was following the birth of his second son, Kieran Daniel O'Donnell, that Pat had decided to quit the Navy and devote more time to building a business for his growing family.

Paul Finnian O'Donnell had been born soon after and there was no Irishman prouder of his three sons than Patrick O'Donnell!

Despite the difficulties of the times, Pat slowly built up a successful taxi business and auto repair service and at last, he was beginning to enjoy the benefits of his years of scrimping, saving and exhaustive long hours.

During his years on board the cargo ships, Pat had developed an interest in boxing and, on his return to Belfast, he had joined the local boxing club, soon becoming very proficient and skilled enough to win many tournaments. A hard man and an experienced brawler, Pat had also taken part in many of the bare-knuckle fights that took place in closed warehouses and empty barns; where large sums of money had changed hands on the outcome of the fights.

Then the troubles had flared up again in Northern Ireland, and it had affected the taxi business quite badly; people didn't want to go clubbing or spend their evenings in the pubs. Pat had been forced to let some of his drivers go. Even the garage takings were down but it was not all bad news,

Cathleen was pregnant again and on her last visit to the hospital, she had asked and been told that the child she carried was a little girl.

Pat had been overjoyed, he had so much wanted a daughter, a little girl who would grow up just like her beautiful mother, she would be Maria Cathleen O'Donnell, Maria for his mother and Cathleen for his wife.

Cathleen was so happy; she loved her three boys dearly and

now they would have a little sister to look after and love. She was due at the end of December, a Christmas baby only a few more weeks to go. Cathleen had hoped that her baby would be born just before Christmas so that her baby would be home in time to spend the holidays with the family. It was a happy time in the O'Donnell household despite the problems in their volatile community.

Preparations for the Christmas celebrations were well underway. And despite her stage of advanced pregnancy, Cathleen was still busy, putting up the Christmas decorations, making Christmas cakes and writing Christmas cards.

It had been one lunchtime in the middle of December when she had popped into the garage to see Pat.

"I'm going into the city centre," she had said, smiling, "while the boys are at school, I need to do a bit of Christmas shopping, Bran wants me to buy something special for him."

Pat had offered to take her into the shopping mall in a taxi, but Cathleen had said no. Pat knew why she hadn't got his Christmas present yet and he knew that she didn't want him to find out what she was buying him.

"We have a perfectly good bus service that goes right into Victoria Park," she said laughing, kissing him as she left to walk the short distance to the bus stop. "I'll see you later!" she waved.

Pat grinned to himself. His Christmas present was always such a big secret. Cathleen and Bran always made such a big thing of wrapping the gift carefully, so that he could have no idea of what it contained until the family opened their presents on Christmas Day when they got back from early morning Mass.

Pat had been working in the garage that afternoon. The radio was playing in the background, the usual pre-Christmas songs and jingles. Pat was whistling joyfully along to 'well here it is –

Merry Christmas' when the music suddenly stopped.

A sombre voice interrupted the programme,

"News is just coming in of massive explosions in the centre of Belfast; at two fifteen this afternoon the Victoria Park Shopping Mall was rocked by a series of explosions…"

2

As Bran made his way to the office, his father excused himself from the drivers to whom he had been talking and followed his son into the building.

Bran climbed the stairs passing Mickey Lee, one of their driver's. Mickey was just on his way out to pick up a fare from the station. He grinned as Bran made his way up to the office.

"In the shit again Bran?" he asked.

"What's new!" Bran scowled, as he made his way up to the room where his younger brother Kieran was operating the radio link.

Kieran at twenty years of age was still too young to hold a cab drivers licence and so was learning the business by managing the bookings and directing the drivers.

"Oh! So, you've decided to honour us with your presence have you?" he asked.

Before Bran could reply, his father stormed into the room.

"Where the friggin' hell have you been you lazy bastard! I've had to rearrange all the bloody pickups because of you!"

"Where I've been is my business," Bran said reaching for the keys of the private hire cab he drove.

Kieran laughed. "He's been tomming up town! All those hot arsed students flashing their knickers at the flash motor, I bet there's been more than one bit of skirt lost her cherry in the back of that car!

"Grow up Kieran," Bran said tiredly, he was fed up of listening to his younger brother's coarse comments and sexual innuendos.

"Business is bad enough without being screwed by you!" Pat continued angrily. "I'm losing money because there's no bloody minibus driver for the airport pickups!"

"Well get one of those two lazy bastards out there to do it!" Bran said as he pushed past Pat on the way to the door. He grabbed his list of pickups from the desk as he walked out.

The big diesel roared into life as Bran pulled on his seatbelt and flicked on the radio. He looked at the first pickup on his list; Friggin' Tesco He sighed and headed out into the busy evening traffic. Friggin' Tesco! He thought about Jason drinking coffee in his cosy little flat. That was a different life, different Bran. He pressed the mike button on his radio.

"Kieran! Was it you who logged me in for the bloody Tesco runs? You bastard!"

"Well get off yer fuckin' arse and get into the garage on time in future!" Kieran swore, "Mick took the out of city runs when you didn't turn up! What's she like anyway? And don't say you were at the Gym again 'cos Dad rang there when he got the last-minute Airport pickup."

"So, who took the airport run?" Bran said, ignoring Kieran's question.

"That's what pissed him off," Kieran said, "we were already one driver down and then you didn't turn up, Dad had to let the fare go! City Ride Black Cabs got the job!"

Bran could see why Pat was so angry; City Ride was a big rival taxi company, one of a number that were based right in the centre where they were able to pick up the choice jobs.

Bran pulled up in front of the Tesco superstore; it was busy with late-night shoppers, the car park, full of impatient drivers, shuffling from lane to lane as they vied for spaces closer to the store entrance. A young woman hurried over to the cab.

"Can you take me to Bristol Avenue?" she asked.

Bran got out of the cab and opened the boot; she had two shopping trolleys loaded with groceries. He started stacking the bags in the taxi. Bristol Avenue was only a couple of streets away, the fare came to one pound fifty, Bran carried all the shopping bags to the woman's doorstep and received a fifty pence tip for his trouble.

"Don't spend it all at once!" He said to himself as he drove back to Tesco.

As he sat in the line of Taxis waiting for fares outside the superstore, his thoughts drifted back to when they had first moved to Liverpool. Fifty pence had been a lot of money then! And every fifty pence had been important.

Bran remembered so clearly, the ferry journey from Belfast. He had been almost sixteen years old and had just sat his school-leaving certificate. Bran's two little brothers had huddled close to him on the big ferry, for once amazingly quiet, a bag of crisps and a can of cola still unopened in their hands.

Their Dad, Pat O'Donnell sat silently looking out of the window, deep in thought as he watched the foam-topped waves, the wake from the bow of the big Stena Ferry as it ploughed its way through the choppy Irish sea, heading for their new life in Britain.

Bran watched as his father repeatedly took the silver flask from his jacket pocket. Pat O'Donnell had always liked a drink, but that had been in the pub with his mates after he had finished work, but since Cathleen had been killed, it seemed that whenever Bran saw him, he had a glass or a flask or a bottle in his hand, and a brooding, dark look on his face.

After Cathleen had died, Pat had drunk to get over the heartbreak of those bleak days; but the sorrow turned to anger and frustration; the alcohol seemed to intensify the anger and the frustration found its outlet in the only targets Pat O'Donnell could reach, His boys! In particular, his eldest son Bran!

"When are we going home, Bran?" Paul had asked.

"We're going to a new home Paul," Bran had explained.

"I want to go home!" Paul had said, his six-year-old voice very small and trembling as a fat tear rolled down his cheek.

Bran glanced at Kieran, the eight-year-old had said almost nothing for the entire journey, his young face set in a hard scowl as he stared determinedly out across the water.

Bran didn't know what to do for the distressed youngster, he looked across at his father, worried that Paul's complaining would anger him, but Pat still sat gazing out at the waves. Bran pulled a grubby hanky out of his pocket and pushed it into Paul's hand.

"Here, blow your nose," he said, remembering with a pang, that this had been his mothers' favourite way of resolving an upset!

The eight-hour journey from Belfast to Liverpool seemed to go on forever, until, finally; the big ferry docked unceremoniously at the busy quayside.

The port of Liverpool was big and noisy and frightening. Crowds of people poured from the boat, jostling their way to the exits, pushing past the three boys who had been told gruffly by their father to wait there.

"If I have to come lookin' fer ye; y'll effin' know about it." Pat had growled at Bran. "Stay here!"

Paul had clung to Bran when their Dad had gone to pick up

the car, terrified of being on his own in this strange place, crowded with strange people. And then Kieran's shrill eight-year-old voice as he pointed an accusing finger at Paul.

"Bran! Bran! Our Paul's wet himself, Bran! Bran!"

"Bran!" The sharp rap on the roof of the taxi brought Bran out of his daydream.

"O'Donnell! Move yer fuckin' cab, you're holding everyone up!"

"OK, OK," Bran said as he turned the ignition and moved the cab down to the end of the taxi lane. He glanced at his watch, nine fifteen; another hour before he could head off to the Capital Centre to pick up the couple that had booked a taxi from the bowling alley to a club in town.

The back door of the taxi opened and a little grey-haired old lady climbed in, pulling her shopping trolley behind her.

"Can yer tek mi t't Gala Bingo 'all luv?" she said.

It was going to be a long night!

The radio had been silent for some time now and Bran had spent the last half hour parked up at the Capital Centre, no one seemed to want a taxi tonight. Bran picked up the radio mike.

"Log me off Kieran," he said, "I'm on my way back into the office." There was no reply.

"Kieran?" Bran said again. "Kieran?" Now where the hell had he disappeared too?

A couple of minutes later Bran found out as he pulled into the garage on Allen Street. Parked in the centre of the yard were three sporty cars, their occupants standing in a group chatting and admiring the flashy customised additions to their vehicles.

Kieran was standing in the yard talking to them.

Bran drove the cab up to the group. The electric window dropped as he stopped next to Kieran.

"So, this is why I can't get any reply on the effin' radio."

"Chill, bro," Kieran said. "It's fuckin' dead tonight anyway!"

"Yeah, and if Dad knew you left the office unattended, you'd be effin' dead as well!" He swung the taxi round, reversing between two of the cars on his way to park up for the night.

"And get this crap out of the yard!" He said, "Or I'll get it out for you!"

"Well, seeing as you are so bloody important," Kieran spat. "You can lock the bloody place up!" and he pulled a bunch of keys from his pocket and threw them through the open window of Bran's cab then he walked across the yard and climbed into his souped-up Peugeot GTI. Revving the engine and spinning the wheels to create clouds of foul-smelling rubber smoke, Kieran and his friends drove off, heading towards the centre of town.

With a sigh, Bran retrieved the bunch of keys from the floor of the taxi and reversed the cab neatly into its allocated parking spot. Tucking the pouch containing the nights' takings into his back pocket, he locked up the cab and made his way up the flight of stairs into the taxi office.

The place stunk of stale cigarette smoke; the ashtray on the desk was overflowing with stubs and at least a dozen empty lager cans stood dotted around the office. Stupid bastards! Bran thought as he cleared up the mess left by Kieran and his friends.

Kieran would never get his cab drivers licence if he got pulled for drink driving. Bran shook his head as he locked the takings in the safe. Friggin' boy racers!

Twenty minutes later, he was pulling into the drive at home; Kieran's car wasn't in its' usual spot, so he was still out on the town somewhere. Bran sighed; Kieran had always been a bit wild, always getting into one scrape or another, always coming to him when he needed someone to get him out of trouble!

Bran yawned, it had been a long day; he couldn't believe that only eight hours earlier he had been in Jason's bed, it seemed like days ago!

He climbed wearily out of the Audi and walked to the kitchen door; the light was on so Pat would probably still be up.

He walked into the warm kitchen and hung the car keys on the hook by the Aga, the solid gold key fob, shaped like an anchor glinted as the light caught its polished edges. He made himself a coffee and wandered through to the study, Pat was sitting on the leather settee, a glass of whiskey in his hand and a half-empty bottle on the table.

"Bran," his father waved the glass of whiskey in his direction, "Brandon O'Donnell, come and have a drink with your old man," he slurred. Bran picked up the whiskey bottle, screwed the cap back on and put it back in the drink's cabinet.

"I think you've had enough tonight Dad, it's late and I'm tired."

"Aye, you're a good lad Bran, to be sure!" The Irish accent was always more pronounced when Pat had been drinking "But there's always time for a wee nightcap."

"C'mon, Dad," Bran said, "let me give you a hand up the stairs, you need your sleep, we have a full day tomorrow."

"I'm alright Bran," he said, staggering to his feet. "I'll just have a wee chaser; it'll help me to get off to sleep."

"I'll make you a coffee, Dad," Bran offered.

"Stuff the coffee! Wha' did you do wit' ma whiskey?"

Pat stumbled across the room heading for the drinks cabinet.

"I'll bring you a whisky up to the bedroom," Bran said, steering his father towards the stairs; these tactics had worked in the past. Hopefully, they would work again. Once Pat was in bed, it wouldn't be long before he would fall asleep.

"You're a good lad Bran," Pat said again, patting his son's arm as he was guided towards the stairs "A good lad!" he flung his arm around Bran's shoulder, the whiskey on his breath almost overpowering.

"When are you going to make me a granddad son?"

Bran sighed as Pat's bleary thoughts rambled onto his favourite subject; the continuation of the O'Donnell family line!

"There are a lot of nice Irish lasses here in Liverpool, you could have your pick of them Bran boy, good looking stud like you. Ah, you take after your mother there son, she was a handsome woman Bran; a handsome woman!"

Bran smiled as he thought to himself, if only you knew, Dad, if only you knew!

With his father safely settled in bed, Bran made his way down to the kitchen and a much-needed cup of coffee. He glanced at the clock; it was three in the morning and still no sign of Kieran.

Bran turned off the lights and headed for his bedroom, Kieran was old enough to look after himself. As he put his head on the pillow, his thoughts turned to Jason; it had been a long, long day, but not a bad one!

Next morning as Bran walked down the stairs into the hallway, he could hear voices coming from the kitchen, Paul and Kieran were deep in conversation.

"What time did you get in?" he asked Kieran as he poured himself a mug of coffee and took a slice of toast from the plate in front of Paul. Kieran shrugged his shoulders.

"Late," he said yawning, he leant back in the chair and lit a cigarette, drawing deeply and blowing the smoke into the air.

"Do you have to smoke in the bloody kitchen?" Bran asked.

Kieran didn't reply; he just raised his hand with the middle finger extended.

Bran helped himself to another piece of toast.

"Do you want a lift to the Uni Paul?" he asked, "I've got to pick up some auto parts this morning, the Uni's not much out of the way."

"Yeah thanks, Bran," Paul said cramming the last piece of toast into his mouth. "I'll be glad when I've passed my test and got my own car."

"Well," Bran said, looking meaningfully at Kieran "I just hope that when you do, you have a bit more sense than SOME in this family!" Kieran looked up at his older brother and said quite amicably, "Get stuffed!"

"Dad still in bed?" Bran asked as he waited for Paul to get his course work together.

"Yeah," Kieran nodded "I take it he had a skin full last night?"

"That reminds me," Bran said. "What were all those bloody lager cans doing in the office?" Kieran didn't answer.

"Should I take Dad into the office with me or are you picking him up later?" He said, changing the subject.

"Take him in with you, Kieran," Bran said. "I might not get back here today."

"Oh, and where are you beggaring' off to again?"

"What! After I've dropped Paul off, collected the spares, been to the bank and the post office and done a dozen other bloody jobs that everyone seems to think just happen by bloody magic!"

Bran shook his head.

"C'mon, Paul!" he yelled, "I haven't got all fuckin' day!"

3

It was four thirty when Bran finally made it to the garage. Jane, the daytime receptionist was operating the radios. Jane had been with the firm for years and considered herself a surrogate 'auntie' to Pat O'Donnell's boys. She was pretty busy organising all the school runs so Bran didn't interrupt her, he put the replacement water pump down on the desk and poured himself a coffee.

"Has Pat been in?" he asked when she paused for a few minutes, he handed her a cup of coffee, black with no sugar.

"Thanks, Bran," she said sipping appreciatively at the hot liquid. "No, I haven't seen Pat or Kieran yet, and I hope Kieran won't be late," she said, "I have to leave on the dot at five." Her thin, pinched face formed a worried scowl as she peered over her glasses.

"Don't worry, Jane," Bran said as he looked through the office window into the parking area below. "Kieran's just arrived," he watched as his younger brother climbed out of the nippy little Peugeot. Kieran was on his own, Pat must have decided to take the day off. Bran frowned and hoped that his Dad wasn't going to start where he left off the night before and hit the whiskey again.

Bran expected Kieran to head straight for the office, but Kieran lingered by his car for a while, talking to someone on his mobile phone. Bran watched his brother for a little longer, he was pacing backwards and forwards, the conversation appeared to be getting quite heated.

"You take off Jane," he said, "I'll hold the fort till Kieran's finished gabbing."

"OK, Bran," she said putting on her warm waterproof coat and grabbing her handbag. "See you tomorrow!"

Bran watched Jane walk across the yard, her straggly auburn hair blowing in the wind and her coat flapping around her thin legs. She waved to Kieran as she headed for the gate, but Kieran didn't seem to notice her, he was still completely immersed in his phone conversation.

Bran watched until Kieran finally ended the exchange. From Kieran's reaction, Bran guessed that the conversation had ended somewhat abruptly. At last Kieran headed towards the office.

"What was all that about?" Bran asked as Kieran threw his leather jacket onto the desk and poured himself a coffee.

"What was all what about?" Kieran said.

"The phone call," Bran replied. "It looked like you were getting quite uptight."

"What the fuck has it got to do with you!" Kieran swore. "Just keep out of my business!" Kieran threw himself down into his chair.

"Bloody spying on me now!" he muttered. "Since when did you become my keeper?"

"Where's Dad?" Bran asked, choosing not to get into a slanging match with Kieran. "I thought he was coming in to do the paperwork this afternoon?"

"He decided to do it tomorrow," Kieran said, checking the bookings sheets; he looked up at Bran "Are you working now, Mrs Henderson wants picking up at the hairdressers and she's asked for you if you're in!" Bran grinned. "I'm definitely not working then!"

Mrs Henderson was a rather matronly woman who had a bit

of a crush on Bran; she tipped well, but some things just weren't worth it, and Mrs Henderson was one of them!

"I'm going to take off for a couple of hours," he continued, "I'll be back at eight."

"Make sure you are!" Kieran said as Bran left the office "Or you'll be doing the effin' Tesco runs again!"

It only took Bran a few minutes to get from the garage to the flats where Jason lived; he parked the Audi round the back and let himself into the main building.

He made his way up the three flights of stairs and tapped softly on the door. There was silence for a moment, and then a voice said, "Who's there?"

"It's me, Jay," Bran said quietly.

The door was thrown open and a beaming Jason ushered him into the room. Jason put his arm around Bran's waist and hugged him.

"This is a nice surprise," he said, "and I'm so glad you've come 'cause I've just finished it and I want your opinion!"

Bran grinned, the painting Jason had been working on in secret for weeks, the painting that Jason wouldn't let him look at until it was finished; at last, he was going to get to view the finished piece. This work, as Jason had explained, was just for them; it wasn't intended that anyone other than they saw it. It was a celebration of their lives; their meeting and their sexuality.

Jason led Bran through to the study, the canvas was positioned on the big artist's easel. The painting was a riot of colour, the intricate images merged on the canvas; the contrasting play of light and dark reflected the subject matter and yet the whole thing seemed so balanced.

Bran was amazed at the detail Jason had managed to get into

the painting; how the images represented minute fragments of their lives and still seemed to present a complete picture; the more Bran studies the painting, the more he found that absolutely stunned him. Portraits of both he and Jay took centre stage, they faced each other the palms of one hand pressed against the others. The image seemed to turn to mist as it entwined; through the mist a taxi was emerging; behind them an Irish shamrock overlaid a red rose; an outline of the map of Ireland was surrounded by an explosion; the Gay movement 'rainbow' arched above; an angel looked down from the rainbow that became on one side the amnesty international candle and on the other a figure of two men embracing. Two male symbols were entwined, and a paintbrush and pencil were crossed beneath the mist-shrouded taxi. As Bran looked, he found more and more symbols, the doves of peace, the Irish flag, Liverpool football clubs' big red Liver Bird; the Gay Pride ribbon.

"That's fabulous Jay!" he said ruffling the blonde hair affectionately. "You are such a talented little bugger!"

Jason grinned. "I'm glad you like It." He said, then added wickedly, "because I'm going to present it as my end of year piece!"

Bran looked at the painting again, the explicit images, the beautiful portraits, the very personal subject matter, he glanced a little worriedly at Jason. "You are kidding?" he asked.

A big grin crossed Jason's face. "Of course, I'm bloody kidding!" he laughed. "Anyway, I wasn't expecting you to call today. To what do I owe this unexpected pleasure?"

Bran shrugged his shoulders. "Fancied a coffee, wanted someone to talk too, wanted to see you again,"

A few minutes later, when Jason had washed the oil paint from his hands and put away the painting, they sat at the kitchen table, sipping the hot aromatic coffee.

"So, what is it you wanted to talk about?" Jason asked, putting a reassuring hand on Bran's arm. Bran put his hand over Jason's and stroked it affectionately.

"You'll probably think I'm over-reacting," he said. "But I'm worried about my younger brother Kieran; he's been really edgy lately; one minute he's depressed, the next minute he's flying off the handle at nothing; there's something going on and I can't just put my finger on it!"

"It's probably hormonal," Jason suggested, "he's just at that 'funny' age; has he got a steady girlfriend?"

"Who knows," Bran said shrugging his shoulders. "He disappears off at night with his boy racer buddies and we don't see him again till the early hours of the morning."

"Just like the majority of the students at the Uni." Jason smiled. "I wouldn't worry; he'll probably grow out of it pretty soon."

"I hope so," Bran laughed. "He's starting to annoy me!"

"What about your youngest brother, Paul?" Jason asked, "He's at Uni now isn't he?"

Bran nodded, he was so proud of his little brother,

"Yeah! He was the one that got all the brains in the family, Business and marketing, it's his first year, he'll be the one that takes over the running the firm when anything happens to Pat; me and Kieran will end up working for him!"

"Well let's hope that won't be for quite a while yet," Jason said.

"I'm not too sure about that," Bran was quite sombre, "Pat's been drinking quite heavily just lately and he's not as young as he used to be; all that alcohol has got to take its toll somewhere, a lifetime looking at the bottom of a glass…"

Bran's thoughts slipped back to his home in Belfast, those dark difficult times after the funeral. People had been so supportive in the days after Cathleen was killed. The terrorist bombing of the busy shopping mall just a few weeks before Christmas devastated their community; there didn't seem to be one person that this atrocity hadn't affected personally; everyone knew someone who was either killed or injured on that terrible afternoon.

Friends and neighbours had tutted and clucked over Cathleen O'Donnell's three poor wee motherless boys. In the days that followed the bombing, it felt as though he was being battered by some giant unseen storm.

Bran had tried to make sense of the traditional rituals and religious formalities that took their mother away from them. Bewildered and dazed; he was barely able to understand the solemnity of the procedure himself but it was left to him to try and help his two younger brothers to come to terms with the tragic events; and to survive the tidal waves of emotions that swamped their young lives; when he turned to his Dad for help; understanding; love! He met a cold stonewall of denial, and more often than not, a harsh word or the back of a hand.

Pat O'Donnell tried hard to shut out the memories that were so painful, but every time he looked at the boys, their faces turned to him for love and understanding; he saw Cathleen. Especially Bran. Bran, who had his mothers' eyes; his mothers' smile; and his mothers' gentle ways.

In the days that followed the funeral, fewer and fewer people called or spoke to them in the streets. Pat O'Donnell had started drinking, and when he drank, he became argumentative and aggressive. Soon no one wanted to risk a confrontation; they left the O'Donnell family alone. Bran remembered how they had tried to pull the fabric of the family back into some sort of a routine. Life must go on! But life had changed; nothing was the same; nothing would ever be the same again!

He remembered coming home from school on cold dark winters nights and making Kieran and Paul wait outside while he went in to see if their Dad had got back from work. If he was home, it usually meant that business had been poor and he would be in a foul mood, If the Vodka or the Whiskey bottle was on the table, Bran would smuggle the two boys up to the bedroom with a promise to bring them some tea in a little while if they kept quiet and stayed out of their Dad's way.

Memories came flooding back, fifteen-year-old Bran cooking for the family, trying to make a meal out of the hotchpotch of ingredients in their meagre kitchen cupboards. As usual, Pat had been drinking again.

"What the fuck do you call this shit!" he had said, slinging the plate of stew across the table at Bran.

"Yer fuckin' useless!" he had said. It seemed that no matter what Bran did or tried to do, it was never enough; never right, never as good as his mother would have done!

Bran shook his head; it didn't seem all that long ago!

"Hey!" Jason interrupted his thoughts. "Where are you Bran?" he said, his hand reassuringly on Bran's arm. "You were miles away then!" Bran smiled, but the smile didn't reach his eyes.

"Not a good place Jay," he said quietly and then he glanced at the kitchen clock; "and I'm going to have to leave now; I need to get back to the office so that Kieran doesn't stitch me up with all the crap jobs again tonight." He stood up and drained his coffee cup, and then he leaned across the table and kissed Jason affectionately on the lips "And I really love the painting Jay, it's great!"

Back at the taxi office, things were beginning to get quite busy. Three of the drivers were sitting round the office chatting and drinking coffee. Bran picked up the keys to his cab and headed for the door.

"Bran," Kieran said putting his hand over the mouthpiece of the phone, "Can you pick a fare up from sixty-eight Fairthorn Close to the railway station?" Bran nodded.

"The cab's on its way Mrs Evans"' he said, "should be with you in about;" he paused and looked up at Bran who held up both hands; the fingers splayed.

"Ten minutes Mrs Evans… Your welcome… It's no problem… enjoy your trip…" He paused for a second as he took another call over the headset. He scribbled an address down on his notepad.

"Jimbo," he said turning to one of the drivers.

"Pick up at twenty-seven Greenhaven Close; a Mister Andrews, going to an address in Knowsley."

Jimbo tossed back the remnants of his coffee, "See you later," he said to the men he had been chatting to, and he disappeared down the stairs, following Bran out into the yard.

The next couple of hours were quite hectic, but by eleven thirty the jobs were becoming less frequent.

"Log me off Kieran," Bran said as he headed back to the garage, "I still have that water pump to replace on the Carlton, I'll make a start on it tonight." There was no reply from the office.

"Kieran? Are you there Kieran?"

Now where the fuck has he disappeared too Bran thought.

"Kieran!"

The radio crackled into life.

"Keep yer knickers on Bran!" Kieran's voice came over the loudspeakers, "I was on the phone!" he sounded a little agitated.

"It's a bit effin' late to be starting on the Carlton Bran; why don't you do it tomorrow?"

"Pat will want us to go over the books with him tomorrow Kieran," Bran explained, "besides which, I could have most of the repair done tonight, it should only take a couple of hours at the most!"

"Please yourself," Kieran snapped, and the radio went dead. Now what's rattled his cage, Bran thought to himself!

He pulled in through the gates; the yard was dark and deserted. He drove slowly across the silent yard, only the faint light from the office window showed that he was not alone. It certainly looked like he was the last driver in; all the other Taxicabs were parked up for the night. He went up to the office and handed the nights takings over to Kieran and poured himself a cup of coffee.

"If you want to go home Kieran, I'll lock up," Bran said as he pulled on a pair of overalls and unpacked the replacement water pump, "no point us both being stuck here."

"Yeah, later perhaps," Kieran said absently.

Bran shrugged his shoulders. Kieran was so moody these days, he just couldn't weigh him up. He made his way down the stairs and across the yard to the mechanics bay. Turning on the lights and popped the bonnet on the Vauxhall Carlton.

He rolled the toolbox over to the car and got to work. He was well into the job, having removed the faulty pump when Kieran appeared with a cup of coffee.

"Thanks, Kieran!" Bran said as he paused and wiped the oil from his hands onto the rag he had tucked in his overall pocket.

"How long are you going to be Bran?" Kieran asked, drawing deeply on the cigarette he held.

"An hour, maybe an hour and a half," Bran replied, "should be finished by then."

Kieran wandered back towards the office and Bran put down his coffee and continued the repairs.

About fifteen minutes later, Bran paused when he thought he heard a car leaving the yard, he glanced over to where Kieran's Peugeot was parked, it was still there, perhaps it was his imagination or a car on the road outside, he yawned, he was getting tired, perhaps Kieran was right, perhaps it would be better to finish it in the morning. He yawned again and began to put the tools away. Then he thought 'what the hell!' it's nearly finished, why stop now; when he could have it completed in an hour. Picking up the spanners again he carried on, shrugging off the niggling pain in his back and aching shoulders.

About half an hour later he heard a car engine again, he walked to the door of the mechanics bay and looked down the yard, there was no sign of any movement and Kieran's car was still where he had parked it earlier. Strange, Bran thought, it just sounded like someone driving into the garage, but everyone was back, he shook his head, he really must be getting tired. Then he heard another car, this one he recognised, it was Kieran's Peugeot he watched as the sporty little car disappeared out of the gate. Finally, the water pump was replaced, and he dropped the bonnet on the car, he would give it a test drive in the morning, for now; he just wanted to get home, have a shower and climb into his bed.

Sitting at the big table in the spare room next to the office. Pat flicked through the pages of the diary while Bran sorted the bills and receipts into order.

Once a month the books were brought up to date, it was a job that he hated but he realised that it was an important part of running a business; he glanced over at Kieran who was checking the radio logs.

"I'll be glad when Paul has finished his business course, then he can take over this job."

Kieran didn't answer; he was busy counting.

They had only been in the room for about an hour, when Jane came through from the office, her pinched face made to look even more severe by the worried frown she wore.

"Mister O'Donnell," she said, addressing Pat. "There's a policeman here to see you."

Pat looked up, puzzled. "What the hell?" he said. "You'd better tell him to come in then."

The officer was from a local station, Sergeant Carver, and he worked mainly on the traffic division.

"Just a word of warning Mr O'Donnell," he had said, taking out his note pad and referring to it.

"At one twenty this morning, one of your drivers was observed exceeding the speed limit and driving without due care and attention."

"Impossible!" Pat said angrily. "My lads finish at twelve thirty unless there's been a booking and I know none of my cabs was out last night!"

"There will be no further action taken Mister O'Donnell and no charges pressed," he paused. "On this occasion, - but just be aware that we will be keeping an eye on your vehicles, just have a word with your drivers will you."

"I'm telling you!" Pat said raising his voice, "none of my bloody cars was out last night!"

Bran glanced over at Kieran and was quite surprised to see how pale he suddenly looked.

"P46 KWH," the sergeant said, referring again to his notebook.

"That's one of my cabs, yes; but I don't see how? You must have got the damn registration wrong!" Pat said angrily.

Bran remembered the sound of a car leaving the garage and returning half an hour later, the only two people there had been him and Kieran! He looked over at Kieran, he looked sick!

"It was me, Dad!" Bran said, "I was working on the car late last night, putting that new water pump in, I took it out for a test drive; I guess I didn't realise I was going as fast as I was; I'm sorry."

"I'll fuckin' sorry you, you stupid bastard!" Pat said glaring at his son.

"It won't happen again sergeant," he said as he walked out of the room with the officer. "You can take my word for that!"

When Pat returned, he was livid.

"Well you made me look a right bloody idiot!" he said, "Bloody police knocking on the door in the middle of the morning, made me out to be a right dick head you did!"

"It was one in the morning, I didn't think..."

Pat's backhanded blow rocked Bran.

"Well that might help you to effin' think in the future!" he said. "You ever show me up like that again and I'll make you wish you had never been effin' born! Sorry about the language Jean," he said turning to his receptionist, then he turned back to Bran. "Now fuck off out of my sight and let me and Kieran get on with some work!"

Bran looked across at Kieran, he had his head down, refusing to meet Bran's glance. Bran didn't say anything; he just turned and walked out of the office. He drove his Audi TT down to the docks road and sat gazing out across the Irish Sea.

The secluded lay-by on the waterfront had always been his favourite place to come when he needed somewhere quiet just to sit and think; he touched his mouth gingerly. Pat's backhander had cut the inside of his lip; he could still bloody hit, Bran thought angrily. The anger was directed more at himself; six foot two, twenty-six years old and he still let his Dad smack him in the face. Some things didn't change, even after all these years.

His thoughts drifted back across the water to their terraced house in the heart of Belfast and the time when his mother had been there to stand between Pat's temper and her sons.

He remembered how her long black hair used to swing around her face when she stood up to her husband, something quite uncommon in Irish marriages.

"Patrick O'Donnell, don't you dare raise your hand to those boys!" And he had listened to her and Bran had felt safe.

He remembered the flowery dresses she wore, bright splashes of colour in those dark depressing times; the little songs that she sang in the kitchen, haunting little melodies that he still heard in his dreams sometimes and that she always smelled of baking.

Then she was gone, and Pat started drinking and there was

no one to say "Patrick O'Donnell, don't you dare raise your hand to those boys!"

There was no one to take them to Church on Sundays, Pat had never been one for Church going; that had been Cathleen's role, every week; their faces scrubbed, and their hair brushed. Dressed in their Sunday best they would go off to mass and they would sit quietly with their mother, happy in the knowledge that if they behaved themselves there would be chocolate and sweets on the way home!

There had been no more chocolate or sweets and Father James had called, concerned that he hadn't seen the O'Donnell boys in church for a while. So Pat had insisted they go to the local Catholic Church Sunday school once a fortnight.

Bran had hated it; it was boring and tedious, learning all the long religious ceremonies, but there had been another reason Bran had hated the fortnightly trip to the Church, Father Ryan, the Priest who taught Sunday School; a middle-aged man from Antrim had noticed Bran's good looks; he would stand close behind him and lean over to listen to Bran recite passages from the prayer book.

Bran would feel him touching his shoulders, pressing himself against his back! He would put a hand on Bran's waist as he walked out of the room, then one day he asked Bran if he would stay behind and help him to collect the hymnbooks and return them to the Church Vestry.

Bran couldn't tell anyone, hadn't dared tell anyone what the Priest did when they were alone in that small room; no one would believe him; they would say it was his fault! So he had endured the pain and the humiliation and the shame in silence. It was a deep dark secret that he had lived with and dealt with on his own; that was until he had met Jason and at last found someone with whom he could share his secret, someone who would understand; someone who was not judgemental; someone who would help him to overcome the crushing feelings of guilt and self-loathing.

Jason!

Bran flipped open his mobile phone.

"Where are you, Jason?" He asked when he heard the familiar voice.

"At home."

"You're not going to the Uni today are you?" Bran asked.

"No, Friday's my free day, why? Are you OK, Bran?" Jason could hear the tension in Bran's voice.

"I'm on my way round, Jay," he said. "I need some company."

He turned the Audi around and headed towards the City centre. Twenty minutes later he walked through the door of Jason's flat and into the arms of the one person he could talk too.

"Why do I put up with it, Jay? Why?" he said shaking his head. Jason could see that he was upset.

"Shush now," Jason said quietly, placing his fingers on Bran's lips. Bran winced and pulled away, his cut lip still painful.

Jason shook his head and sighed; he wrapped his arms around Bran and pulled him into his embrace. Jason was only too aware that Patrick O'Donnell liked to use his fists.

"Oh, Bran!" He said gently massaging his neck with the tips of his fingers as he felt the hard knots of tense muscle. "What happened this time?" He pulled his lover close, knowing that he needed the contact; needed the reassurance; needed someone to tell him that it was all right!

Bran burrowed his face into the sweet-smelling blonde hair. It had been a long time since he had felt this uptight; this emotional. He hated himself for being so weak, so easily affected by his fathers' anger. Pat had always made him feel like this, right from his teenage years, he had always felt intimidated by his father. But now! Now he was twenty-six years old for Christ's sake!

Waves of emotion washed over him. It was as though being here; now, had triggered a release switch in his mind. This was the one place where he felt he belonged; the one person he felt understood him. Here he could give in to the emotions that he could never reveal at home.

"It's OK, Bran," Jason said softly as he gently massaged Bran's back.

Jason put his hands gently on either side of Bran's face and looked into those dark brown puppy eyes, they were full of tears; the long eyelashes sparkled with moisture.

"Jay…," Bran began.

"Shh," Jason said as his half-open mouth covered Bran's lips.

This time Bran didn't wince or pull away, the pain of his cut lip was forgotten in the passion of their kiss.

Jason undid the buttons of Bran's leather jacket as he felt the warm hands slip beneath his t-shirt and slide up the bare skin of his back. He undid the buttons of Bran's shirt and ran his hands lovingly down the firmly muscled torso. Their passionate kissing continued as Bran's shirt and jacket slid to the floor.

Jason undid the button and slid open the zip of his jeans, his arousal becoming very obvious.

Bran unzipped his pants and they fell to his ankles; quickly followed by his boxers; he paused for a moment, enjoying the sensation of complete freedom then he ran both hands down Jason's waist and peeled off the tight jeans. Jason grasped the bottom of his t-shirt and pulled it up and over his head. Stepping out of the jeans, he dropped the t-shirt and pressed his naked body against his lover.

The sensation of skin on skin was electric; Bran held Jason close, enjoying the intimate feeling of heat against his bare flesh.

Placing his hand on Bran's chest, Jason pushed him away and glanced down at Bran's firm erection.

"It's been a long time since you took the lead, Bran," Jason said as he led his lover towards the bedroom. "Far too long!"

Later, as they lay side-by-side in Jason's comfortable bed; drained from their intense lovemaking; Bran, at last, told Jason about the visit by the police sergeant and the events of the night before and how he now believed that it was Kieran who had taken the Cab out for a joy ride.

Jason ran his fingers gently over the bruise that was appearing on Bran's cheek.

"When are you going to stop taking the punishment for the things your brothers do?" The blue eyes were dark with concern as that searched his face, as they rested sadly on yet another bruise caused by Patrick O'Donnell who had been, once again, too quick to use his fists!

Bran looked away, he couldn't answer Jason because he didn't know; he didn't know why he still protected them from Pat, but it was what his mother would have done, what he had been doing since she died.

"Kieran will be applying for his Taxi Drivers License next year, being caught speeding in a vehicle he wasn't insured to drive wouldn't have gone down very well."

"Did he say why he had taken the cab out?" Jason asked.

"We didn't get chance to talk," Bran laughed. "Pat was too busy throwing me out of the office!"

"Your brothers are going to have to stand on their own two feet one-day Bran," Jason said. "You can't be there for them all the time."

"I can try," Bran said simply.

It was sometime later, as they sat drinking coffee in the kitchen that Bran's mobile phone received a text message, it was from Kieran; just one word – sorry!

4

Charlies Gym was very popular with many of the young up-and-coming businessmen from this part of the City. It was quite expensive to be a member, but the facilities were excellent. In addition to the gym, members had access to, amongst other things, a private pool, Jacuzzi, sauna and sunbeds.

Bran was a regular visitor and often stopped at the gym on his way to the taxi office. Today was one of those days. He felt that a good workout on the equipment would help to calm him down and get rid of some of the tension and the stress that the last couple of days had built up.

He pulled the sports bag from the wardrobe and carefully folding his black chinos and a clean white shirt, he put them in the bag along with a clean pair of boxers, his socks and a pair of soft leather shoes. His bag of toiletries was tucked into the end compartment of the roomy bag and a clean white towel placed over his clothes.

He unwrapped the damp towel from around his hips and used it to rub dry his newly washed hair. The thick dark brown hair stuck out in untidy spikes, made black by the moisture that still made the strands of hair stick together, a bit like a startled hedgehog he thought, grinning to himself. He ruffled his hair with his fingers, but that didn't improve the style any. He reached for a comb from the bathroom cabinet and raked the unruly mop into some semblance of order.

He slipped his tracksuit over his shorts and vest and pulled on a pair of gym socks before stepping into a pair of Nike trainers. Grabbing up his sports bag and flipping his leather jacket casually over his shoulder, Bran made his way downstairs and strolled into the kitchen. Kieran and Pat were both sitting at the kitchen table drinking coffee.

Kieran looked up from the newspaper he was reading and flicked the ash from his cigarette into the ashtray.

"Off to your 'keep fit club', bro?" he skitted, swinging his arms back and forth in a mimicry of exercise. "Poncing round the gym with the 'would be' suits?" He laughed, "I bet half of them are puffs!"

"It wouldn't do you any harm to look after yourself a bit better, Kieran," Bran grumbled. "You could kick that habit for a start," he said indicating the half-smoked cigarette between Kieran's fingers, "and you're starting to get a beer gut."

Kieran looked down; there was the tiniest roll of skin protruding over the top of his tight jeans. "Three sugars in the coffee again?" Bran grinned as he walked over to the Aga to retrieve his car keys from the hook on the wall.

Pat smiled. "He's got a point, Kieran," he said. "I've heard you wheezing when you've been climbing up the stairs to the office."

"Bugger off!" Kieran said, frowning slightly. "I'm fit enough!"

"Well you should be fit, Kieran," Bran laughed. "All the weight training you do; lifting those heavy cups of coffee all day every day!"

"Piss off!"

Bran grinned and headed for the door, but he did notice, with a little smile, that Kieran had stubbed out his half-smoked cigarette.

Charlies was busy as usual. Bran found a place to park the Audi. He backed it neatly between the BMW and the RAV 4. The car bleeped reassuringly as he activated the alarm system.

An early morning club member was just leaving as Bran walked towards the ornate double doors. He nodded briefly as he passed the man, whose round face was pink and shiny still, from the exertion of his recent workout.

The doors swung open automatically as Bran stepped into the very stylish, modern reception.

He handed over his membership card to the pretty receptionist and she swiped it deftly through the registration computer system.

"Good morning Mister O'Donnell," she said brightly, "would you like to make an appointment to see your personal trainer this morning; Keith is available?"

"No thanks," Bran said as he signed the register. "Some other time perhaps." He swung his bag up onto his shoulder.

"Is there anything else we can offer you today Mister O'Donnell?" she continued, "we have a special offer in the tanning studio, or you might like to take advantage of the introductory Shiatsu massage offer?"

Bran smiled "I might need it after the circuit training session," he said, "it's been a few weeks since I last came here."

She grinned at him. Her eyes slid appreciatively up and down his body.

"It certainly doesn't show Mister O'Donnell," she said cheekily.

Bran smiled and winked at her. She giggled and blushed. Bran laughed softly to himself as he made his way through to the locker room. He nodded occasionally to the people making their way to and from the various fitness suites.

Once in the locker room, he stashed his sports bag and began his routine of stretch exercises before making his way to the gym.

"All right Bran!" a voice called from across the room. Bran paused his stretch exercises and glanced up. It was a young black guy he had seen in the gym a few times in the past. A friendly sort, and good company when he was working out on the equipment.

"Hi Ross," he said as he stretched his thigh muscles, warming them up for the coming exercise. "You been here long?"

Ross shook his head. "No; just arrived. Want some company?" He asked, indicating the gym. Bran nodded.

"Great!" Ross grinned. "Hey, do you fancy a game of squash later?"

"You're a glutton for bloody punishment," Bran laughed as they headed for the first piece of equipment on their circuit training session.

Bran easily kept pace with Ross as they worked through the routine of warm-up exercises. Step-ups; press-ups; abdominal curls. The exercises were repeated two or three times until they were both ready to step up the pace.

Bran stripped to his singlet and shorts as they worked through the various pieces of equipment. Before long they were both sweating freely, and the conversation had died as they concentrated on their breathing exercises.

The circuit ended with a session on the weights followed by some gentle exercise designed to allow their stretched muscles to relax and their thumping hearts' and ragged breathing to return to normal.

Bran wrapped his towel around his neck and glanced across at Ross.

"Sauna?" he suggested.

Ross nodded, still too breathless to answer.

"I don't know about a sauna," he said, eventually regaining the ability to speak. "I think a bloody iron lung might be more appropriate!"

Bran leaned back against the wooden slats of the benching in the sauna and closed his eyes. He took a long drink from the bottled water he carried, on the bench just above him; Ross did the same.

"I wish I had the room for one of these at home," Ross said, wiping his chest with a towel. His skin; the colour of dark chocolate, glistened with sweat. Bran glanced up, stretching appreciatively as the wet heat soothed his tired muscles.

Ross was laying on his back, enjoying the slightly elevated temperature of the higher benches, his swimming trunks leaving nothing to the imagination.

Bran grinned; 'Bloody hell!' he thought. 'It's right what they say about black men'. Through half closed eyes he studied Ross surreptitiously, he was one hell of a good-looking guy. The film of perspiration accentuated the smooth lines of the body, honed to perfection by regular workouts. The lean hips, well-defined six-pack and impressive pecs would have stirred a feeling of envy in most men.

With a slight shock, Bran realised that the feelings stirring deep within him weren't feelings of envy.

He shook his head and tore his eyes away from the impressive bulge in Ross's trunks and glanced up. His heart seemed to miss a beat as he realised that Ross was watching him intently. Their eyes met and they held the gaze; an unspoken understanding passed between them.

"You got any water to spare?" Ross asked, propping himself

up on one elbow on the bench just above Bran. Bran reached down for a water bottle then lifted it above his head, handing it to Ross. Ross took the bottle.

"Thanks, Bran," he said, his fingers briefly caressed the back of Bran's hand.

He drank deeply from the bottle and let a little of the water trickle over his face and chest.

"Do you fancy a drink later?" Ross asked, "There's a nice quiet little pub a couple of miles down the road."

Bran looked up; Ross was watching him through half closed eyes, his long dark lashes fluttering against his black skin, like the wings of some exotic, sensuous bird.

Bran sighed; he so wanted to place his hand on that beautifully muscled thigh. His heart was beating strongly, he could feel it pounding against his ribcage; his face was only inches away from Ross'; from those beautiful dark full African lips.

Ross moved slowly forward. Bran noticed how pink his tongue was as it ran provocatively across his upper lip.

There was a sudden movement of air as the sauna room door opened and a middle-aged man with a towel wrapped around his waist walked in.

Ross didn't miss a beat; he handed Bran the now empty water bottle and sat back on the bench.

"Thanks for that!" He said breezily. "Now about that drink?"

"I can't Ross," Bran said regretfully. "I've got to go to work when I leave here."

Ross frowned; he seemed quite crestfallen.

"What about one night?" he asked hopefully.

Bran paused, shaking his head slightly; he was tempted, so very tempted, but the image of blonde hair and blue eyes flashed through his mind.

"I'm sorry Ross," He said, shaking his head "I really am sorry," he lowered his voice, "but I have a partner."

Ross shrugged his shoulders and sighed and leant back on the wooden bench, his hands behind his head.

"Lucky guy," he said quietly as he closed his eyes and relaxed, enjoying the soothing heat of the sauna.

5

Friday night was always a hectic night for the taxi firm and they were kept busy running between clubs and pubs. When Bran finally finished at twelve-thirty, Kieran was still in the office, waiting for some of the late pick-ups to return.

"You go home Bran," he said, "No point us both staying here; I'll be home when everyone's back."

"I'm in no hurry, Kieran," Bran said, thinking that he would keep his brother company for a while.

"Look! I don't need effin' babysitting," Kieran snapped. "I'm perfectly capable of locking up without you to help me!"

"Fine!" Bran said, grabbing his jacket and car keys, and without another word, he left the office and drove home.

The lights were on in the big house, Bran sighed, this meant Pat was still up and if he was up at this time of night he was drinking again. Sure enough, Bran walked into the study to find Pat with a glass in one hand and a bottle of Vodka in the other,

The house was a mess, the study was full of old magazines and empty coffee cups. The smell of cigarettes and old ashtrays seemed to fill the room. Some of Paul's clothes hung over the bannister rail and a pile of his textbooks sat on the floor by the study door.

"Why don't you go to bed Dad?" Bran asked as he watched Pat pour another measure of Vodka into his glass.

"I wanted to talk to you, Bran." His father slurred the words, swaying a little in the chair as he reached over to place the bottle somewhat unsteadily on the table. "Have a drink," he said pointing towards the almost empty bottle.

"I'll make us both a coffee Dad," he said and disappeared into the kitchen.

The kitchen was a mess, coffee had been spilt on the work surface, dirty dinner plates were stacked in the sink and half empty pans still sat on the cooker hob. The bread and butter lay open next to the toaster, which was surrounded by crumbs.

The cleaner who came in every Monday morning would be well pissed when she saw the state of the place!

Bran found two clean cups and made two strong cups of coffee, and carried them through to the study. Pat had finished off the last of the Vodka. Bran put the cup down on the table beside Pat and settled into one of the comfortable leather chairs to enjoy his coffee.

"It's all my fault!" Pat said suddenly; he swayed alarmingly as he tried to focus on his son's face. "I 'spect you to be a'the office an' y'wont meet any lasses there will you?" Pat shook his head. "You should have been born first; you should 'ave been mi eldest, that useless brother of yours is a waste of time! Family comes first. It's the old way, the Irish way, the way it's got to be!"

His confused ramblings made no sense to Bran "When are you going to take a wife Kieran; you'll need to bring yer son up to be an O'Donnell."

Bran realised that his Dad was confusing him with his younger brother and shook his head sadly, even drunk, Pat couldn't find anything good to say about him.

"It's my fault, yer should 'av a woman son, I push you too hard!" He made a grab for the coffee and knocked the cup off the table.

"I'll do it! I'll clean it up," he said staggering to his feet. Bran caught him as he fell over the coffee table.

"C'mon, Dad," he said and helped his father towards the stairs.

"Yer a good boy, Kieran," Pat said as he was helped up the stairs. "One day you'll make some lass a good husband!"

Pat was soon settled in his bed and Bran was left to clear up the mess that he had created, he cleaned up the spilt coffee, put away all the magazines and emptied the ashtrays, then he started on the kitchen, It didn't take long to get it looking a little more respectable; as he put away the last pot and wiped down the last section of the work surface he glanced at the clock, it was nearly two forty-five in the morning and there was still no sign of Kieran, wandering back to the study, he poured himself a whiskey and picked up one of the magazines Pat had been reading. 'Skin Deep'. It was a monthly journal all about tattoos and tattooing. Bran looked at the pictures of dragons and knives and snakes and flames and skulls; Pat was still living in hope that he would join him on his regular visits to the tattoo shop and have some weird designs engraved into his skin!

He sat back and sipped the whiskey and his thoughts drifted back to his first visit to a tattoo parlour, down by the docks in Belfast, it had been after the terrorist bomb had killed his mother in the shopping centre just weeks before Christmas. Pat had been distraught and had talked about having a tattoo as a remembrance piece for Cathleen and he had insisted that Bran should be with him when he had it done.

Bran remembered that day very clearly, it had been raining; everywhere seemed cold and dark and miserable. He walked with his father down the narrow back streets towards the old docks, the buildings were close together and depressing, windows were boarded up or broken and graffiti was daubed everywhere.

At the end of one street was a grubby shop window that had been painted black with the word TATTOOS printed in white across it.

Pat pushed the door open and ushered Bran inside, it was dark and smelled of stale bodies and cigarettes.

A big man wearing a grubby vest sat in a chair behind a small table, his arms were covered in tattoos and Bran remembered how stained his fingers were from the cigarettes he smoked, and the ink he used.

"Brought the lad in for a tattoo Pat?" he said reaching out towards Bran. Bran had moved warily behind his Dad, backing away as the two men laughed.

Bran had watched, horrified as the tattooist had punched thousands of pinprick holes in his father's shoulder, wiping the blood away to leave the skin inflamed and angry and covered in dark hateful symbols.

The tattoo he chose to remember their mother by wasn't one of love and tenderness, but one of bitterness, anger and hostility.

"Right; you now!" His Dad had said, pushing Bran towards the grubby black leather couch. Pat and the tattooist had laughed at the look of terror on Bran's face as he had tried to free himself from his fathers grasp; laughed at the joke they had played on him!

The sound of a car crunching over the gravel drive brought Bran back to the present; he shook his head and tossed the magazine onto the coffee table.

Kieran! Bran glanced at the clock; it was three twenty-five. He walked through to the kitchen just as Kieran was walking through the back door.

"Where the hell have you been?" Bran asked.

"Yeah and it's good to see you too bro," Kieran grinned.

"Do you know what time it is?" Bran said. "Where have you been till now?"

Kieran smiled and shrugged his shoulders "Just chill Bran, you're so wired; loosen up; just go with the flow bro!" Kieran laughed.

"Have you been drinking Kieran?" Bran asked because Kieran was definitely not himself.

Kieran peeled off his leather jacket and threw it onto the kitchen table.

"Later, Bran," he said, heading for the stairs "I'm shagged!" He paused for a moment, but didn't turn around, "and no! I haven't been drinking!"

He made his way towards his bedroom leaving Bran somewhat puzzled at his brothers' strange behaviour.

Bran turned off the kitchen lights and locked the doors. He picked up Kieran's jacket to hang it on the stand in the hall. As he carried it through from the kitchen, he thought for a moment about going through the pockets, seeing if there was a clue to where Kieran had been till now, but he shook his head and hung the coat on a spare peg, he hadn't quite got to the point of going through his brothers pockets just yet!

The weekend was always busy and Kieran and Bran both worked very long days, all the Taxis were out on Saturday, it was one of the busiest days of the week and they had bookings till two and three in the morning.

The drivers were in and out of the office all day and Kieran was kept busy keeping up with the jobs that came in on a regular basis.

Friday nights and Saturday nights were hectic. Kieran and Bran often worked through till the early hours of the morning, but tonight was Sunday night, and they would be finishing, as always at eleven on Sunday night.

Tonight, for some reason, Kieran seemed even keener to finish and get home.

Bran emptied the safe and counted the weeks' takings, ready to deposit it in the bank first thing in the morning.

"OK, Kieran," he said at last, "that's it, let's go home." Bran tucked the money pouches into his inside pocket and made his way down to the garage where his Audi was parked. He saw the lights go out behind him, as he drove through the gate, Kieran couldn't be far behind. He hadn't gone more than twenty-five yards down Allen Street when a big dark green four by four almost ran him off the road.

"Wankers!"' He shouted, more from surprise than anything else. He hadn't expected to see any other vehicles on the road at this time in the morning.

He continued down Allen Street heading for home, he thought about his brother, leaving the garage and hoped Kieran didn't run into them as he was stopping to lock the big outside gates. He had gone quite a way down the road when he realised that there were no headlights following him, surely it wouldn't take Kieran all this time to lock the gates, he slowed down to a crawl, watching his rear view mirror all the time, expecting to see the headlights of Kieran's Peugeot appear at any moment. As time passed and still no headlights appeared, Bran began to feel apprehensive.

Now what! He thought to himself, and he turned the Audi around and headed back to the garage. The gates were still open and Kieran's Peugeot was parked just inside the yard. Parked next to it was the big green four by four he had passed on the road.

What the hell? Bran said to himself as he looked up to see the lights were still on in the office. What the hell was Kieran playing at now!

Bran started to climb the stairs to the office; he could hear voices, angry voices.

"That was your last fuckin' chance O'Donnell!" one was saying "You've had as much time as your going to get; no more fuckin' excuses!"

"First thing in the morning Doug, I swear; first thing in the morning," It was Kieran; he sounded terrified.

"Too late," the voice said, "time's up!"

Bran flung open the office door.

"What the fuck's going on?" he said, swiftly taking in the scene before him.

There were four men in the office. Kieran was being held in a chair by two of them. Another man was sitting on the edge of the desk. This must be the man he had heard speaking, Bran assumed rightly. Kieran had called him Doug. The fourth man was holding Kieran's ankle; forcing it back around the leg of the chair. In his hand he had what looked like a rubber flashlight, but it had a grip and a trigger! And he had it held against Kieran's leg.

One of the men swiftly moved to the door, effectively blocking Bran's way out. Bran looked round at the four men; he knew he was no match for them.

"What the hell are you doing?" Bran shouted. With a stomach-wrenching lurch of horror, Bran realised that the man was holding a captive bolt humane killer, the ones they used at the abattoir to kill cattle; those things would go through the skull of a cow as easily as a spoon went through the shell of a boiled egg and he had it pressed against Kieran's kneecap!

Bran looked around at the group of men who were holding his brother; they weren't amateurs; they were relaxed and confident. Bran had grown up in Northern Ireland; he knew a punishment squad when he saw it!

"What's going on Kieran?" Bran said again, trying to give himself some time to think as he assessed his options.

"Nothing that concerns you O'Donnell; if you're smart you'll walk away and pretend you've seen nothing," said the man called Doug who was sitting on the desk.

"Of course it effin' concerns me; that's my effin' brother you've got there!"

"Take my advice O'Donnell," Doug said quietly "Just walk out of here now while you still can; my business is with your brother, not you; not yet."

"What makes you think I won't go straight to the police?" Bran said playing for time as his mind worked overtime; frantically trying to come up with an idea that would get them out of this desperate situation.

"You're too bright for that," Doug laughed. "I believe you have another brother – Paul, isn't it? – Clever kid; would be a shame if he had an 'accident' on his way home from the University one night."

"Just get out of here, Bran," Kieran groaned.

"That's the first sensible thing your brothers' said since we arrived."

"I'm not going anywhere Kieran," Bran said, "what do these men want? What the fuck have you got yourself mixed up in?"

"Your little brother has a habit; a rather expensive habit, one that he can't afford. So, I'm afraid we have to make an example, send a message to all the other fuckin' Coke heads who think they can rip me off; nothing personal, but business is business and the kid owes me a lot of money!"

"Cocaine?" Bran said stunned, looking in disbelief at his brother. He turned back to the drug dealer.

"How much?" Bran said. The man raised his eyebrows.

"Three grand," was the reply.

"Three grand!" Kieran objected. "I only owe you two!"

The man sitting on the edge of the desk slid down and walked over to Kieran, he twisted the front of his shirt in his hand, he pulled Kieran forward till he was just inches from his face.

"That's before you tried jerking me off you little prick!" He said quietly and pushed Kieran back hard into the chair.

Bran took the weeks takings from his jacket and tossed it on the desk.

"There's two thousand four hundred here," he said. "I can have the rest here in twenty minutes."

Doug opened the pouch and glanced at the cash inside; Thinking for a moment he paused, he looked over at Kieran and then at Bran,

"I think this little lesson might be more profitable in the long run."

"A Liverpool cabbie has a very big family," Bran said quietly, "and the O'Donnell's still have connections in Northern Ireland, if you get my drift." He pushed the pouch containing the money across the desk towards the drug dealer.

"Three grand," he said, stepping back and holding up his

hands. "Three grand and no problems."

The drug dealers' gaze narrowed, as he looked hard at Bran.

"Is that meant to be a threat?" He asked.

Bran shook his head.

"No threat," he said, "just a good business offer."

The man thought for a minute and then nodded and smiled, he signalled to the man with the humane killer who moved away from Kieran and handed the bolt gun to his boss.

"Twenty minutes O'Donnell," he said, "if you're not back here in twenty minutes with the cash, your brother loses a kneecap; five minutes after that he loses the other."

Bran nodded.

"I'll be back, Kieran," he said, "just stay calm." He headed towards the door.

"And O'Donnell; any sign of trouble; any sign of the police…"

Bran watched as he stood beside Kieran and placed the humane killer beneath his brothers' right ear; the meaning was very plain.

Bran had money at home, He knew he could get there and back in less than twenty minutes, as long as nothing delayed him. He pushed the thought of what would happen if he didn't get there in time out of his mind as he sprinted for the Audi and raced out of the yard heading for home, seven minutes later he was leaping up the stairs two at a time heading for his bedroom, he grabbed the box from his wardrobe; there was a couple of thousand pounds in there, money he had saved from tips and the occasional car deal.

Ten minutes, he had ten minutes to get back to Allen Street.

"Bran! Is that you?" it was his Dad! Bran ran down the stairs and flung open the door. "Bran! Get back here!"

There was no time to lose, no time to explain. Ignoring Pat's shouts, Bran ran out of the house and jumped into the Audi. The tyres spun and shot gravel across the drive as he raced out onto the road and headed back to the garage.

Back in the taxi office, Kieran was watching the clock.

"Sixteen minutes," Doug said smiling, "another four minutes O'Donnell and you can say goodbye to your football career."

The man who had held the bolt gun against Kieran's knee laughed.

Seventeen minutes; where the hell was Bran? Eighteen minutes, Doug walked over to the desk and picked up the humane killer.

"He'll be back Doug!" Kieran said, his voice tight with panic.

"For Christ's sake Doug you don't need to do this, you've got most of the money there, Bran will be back with the rest!"

Doug walked over to the chair where Kieran was being held, he nodded to one of the men who grabbed Kieran's ankle and pulled it back hard behind the chair leg, bending his knee joint and holding it steady against the solid wooden frame.

Doug looked up at the clock.

"Nineteen minutes kid," he grinned, "Unlike you; when I say I'll deliver, I mean it!" he nodded to the two men holding Kieran. "Keep him still!" He said as Kieran struggled against their grip. "I'm going to enjoy this." He pushed the captive bolt gun hard against Kieran's kneecap.

Headlights swinging into the yard suddenly illuminated the office; there was the slam of a car door.

"It's O'Donnell," one of the men said almost apologetically, looking out of the window as Bran sprinted towards the office.

Doug sighed and slowly lifted the captive bolt gun from Kieran's knee. He looked up at the clock, there were less than thirty seconds left.

"This time you were lucky O'Donnell," he said as Bran walked into the room.

"Next time you won't be as lucky."

Bran counted out the cash and tossed it onto the desk.

"There won't be 'a next time'," he said.

Doug picked up the money.

"That's what they all say!" He swung round and hit Kieran hard across the face with the bolt gun! Two of the men grabbed Bran as he lunged for Doug "and that!" Doug said as a trickle of blood ran from Kieran's nose. "Was for fucking up my night!"

The four men turned to leave; Doug, the last to go, paused as he walked through the door.

"Pleasure doing business with you gents," he said, and then they were gone.

Neither Kieran nor Bran spoke or even dared to breath until they heard the Range Rover drive out of the yard.

"Are you alright Kieran?" Bran asked. Crouching down beside his brother who was still sitting in the chair he had been held in for the last thirty minutes.

Kieran was shaking; his face white; the shock seemed to hit him all at once, he wiped the blood from his nose on the back of his hand.

"I'm sorry Bran; I'm sorry: I'm sorry."

Kieran leant forward and put his head into his hands, they were shaking violently.

Bran wrapped his arms around his brother.

"You're OK now, Kieran," he said. "It's over."

"If you hadn't come back for me Bran…" Kieran's voice faltered.

"They were really going to do it! They were going to blow my kneecaps away! They could have killed me Bran; at best I would have ended up crippled! With my kneecaps shattered!"

"You don't fuck about with drug dealers Kieran." Bran said quietly, "and we're not out of the shit yet." Bran shook his head,

"We still have to find a way to tell Pat where two and a half grand of the firm's money has gone!"

"He's going to friggin' kill me; isn't he?"

Bran slid open the bottom drawer of the desk, Pat always had a spare bottle somewhere in the office, he wasn't wrong; he took out a glass and the half bottle of Irish Whisky and poured Kieran a stiff drink.

"Drink that, it will help a little." He handed Kieran the glass; his hands were shaking so much he spilt most of it. "You're in no state to drive anyway," Bran said. Kieran tipped back the glass and shuddered as the neat whiskey seared his throat.

"Now how the hell did you get mixed up with those characters?"

Before Kieran could speak, Bran's mobile rang. He glanced at the caller display; it was Pat.

Bran paused for a moment; then answered the phone.

"Dad?"

"What the friggin' hell are you playing at Bran!" he stormed.

"Where the fuck are you?"

Bran looked over at Kieran.

"He's going to have to know sooner or later, Bran," Kieran said. Bran nodded.

"Dad, we've had some trouble here," he said, "but it's sorted now, we're on our way home, I'll tell you about it when we get in."

"C'mon, Kieran," he said. "Let's go home!"

The trauma that followed the revelation that Kieran had been snorting Cocaine was nothing compared to the blow up that followed Bran's revelation that he had handed two and a half thousand pounds of the firm's money over to the drug dealers.

"Every penny you'll pay back!" Pat had bellowed at Kieran. "Every fuckin' penny! You're working for nothing till that's repaid and if you ever so much as roll a joint in future, you won't have to worry about the dealers, 'cos I'll break both you're fuckin' legs; Stupid bastard!"

The next few days proved to be really difficult for Kieran; Pat was giving him a real hard time over the loss of the weeks' takings; Bran, as always, tried to head off the worst of Pat's temper, but he was out working most of the time; Kieran was stuck in the office; an easy target for Pat's vitriolic tongue.

"I can't take much more of this, Bran." Kieran had confided to his brother one night when Bran came in after his last fare had been dropped off.

"He's friggin' driving me nuts'! I can't do a friggin' thing right!" Kieran paced backwards and forwards across the office.

"I daren't breath when he's in the office; he's got me so my nerves are shafted," he said holding out a shaky hand.

"I'll have a word with him, Kieran, see if I can get him to ease up on you a bit." He watched his brother for a few moments.

"A lot of what you're going through is because you've stopped using." Kieran stopped his pacing for a moment and looked at Bran. He sighed.

"Yeah; I know," he said and shook his head. "One line, just one line and I would feel great, I could get through this."

"That's not the answer Kieran."

"I know," Kieran said, "But it doesn't make it any fuckin' easier!"

"One day at a time Kieran," Bran said, "one day at a time!"

6

Time passed slowly, especially for Kieran who had begun to dread hearing his fathers' footsteps on the stairs leading to the office. Never had he wished he had his taxi drivers license more than he did now!

How he wished that like his brother, he could just walk into the office, pick up the keys to his cab and disappear into the hustle and bustle of the City streets!

Business was picking up and Pat was talking about taking on a couple more drivers and extending the hours to twenty-four, seven.

"You'll need someone extra for the office." Kieran reminded him. "Me and Jane can't cover that many hours between us!"

"I'll think about it," Pat scowled.

They had managed to operate a twenty-four-hour service in the past; when business had been booming and the cars were always busy, but when the economy in Liverpool took a nosedive, so did the Taxi trade; along with all the other small businesses in the area. After all, apart from the clubbers, there wasn't much call for Taxis in the early hours of the morning.

That was until the government revised the licensing laws and extended the opening hours. Now, instead of the usual eleven o'clock rush, late-night drinkers needed Taxis at one and two in the morning. Pub-goers weren't booking Taxis in advance anymore, because they could just keep drinking till one was available. Pat was losing out on jobs because his drivers didn't work a twenty-four-hour shift system.

Times were changing, and it had become blatantly obvious;

especially to the boys' that things needed a serious overhaul!

"Paul came up with some pretty good ideas," Kieran said, reaching for his coffee. "We do need to update the system, getting a bloody computer in the office would be a start!"

Pat scowled again. "Fucking technology," he growled.

"He's got a point, Dad," Bran said as he watched some of the cars leaving the yard. He put his coffee mug on the filing cabinet next to the window.

"Just look at the difference bringing in the hands-free headsets made; Kieran and Jean can get through twice as many phone calls now."

Pat grunted. "Yeah, but the headsets' didn't cost me a couple of grand!"

Kieran grinned. "You've got to speculate to accumulate Dad."

Pat turned and glared at Kieran. "That's friggin' rich; coming from someone who cost the firm over two grand not so friggin' long ago!"

The comment was like a physical blow to Kieran.

"Kieran's paying the money back Dad!" Bran said, his heart going out to his younger brother.

"It's OK, Bran," Kieran said. "Dad's right; I made a stupid mistake, and I paid for it." He took his headset off and laid it on the desk next to the radio. "I need a break." He said, picking up his cigarettes and walking towards the office door.

Bran could see he was upset; he could almost sense the feelings of hurt and distress that surrounded Kieran like a dull grey rain cloud that wouldn't blow over.

Pat had been hazing him for a couple of weeks about the money he handed over to the drug dealers for cocaine.

Kieran took a cigarette out of the packet, lit it and inhaled deeply. He paused at the door on his way out.

"Oh, just one thing," he said over his shoulder as he walked out. "Just how much of the firms' money have you pissed up against a bloody wall when you came home drunk out yer skull every fuckin' night! Just think about that one Dad!" he said.

"Bran," Pat's voice was unmistakable, even over the crackly taxi radio. "Pick up Sean Driscoll from 'The Ferryman' in twenty minutes will you and bring him back to the office."

'The Ferryman' was a popular, if somewhat rough Irish Pub down by the Victoria docks; Bran knew it well as it was one of Pat's favourite haunts. He had picked his Dad up from 'The Ferryman' on many occasions.

It had been driving home from 'The Ferryman' just once too often after a late night drinking session that had caused Pat to finally lose his driving licence; but he hadn't seemed to mind that, after all, he had two sons with cars of their own at his beck and call and a fleet of Taxis whenever they weren't available.

Bran guessed, quite rightly, that his Dad was quite happy to have been banned from driving because it meant that he could get as blathered as he liked and he didn't have to worry about getting pulled or totalling another car. There would always be someone to make sure he got safely home."

It was four fifteen. Crowds of youngsters were milling around the University, blocking the footpaths and spilling out onto the roads, their rucksacks and bags slung over their shoulders, their outlandish clothes and weird hairdos' marking them as students.

The traffic was beginning to build up to the teatime rush

hour, slowing Bran's progress as he headed towards the Docks.

"Get out the bloody road!" Bran yelled as he had to stop suddenly, his way barred by a gang of students sauntering across the street.

"Get stuffed!"

"Fuck off wanker!"

"Piss off."

The usual replies were accompanied by the time-honoured two-finger salutes.

The road cleared and Bran drove on, hearing the thud of a shoe against the Taxis side panel as he passed the group, he ignored it, it was par for the course in this part of the City.

Jason would probably be making his way to the flat by now. A shiver of anticipation ran through Bran as he visualised Jason walking round the bedroom; as soon as he had dropped this guy off at the office, he was going to call at Anncolm Heights!

He pulled into the car park at 'The Ferryman' and checked his watch; he was ten minutes early. His mind was still very much on Jason. He knew that Jason liked to shower as soon as he got in from the Uni and he smiled as his mind wandered to an image of Jason, naked in the shower.

Pulling up in front of the pub, he killed the engine and closed his eyes. In his mind's eye a clear picture of Jason formed; the water washing the soapy lather off his gorgeous baby soft skin.

He imagined himself naked in the shower with Jason, skin on skin as they shared the intimate pleasures of a hot shower. His mind travelled across Jason's shoulders, covered in slippery, foaming shower gel and how he would run his hands down that beautiful wet body; The erotic thoughts caused a stirring in his crotch as his manhood strained against the fabric of his chinos and he reached down to adjust to a more comfortable position. He smiled to himself as he thought about playing out his fantasies later that night.

A tapping on the cab window shocked him back into reality with a jolt. He grabbed the newspaper from the passenger seat next to him and dragged it across his lap to hide the very obvious erection; he hadn't expected the fare to come out of the pub looking for him.

He pressed the button and the electric window slid down.

"It's Bran, isn't it?" the strong Belfast accent was unmistakable.

"I'm Sean Driscoll; I'm an old friend of your fathers, and this is my lass, Lisa." He beckoned over the young woman who had been standing unnoticed by Bran, in the shadows of the pub porch.

"Your fathers' told us a lot about you, Bran."

Bran felt he should get out of the taxi and open the doors for them, but just at that moment he didn't dare; his aroused state was still very evident.

"Right! Yeah! OK!" Bran squirmed uncomfortably in his seat, wishing that Sean Driscoll and his daughter would stop staring in through the open window.

"I haven't seen your Dad in a long time; met him on a cargo ship but lost touch when he left Belfast. We've been over here a couple of months; the missus was looking for a taxi in the yellow pages and spotted your name, I didn't think it could be the same O'Donnell, so I rang up; had a nice long chat with your father."

"Right," Bran said again, "he's waiting back at the office do you want to jump in?" he asked nodding towards the back doors.

"Yeah, sure," Sean said.

"Is that today's?" He asked, indicating the newspaper on Bran's lap.

"No!" Bran said quickly as he crumpled the front page. "It's an old one, I was just using it to… to clean the windows.

Sean gave him a quizzical look but shrugged his shoulders.

"Oh," he said.

"Do you want to get in?" Bran said hopefully. "Pat's waiting back at the office."

Sean opened the back door and Bran breathed a huge sigh of relief as the young woman; Lisa, moved away from his open window and climbed into the back of the taxi. Sean walked round the vehicle and climbed into the other side.

Relieved to at last be moving, Bran pulled out of the car park onto the main road. It must have looked a bit strange, driving along with the newspaper spread across his lap, but Bran wasn't taking any chances!

The rush hour traffic crawled through the busy City centre as Bran made his way across town towards Allen Street.

"So what made you move from Belfast?" Bran asked as the taxi stopped at the lights of a big junction that was crammed with slow moving vehicles.

"Business," Sean said, "we're only here temporarily while I set up a few contracts, my son, Danny is looking after things at home. Lisa here," he indicated the pretty young woman who sat next to him "Wanted to see some of the sights in England; the missus wouldn't let her come on her own, so I'm stuck with both of them." He grinned at his daughter.

It was obvious to Bran that 'being stuck with both of them' wasn't the hardship that Sean tried to make out!

"So what business are you in?" Bran asked as the traffic began moving again.

"Construction," Sean said. "Mainly high rise and offices, but we're looking at some big residential projects round Kirby and Croxteth."

"Big firm then?" Bran asked.

"It pays the bills," Sean replied.

They were soon on the long straight road that led to the O'Donnell Garage and Taxi Office. Thankfully Bran felt the throbbing in his trousers slowly subsiding as his cock assumed a more manageable size. Cautiously he removed the newspaper and glanced down at his lap.

Thank Christ, he thought, things were almost back to normal, he would have to kerb his fuckin' imagination in future!

Bran pulled into the yard and stopping outside the office, he jumped out of the taxi to open the door for Lisa.

"Thanks," she said, grinning at him as she straightened her jacket and looped her bag over her shoulder.

"This way," Bran said as Sean Driscoll joined his daughter, He opened the office door, standing back to let them enter before him.

"Follow me," he said, passing them and heading for the stairs, "I'll show you where the office is."

Sean and Lisa Driscoll followed Bran into the office where Pat O'Donnell waited to greet his old friend.

"Don't disappear, Bran," Pat said as he saw Bran making for the door.

"I want you to take us back to the house, Sean and I have a lot of catching up to do."

"Ah'hem!" Kieran coughed noisily to attract his Dad's attention. "Are you not going to introduce me?" he asked, looking round Sean to where Lisa stood shyly at the back of the room.

"Oh, yes, Sean this is Kieran, my second eldest, Paul, the youngest is at University, Business studies, he'll take over the firm one day no doubt."

"Dad! Forget Paul," Kieran said exasperated. "Who's this lovely young woman hiding in the corner?"

Sean laughed.

"This is Lisa, my daughter, she's just finished her final year at Queens University in Belfast, Ecological science and land management," He grinned.

"It took me a month to remember what the subject was, let alone anything about it."

"Brains as well as beauty," Kieran smiled.

Lisa squirmed in the corner and blushed to the roots of her hair!

"Stop embarrassing the lass," Pat said.

"Oh, don't worry, Pat." Sean smiled.

"Lisa can take care of herself; believe me!"

The ten-minute journey back to the house was pleasant, the conversation light and chatty; the weather, the flight over from Belfast; the house Sean and his wife were renting on the outskirts of Liverpool; Pat's taxi firm and Paul's promising academic achievements.

Bran turned into the drive at home, the gravel crunched with a familiar sound as he pulled up opposite the big front door, he jumped out and opened the door for Lisa, she smiled as she took the hand he offered her as he helped her out of the taxi.

The house was warm, and, Bran was relieved to find, relatively tidy; the cleaner must have been in that morning.

Pat led his visitors through to the study.

"Get the coffee Bran," he ordered. "Have a seat, Sean," he said indicating the comfortable leather settee.

Bran headed for the kitchen. He put the kettle on the Aga and pulled four mugs down from the shelf.

"Can I help?" It was Lisa; she had followed him from the study. "Those two will be talking about boats and cargos and old times for ages," she said, looking round the spacious kitchen.

"Oh! An Aga!" she walked over to the huge cast iron cooker and leant against it, enjoying the heat that radiated from its reassuring bulk.

"I've tried to talk mum into getting one of these, but she's into all these hi-tech gadgets."

She ran her fingers over the polished enamel surface, enjoying the warmth of the metal beneath her hand.

"And I love the colour," she said. "British Racing Green isn't it?"

Bran nodded as he reached for the coffee jar that sat on top of the microwave.

"Doesn't get used very often," he said, "but when you get in on a dark winters night, wet through, frozen to the bone and dog tired, the kitchen's always warm, the kettles always near to boiling and it's just the right height for leaning on."

He spooned coffee into the four mugs.

"So, how long are you over here for?" Bran asked, making polite conversation. Lisa shrugged.

"All depends on Dad," she said.

"How quickly he can sort out these contracts and set up a base here in Liverpool, then Danny will probably come over and run things from here."

"Danny?" Bran asked.

"My brother."

Lisa reached for the jar marked 'sugar' and put it down next to the mugs.

"Dad has two," she said, "none for me."

"Milk's in the fridge." Bran indicated the big, brushed steel fridge freezer over in the corner. Lisa opened the fridge and pulled out the two-litre bottle of milk from the bottom shelf. She was mildly surprised to see that the fridge was reasonably well stocked. She knew that if this had been a fridge in a flat belonging to any group of male students back at Queen's it would probably have contained a two-week-old pizza, a packet of bacon and a couple of cases of beer, but then this top of the range fridge freezer wasn't the sort of thing that you found in the usual student dive!

"No beer?" She said, turning towards Bran, the milk in one hand, and the open fridge door in the other.

"There's a fridge in the study." He grinned, we got fed up of trailing backwards and forwards to the kitchen all the time!"

Lisa laughed and closed the fridge door. She put the milk down on the unit next to the Aga.

"So what do you and your brothers get up to when you're not working?" she asked.

"We don't get a lot of free time," Bran explained. "But when we do, it's the usual; pubs and clubs."

Between them, they took the four coffees through into the study.

"I'll get back to work Dad"' Bran said as he finished his coffee, "Get Kieran to radio when you want picking up."

"Hang on, Bran," Sean said as Bran made for the door. Bran paused, puzzled. "Is your cab booked for the next couple of hours?" he asked.

Bran shook his head and glanced at Pat. "You haven't got me down for any runs have you?" he asked.

"Nothing on the books," Pat confirmed.

"That's good," Sean continued. "Because I would like to hire your taxi for a couple of hours if that's OK with your Dad."

Sean put his arm around Lisa's shoulders. "Lisa would be bored stiff listening to two old sailors reminiscing, so I would like you to spend a couple of hours showing her some of the sights around Liverpool."

Bran glanced across at his Dad, his evening with Jason rapidly disappearing.

"Of course, the lad will do that for you, Sean," Pat said.

"Only if that's OK with Bran?" Sean had noticed the fleeting look on Bran's face.

"That would be fine, Sean," Bran smiled reassuringly. "It's not a problem, really; I would love to show Lisa something of the City."

"Well that's settled then; just tell me what I owe you when you pick us up later."

Pat tried to wave off the suggestion that Sean should pay for the taxi, but Sean wouldn't hear of it.

"Business is business," he said, "and a fare is a fare."

A few minutes later he stood at the door with Pat and waved as Lisa climbed into the front passenger seat next to Bran. She pulled on her seatbelt as Bran pulled smoothly out onto the road.

"Thank Christ for that!" She exclaimed. "I thought I was going to be stuck with him all bloody day!"

Bran was shocked! But not as shocked as he was with what happened next.

Lisa slid her hand across onto his thigh; he could feel the heat of it through his chinos.

"So just what are you going to show me Bran?" she grinned wickedly. Bran took a deep breath.

"Look, Lisa, I really am very flattered." He wriggled uncomfortably beneath her touch.

"But that is rather distracting when I'm trying to drive!"

She laughed as she removed her hand.

"Sorry Bran," she grinned. "I couldn't resist teasing you; I'll behave myself, honest!"

Bran cast a sideways glance at the young woman who sat beside him; a mass of dark brown wavy hair surrounded the laughing face with its' pert little pixie nose and elfin features;

"somehow," Bran thought to himself. "I don't think this one could behave herself if she tried!"

Bran proved to be an excellent tour guide and he kept Lisa amused with his anecdotes about the City.

He walked with her up the steps of the Metropolitan Cathedral.

"You know what the locals call this building?" He asked. Lisa shook her head.

"Paddy's wigwam." He grinned. Lisa chuckled, "Well it does look a bit like a very big teepee!"

As they walked round the Albert docks and gazed up at the buildings known as The Three Graces, Bran was relaxing and starting to enjoy Lisa's company; true to her word, she was 'behaving herself' and apart from the occasional hand she placed on his arm, she left his body alone!

They took some time to look round the Beatles Experience Exhibition; both of them too young to remember 'The Fab Four'.

Back in the taxi, Bran headed for Matthew Street and the Cavern Club and they sat and drank coffee at a street café, watching crowds of people hurrying by. And as evening approached, the light faded only to be replaced by a magical kaleidoscope of colour as the night-lights of the City twinkled into existence.

"C'mon," Bran said, taking her hand and pulling her to her feet. "There's one place I want you to see.

The impressive entrance to Liverpool's' China Town towered majestically above the entrance to Nelson Street, lit by floodlights that brought the detailed carvings to life.

"This is the oldest China Town in Europe; the traditional Chinese gateway is over forty feet high. It was built by workmen from Shanghai and contains two-hundred hand carved dragons." Bran paused, embarrassed. "Shit!" he said grinning, "I sound just like one of the poxy council tour guides!"

Lisa put her hand on his arm.

"You sound OK to me Bran O'Donnell."

They were still walking through China Town when Bran's mobile rang. It was Pat.

"Bran, come and pick Sean up, you can take him and Lisa home now." Bran turned to Lisa. "End of the tour I'm afraid."

They turned and walked back towards the taxi; Lisa looped her arm around Bran's with a familiarity that Bran wasn't comfortable with.

Lisa glanced up at him and unhooked her arm so that she could go and look in one of the colourful shop windows.

"I will have to come and do some serious shopping here." She said breezily, as they walked side by side down Nelson Street.

This time she didn't loop her arm in Bran's.

It was quite dark when they got back to where Bran had parked the taxi; he walked round to the passenger door and opened it for Lisa.

"Thanks, Bran," she said, "it's been a super couple of hours." She wrapped both her arms around his waist; she grinned wickedly as he froze, like a startled rabbit caught in the headlights of a car!

"Thank you for being such a lovely tour guide," she reached up to kiss him; he turned his head so that she could kiss his cheek. Lisa smiled "You are a sweetie," she said as she slid into the passenger seat, "Let's go home shall we?"

The gravel crunched as the taxi pulled smoothly up to the front door; Pat and Sean Driscoll were waiting, still chatting; illuminated by the beams from the bright security lights that were fixed to the outside walls.

Bran got out of the taxi and walked round to open the door for Lisa. She smiled sweetly as she climbed gracefully out of the passenger seat. Pulling her wavy brown hair free of her jacket collar, she looped her handbag over her shoulder and walked over to her father.

"Had a good afternoon, honey?" he asked, kissing her lightly on the cheek.

"Wonderful!" she beamed. "Bran has been an absolute gem; I don't think I've enjoyed myself so much for ages; the time just flew by!"

Sean looked up at Bran and beamed.

"My pleasure," Bran said shrugging his shoulders and feeling quite embarrassed.

"It's much appreciated Bran," Sean said, "let your Dad know how much this afternoon came to because he's going to set up an account for me; I'm going to be needing transport while I'm over here, so I hope you will be driving for us again."

"Any time," Bran said.

Pat walked over to the taxi and opened the back doors for Sean and Lisa and closed them carefully once they had got in; he opened the front passenger door and climbed in as Bran slid into the driver's seat and pulled on his seatbelt.

"Take Sean and his lass home and then you can drop me at the office," Pat said as Bran pulled out into the busy evening traffic.

The house Sean and his wife were renting was a big detached three-bedroom property in a nice leafy part of Liverpool.

Bran pulled the car into the drive and got out to open the door for Lisa; Sean climbed out of the other door.

"I'll be in touch Pat," he said, leaning into the taxi.

The two old friends shook hands.

"Good to see you Sean," Pat said. "Brought back some good memories!"

Sean nodded and straightened up.

"Been nice meeting you too Bran," he said, extending his

hand. "Thanks for looking after Lisa."

"My pleasure." Bran grinned and grasped the outstretched hand; he felt the rustle of paper in his palm.

Sean nodded and releasing Bran's hand; put his arm around his daughters' shoulders and ushered her towards the front door.

"Bye Bran," she called. "Thanks again."

Bran looked down at the notes in his hand as Sean and Lisa disappeared into the house; two twenties!

"C'mon!" Pat said. "Get a move on; I need to get back to the office now."

"Yes, sir!" Bran said, pushing the two notes deep into his back pocket. "Right away sir!"

"Nice young woman that," Pat commented as they made their way towards Allen Street.

"Yeah, they both seemed very nice." Bran agreed, thinking about the forty-pound tip in his pocket.

"Good Irish family," Pat said. "Pretty lass; bright as well!"

Bran sighed, "Don't start Dad!" he said.

"Well you could do a lot worse Bran O'Donnell; successful business; companies all over Europe and Sean tells me she hasn't got a boyfriend at the moment."

"For Christ's sake Dad; leave it out!" Bran groaned.

Pat continued as though he hadn't heard Bran.

"You know what they say son; marry for love, but love where there's brass!"

Bran put his foot down a little harder on the accelerator; the sooner they got back to the garage the better!

7

Bran closed the taxi door and smiled as he watched the young couple make their way, somewhat unsteadily up the garden path to the front door of their house. The woman who looked to be in her early twenties, hugged a huge bouquet of red roses in one arm, her other arm was firmly wrapped around her husband's waist. Bran grinned as he watched their giggling attempts to unlock the door and their final passionate kiss on the doorstep before disappearing into their home.

It had been their first wedding anniversary, celebrated by a romantic candlelit meal, champagne and roses. Yeah, lots of champagne, Bran thought. It had been a good job and - a ten-pound tip! There were rose petals all over the back seat and the cab smelled like a flower shop! Bran grinned; again he could live with that!

Sliding into the driver's seat, Bran pulled on his seatbelt; he was just about to turn the ignition when his mobile phone rang; he flipped it open.

"Yeah!" he said, wondering who could be calling him on his personal mobile at this time of night.

"Bran?" the voice was weak, almost inaudible. "Bran?"

"Jay, is that you?" Bran could only just recognise Jason's voice. "Reception's bloody terrible, I can hardly hear you!"

"Oh, God… I'm hurt, Bran,"

Bran was shocked at the faltering sound of Jason's voice.

"I need you, Bran! Help me; please!"

A cold icy lump seemed to form in the pit of Bran's stomach.

"Jason! What's happened, where are you?"

"On Campus Bran, the lane behind the students' bar."

Bran didn't hesitate; he swung the taxi onto the main road and stomped on the accelerator.

"Jay, what's happened? Do you need an ambulance? Bran asked as he raced towards the University.

"No!" Jason said, "no ambulances, just get me out of here Bran, just get me away before they come back!"

"Hang on Jay, I'll soon be there, just hang on!"

Bran had a good idea what had happened, he could tell from the horror and dread in Jason's voice. Gay bashing was considered a sport in certain areas of Liverpool and the student bars were considered a good place to 'go hunting' and Jason was such a sweet soul, so very gentle; an easy target because in a lot of ways he was so very innocent.

Bastards! Bran thought as he raced towards the University. Effin' bastards!

The main student bar was on the edge of the Campus, the entrance to the bar was well lit on the main road to the central complex; running parallel to the main road and to the rear of the bar was a short cut that went to the halls of residence, Bran had transported many students to and from the docks, the station or the airport, to the halls of residence and he knew the lane well, it was quiet, secluded and not very well lit; something that many of the young female students had complained about bitterly on many occasions!

He swung the taxi into the Campus and headed for the halls of residence.

The Student bar was still busy, but the lane at the back of the bar was deserted. The taxi rolled slowly down the lane, Bran searched the shadows for any sign of Jason, and then down by one of the lock-up garage blocks, he spotted a figure huddled in a dark corner.

He threw himself out of the taxi and sprinted to where Jason lay hunched in the shadows cowering in fear and pain. The light from the cab's headlights was enough to show Bran that Jason was badly hurt, his blonde hair was matted with blood and the fresh bruises on his face were very evident.

"No!" Jason whispered; his voice full of panic as Bran crouched down by his side. "Jason, it's me," he said reaching out to touch him. Jason flinched and pulled away from him. It was then that Bran realised that Jason's jeans had been ripped down to his knees, exposing his buttocks, Bran could see the livid bruises and muddy marks of the shoes and boots that had repeatedly kicked him as he lay exposed and vulnerable in the muddy lane. Not content with the physical assault, his attackers had gone out of their way to humiliate Jason as well.

"Effin' bastards!" Bran swore as he took off his jacket and wrapped it around Jason's shoulders, Jason's shirt was torn and his jacket was wet through, Bran could smell the reason for that, his attackers had urinated on him as he lay almost unconscious from the vicious kicking!

"Can you walk Jay?" Bran asked as he tried to help Jason to his feet. Jason's legs just buckled underneath him.

"Get me out of here Bran," he pleaded, "get me away before anyone sees me like this."

"I'll get the cab; don't worry, Jason, it'll be alright." He ran back to the cab and noticed, with another angry surge, that Jason's portfolio of artwork had been ripped into pieces and trampled into the mud. He drove down to the lock-up, and, grabbing a rug from the boot he knelt beside Jason and gently wrapped the rug around him.

"Come on Jay," he said, putting his shoulder beneath Jason's arm, "Let's go."

He lifted Jason who cried out as the sudden movement caused him more pain.

"Wait!! Jason said, and he leant against Bran whimpering in pain as he slowly pulled his jeans up over his hips.

Bran helped Jason into the back of the cab; every step he took seemed to cause him pain. Bran was worried because there were times when Jason seemed to be drifting into unconsciousness; head injuries were serious things and there was a lot of blood in his hair.

It didn't take long to get from the University to Liverpool City General. It was Friday night and the Accident and Emergency department was heaving with the usual binge drinkers, drug takers and victims of domestic violence as well as road traffic accident and assault victims.

Leaving the cab by the accident and emergency entrance, Bran ran in to find a nurse or a porter, anyone who could help him to get Jason some much-needed attention. A nurse immediately organised a porter to bring a wheelchair.

"Bran?" a familiar voice caught his attention. "Bran are you alright? Has someone from the firm been hurt?"

It was Mike Cooper, one of the O'Donnell's Taxi drivers.

"I'm fine, Mike," Bran replied, "just brought someone in from the Uni." He looked through the glass doors; two porters were helping Jason out of the back if the cab and into the waiting wheelchair.

"What are you doing here Mike?" Bran asked, wondering what was taking these flaming porters so long!

"A guy fell through a plate glass door and cut his hand up pretty badly, I'm waiting for him to have stitches put in then I can take him back home, he couldn't drive himself."

At that point, the porter wheeled Jason over to where Bran was standing with Mike.

"All the triage rooms are in use at the moment but as soon as one is free the nurse will come and take him through; you sit tight," the porter said to Jason, "a nurse will be with you soon."

"Are you OK?" Bran said quietly to Jason, he was very aware that Mike was listening to every word.

"I didn't want to come here Bran," Jason said, "I hate fuckin' hospitals, all that prodding and poking, and they ask too many fuckin' personal questions!"

"I know him," Mike said quietly to Bran, just out of Jason's hearing "I'm sure he's one of those poncy art students, I'm sure I've picked him up from the art gallery before now; looks like he's been cruising the wrong district!" Mike smirked.

A sudden panic gripped Bran, what if Mike started to put two and two together, what if Jason said or did something that made their relationship obvious. Bran could just imagine the reactions that would sweep through the office, the family, before long every friggin' taxi driver in Liverpool would know!

He jumped as the nurse touched him on the arm before she bent down to talk to Jason.

"There's a triage room free and the doctor can see you now." She looked up at Bran.

"This may take a little while," she said. "Would you like to come through and keep your friend company?"

Bran was torn, he wanted to be with Jason, but was so very aware of Mike listening to the conversation, he didn't know what to do, what to say; he just wished he was somewhere else, anywhere else but here. He was aware that Jason was looking up at him, waiting for a response. Mike was watching him, listening to him. He wondered if they could hear his heart beating and the panic grew and grew!

"No… err no," he faltered. "I'm just the taxi driver."

"Oh, I see," the nurse said, standing up and taking hold of the wheelchair handles.

Bran glanced down at Jason. He thought he would never get the memory of that moment from his mind. Jason's expression was heart-breaking. There was such a look of utter disbelief and betrayal in those baby blue eyes.

The nurse started to wheel Jason towards the triage room.

"Wait!" Jason said, and he dug painfully into his jeans pocket, he thrust a bloodstained ten-pound note into Bran's hand.

"Keep the change!" he said bitterly.

"Hey, Bran!" Mike said. Bran dragged his gaze away from those accusing blue eyes.

"When you get back to the office, will you let Kieran know I'll be stuck here for a while," Mike continued, "Friday night and all that!"

"Yeah, sure," Bran said turning back to where Jason had been, but it was too late, the nurse was just pushing the wheelchair through the doors into the triage room.

Bran looked down at the ten-pound note in his hand.

"Fuck!" he said under his breath "Fuck!"

The hospital porter tapped him on the shoulder.

"Is that your cab outside?" he asked. Bran nodded "Move it

will you mate; it's making it difficult for the ambulances to turn around."

"Right, sorry," Bran said absently, and he wandered out to the cab. He felt absolutely gutted; he couldn't get the look on Jason's face out of his mind.

Later that night, Bran tried to contact Jason, both on his mobile and his landline and could not get a reply from either; of course, he remembered; Jason had a head injury, they would probably keep him in overnight. Bran wondered if he should ring the hospital, but they wouldn't tell him anything anyway. He would ring Jason at home tomorrow night; surely he would be home by then.

Saturday was one of their busiest days, Pat had booked four Taxis for a late night pick up from one of the clubs in town, a stag night party that was supposed to finish at one thirty in the morning, by the time all the guests had been found and organised into their relevant cabs, it was twenty past two. Bran finally made it back to the garage at ten to three. Far too late to call Jason, but Sunday was his day off; he would call round at the flat and see how he was, if he needed anything and hopefully he would get the opportunity to apologise and try to make up for being such a dick!

It was the afternoon before Bran got the chance to get out of the house and phone Jason. There was no reply from the mobile. Bran sat in the car for a while and tried the number again. Still there was no reply from Jason's mobile; Bran tried the landline, surely Jason would be at home. There was no reply from the landline either, becoming a little worried; Bran decided to ring the hospital. Eventually, he was put through to the ward that Jason had been admitted to for observations only to find out that he had been discharged on Saturday morning.

Bran drove round to Anncolm Heights and let himself into the block of flats; he walked up the three flights of stairs and quietly knocked on the door to Jason's flat.

"Jason, it's me, Bran." He knocked again; there was no sound from inside. "Jason?"

Bran sighed and headed for the stairs, perhaps he was staying with friends for a couple of days, or he may have gone home to his parents for the weekend. He took one longing look back at the impassive door and walked slowly back down the stairs.

Jason should be back at Uni tomorrow; Bran wondered if he would be ready to go back to the campus, after all, that's where the attack had taken place. He would ring again tomorrow.

Bran hated Mondays; the trek into town to deposit the previous week's takings in the bank; the struggle to find a parking space and then the tedious stand in the long queues, waiting to get to a teller. Banks were such boring places, there wasn't even anything interesting to look at while you were waiting, and then the teller always insisted on re-counting the cash. Then there was the trip to the filling station to settle the firms' account and last but not least; the weekly shop at Tesco.

All terribly exciting stuff! Bran thought to himself as he loaded the bags of groceries into the back of his Audi.

He slid into the driver's seat and paused for a second; then he flipped open his mobile phone, Perhaps Jay was at home now.

But again, there was no reply to any of his calls. This was rather strange and somewhat disconcerting. Where had Jason disappeared too?

Kieran was waiting for him at the door when he arrived back

home, and helped to unload the groceries.

"I never really got the chance to thank you properly for pulling me out of the shit with Doug the other week, Bran," he said as they emptied the bags into the kitchen cupboards. "And before that, you took the blame when I got caught speeding in one of the taxis."

"Yeah." Bran smiled ruefully rubbing his chin. "I remember that well; what possessed you to go joy riding in one of the cabs anyway?"

"I needed a fix; the only place I could get it was the City centre and the dealers were looking for me; they knew my car, but Taxis come and go all the time." Kieran shook his head "I thought that if I could get there and back quickly you might not notice the cab was missing." Kieran put the last bag of chips into the freezer, and reaching into his pocket, he pulled out a wad of notes.

"Six hundred pounds Bran," he said, pushing it into his brothers' hand.

"But you've not paid Pat off yet," Bran said as he looked at the notes in his hand.

"I just wanted to make sure you got your money back Bran."

"I could have waited," Bran said.

"I know," Kieran smiled; the two brothers looked at each other.

"You've had to wait far too long." And in that split second an understanding passed between them, an understanding that spanned the years.

"Bran!" Pat shouted from the study. "Get off yer ass! Paul wants picking up from the Uni!"

Bran sighed and bowed his head.

"A woman's' work is never done!" He laughed.

"Do you want me to go?" Kieran uncharacteristically offered.

Bran was almost tempted to accept the offer, but his car was parked outside the door and it would give him another opportunity to ring Jason on his way to the Uni.

At the first opportunity, Bran rang Jason's mobile; once again the phone rang and rang but was not answered.

Bran rang Jason's home number, the phone rang for a while; "Pick up Jason! Pick up!" Bran said to himself. He felt a sudden rush of relief as the phone was answered and Jay's quiet voice said "Hello?"

"Jason; It's me…I…" There was a click as the phone went dead.

Bran redialled the number; he got the engaged tone. He tried again; still the engaged tone; what the fuck!

Bran rang Jason's mobile. The pre-recorded message played in his ear "This number is currently unavailable."

Bran's heart sank; Jason had put the phone down on him. His first reaction was to turn the car around and head for the flats at Anncolm Heights, but he was on his way to pick Paul up from the Uni. His mind was in turmoil; he hadn't expected Jason to react this way. Then that terrible feeling of guilt washed over him; he had been a right bastard; he had turned his back on the man who had come to mean so much to him; denied that he knew him and then left him stuck in the friggin' hospital!

"What do you expect you stupid bastard!" he said to himself "Fuckin' flowers!"

He pulled into the Campus car park; Paul wasn't in the usual pick up place. Bran rang Jason's home number again.

Jason answered the phone.

"Jason please don't," … '*Click*' … "Put the phone down." Bran's voice tailed off; he was talking to a dead phone.

"Shit!" Bran swore. "Shit!"

This was turning into a bigger problem than he thought.

He was just about to try the number again when the passenger door opened, and Paul slid into the seat. He put his books on the floor and pulled on the seatbelt.

"What a shit day!" He complained. "Nothing but effin' case studies."

Bran dropped his mobile into his pocket and slipped the Audi into gear.

"How about letting me drive Bran!" Paul suggested hopefully.

Bran coasted out onto the busy main road and glanced across at Paul.

"In your dreams little brother!" he said.

8

Kieran's voice was clear over the radio.

"Have you dropped off that station fare, Bran?"

Bran yawned, it was late and he had been working all day.

"Yes, just about to head for the garage, I'm knackered!"

"Are you anywhere near Fennel Street?"

"Close enough, why?"

"Can you do a run from the Bird and Baby to Ormerod Street?"

"OK," Bran said, yawning again, "make it the last one for me Kieran, I'm shagged! You got a name?" he asked.

"Smith," Kieran said, and the radio went dead.

Great! Bran thought as he swung the cab around 'Smith' had better not be friggin' bombed. The last thing he needed at this time of night was some Piss head throwing up in the back of the cab.

The Eagle and Child Pub had a reputation of being a drinker's pub, the car park was crammed with vehicles; so much so that it took Bran quite some time to manoeuvre his way to the Pub entrance. There was no one at the door so Bran locked up the cab and walked into the pub.

"Cab for Smith," he announced.

A man who looked to be in his late twenties was standing at the bar, he had a part drunk glass of lager in his hand.

"Yeah! Over here mate," he said, raising the glass, "be with you in a minute," and he began drinking the remainder of the pint.

"I'll wait outside," Bran said and turned to leave.

A hand reached out and touched him on the elbow, he looked down, and it was Keith, one of the City Ride drivers.

"Hi, Keith," Bran said, pausing for a moment "Having a night off?"

"You know what they say, Bran! All work and no play…"

Bran laughed.

"Yeah, I certainly seem to be seeing more work than play these days," he said.

Keith beckoned him a little closed, his face serious for a second; he nodded his head towards the punter Bran had come to pick up.

"Be careful with that one Bran," he said, "He can get a bit funny."

Bran looked up; the man had almost finished his drink.

"Thanks for the warning, Keith," he said and walked out to his cab.

Bran radioed the office.

"On my way to Ormerod Street Kieran," he said to his brother.

"Should be back at the garage in about thirty minutes." He had just clipped the radio mike back in its holder when the front passenger door was opened and the Smith guy slid into the seat, then both back doors opened as three more men climbed into the back of the cab.

"Hey! I'm only supposed to carry three passengers max," Bran pointed out.

"C'mon mate!" one of the men behind him said. "There's

plenty of room here in the back!"

"We'll make it worth your while," Smith said, "you can't leave one of us here, it's a hell of a long way to Ormerod street!"

Bran pulled on his seatbelt, he didn't like having this many men in the cab, but at least they didn't seem to be drunk.

What the hell, Bran thought, it would be quicker to take them to Ormerod Street than it would be to argue.

The taxi pulled smoothly out onto the main road, it was quite a way to the Ormerod Road Estate, it was a good job; with or without a tip! It was a job Bran really couldn't afford to turn down, especially as it was the last one for the night. The four men were very quiet and seemed to spend most of their time texting messages on their mobile phones. It was eleven forty-five and the City Centre was still buzzing with activity, Bran made his way easily through the heavy traffic, at last the flow of vehicles became lighter and lighter until only one or two other cars passed the cab, Ormerod street was in the centre of the Ormerod Road Estate, it was a veritable rabbit warren of housing association properties and flats but one that Bran knew well as quite a few of their regular customers lived in this area.

"Here will be fine, mate," Smith said as they turned the corner into Ormerod Street.

"That will be eleven pounds," Bran said turning to the man in the front seat.

One of the three in the back of the cab laughed.

"You've got to be bloody joking," Smith said, "if you think we're paying eleven effin' pounds for a poxy taxi cab you're effin' mistaken!" The three men in the back got out of the taxi, they were laughing. Bran got out of the cab. Smith was climbing leisurely out of the passenger side. Bran held the door, preventing him from leaving the taxi.

"That," Bran repeated, "will be eleven pounds!"

The three men had stopped laughing, they were moving towards Bran.

Bran slammed the taxi door and heard the howl of pain as Smith's hand was crushed between the heavy door and the metal frame.

One of the others swung his fist at Bran. Bran ducked and drove his fist into the stomach of his attacker. The man doubled up gasping for breath. A second man launched himself at Bran, sending him crashing into the side of the taxi. Two of them rushed at Bran, trying to pin him against the vehicle. Bran brought up his elbow and smashed it with all the force he could muster into the face of the nearest man, blood splattered from his broken nose; the other mans' fist crashed into the side of Bran's head.

"Y' frikin' wanker!" the first man swore through the blood that ran across his face "you've broke mi fuckin nose!" He swung his fist at Bran's face, the heavy gold ring he wore sliced the skin beneath his eye. Bran retaliated quickly, his fist catching the man squarely on the jaw, snapping his head backwards, he fell silently in a heap beside the taxi, Bran felt a sharp pain behind his knee as one of them kicked him, unable to stop himself, he fell to one knee; he gasped as the men kicked him again and again, the impact of heavy boots almost causing him to fall as they smashed into his lower back, turning, he pushed himself up, his back against the taxi. Smith had climbed out of the passenger seat, A Stanley knife in his hand!

"You effin' Irish bastard!" Smith swore. "You're going to effin' regret that!" and he swung the knife at Bran's face. Bran blocked the attack with his left forearm and drove his right fist into Smith's groin. Smith screamed and dropped the knife, clutching his damaged genitals.

The two men still standing rushed Bran,

Bran pushed himself to his feet, and without thinking, brought his foot up to meet the attack; it was a technique he had been taught at the martial arts club Pat had insisted he join. His foot caught one of his attackers squarely on the jaw; the man fell without a sound.

Bran turned towards the fourth man. The man backed off, looking at his companions. Bran took a step towards him. He turned and ran off down the street.

Bran turned to Smith, who was still moaning and nursing his injured balls. Grabbing him by his collar, Bran hauled Smith to his feet and pushed him up against the side of the taxi. Going through Smith's pockets he eventually found a wallet.

"That," he said, counting out the money in front of Smith, "will be eleven pounds!" Bran pocketed the money and thrust the wallet back into Smith's jacket, then he pushed him away from the taxi and climbed into the driver's seat, and without a backwards glance, drove off down Ormerod street, leaving Smith and his friends wondering what happened!

Bran pulled into the garage; he parked the cab in its usual spot and headed wearily for the office. Kieran was talking to a driver over the radio and Pat was deep in conversation with another of the drivers who had obviously just finished working as well.

"No, it doesn't hurt; stings a bit, that's all," Pat said showing off his latest tattoo.

The driver rolled up his sleeve to show the Celtic band tattooed around his arm "Got that done in Manchester," he said.

Pat nodded, admiring the clean lines of the tattoo.

"You will have to call in at Rick's Place, where I get mine done he said, "Rick's a bit of a weirdo, but he's a bloody good tattooist!"

Bran shook his head and smiled, Pat and his bloody tattoos, he was always getting on at him to have a tattoo done; 'It'll make a man of you, son!'

He walked over to the small kitchen area and poured himself a coffee from the pot that stood on the hot plate; he strolled over to Kieran and handed him the pouch containing the nights' takings.

"Thanks," Kieran said taking the pouch from his brother, and then he looked up at Bran.

"What the fuck happened to you!" he exclaimed as he caught sight of the cut under Bran's eye.

Pat and the driver stopped their conversation and hurried over to check Bran's injuries.

"How the hell did you let this happen?" Pat asked.

"That last fare; the Smith guy." Bran said, continuing to drink his coffee. "Him and his mates decided they weren't going to pay for the ride; they were mistaken!"

Pat examined the cut, pushing the skin to see just how deep it was.

"Ouch!" Bran exclaimed, pulling away from his fathers probing fingers "Fuck off, Dad: that bloody hurts!" he said.

"Needs stitching," Pat said.

Bran shook his head.

"Oh, no! No hospitals! There's some micropore in the first aid box," he said, "that's all they would put on it at the General anyway."

Kieran pulled the first aid box down from the shelf. Bran was relieved when Pat finally completed his ministrations and declared that he was at last fit to drive home.

"Now I really do need a whiskey!" Bran said as he carefully prodded the strips of micropore that held the edges of the cut together.

Bran started to get up from the chair but sat down again very quickly as the torn muscles above his right hip caused him to swear as pain stabbed through his lower back.

"What's wrong with your back?" Kieran asked, seeing Bran wince.

"One of the bastards kicked me," he said.

"Get your shirt off Bran."

"Oh, C'mon! I'm alright Dad, honest!" Bran said, wincing as he rubbed the painful area.

"Do as your told," Pat said opening the first aid box again.

"It's nothing," Bran objected "just a bit of a bruise if that, it'll be OK tomorrow." He stood up and reached for his leather jacket. "It's fine!" he said, "I just want to go home and get some sleep."

"I'll be the judge of that," Pat said, "and you're going nowhere till I've looked at your back!"

Bran sighed, he knew better than to try and argue with Pat, his Dad would not give in. He tossed his leather jacket onto the chair and somewhat reluctantly and very gingerly, pulled his shirt over his head.

"Jesus!" he heard Kieran exclaim.

Pat examined Bran's back carefully, a huge deep purple bruise extended from his ribs to his right buttock.

"The muscle's torn," Pat said as he felt carefully around the injury. "That'll be real painful for a couple of days."

"Tell me about it!" Bran said wincing as his father pressed the discoloured skin. Pat searched in the first aid box for a small jar containing some dark brown evil-smelling ointment. He carefully smeared some over the bruised area. "It's what boxers use," he said, "it will help take down the swelling."

"It bloody stinks!" Bran said wrinkling his nose "What's it effin' made of?"

Pat grinned. "It's better if you don't know," he said, putting the precious ointment back in the first aid box.

Bran carefully put his shirt back on.

"It had better not stain," he said, "this shirt cost me a friggin' fortune!"

"I'll get one of the drivers to take you home, Bran," Pat said and take the day off tomorrow."

"I don't need taking home Dad," he said. "I'm perfectly capable of driving and if I feel rough tomorrow, I'll take a couple of paracetamol!"

The last thing Bran wanted was to be stuck with one of the firms' drivers, he had intended calling at Jason's flat on the way home, Jason still wasn't answering his texts or the landline. Bran was starting to worry about him, and he still felt real bad about leaving him at the hospital the other night, Jason had obviously been upset. Bran knew how sensitive Jay could be. He had to talk to him. He didn't know what he was going to say, but he couldn't let this guy just walk out of his life.

The black Audi TT pulled into the car park at the side of the flats. Bran turned the engine off then killed the lights; he sat for a few minutes wondering what he was going to say. He looked up at the dark building, the light was on in Jason's flat; he was still awake.

It's no good sitting in the car like a fuckin' dummy, he thought; get off your fuckin' arse and go and tell him your sorry!

Another niggly little voice was saying that he could always come back tomorrow, the same voice said, what if he's not alone; what would you do then?

He shook his head; the thought of Jason with someone else was not a nice thought. Perhaps it would be better if he just drove away; tried ringing him again or came back another day.

Fuck it! Bran thought, and he climbed out of the Audi and walked over to the entrance to the flats. He punched the security code into the number pad by the door; he heard the 'click' of the lock mechanism and pushed the door open. It was three flights of stairs up to Jason's flat and by the time he got there his bruised back was giving him hell. That same doubting little voice was still there, in his head; there's still time to go back to the car it was saying, you could always come back tomorrow!

Bran pushed that voice to the back of his mind and rang the doorbell.

There was no answer, he rang it again and this time he rapped on the door with his knuckles.

"Jason! It's me!" he said.

There was no sound from inside the flat.

"Jason!" He said a little louder "Come on, open the door, I need to talk to you!" Still there was no sound from the flat.

"Jason!" he said loudly "I know you're there, stop pissing about and let me in!"

He hammered on the door.

"Jason!" he shouted. "Open this effin' door; NOW! Or I'll

open the effin' thing for you!!!"

Down the hall, a door opened and a middle-aged man stepped out of his flat.

"Do you know what time it is!" he said angrily.

"Yeah! Time you pissed off back into your effin' flat you wanker," Bran snarled.

"I'm reporting this to the landlord," the man said, "it's bad enough with one bloody puff!" Bran started towards the man who shot back into his flat and slammed the door.

"And keep your effin' nose out!" Bran yelled at the closed door. He turned back to Jason's flat. "Jason, I'm not going till you open this door!" he said. "For Christ's sake Jason, let me in!"

There was the click of a key being turned in the lock and the sound of the bolt being drawn back.

Bran pushed the door, it opened, and he stepped inside closing it behind him. Jason was walking towards the kitchen; he was limping and obviously still in some discomfort; his back to Bran.

"I don't remember ordering a taxi," he said quietly.

"Jason I'm sorry, it was a stupid bloody thing to do, I never meant to hurt you, please don't do this!"

Jason turned to look at him; the bruises on his face were very evident, even though they were beginning to fade.

"I should never have left you at the hospital, Jay," Bran said, "I should have stayed with you; brought you home and made sure you were OK."

"You couldn't even admit that you fuckin' knew me!" Jason said accusingly, "what was it, Bran? Were you afraid that I was going to shout out to the world that we were lovers?"

"I'm not as strong as you, Jay," Bran said quietly, "you know my background, my family; my Dad's gone through so much, worked so hard to keep us together after mum died. If I came out, told him I was gay it would kill him! He sees me bloody settled down with some fine Irish Catholic lass and a horde of fine Catholic grandchildren running around."

"And what about you Bran?" Jason asked. "Are you going to live a lie, because that's what your Dad wants?"

"I don't know how I'm going to do this, Jay," Bran said sadly.

"I don't know how long I can pretend to be something I'm not!"

"Huh!" Jason said. "You did a fuckin' good impersonation the other night!"

"I know, and I'm not proud of it, believe me!"

Jason looked up at Bran; his blue eyes were full of hurt and accusation.

"When I was lying in the mud in that lane, having the shit kicked out of me, all I could think of was that I had to keep hold of my mobile so that I could phone you; you would know what to do; you would take care of things; you would be there for me when it was all over!" Jason turned away so that Bran wouldn't see the tears that pricked his eyes.

"And what did you say?... No! I'm just the fuckin' cab driver!"

Bran stepped forward and put his hand on Jason's shoulder. Jason shrugged it off. Bran wrapped both arms around Jason, pulling him back into his embrace. He rested his cheek against Jason's long blonde hair.

"Don't do this Jason," he said softly as he felt the resistance to his touch. "I'm sorry, I really am so very sorry, I wouldn't hurt you for the world, I love you, Jay, you know that."

Jason sobbed. "What you said hurt much more than the kicking I got from that gang of homophobes, Bran."

"Yeah! I'm a complete prick, I know it!" Bran said, kissing the soft blonde hair that curled around Jason's neck. "Will you forgive me?"

Jason turned to face Bran; he looked up into those gorgeous soft brown eyes. He shook his head and smiled. How could he resist that puppy dog look! He wrapped his arms around Bran's waist, "You're a friggin' bastard," he said, "and I have missed you… and what the fuck is that smell?"

"If you'll stop squeezing me," Bran said grimacing with pain,

"I'll tell you!"

"Bran, what happened to your face?" Jason said, noticing the cut below his eye.

Bran grinned. "Poetic justice," he said.

"You're not the only one who's had a kicking lately, Jay," he explained about the fare to Ormerod Street.

"At least they didn't piss on you!" Jason said with a wry smile.

"Well if you ask me," Bran said grinning, "my Dad went one better when he plastered my back with this foul-smelling shit!"

"You do smell a bit like something you'd find lurking at the bottom of a wheelie bin." Jason grimaced.

"Mind if I have a shower?" Bran asked.

"Mind! – I insist!"

Later, clean, smelling a little sweeter and wrapped in one of Jason's soft white bathrobes, Bran relaxed in the lounge, so relieved that Jason was at least still speaking to him.

"I thought I'd really blown it with us Jay; that was a terrible feeling, I don't know what I would have done if you hadn't let me in."

"I nearly didn't, Bran," Jason admitted. "You are ashamed of our relationship and that's not easy to live with."

Bran hung his head; he knew it was the truth, but it didn't make it any easier to deal with.

"We're not like other men, Bran," Jason said, sitting down gingerly in the easy chair opposite, his bruised backside was still tender and painful. "Something in our genes made us what we are and there's no getting away from it; you can pretend all you want, but in the end; you have to admit that you are homosexual." He leant forward and put his hand on Bran's knee.

"Bran you have to admit it to yourself before you can admit it to anyone else." He said.

Bran couldn't meet Jason's gaze, but he knew he was right; Jason was usually right about these things.

"I wish I had your strength, Jay." He said, shaking his head. "I wish I had the guts to tell Pat that we have this relationship; that I have a gay lover! Hell! That would be something." He said, looking up at Jason "Not only a gay lover, but a gay Protestant lover!"

Jason laughed out loud "A Catholic father's worst nightmare!"

Bran laughed. "It's not funny Jay! I don't know what he would do first, have me excommunicated or castrated!"

Jason grinned wickedly.

"I could live with the excommunication." He said; he

watched Bran carefully; very aware of the turmoil that was taking place in his mind. Jason could remember the heartache and trauma that he had gone through when he came out to his parents; after the initial shock, they had been sympathetic, and really not surprised that their sensitive, artistic son had been gay. All the same, they had been very quick to suggest that he went off to University. Jason wondered how he would have coped if his parents had been homophobic bigots, or if his mother hadn't been there to listen and sympathise. He guessed his life would have been very different and certainly a lot harder!

"Shit!" Bran said glancing at the clock. "Look at the time; I really should be going!"

"Stay here." Jason said simply, "I think we could both do with a bit of company tonight."

Jason's bed was warm and comfortable. It felt so right just to be lying in Jason's arms, and as he drifted off to sleep, the garage on Allen Street seemed a million miles away.

9

"What the bloody hell's up with you today?" Kieran said as he spooned his usual three sugars into the mug of coffee.

Bran looked up from the table, vaguely aware that Kieran was talking to him.

"I've asked you three times if you want a coffee!"

Bran didn't answer; he just shook his head and continued staring out through the window. His thoughts still spinning round and round from the conversation he had had with Jason the night before. There were so many questions he asked himself, yet there didn't seem one to which he could put a logical answer. Why was it so important that no one found out that he was gay? Was he really so weak minded that he couldn't live with his own sexuality; was he going to pretend he was something he wasn't all his life! Or was it that he was afraid of what his father would say; how he would react. It would be just another way that Bran had failed to live up to his expectations. Bran knew that this was something else that would be thrown back in his face; he could hear the words in his head. "Yer fuckin' useless!"

He knew that he had let Jason down so badly. Jason, sweet innocent Jason, who knew who he was and what he was and was perfectly happy with it! Jason was gentle, quiet and inoffensive and so much stronger than he was!

"You're in a bloody funny mood today," Kieran commented. "Have a fight with the girlfriend? Is that why you didn't come home last night?"

"Something like that." Bran replied. His head felt like it was full of cotton wool; he didn't really feel like getting into the usual long complicated fabrication with Kieran, he always felt uncomfortable; lying about where he had been or who he had been with.

"Flowers!" Kieran said. "Or a nice little bit of jewellery; works every time for me!"

"I think this is going to take more than a few wilted roses, Bro," Bran said shaking his head.

"Well stuff her then Bran, there's plenty more fish in the sea!"

"Yeah, right," Bran pushed the kitchen chair back as he stood and stretched. "Thanks for the advice, Marjorie!" He walked over to the Aga and took his car keys from the hook on the wall.

"You could always take a leaf out of Dad's book." Kieran laughed and lifted the sleeve of his T-shirt. "A nice flowery love-heart with her name written across it tattooed on your arm."

"Yeah, and 'Piss off Kieran' tattooed across my arse!" Bran scowled.

"Where are you going now?" Kieran asked as Bran picked up his leather jacket.

Bran shrugged his shoulders.

"Not sure," he said. "See if I can clear my head a bit."

"You've got a couple of theatre runs just before eight o'clock," Kieran reminded him.

"Yeah, I'll see you at the office later," Bran said as he walked out of the kitchen door.

He climbed into his sporty little Audi TT and turned the ignition. The engine roared into life. Bran sat at the wheel for a few moments, before pulling out of the drive; he didn't need to think about where he was going, he automatically turned and headed for the flats at Anncolm Heights.

An idea was starting to form in Bran's mind, a crazy idea. One that he knew Jason would object to; but he would cross that bridge when he came to it!

"A Tattoo!" Jason was stunned. "What do you mean by a tattoo?"

"You know, one of them permanent picture things on your skin," Bran said between mouthfuls of lasagne. He hadn't realised just how hungry he was until he had arrived at the flat and found Jason just about to have lunch; homemade lasagne; and it smelled bloody wonderful!

Bran helped himself to another piece of the hot crusty garlic bread.

"Your passengers are going to love you tonight," Jason grinned, "and you know exactly what I mean! What on earth has made you think about having a tattoo?"

Bran paused; the fork full of steaming lasagne hovered above his plate, forgotten for the moment.

"I guess it was something Pat said once when he was talking about his tattoos. He said that the tattoos defined who you were; what you were." He put the fork full of lasagne back on the plate uneaten.

"He once told me about tribal tattoos; how some cultures used them as a sign that they had become a man and that it was their way of showing the rest of the tribe that they accepted everything that went with growing up, including pain! It was a commitment to a way of life; a rite of passage."

"So, what are you going to do?" Jason asked as he poured

himself another glass of red wine, "Have GAY PRIDE tattooed across your forehead! This isn't the jungle Bran!"

"You've lived in Liverpool long enough, Jay," Bran said. "It's more of a jungle out there than it is in fuckin' South America!"

"It's a stupid idea Bran; what difference would a tattoo make."

"Would it really bother you if I had a tattoo?" Bran asked.

Jason thought for a moment.

"No; I guess not, if that's what you really want and if it would make you feel better."

Jason shrugged his shoulders.

"It didn't bother you, that time I had that piercing done; well not a lot."

Bran cringed.

"It wasn't so much that you had the piercing; it was ***where*** you had the piercing that got me!"

"The thing about a piercing, Bran," Jason reminded him, "was that when you got tired of them, you could take them out."

Bran looked down at his chest.

"What do you reckon then Jay? A couple of nipple rings and an eyebrow bar?"

Jason laughed and drained off the remains of his wine.

"Finish your lunch while I get my files together," he said pushing his chair back from the table and heading into the lounge. "Then you can drop me off at the Uni; I have a tutorial this afternoon."

Bran looked up, a little concerned.

"Are you up to going back to Uni Jay?" He asked.

"That's what the tutorials about," Jason said. "I've had a few days off now; I can't stay away forever and I'm missing too much work." He smiled, "I don't think there'll be any more trouble now; I think last time was just a misunderstanding…"

"Misunderstanding my arse!" Bran swore.

"I was trying to be friendly," Jason explained. "I guess it was taken the wrong way."

"Don't make excuses for the bastards Jason," Bran said.

"I'll just have to be a bit more careful who I speak too."

"It's not right Jay; if some of these morons are at Uni, you should report them; get them thrown out!"

Jason shook his head.

"I don't think that would be a good idea," he smiled. "Now shut up, finish your lunch and drink your coffee, or I'll be late for my tutorial!"

"You're Bran O'Donnell, aren't you? Pat's son?" Bran nodded. "Your Dad not with you?" Rick asked, looking past Bran, expecting to see the head of the O'Donnell family walking into his studio.

Bran shook his head.

He had been to The Ink Spot a couple of times with his Dad, but it seemed strange, walking into the tattoo shop on his own.

He glanced around the big reception room, comfortable black leather settees were dotted around, framed photographs of stunningly beautiful tattoos hung from the walls, tattoo magazines were scattered on the glass-topped coffee tables and the rich smell of freshly ground coffee hung on the air.

"I wanted to ask you about having a tattoo done," Bran said.

"Pat got to you, at last, did he?" Rick grinned.

"Sort of," Bran said, "but he doesn't know about this and I would prefer it to stay that way!"

"Oh!" Rick smiled "Going to be a surprise is it?"

"Oh, yeah!" Bran said. "It's going to be a friggin' surprise all right!"

"Have a seat," Rick said pointing to one of the leather settees, "I'll get us a coffee."

Rick disappeared into the back of the studio and came out a couple of minutes later with two cappuccinos and a file of tattoo designs.

"You've never had a tattoo before have you?"

Bran shook his head.

"OK, so what are you looking for?" He flipped open the design book "Tribal? Traditional?"

Bran glanced at the book, then looked round the walls at the photos of the big tattoo jobs displayed for their beautiful artwork.

He nodded towards a full back piece of a Native American design of wolves and eagles.

"Something like that!" he said.

"Fuck off!" Rick said grinning "Come on, be bloody serious." He pushed the book of designs across the table towards Bran. "What do you want doing?"

"I am serious," Bran said. "I've never been more serious in my life!" He pulled an envelope from his jacket pocket and took out the photograph inside it, he handed it to Rick.

"That's what I want doing." He said.

Rick looked down at the photo Bran had handed him.

"I want you to do elements from that painting."

The first thing Rick noticed was the intricate colourful artwork of the painting shown in the photograph and then as he studied what was a stunning piece of work, he began to realise what the subject matter was.

"No fuckin' way!" he said dropping the photo on the coffee table "Your Dad would effin' kill me!"

He picked the photo up again, fascinated by the emotive image. He looked at the photo and then at Bran, the whole thing was a celebration of the relationship between two gay men, and Bran was one of them!

"Does your Dad know about this?" Rick asked.

Bran laughed.

"Nobody knows about this, do you think if Pat knew I would still be walking!"

"Well, a piece like that covering your back just might give him a bit of an inkling." He gave the photo back to Bran.

"I can't do it," he said. "You know, once something like that's been done, you can't change your mind; it's there for life!"

"I'm not going to give up on this Rick, this is important to me, it's something that I have got to do."

"Just go home and think about it, Bran, I'm sure you will realise what a stupid idea it is if you give it some thought."

"I've been giving it some thought for a long time now," he said, "and I will have the tattoo I want, even if I have to go down to one of the tattoo booths down by the docks!"

"Oh, for fucks sake, Bran," Rick said, "keep away from those cowboys, the places are filthy, their equipment isn't sterilised and God only knows where they get their needles from and if you went in there with that photo, you would be lucky if you didn't leave with your balls shoved up your arse!"

Bran picked up the photograph and pushed it back into his inside pocket.

"Look, Rick," he said, "you have a reputation for being clean, professional and a bloody good tattooist, that's why I came here first. I would prefer it if you would do this for me, but if you won't, I'll go somewhere else and take my chances."

He stood up to leave. "Thanks for the coffee," he said.

"Wait," Rick said as Bran walked towards the door. "Look, can you call back tomorrow, and we'll talk about it then?" he walked over to Bran and held out his hand. "Leave the photo with me, I'll have a look at it again tonight, and you promise me that you will give this some real serious thought, something like that would take a long time, would hurt like hell and be bloody expensive."

"Tomorrow then," Bran said, he paused in the doorway. "You won't say anything about this to Pat, will you?"

"Not if you don't want me to."

The door closed silently; Rick watched as Bran climbed into his black Audi. He looked again at the photo as the car pulled away and wondered who had done the artwork.

Pat O'Donnell's son, a freakin' shirt lifter. Jesus Christ! Rick thought; I wouldn't like to be him when Pat found out about that!

Bran sat for some time in the comfort and isolation of his black Audi TT. His heart was pounding against the walls of his chest. He had finally admitted to someone that he was gay; that he was a homosexual; that he wasn't normal! That was it; that was the problem; all his life he had been told that he wasn't good enough, he didn't match up to the other boys; he didn't like football or fighting or anything else that began with 'f'. He wasn't normal. His mother had recognised the gentleness in him and had kept that part of him safe from Pat. His Dad had said if he didn't look after his two brothers; if he wasn't good enough to look after his two brothers, they would all be sent into care. The Sunday School Priest had said that he wasn't normal and that if he told anyone he would be taken away and put in a home. He closed his eyes and put his head down into his hands. His head was completely messed up but somehow, he seemed to be able to think better when he was alone in the car. It was almost as if the metal shell formed a barrier between his thoughts and the world beyond the stylish bodywork.

Rick had given him quite a lot to think about. Just why was he contemplating having this tattoo done, what made it so important just at the moment.

Bran was ashamed, ashamed of the fact that he couldn't admit to his family and friends that he was homosexual. He was; as Jason had so eloquently put it, in denial; unable to admit even to himself that he was gay.

Perhaps walking into the Tattoo Studio was the first step on that difficult journey.

Bran pulled into the garage just in time to see a recovery vehicle offloading one of the Taxis; the near side panels were caved in and the bonnet and offside headlights were mangled.

Bran climbed out of his Audi and walked over to where Kieran was directing the recovery vehicle driver.

"Anyone hurt?" he asked.

Kieran shook his head.

"OK!" he shouted to the driver, as the taxi rolled fully off the trailer and came to a halt. He bent down and unhooked the winch wire.

"Whose cab is it?" Bran asked, walking round to assess the damage "Or should I say; whose cab WAS it?"

Kieran was signing the forms that the recovery driver handed to him.

"Mike Coopers."

Bran looked round.

"Where is he?" he asked; there was no sign of the taxi driver.

"Got himself taken to hospital; whiplash. He'll be putting in a nice fat claim for personal injuries."

"So, what happened?" Bran asked. "I take it Mike wasn't at fault?"

Kieran handed the paperwork back to the driver who pulled off the top copy and gave it back to Kieran.

"Cheers mate," he said pulling himself up into the big yellow recovery vehicle.

Kieran and Bran walked towards the office as the breakdown truck pulled smoothly out of the yard.

"Apparently," Kieran said, "some jackass pulled off a garage forecourt; hit Mike's cab side on and knocked it into the oncoming traffic."

"Police involved?" Bran asked.

"Yeah; took statements from everyone but I think they'll just let the insurance companies sort it out."

Kieran sat down behind his desk and threw the recovery vehicle invoice into Pat's 'in' tray.

"You told the old man yet?" Bran said.

Kieran shook his head. "He'll be well pissed, that means we're another fuckin' driver down."

"Let me know how he takes it?" Bran said grinning as he

picked up the keys for his cab.

"You can ask him yourself," Kieran smirked. "Mick was supposed to be picking Dad up today; so, I guess you're the lucky runner up bro!"

Kieran had been right; Pat was well and truly pissed off and complained all the way back to the office. His mood wasn't improved when he saw the mangled wreck of the taxi in the garage.

"More effin' expense!" He swore. "I suppose the stupid bastard will expect me to replace his effin' cab!"

"The insurance will cover that surely Dad," Kieran said.

"Could take months to get paid out," Pat grumbled. "You know how these bloody insurance firms like to drag their feet."

"What about Dobbins' cab?" Kieran ventured.

"Dobbin?" Pat asked.

"Geoff Gee," Bran prompted.

Pat's face still wore a look of puzzlement.

"Geoff Gee – GG – Dobbin," Bran explained.

"Well, why the hell didn't you say so in the first place," Pat turned to Kieran. "So what about Geoff's cab?"

"It's been parked up since Geoff broke his ankle playing football; Mike could use that till Geoff is fit to drive again."

Pat thought about that for a moment.

"That's not a bad idea but check with Geoff first," he said grudgingly. "It's about time you used your bloody head and started earning your keep." He turned to Bran. "And have you nothing better to do than sit on yer arse all day drinkin' coffee?"

Bran drained off the last of his coffee and headed for the door.

"I'll go over Dobbins' taxi. He said, reaching for the keys. "It's not been out for a while."

"Well don't spend all bloody day on it," Pat said.

As he left, Bran heard Pat's voice raised in anger.

"Fuckin 'ell! Where did they bring it from? Fuckin' Glasgow!"

Bran smiled; Pat had found the recovery firms' invoice!

Bran was back in the office when his youngest brother walked in; he tossed his rucksack onto the desk and threw himself into one of the empty chairs.

"I've had to walk all the bloody way! I thought you were going to pick me up from the Uni Bran?"

"Sorry, Paul," Bran said. "Been a bit of a funny day today; anyway, the walk will do you good!"

Paul threw a dirty look in Bran's direction.

"Hey Kieran," he said, "did you hear about the poof at Uni that got a good kickin' the other night; one of them effin' art course fairies."

"Yeah," Kieran said, "Mick told me something about it; it was Bran who took him to the General apparently, Mick was there when they arrived."

Kieran turned to Bran. "He was bloody lucky you were there; Mick said he was in a bad way."

"You should have run over the bitch Bran." Paul spat. Bran couldn't believe the venom in Paul's voice. "Dirty bastards!" Paul continued. "Well he won't be having any bum fun for a while, not after the kicking his lily-white arse got!

"You should have seen him, Kieran!" Paul laughed, oblivious to the look of horror on Bran's face. "Crawling through the mud with his keks round his friggin' ankles getting' his arse kicked; they want their dicks' cutting off, the bloody lot of them!"

"That was fuckin' brave of you!" Bran spat. "A gang of you beating up one bloke on his own!"

"He'd been asking for it!" Paul said. "Trying to chat blokes up in the student bar! Well, he hit on the wrong one this time!"

Bran turned and walked out of the office; he felt sick, physically sick! His conversation with Jason came rushing back. 'I was just trying to be friendly, I guess it was taken the wrong way'

Paul! His own brother! Paul had been one of the gang that had attacked Jason!

Bran only just made it down the stairs before he threw up.

Paul! His baby brother Paul! His deep hatred of homosexuals had suddenly been made so very clear! Bran wondered if Jason knew that Paul was his brother! Of course, he bloody knew! And he had never said anything; he must have known that Paul was one of his attackers. Shit! He thought; what would happen if Paul ever found out that he was gay; could he find himself being beaten up down a dark alley somewhere by his own brother!

Bran sat in his cab and stared out of the window for ages, looking at nothing in particular. In his mind, he kept seeing the look on Paul's face as he described the degradation and humiliation of a soul as sweet and gentle as Jason. He kept hearing Paul's voice. "You should have seen him; crawling through the mud with his keks round his friggin' ankles!"

Bran knew he couldn't do it anymore. He couldn't pretend to be something he wasn't. He couldn't laugh and joke with Paul, knowing how Paul felt about gays', knowing that Paul had been among those who had hurt Jason and then laughed about it.

He had to tell them; tell Pat that he had another reason to say he was useless; a failure. He had to tell Paul that the man he nearly killed was the man he slept with. He had to tell Kieran that his big brother, the brother he looked up to; the brother he idolised was nothing but a friggin' poof!

But how? How could he tell them that he had lived a lie for the last fourteen years?

The tattoo!

Once he had the tattoo done, there would be no turning back.

He laughed. It was a harsh laugh, a laugh devoid of humour.

Pat had always said that he should get a tattoo; that it would make a man of him. Bran wondered if Pat would feel the same when he saw this one?

10

The tattoo studio was quite busy when Bran next called. The receptionist greeted him with a smile. He could hear the sound of the tattoo machine in the room at the back.

"Have you got an appointment?" She asked.

Bran shook his head.

"I just want to talk to Rick about a tattoo I want doing."

She smiled again.

"My name's Melanie by the way; what's yours?"

"Bran."

"Rick should be finished in about half an hour Bran; would you like to look at some design books?" she reached for a big black folder behind her. "So where do you want the tattoo doing?" she asked, looking him up and down. Bran got the distinct impression that Melanie was already imagining him practically naked on the couch.

"Rick knows what I want doing." He said feeling slightly uncomfortable under the somewhat obvious assessment of the size of his bollocks!"

"So what can I do for you till Rick's finished?"

"I'll be just fine thanks," he said, reaching for a magazine – ANY magazine!

Melanie smiled.

"Then how about a coffee while you wait?"

"That would be great," Bran said relieved.

"Take a seat," she said pointing to one of the comfortable

leather settees "I'll bring it over."

The coffee came in a little jug with hot milk, a bowl of brown sugar crystals and a stylish cup and saucer.

Melanie stretched across the coffee table to put the small tray down in front of Bran. "Is there anything else I can get for you?" she asked, leaning forward so that her ample bosom and deep cleavage were very prominently displayed for Bran's view.

"The coffee's just fine thanks," Bran said smiling to himself.

"You haven't been to the studio before have you?" she asked, looking him up and down appreciatively; "I'm sure I would have remembered anything you had done here!"

"Can I show you anything?" she said suggestively. "I'm sure I could help you to make your mind up on any piece you were interested in."

Bran sipped the hot coffee, "No thanks," he said, "Rick knows what I want doing," he repeated.

Melanie pouted.

"Rick does some beautiful tattoos of birds," She sat on the coffee table in front of Bran and pulled her top down off her shoulder.

"Would you like to see my Blue-Tit?"

"Melanie!" Rick snapped as he walked back into the studio followed by a guy with cling-film wrapped around his upper arm. "Piss off back to your desk and stop annoying the customers!"

He turned to the man whose tribal armband he had just finished. "Melanie will give you an aftercare leaflet and book your next appointment Martin," he said, "and I'll see you in a few days time to finish off."

"Thanks, Rick," Martin said looking appreciatively at the

bold design around his upper arm.

"Sorry about that Bran," he said as they watched Martin head for reception where Melanie waited, "she's like a freakin' bitch on heat at times," and he grinned at Bran. "But most of my customers quite like it really so what the hell; as long as I don't catch her shaggin' them on the tattoo couch!"

"Melanie!" He shouted across the studio. "When you've finished there, I'll have a coffee!"

He sat down on the chair opposite Bran.

"I take it you've come in to talk about this back piece?" He said.

Bran nodded.

"You know something like that could take days, perhaps weeks to complete."

Bran shook his head.

"I want it doing in one day, Rick."

"No way Bran, I couldn't do that!" Rick said aghast! "Do you realise what that would entail; a piece like that would take…" he made some quick mental calculations. "It would take eight, maybe nine hours of non-stop work; do you realise just how painful that would get?"

"It could be done in one day though?" Bran asked.

"Yeah but…"

"Then that's what I want!"

"Shit Bran!" Rick swore, "Do you know what you're asking me to do!" he looked at Bran; a spark of understanding beginning to dawn. "This isn't just about the tattoo is it?", he asked, "you know this is going to be freakin' agony don't you."

Bran looked Rick straight in the eyes.

"My life has been hell Rick, just one piece of shit after another; but now I've found something – someone who has changed that. They say that pain can be very cleansing and that in some tribal cultures a tattoo can show that a boy has made the transition from a youth to a man; I need to do this Rick. I know that once I start, there's no turning back. I know I can get through this; and if I can get through this, I can get through anything! Besides which, if Pat saw this tattoo before it was finished, he would make damn sure that I didn't come back."

"OK, Bran," Rick said. "I'll do it, but not just yet. I want you to think about it for a bit longer, and I need to clear a full day in my diary, it will be a few weeks before I can do that.

Give me a ring in a couple of weeks; I should have a better idea of when I have the time free and if you're still one hundred per cent sure; I'll do your back piece for you!"

"It will take me a while to prepare the artwork and do the tracing; there's a lot to be done before I can actually do the tattoo."

"Don't leave it too long, Rick," Bran said.

"What about your partner?" Rick asked. "How does he feel about you having this done?"

Bran thought for a while.

"OK, I guess." He looked across at Rick. "I don't suppose he is one hundred per cent thrilled with the idea, but he understands why this is important to me, and I guess he's a little flattered really."

Rick shot Bran a quizzical look.

"Jason is an artist; He painted the original."

Rick nodded.

"I can understand that," he said. "I feel that every time

someone walks out of here with one of my original designs on their skin!"

Bran got to his feet and held out his hand to Rick.

Rick looked him in the eyes as he grasped the outstretched hand; it was a strong, positive handshake.

"I hope you know what you're doing, Bran," he said.

Bran nodded "So do I, Rick," he said as he headed for the door. "Bye, Bran." Melanie smiled as he left the studio. "Come again - real soon." She grinned cheekily as he walked out into the watery sunlight of the cold Liverpool afternoon!

Bran knew everything would change once the truth was known. He had a good idea how Pat and Paul would take the news, but he wasn't too sure about Kieran; he felt closer to Kieran than to anyone else, and in a way, that made him sad, because he knew that Kieran would be disappointed in him. He knew Kieran would feel betrayed; would feel that Bran had betrayed that trust they had between them. The friendship that had formed over the years; a friendship based on a lie!

He hoped Kieran would be the one who might try to understand. But he knew that Kieran lived in the world of Irish Catholic values, rough taxi drivers and boy racers. It was asking a lot for Kieran to sympathise or support his brother – the queer!

Bran knew it wouldn't be long before his life would be changed forever. He felt as though he should spend some time with Kieran and get to know his wild younger brother while he still could.

The opportunity to do just that came sooner than Bran had expected; when one evening, Kieran had suggested they had a drink together and then went 'clubbing' at one of the popular nightclubs down by the docks. Bran gave it some thought, and then; much to Kieran's surprise; said "OK; why not!"

11

Kieran put another pint of Larger down on the bar in front of Bran; the pub was crowded and noisy, the air thick with blue tobacco smoke. He had to shout to make himself heard over the loud music and babble of voices.

"Get that down you, bro!" Kieran said as he drained the last of his pint of Lager, "Then we're outta here; I've promised to meet someone at The Fizz!"

The Fizz was a big fancy Night Club down by the Albert Docks, Bran knew it well; he had picked up many fares to and from The Fizz. It was very popular with the twenty to thirty age groups.

"I'll drop you off there," Bran said as he drank the Lager. "No point me staying; I've drunk too much now!"

"Bollocks!" Kieran said, "leave the bloody Audi here! I've ordered a taxi for us."

"No way am I leaving my car on this effin' car-park!" Bran said, "it would be in a chop shop and stripped down to the chassis before we got to the end of the road."

"OK!" Kieran said; he wasn't going to take no for an answer "I'll get one of our drivers to take it back to the garage for you."

Bran shook his head and swallowed the remainder of his pint.

"OK," he said reluctantly. "But make sure it's someone sensible!"

Kieran laughed and flipped open his mobile phone.

They'll be ten minutes," he said as he closed the cover of his phone. "Just time for a quick one!"

"Bacardi and coke and a Whisky and dry," he ordered. "Just to get us in the mood," he said grinning at his older brother. "Loosen up Bran; you're not working till eight o'clock tomorrow night; it's about time you had a break!"

"I'll probably live to regret this." Bran grinned as he tossed back the Whiskey chaser. "But what the hell!"

The O'Donnell cab pulled up in front of the pub and Bran handed his keys to the extra driver, who had come to pick up his Audi. Soon they were heading into town and The Fizz Night Club.

There was a real party atmosphere at The Fizz; the bars were busy and the darkened dance floor crowded. They had no trouble getting past the beefy bouncers at the door. O'Donnell's Taxis were regular visitors to the Club either picking up or dropping off clubbers and Bran often chatted to the bouncers as he waited for a fare to appear.

It didn't take Kieran long to meet up with some of his friends who he introduced to Bran.

"Is Marie here yet?" he asked looking around the crowded bar area for that wild mop of brunette hair with its jazzy red highlights.

"Haven't seen her yet," someone said, "but if she's here; she will be down there; listening to the band." Kieran looked across the sea of dancers towards the low stage at the far end of the building where a live band was belting out heavy rock.

Kieran turned to Bran.

"Your turn to get the drinks in bro," he said, "I'll have a Vodka and Blue Aftershock on the rocks."

"What the hell is that?" Bran asked.

Kieran grinned.

"Try it Bran; you'll get a taste for it, trust me!"

He indicated the corner of the bar where he had spotted some of his friends. "I'll be over there."

Kieran was laughing over some comment Bran had made about the clubbers gyrating on the dance floor and he was just starting on his second drink when a voice just behind him caused him to swing round.

"I hope there's one of those for me Kieran O'Donnell?"

"Marie!" Kieran said jumping to his feet and sweeping the young woman off her feet. He pulled her into a close embrace, running his hands down her skimpily clad body. He slid his hands over her buttocks and squeezed the pert little bum affectionately. She wrapped her arms around his neck and kissed him passionately.

"Where the hell have you been hiding Kieran?" she said pouting. "I haven't seen you in ages!"

"Working honey; you don't get much free time when it's a family firm." He turned and indicated Bran. "This is my big brother, Bran," he said.

"Hi, Bran." Marie grinned and turned to speak to someone in the crowd behind her. "Sarah! Come and meet Kieran O'Donnell; him and me go way back!"

The tall willowy figure with waist length blonde hair excused herself from the group of male admirers and joined her friend Marie.

"Hi!" she smiled. "I've heard a lot about you, Kieran O'Donnell!"

"All good I hope," Kieran said.

"What do you think?" she said laughing.

"Well are you two tightwads going to buy us a drink or do we have to buy our own," Marie said playfully jabbing Kieran in the ribs.

"Sure hon.' what would you like?"

Sarah leaned across the table where Bran was sitting.

"You must be Kieran's brother Bran?" she asked, and she looked questioningly at the glass in front of him.

"That looks, quite interesting," she said. "What is it?"

Bran picked up the glass and sipped the blue liquid.

"Your guess is as good as mine," he said grinning.

"Good!" Sarah said; "I'll have one of those, Kieran, please."

Kieran was soon back with four more of the tall glasses of ice with Vodka and Blue Aftershock. He had a can of Red Bull, which he shared between the four drinks.

"Gives it a bit of a fizz," he said when Bran cast a questioning glance in his direction as he topped up the glasses "Gives you energy for the dancing," Kieran said.

"What bloody dancing!" Bran said laughing.

"Oh, you'll soon get the hang of it 'old man'," Kieran said as he pulled Marie down onto his lap.

"Haven't seen you here in the past Bran O'Donnell," Sarah said as she slipped into the seat next to Bran.

"That's because I've never been here before; well never on the inside; picked plenty of fares up from here late at night." He took another sip of the Vodka blue; Kieran was right, it was certainly going down very easily!

"So, you're a taxi driver?" Sarah asked.

"Yeah," Bran said, "not very exciting I'm afraid!"

"Sarah; come and dance!" Marie said pulling her friend to her feet. "C'mon Bran!" she tugged at his sleeve and then caught hold of Kieran's hand. The lure of the dark dance floor with its smoky strobe lights and flashing laser beams drew Marie towards the music. "C'mon Kieran; you used to be a pretty hot dancer!"

"What do you mean; used to be?" Kieran objected as he got to his feet laughing.

"C'mon, Bran," he said.

"Perhaps later," Bran grinned, "when I've had a few more of these!"

"Kieran," Marie said pouting as she pulled him away from the table and towards the pulsating dance floor. Laughing, Kieran shrugged his shoulders and surrendered himself to Marie's wishes. Bran raised his glass in salute as they disappeared into the darkness and the sea of bodies.

Bran leaned back and watched the gyrating dancers highlighted by the electric blue strobe lights. He was impressed; Kieran wasn't a bad dancer after all!

Two black youths strolled up to the table and sat in the chairs opposite Bran.

Bran looked at them over the top of his glass, waiting for them to speak.

"You Kieran's brother?" one of them asked.

Bran took a sip of his drink.

"What if I am?" He said cautiously.

The two youths looked carefully around and leaned across the table. One of the slipped his hand inside his jacket pocket and then slid it surreptitiously across the table towards Bran, there were three or four small plastic bags containing white powder beneath his fingers.

"You interested?" He asked.

Bran took another sip from his glass, then, very slowly and very carefully he put it down on the table in front of him. He leaned across to the youth who was trying to sell him cocaine and very quietly said, "If you come anywhere near me or my brothers with that shit; I'll rip your fuckin balls off and shove them and yer fuckin coke up yer fuckin arse; now piss off you wankers' while you still can."

"Watch your mouth mother fucker!" one of them snarled getting noisily to his feet.

"Hey what's going on, bro?" It was Kieran.

"You want to keep your fuckin' brother on a fuckin' leash O'Donnell," the drug pusher said. "Before someone gets hurt!"

Kieran looked over at his brother and smiled.

"Lucky I came back when I did then," he said, turning back to the black youth, "because Bran could take you two morons without raising a sweat; now piss off."

"You'll come crawling back O'Donnell," the drug pusher snarled, "and when you do, you'll find the price has gone up… way up!" he pushed the bags angrily back into his inside pocket. "And you'll have to fuckin' beg for it!"

Kieran clenched his fist, his eyes blazing.

"Not now Kieran," Bran said, putting his hand over Kieran's fist as he nodded to where Marie and Sarah were walking towards them.

The two black youths moved away from the table.

"Beggin' O'Donnell, on your fuckin' knees beggin'!"

Bran held Kieran back as the two youths disappeared into

the darkness that surrounded the mass of dancers.

"What was that about?" Marie asked as Kieran; breathing hard, fought to regain his composure.

"Nothing," Bran said, "mistaken identity, a misunderstanding and a pair of nob-heads that don't know when to shut up!"

"Oh, yeah," Marie grinned wickedly, running her hand down Kieran's cheek, "and who were the black guys?"

Kieran grinned at Bran who drained the remainder of his drink.

"Can't leave you on your own for five minutes without you causing trouble can I?"

"C'mon, Bran," Marie said grasping his hand and pulling him towards the dance floor, "with a body like yours; you must be able to dance!"

The Vodka Blue had made Bran a little more adventurous than normal and laughing he allowed himself to be pulled onto the crowded dance floor. A couple of minutes later, Kieran joined them, he handed Bran another glass of the Vodka Blue. Bran grinned and took a mouthful of the drink and swallowed. He gasped, his eyes watering. "Bloody hell!" he said; that was a damn sight stronger than the last one!

"Triples," Kieran grinned. "Saves time."

"You could have friggin' warned me, bastard!"

Kieran shrugged his shoulders and wrapping his arms around Marie, surrendered himself to the beat of the music.

Bran took another, more cautious drink.

There was a slender arm around his waist and a lithe sweet-smelling body moved provocatively against his, Sarah swept back her long blonde hair. She reached for Bran's drink, her elegant fingers covering his as she guided the glass to her lips.

She sipped the drink and smiled up into his eyes as her hand travelled up his arm and around his neck.

The rhythm of the music was hypnotic; like a drug dulling Bran's senses as he swayed in time to the beat. In the darkness of the club with its flashing coloured spotlights and strobe effects, he felt like a different person in a different world…. Finishing the drink, he put the glass down and ran his hands up through the long blonde hair.

Sarah tilted her head back as his hot lips descended on hers' His hands moved down her back and massaged her silky thighs before cupping her firm little arse and pulling her close against his body. The music seemed to become part of him and the room began to spin. He looked down at the blonde hair and blue eyes that gazed up at him. He kissed her again, the kiss was passionate, hungry; but the hunger was for a different pair of blue eyes and a different head of blonde hair.

Bran opened his eyes carefully. His head felt as though it was about to explode.

He was in a bed, but it wasn't his bed and there was a naked leg draped across his naked body. An elegant hand lay across his bare chest.

Shit! He thought. Where the hell am I? He turned and looked slowly across at the head that lay on the pillow next to him; at the mass of long blonde hair curled round the face of the beautiful woman who slept soundly beside him.

Sarah! Oh, God! What the hell was he doing in bed with Sarah! He moved slightly to one side. The leg entwined itself around his hips and the hand moved around his waist. Still asleep, Sarah nuzzled into his neck; her hair cascaded across his chest. Shit! What the hell HAD he been doing in Sarah's bed?!

Carefully, and as quietly as he could, so as not to wake her, Bran extricated himself from Sarah's embrace and climbed out of the bed. The room swayed alarmingly as he stood naked and totally unaware of where he was or how he had got here.

When the room finally stopped spinning, he looked around; what the hell had he done with his clothes?!

There was a small silky dressing gown at the bottom of the bed; lifting it carefully, so as not to disturb Sarah he wrapped it around his hips and quietly let himself out of the bedroom.

The lounge was small and cosy with a big table against the wall that was covered in textbooks and papers. Sarah must be a student at the Uni.! Various scenarios involving Jason and Sarah ran through Bran's head, each one more horrifying than the last. He banished the mental pictures from his mind and hoped fervently that she wasn't studying Art!

There was still no sign of his clothes. There was another door leading off from this room, he walked through it.

The first thing he saw was his brother Kieran's bare arse rising and falling as he screwed the woman who lay beneath him!

Pausing, Kieran looked over his shoulder at his brother.

"Do you friggin' mind!"

"Kieran you bastard! Where are my bloody clothes?" Bran asked.

"How the fuck should I know?" Kieran said puzzled.

A tousled head of brunette hair appeared from beneath Kieran's shoulder.

"Hi, Bran," Marie grinned up at him from beneath his brother's naked body, "you feeling any better now?"

"Sorry, Marie," Bran said, suddenly realising where he was.

"Kieran, where are my clothes?"

"I think you left most of them in the taxi that brought us here," Kieran said wickedly.

Marie smiled when she saw the look of panic on Bran's face.

"Take no notice of him Bran, I think you'll find them on the bathroom floor where you left them."

Kieran pulled the duvet up over his naked butt.

"So piss off Bran you pervert." He laughed and lowered his body down onto the eager young woman who lay beneath him as her bare legs snaked up to wrap tightly around his waist.

Bran found the bathroom, his clothes were indeed scattered all over the floor, as were various frilly undergarments that obviously belonged to Sarah.

Bran bent down to pick up his clothes; it was a mistake, as the room spun alarmingly and he staggered sideways, the effects of the alcohol from the night before still playing havoc with his balance.

He clung to the washbasin, desperately hoping that the dizziness and the nausea would pass.

Two slim arms wrapped around his waist and a voice said in his ear "You look terrible Bran; come back to bed before you hurt yourself."

Sarah guided him back into the bedroom and he collapsed in a heap across the bed.

Smiling, She pushed his legs up onto the bed and climbing in beside him she pulled the duvet over both of them. Bran rolled onto his side and gathered her into his arms; within seconds he was asleep.

"Bran! Bran! - C'mon Romeo: wake up!"

Bran opened his eyes; the bright light was painful.

"Bugger off Kieran." He said and pulled the duvet around his shoulders.

Since when did he have frilly lace edged duvet covers?

He looked around; this wasn't his room.

Sarah! He remembered being in bed with Sarah! He looked round; had he been dreaming? Because he was certainly on his own in the bed now.

"The girls have gone to the Uni Bran," Kieran said tossing his clothes onto the bed next to him "It's nearly lunchtime!"

"Where are we?" Bran croaked. He ran his hand over his chin; he desperately needed a shave and a coffee.

"Sarah's flat; we came here after we left The Fizz, for a nightcap!"

"A nightcap," Bran said, "the way my head feels it was more than a friggin' nightcap!"

"Bran," Kieran grinned. "You were pissed out of your skull before we left The Fizz; do you actually remember anything that happened last night?"

"I remember you handing me a Vodka Blue on the dance floor," Bran said as he climbed out of the bed and began; with some difficulty, to put on his clothes. "After that – nothing!"

"So you don't remember being in the back of the taxi with Marie and Sarah; or that you spent the entire journey comparing tits'!"

Bran shook his head. "You've got to be joking Kieran!" He said mortified!

"That's nothing, bro," Kieran grinned. "When we got back

here you insisted on stripping off in the bathroom with Sarah and Marie and having a shower with both of them to 'sober up' as you so eloquently put it; before you passed out."

"Both of them!" Bran said, "and what the hell were you doing?"

"Pissing myself laughing!"

Bran shook his head.

"I've got a lot of apologising to do."

"Yeah," Kieran said, trying to keep his face straight. "You can start by apologising to me you bastard! Walking into the bedroom at some ungodly hour this morning when I was halfway through giving Marie a good seeing too; fair put me off my stroke it did!"

"Shit!" Bran said. "Then that wasn't a dream?"

"No, it was a friggin' nightmare!" Kieran lifted his index finger high in the air and then let it slowly curl and droop. "Marie thought it was bloody hilarious!" Kieran laughed. "Then you pissed off back into bed with Sarah! – Thanks a bunch bro!"

Kieran grinned wickedly as he slapped his brother on the shoulder.

"Mind you; I can't fault you there bro she's a sweet bit of eye candy that Sarah." He cocked his head to one side. "Is she as fit in the sack as she looks'?"

"How the hell should I know," Bran said worriedly. "I don't' even remember getting in bed with her let alone what happened after that!"

"Oh, I'm sure she'll fill you in next time you meet." Kieran laughed.

"That's what I'm afraid of!" Bran said darkly. Thinking to himself that if he had anything to do with it; there wouldn't be a 'next time'.

The taxi arrived to take the two brothers back to the garage on Allen Street. Bran pulled his wallet out of his back pocket to pay the driver. As he flipped open the leather fastener, a piece of white paper fell into his lap. He unfolded the paper; it was a phone number and a name – Sarah!

Pat was waiting for them in the office. Bran made straight for the coffee pot; he desperately needed a hot drink.

"Where the fuck did you two get to last night?" he said, "I had to get one of the drivers to pick me up this morning!"

"Clubbing," Kieran said yawning.

"Till this fuckin' time!" Pat shook his head. "Go home and get a couple of hours sleep; I don't want you falling asleep on the job, and Bran, I want you in here at six tonight; a party of ten want taking to Lancaster so you'll need to take the minibus."

"Right," Bran said between mouthfuls of coffee. "And get a friggin' shave you scruffy bugger."

"I'll come home with you, Bran," Kieran said, still yawning as they walked across to the parking bays. Bran swore under his breath; he had half thought about calling at Anncolm Heights and spending a couple of hours with Jason. He rubbed the stubble on his chin; he really could do with a shower and a shave.

He was just about to unlock the Audi when his mobile phone bleeped; he had a text message.

"The doors open," he said turning away from Kieran; the message was probably from Jason!

He flipped open the mobile and pressed the 'read' button.

'Really enjoyed last night – Love Sarah; Kiss Kiss Kiss.

He stared at the message for a moment.

"Kieran," he said slowly. "How did Sarah get my mobile number?"

"I gave it to her," Kieran grinned, "you couldn't remember who you were last night, let alone what your mobile number was; well, aren't you going to reply to her."

"What the hell am I supposed to say?" Bran shrugged.

"Glad you enjoyed it! I don't remember a friggin' thing!"

Kieran roared with laughter as he climbed into the passenger seat of his brothers' car.

"How about. Thanks – will try harder next time."

12

Bran walked into the taxi office and threw himself down on one of the office chairs.

"What a bloody waste of a day." He complained. "Nothing but crap jobs and lousy weather!"

"Well there's another crap job for you," Pat said, "you can take me home as soon as Kieran gets here."

"Oh, and this office isn't your personal message taking service," Pat said, "A young lass called Sarah rang a couple of times; wants you to ring her; left her phone number in case you'd misplaced it."

Bran scowled.

Sarah had obviously read far too much into their night at the Fizz. Bran felt a twinge of conscience; he had woken up in Sarah's bed next morning, that at least deserved a phone call and probably an apology as well, but what the hell was he supposed to say to her; sorry, it was all a big mistake; you're very nice but I don't fancy you. What was he going to say that didn't sound like a 'come on', but at the same time, didn't insult her!

"Wake up you dozy sod!" Pat said, reaching for his jacket. "Kieran's just arrived." Bran glanced out of the window.

Kieran's Peugeot was just pulling into the garage. "You can drop me off at the Ferryman for a couple of hours, the footballs on tonight and I might as well watch it there as sit at home and watch it on my own."

Bran opened his wallet, the slip of white paper with Sarah's number was still tucked inside, He'd meant to throw it away; it would have taken some explaining if Jason had found it.

Bran walked out to meet Kieran as he headed for the office.

"Kieran," he began hesitantly, "I need a favour."

Kieran paused. It wasn't like Bran to ask for help with anything, especially from his younger brother.

"This is a first." He grinned, "The wise and wonderful Bran needs a favour from a lesser mortal!"

"Piss off Kieran, this is serious," Bran said looking round to see if Pat was anywhere near.

"I want you to get Sarah to back off." He said, "she's like a friggin' terrier with a bone, texting me every five minutes and now she's ringing the office as well."

"You're dumping Sarah?"

"How can I dump her Kieran, there's never been anything between us in the first place!"

"Shit! Bran! If I had a bit of skirt as fit as Sarah, panting after my arse…"

"Be my guest!" Bran said exasperated.

"You're serious aren't you?" Kieran said incredulously. Bran just looked at his younger brother, his expression giving nothing away.

"There's somebody else on the scene isn't there?" Kieran continued, a grin beginning to form. "You kept that bloody quiet bro you're such a bloody dark horse! No wonder you nearly shit yourself when you woke up in Sarah's bed!"

Pat was walking across the yard towards the two brothers.

"Look; just sort it for me Kieran!" Bran said, "and I'll owe you one!"

"No problem Bran." Kieran grinned wickedly as he headed for the office. He paused and looked over his shoulder. "I'll tell her your gay!"

Kieran checked the bookings with Jean as Bran wrote down the directions to the address in Lancaster. The minibus was in the yard, the engine running.

"The Lancaster party want bringing back at one," Kieran said as Bran slipped on his leather jacket. "What are you doing? Coming back here or staying in Lancaster?"

Bran shrugged.

"No point driving all the way back down the M6 just to turn round and go back to Lancaster." He flipped open his wallet to check how much cash he had.

"There'll be a Warner Brothers or something up there' I'll watch a movie or have a meal," he said, "just make sure Dad knows it's going on my expenses claim this time."

"You'll be lucky!" Kieran laughed. Pat was notorious for forgetting to pay the drivers out of pocket expenses!

"Don't you worry Bran!" Jean said. "I'll make sure you get your expenses, just make sure you get receipts and I'll sort it out with Pat!"

Bran leaned over and planted a kiss on Jean's bony cheek; he towered over her petite form. "You're a star, Jean!" He grinned. "Will you marry me?"

"Get away with you Bran O'Donnell!" she said blushing as Bran wrapped his arms around her bony frame.

"I won't be marrying you, but you can drop me off at the bus stop on your way out."

"Come on," he smiled. The minibus should have warmed up

by now, I'll drop you off at home."

Bran opened the door for Jean and was just about to follow her down the stairs when the phone rang. He paused for a second.

"Oh' Hi Lisa… no, it's Kieran… No, I'm sorry Lisa, he's just on his way out on a job." Kieran gestured Bran to leave with a wave of his hand and mouthed the words "Piss off".

Bran shook his head and turned to leave.

"Yes, I'm sure he will be disappointed to have missed you, Lisa… yes, he's one of our busiest drivers…"

Bran walked slowly down the stairs, Kieran's voice trailed after him, Bran recognised Kieran's tone; it was his best 'chatting up' tone!

"Are you doing anything tomorrow afternoon?"

Bran chuckled, somehow, he thought; Kieran's plans wouldn't exactly match Pat's as far as Lisa was concerned!

Bran slid open the passenger door for Jean and she walked up the steps into the mini-bus and sat in the seat behind the driver.

Bran climbed into the driver's seat. He didn't need to ask Jean where she was going as he had taken her home to her semi-detached house on the Springfield Estate many times.

"Well! Have you got yourself a steady girlfriend yet Bran?" She asked, almost before they had driven out of the yard.

"Not you as well Jean!" Bran said laughing. "I bet Pat has put you up to this hasn't he?"

She shook her head.

"No, Pat hasn't said anything – not to me, that is; but if you had a girlfriend, perhaps he would stop trying to arrange a marriage for you."

"It is pretty obvious isn't it," Bran sighed.

"I told him the other day," Jean continued. "You can lead a horse to water, but you can't make it drink!"

"Thanks for that Jean!" Bran said, grinning. "I think?"

Having dropped Jean off at her cosy little house on the Springfield Estate, Bran headed back into town to pick up the party of ten from the Farmers Arms and take them to Lancaster.

He glanced at the information Kieran had given him. Someone called Jenkins had booked the minibus.

The Farmers Arms was a quiet, family pub, not one that Bran had been to in the past. He pulled up outside the main entrance and stepped out of the driver's door. A young woman in a very short white skirt and wearing a pair of large pink tinsel covered rabbit ears on her head opened the door to the pub, looked at Bran and then turning back to the pub, shouted, "Louisa! The minibus is here, and it comes with its own eye candy!"

Three more young women appeared at the door. One of them was wearing a bright multicoloured curly wig and the other two had headbands with large flashing bobbles on the end of long springs that jiggled about almost as much as the boobs that were just about contained by the skimpy tops they wore.

A Hen party, Bran groaned and made a mental note to himself; 'suggest that they took on some female drivers. He slid open the busses side door as more of the party of ten made their way out of the pub. They were all wearing either wigs or novelty headbands.

A young woman dressed in a pair of black shorts, a strappy black top and knee-length black boots was the first to approach the minibus, she was wearing a pair of pointed black velvet ears and had a long black velvet tail attached to her shorts. At the door she paused. She looked Bran up and down and then slowly licked the back of her hand and rubbed it against one of her fake ears.

"Me – Wow!" She said and climbed onto the minibus.

The young woman with the pink rabbit ears climbed in next.

"Hi handsome," she grinned as she passed Bran. He stood to one side of the door, smiling as the group of partygoers boarded the minibus, trying to ignore the very obvious flirting and poorly disguised sexual innuendos. The last one to get on was Louisa, a young woman in a tight-fitting slinky red dress, she carried a small red plastic pitchfork and had a red forked tail attached to her waistband at the back, while on her head she wore a small bridal veil with two flashing red horns poking through it.

"OK." She said. "Everyone's here."

Bran closed the door behind her and made his way to the driver's door. A chorus of wolf whistles greeted him as he took off his jacket and pulled himself into the driver's seat. "Don't stop there honey!" someone called from the back of the bus. Bran grinned and stretched up, altering the mirror slightly so he could keep an eye on what was going on in the back of the bus. The muscles rippled beneath his silk shirt as he half turned to pull on the seat belt. Catcalls and whistles accompanied the movement.

"Hey, handsome," someone called. "If the strippergram doesn't turn up are you gonna step in and get yer kit off?"

"I think he should get his kit off whether the stripper turns up or not!"

Bran laughed.

"I think you might be disappointed ladies." He said.

"Not from where I'm lookin'," someone shouted.

Bran shook his head and set off towards the motorway, wondering if he would get to Lancaster and back in one piece.

"So where are you ladies heading for tonight?" he asked the woman in red with the bridal veil on her head.

"Funny Girls," she smiled. "They have a great cabaret and I've heard it's really good for a laugh!"

"Is it your Hen Night?" Bran asked, nodding towards the veil she wore. She nodded.

"This time next week I will be Mrs David Ashton."

"Lucky man," Bran said.

"Why thank you!" the reply was accompanied by a broad grin.

The Minibus cruised steadily down the motorway and as the light faded the ten women got more and more excited, singing bawdy songs and telling raunchy jokes.

Bran was relieved to see the lights of Lancaster City Centre and at last, he pulled into the parking bay in front of Funny Girls and his passengers started to step out of the minibus.

"One o'clock back here?" he asked. The future Mrs Ashton nodded.

"What are you going to do till then?" she asked.

"Something to eat and possibly watch a film." He smiled.

"Why don't you come with us?" she said. "It would be a laugh!"

"For who?" Bran said ruefully shaking his head. "I think I'll be much safer with a Little Chef and the local picture house." No amount of persuasion would sway Bran from his intentions and at last the rather disappointed group headed off into the club. Bran looked at his watch; it was eight thirty; four hours to kill. There was plenty of time to enjoy a meal and a film. He climbed back into the minibus and headed into the city, and there would be plenty of time to ring Jason as well!

The meal was good and the film, a comedy; kept him chuckling right to the end. Back at the minibus, Bran chatted to Jason until twelve thirty, eventually having to say goodnight so that he could go and collect his party from the club. It was twelve forty-five when he pulled up in front of Funny Girls. He rolled up his jacket and put it behind his head, making himself as comfortable as he could. These clubbers would be late getting back to the bus; they were always late getting back to the bus. One O'clock would almost certainly be one thirty if not two O'clock!

He was really surprised when; at fifteen minutes past one there was an urgent tapping on the minibus door. It was the future Mrs Ashton. Her veil had disappeared, and Bran could see that she was quite worried. He slid open the side door and waited while she climbed on board.

"Is there a problem?" he asked. Louisa nodded. "We've lost one of our group," she said. "The others are looking for her now, she's only eighteen and she has had just a bit too much to drink; someone saw her talking to a man at the bar about ten minutes ago, but no one has seen her since."

Putting on his jacket, Bran climbed down from the minibus.

"Show me where you last saw her," he said. "I'll help you look; what was she wearing?"

Louisa led the way back into the club. "She was wearing the pink sparkly rabbit ears," she said. Louisa led him through the crowded club to one of the bars towards the back of the building.

" Joyce said she saw Nicola here about ten minutes ago, she said she looked like she had found a friend!"

Bran looked round, there was no sign of the young woman. He remembered her clearly; she had been wearing a very short white skirt and the pink ears and had reminded him of the white rabbit in Alice in Wonderland. Two more of the party came hurrying over.

"We can't find her Louisa; what are we going to do?"

Bran looked round. The bar was quite crowded but he noticed that at the far end of the bar was a doorway that led to a dark corridor. The door was marked STAFF ONLY with a faded sign saying 'toilet's pinned beneath it.

"Wait here," Bran said, and he disappeared down the corridor marked Staff Only. The corridor was poorly lit and obviously used for storage; there were boxes of glasses and beer mats stacked along the wall.

Towards the end of the corridor a door stood open, a dim light shone from the open door and as Bran made his way quietly down the narrow corridor, he thought he could hear the sound of voices and the muted sound of a struggle. He ran the last few yards and burst into what was a small storeroom at the end of the corridor.

A short, stockily built man had the terrified young woman pinned against the wall; one hand was clasped over her mouth while the other groped at the material of her top. Her eyes were wide with fear as she struggled against the stronger man.

Bran didn't hesitate; he grabbed him by the collar and swung him round. The man didn't even have time to even register a look of shock before Bran's left fist smashed into his face. He bounced off the wall straight into Bran's right hook, which doubled him up. Bran was about to finish him off with another left, but the man just crumpled and fell silently in a heap at his feet.

Nicola leant against the wall sobbing, her top was torn, and she had lost her rabbit ears. She wrapped her arms around herself as though she was trying to stop the violent trembling that shook her body.

Bran took off his jacket and wrapped it around the young girls' shoulders.

"Are you OK?" he asked, looking down into her distraught face. She nodded briefly and rubbed the tears away with the back of her hand, smearing her mascara across her cheeks as she did so.

Bran dug into his pocket and pulled out a handkerchief.

"Here, blow your nose."

Bran felt that familiar pang of sadness as once again his mothers' words echoed through his mind.

"Come on," he said. "Your friends are wondering where you are." He put his arm around her shoulders and led her past the prostrate man who still lay motionless on the storeroom floor. She paused and looked down at him.

"Bastard!" she swore.

Bran smiled and nodded. "Go on," he said, "be my guest," and Nicola kicked the unconscious man with all the force she could muster.

"That feel better?" Bran asked. Nicola nodded; a slight smile appeared at the corner of her mouth. "Much." She said.

"Alright, let's go home shall we?" Bran said as he led the way back to the bar. Nicola nodded. "Thank you," she said.

Safely reunited with her companions, Nicola was soon regaling them with the story of how she had been saved by the handsome taxi driver who had rushed to her aid and dispatched her would be attacker so easily. Bran found himself blushing as he was subjected to what amounted to hero worship!

By the time they got back to Liverpool, Nicola had recovered from her ordeal and was quite enjoying being the centre of attention. Just before they reached their destination, Louisa went round the group with an envelope and asked them to contribute to a tip for the driver. Bran thanked them as they left the minibus and slipped the envelope into his pocket.

It was just before three in the morning when Bran arrived home. He parked the minibus on the drive next to Kieran's Peugeot; he would take it back to the garage in the morning.

He locked the doors and headed for the house, pausing under the security light to open the envelope Louisa had pressed into his hand. He counted the notes inside; amazed to find that there was over seventy pounds. He grinned to himself as he walked into the warm kitchen; that was certainly the most valuable rabbit he had ever met!

He looked at the money in his hand and he knew exactly what he was going to do with this unexpected windfall; he would put it with the money he had saved for the tattoo!

13

Bran took a deep breath and walked through the door. Melanie looked up from her desk.

"Oh, Hi." She grinned. "Today's the big day is it?"

The reception was warm and comfortable, and the smell of fresh ground coffee hung in the air.

"Rick's just setting up in the studio," she said. "He won't be long; would you like a coffee while you wait?"

"Perhaps later," Bran said. He felt too nervous to drink anything at the moment.

"This is your first one isn't it?" Melanie asked. Bran nodded.

"It's very ambitious for a first one," Melanie said. "You're very brave!"

"That's not how I feel at the moment," he admitted.

"Don't worry," she smiled. "I've had loads done; it's no worse than going to the dentist."

"I wouldn't fancy the idea of the dentist working on my teeth for seven or eight hours," Bran said darkly.

"Perhaps not the best comparison," Melanie admitted.

"You'll be fine, honest," she smiled. "Rick's pretty good really,"

"Thanks for that vote of confidence, Mel." Rick said as he walked into the reception. "Morning Bran; are you ready for this?"

Bran paused for a moment and exhaled slowly.

"As ready as I'll ever be Rick," he said.

Bran followed Rick through to the studio; it was bright and clean and one whole wall was covered in a huge mirror. A long blue adjustable couch sat in the middle of the room, a large sheet of blue paper was draped over it. At one side of the studio stood a large table with a glass-topped light box set in the middle of it. Rick walked over to this table and beckoned Bran to follow him.

Various parts of the design Bran planned to have tattooed onto his skin were laid out on the table. Rick slid the designs over the lightbox to show how they would be positioned on his back.

"You can hang your shirt over there," he said, pointing to a coat hanger behind the door as he pulled on a pair of black latex gloves.

"The designs are ready to transfer to your back," he said. "I'll put them on and then you can see how they look in the mirror."

Rick rolled a small stainless-steel trolley over to the couch.

"I want you to lie down while I fix the transfers," he said. "But you might find it more comfortable to sit on the chair and lean on the couch while I do the tattoo. Bran stripped off his shirt and climbed onto the couch. Rick swabbed his back with cotton wool balls soaked in antibacterial solution.

"There's still time to back out Bran," Rick said as he tossed the swabs' into a yellow plastic sack. "You can always change your mind you know; right up to the time the needle hits your skin; after that, it's there for life."

"Let's just get on with it, Rick," Bran said. "I'm not pulling out now."

Rick carefully placed the first of the transfers, building up the intricate piece. The process didn't take long, and soon the very striking design was in place. Once he was happy with the layout, he sprayed it gently with a fixing solution then he carefully peeled off the pieces of paper leaving the completed design almost ready to work on. Rick finished off some of the work by hand; joining the various transfers until the places the designs met could not be found. At last, he stood back, pleased with his artwork.

"Have a look Bran; see what you think?" he said. Bran sat on the edge of the couch as Rick gave him a large handheld mirror so that he could look at the reflection in the wall mirror.

Bran studied the design for a few moments. He felt very emotional. The design on his back wasn't exactly the same as Jason's emotive painting, but there were so many elements from it; so much about it reflected his life, his heart and his soul. He gave the mirror back to Rick and just nodded. Right at that moment, he felt an inner strength that he had never felt before. A resolve that he knew would sustain him no matter what.

Rick pushed a strange looking chair over towards the couch.

"An ergonomic kneeling chair," he said as he saw Bran's questioning look.

"Keeps the back straight and helps to stop the muscles getting tired." He showed Bran how to sit on the seat part and then rest his shins on the kneepads'. Bran tried it; despite its strange look, it was surprisingly comfortable. Rick pressed a button to raise the couch to a position where Bran could comfortably rest both arms and leave his back at a good angle to work on.

Rick flicked a switch on the CD player; sixties soul music flooded the studio. He grinned wickedly at Bran.

"Helps to drown out the screams," he joked as he slid the

saddle stool into place behind Bran and straddled it. He pulled the trolley over to his side. He picked up the strange looking tattoo machine and it buzzed into life.

"This might feel a bit hot, or a bit painful at the start, but as we get into it, you'll find it goes kind of numb as the endorphins kick in,"

Bran felt the warmth of Rick's hand on his shoulder and then the first sharp vibration of the needle as it touched his skin.

Bran bowed his head and closed his eyes; the sensation wasn't too unpleasant and as the minutes ticked by, the insistent buzzing sound became almost hypnotic; it was like being annoyed by a large angry wasp.

Rick worked on steadily; every now and again he would pause and wipe the area he was working on with something soft and cool. Bran began to look forward to these brief respites.

His mind drifted back to the long hot summers of his childhood; how they had played on the sun-baked, dusty streets of Belfast; running around all day with only their vests to protect the skin of their young shoulders. Bran remembered the burning pain of his sun blistered back. This felt as though someone was trying to scratch the skin from his sunburned back with a needle.

"You OK, Bran?" Rick asked as he paused to adjust the settings on the machine. Bran nodded. "I've gone through worse."

Rick glanced at the small part of the outline he had completed.

"We've a long way to go yet, Bran," he said. The angry wasp buzzed into life again. Bran closed his eyes and waited for the needle to continue its relentless assault on his now tender skin.

Slowly; carefully; Rick worked his way across Bran's

shoulder. Some areas were a lot more painful than others. Rick could tell from the slightest reactions of the skin; when the pain was particularly intense. During one such session; on a bony part of the shoulder, he called a halt. Turning off the machine, he pulled off his gloves and flexed his fingers, rubbing them to increase the circulation.

"Take five Bran," he said, glancing at his watch; he had been working for just over an hour.

"Get up and have a walk round," he said. "But don't do it too quickly; I don't want to have to pick you up off the studio floor."

Bran stretched his legs and stood up; Rick watched him for a moment; he looked a little pale, but apart from that he seemed to be standing up to the work quite well.

"Melanie!" Rick yelled. "Coffee! Now!"

Bran looked over his shoulder into the big mirror. The black lines of the tattoo outline were stark against the inflamed skin.

"That's just the basics," Rick said. "Once the outline is completed, I'll start again and work on the colour and the shading. Like I said; there's a long way to go yet Bran."

Melanie walked into the studio with two mugs of steaming coffee. She put one down on the table next to Rick and walked across to the couch where Bran was sitting, still naked from the waist up. She looked him up and down; admiring the lean hips and muscled torso. She sighed loudly as she handed him the mug of coffee.

"What a bloody waste!" she said as she turned and walked back into the reception.

Rick laughed; even Bran had to grin.

"That's our Melanie," Rick said smiling. "Tells it as it is!"

"How did you get into tattooing?" Bran asked as they sat drinking the coffee. Rick thought for a while and walked over to sit on the couch next to Bran.

"I studied fine art at Oxford for three years and got a job as a researcher at the Summerfield Gallery in London; it paid well, and I had plenty of time for my own art; the gallery found me a sponsor and held my first exhibition."

He drank the remainder of his coffee. "Then I had some effin' agent appointed by the sponsors telling me what I should paint and how I should paint it. I told them to get stuffed. They tried to say that they owned all my artwork! That the contract I had signed meant that I could only sell or exhibit my work through their agency. Bastards! They started talking about lawsuits and breach of contract so I told them they could have all my work; everything; but before they got their hands on it, I threw paint stripper over every piece; needless to say, they weren't very chuffed; the gallery fired me and the sponsors made damn sure I didn't get another job in that field." He stood up and reached for the box of latex gloves. "I never did fit in with that wine and cheesy biscuits crowd." he said "And now, the artwork I do can't be bought or sold or hung on a wall. Most of the work will never be seen except by the person it's done for. But to that person, the tattoo is special; it becomes part of them; body and soul, and it's there forever. Think about that Bran, you're going to carry my artwork with you for the rest of your life; and when you die, so does the art; but I like to think that when I tattoo your body, I tattoo your soul as well, the spirit of the tattoo will continue on to whatever lies beyond. That's what your tattoo will be Bran; a picture on your soul. That's a big responsibility, so I like to make sure I get it right." He pulled on a fresh pair of the black latex gloves. "And this isn't getting your tattoo done; so let's crack on shall we?"

Bran sat back down on the strange kneeling chair and leant forward, his elbows on the couch and his forehead resting on the palms of his hands. The tattoo machine buzzed into life.

"OK, Bran," Rick said. "Let's get this finished."

The vibrating needle moved slowly over Bran's skin. Somehow, following the coffee break, the pain seemed if anything to be more intense. The areas that had already been tattooed were tender and inflamed and as the waves of pain lapped across his back, Bran closed his eyes and concentrated on the sound the machine made and tried to clear his mind of anything else. The minutes ticked on as time lost all meaning. All there was in Bran's world was pain; the buzzing vibration of the needle and pain.

He thought about what Rick had said; a picture on the soul; His soul, whatever that was, had certainly taken a beating over the years. Perhaps the tattoo would help to heal it. As his mind drifted, he thought about the big old church in Belfast and he remembered standing outside, waiting for his mother's coffin to be carried out.

He had stood alone in the cold dark churchyard; gazing at the stained-glass windows, their images of saints and angels shining out; illuminated by the hundreds of candles that had been lit in the church.

A fifteen-year-old, standing alone, grieving for his mother, wondering how the benign God, pictured in the church windows could have let this happen! The stained-glass windows – the tattoo was like the stained-glass windows through which his soul could be seen. He concentrated on the light that shone through the window.

The brightness of the light spread over him and, as the light intensified, the pain faded into insignificance.

"Bran!" It was Rick's voice that brought him back to the moment. "You OK Bran?" Rick asked. Bran lifted his head and turned to look at Rick. The buzzing had stopped, and he was pulling off his gloves. His back felt as though he had fallen asleep in the sun, he could feel the heat radiating from it. Rick picked up a small plastic spray bottle.

"This will be cold Bran; be warned!"

The fine mist that settled on Bran's back was cold. Rick wiped the solution off with a soft tissue and then sprayed his back again. Bran imagined steam rising as the solution cooled his burning back. This was pure bliss!

"We've been at it for two and a half hours Bran; I need a break and you need something to eat; I'll send Mel out for some sandwiches."

"Nothing for me Rick, I'm not hungry…" Bran started to object.

"It's not an option, Bran," Rick stated simply. "Your blood sugar levels will be crashing around now; you WILL have something to eat because I'm not finishing your tattoo kneeling next to you on the fuckin' studio floor!"

The food was good; Bran hadn't realised just how hungry he was. The sandwiches; followed by a cup of Melanie's wonderful coffee certainly helped to boost his failing energy. He had to admit to Rick, that he had started to feel very lightheaded towards the end of the last session.

"You wouldn't be the first to pass out during a tattooing," Rick told him smiling. "I've had some big hairy arsed bikers in here who have passed out as soon as the needle touched their skin."

"That must be embarrassing," Bran commented.

"Yeah," Rick grinned, "especially when their boyfriends are watching!"

"Yes!" Melanie said as she swept into the studio to retrieve the coffee cups "Nearly as embarrassing as talking to the gay customer about hairy-arsed bikers boyfriends!" she patted Bran's hand condescendingly "Ignore him Bran; He's just trying to be funny; and once again Rick, it's foot…; mouth…; insert former in latter!" and without a backwards glance, she swept out of the studio, leaving both men dumbfounded for a few seconds before they both roared with laughter.

"Are you ready to press on?" Rick asked as he set up more tattoo machines on the trolley. Bran looked dubiously at the kneeling chair next to the couch. Rick had warned him that it would hurt. He hadn't lied. He took a deep breath and sat down, getting himself into a comfortable position leaning on the padded couch.

Rick busied himself preparing the various coloured inks; the dark pigments would be applied first, the yellow and white would be the final ones. He unfolded his original artwork; his colour reference; and laid it on the couch next to Bran. The tattoo machine buzzed into life and Bran tensed, waiting for the first assault on his tender back.

"Try and relax Bran." Rick's hand was on his shoulder as he slid onto the saddle stool behind him. The needle descended, grinding the coloured ink into Bran's inflamed skin. Bran held his breath, as the pain seemed to shoot up unto his neck and down his spine.

"Keep breathing Bran." Rick smiled without pausing. "It'll get easier in a little while."

"How much longer will this take?" He asked through

clenched teeth.

Rick glanced at his watch and studied Bran's back for a moment.

"About another four hours," he said. Bran groaned.

"Now you know;" Rick grinned, looking at Bran in the mirror; "Why most people have a piece this size done over two or three sessions."

It was nearly five o'clock that evening when Rick finally turned off the machine and said, "That's it Bran; all finished."

Bran moved slowly; his back felt like it was on fire.

"Hold still a moment," Rick said. "Just let me wipe this down for you." He picked up the little spray bottle and carefully covered the new tattoo with a fine mist of cooling lotion. He gently wiped off the excess and then sprayed Bran's back once more; finally, he gently smeared a soothing jelly-like ointment over the entire back piece.

"How does it feel Bran?" He asked.

Bran looked up and gave a half-hearted smile; he was exhausted.

"A bloody sight better now you've stopped," he said.

Rick handed him a mirror.

"Take a look."

Rick had taken Jason's artwork to another level; the tattoo was stunning. It was so much more than Bran had even dared hope. The tiredness and pain were forgotten as Bran gazed at the poignant image that was now a part of him. He couldn't speak as the emotions suppressed for a lifetime rose to the surface. It was so beautiful, so very emotional. The tears ran unchecked down his face.

Rick smiled; he knew the power of the tattoo.

"Take your time Bran," he said gently. "Come through to reception when you're ready," and he walked out of the studio, leaving Bran to compose himself.

Sometime later; his back covered in a protective film and with an extensive brochure on tattoo aftercare tucked in his inside pocket; Bran walked out to his car accompanied by Rick who was offering a stream of last-minute instructions.

"Come back in a couple of days time and let me have a look at it, just to make sure everything's OK; and don't let anyone slap you on the back." He grinned.

Bran pointed his car keys at the Audi; the lights flashed as the alarm was deactivated.

"Unusual key ring," Rick said, noticing the heavy gold anchor attached to Bran's keys.

Bran looked down at the gold anchor, now worn smooth with constant handling.

"Yeah, I've had that a long time," he said. "A bit of a good luck talisman really." He looked up and smiled, wondering just how long his luck would last.

"Thanks again Rick," he said, holding out his hand.

"My pleasure Bran," Rick said. The two men shook hands.

Bran opened the door of his car and then paused and turned to look at Rick.

"It doesn't bother you that I'm gay, does it?" it was a statement rather than a question.

Rick looked at Bran; a slight, rather enigmatic smile played across his lips.

"Why should it?" he asked, and with a slight nod of his head, he turned and walked back into the studio.

It was six thirty when Bran got home. The house was deserted; Pat and Kieran would be at the office by now. He carefully peeled off his jacket; his back felt strangely numb. Underneath his shirt, the clear protective film taped across his new tattoo wrinkled as his muscles moved beneath the skin. He took off his shirt and carefully peeled the plastic film from his back; he walked into the bathroom and looked at the tattoo through the mirror.

What the hell had he done! The skin looked angry and inflamed and not at all as he expected it to look, but Rick had said that it would take a couple of days to calm down. He looked again at the striking imagery; it really was quite a stunning design. He couldn't wait to show it to Jason but decided that it might be prudent to wait till it looked a little less painful!

Later, as he took a clean white shirt from his wardrobe and eased it gingerly over his shoulders, he wondered what his Dad would think of the tattoo when he eventually saw it; Pat had on many occasions, called him a wimp because he had refused to go along with him to the tattoo studio. Bran grinned; well his Dad would certainly call him something but somehow, Bran didn't think that it would be 'wimp'.

The lightweight material of his shirt stuck to the layer of healing cream Rick had smeared over his back. It felt strange and Bran wondered just how much of the oily ointment would seep through the material and if the tattoo beneath would be visible. He put his soft leather jacket on over the top of the shirt. Rick had told him to take off the protective plastic film after a couple of hours, but Bran was wondering if that had been a good idea just yet!

Bran took a bottle of mineral water from the fridge; Rick had said he should drink plenty of fluids. Bran didn't know exactly why he should be drinking loads of fluids but if that's what Rick said he should do, that's what he would do!

He picked up his car keys and was just about to leave for the office when the phone rang. It was Pat O'Donnell.

"What do you want Dad?" Bran asked. "I was just on my way into the garage, I'll be there in fifteen minutes."

"Before you do that; call and pick Mrs Driscoll and Lisa up from their house and take them through to the Cavern Walks Shopping Centre; I've no cabs' free just at the moment and it would only take you ten minutes to get out there."

Bran sighed.

"Dad I'm in the Audi, it's not exactly designed for carrying passengers..."

"It's got four soddin' seats hasn't it?" Pat said sharply.

"Yes but…"

"No fuckin buts," Pat said angrily, he didn't like to be argued with. "I've told Mrs Driscoll that you would be there in ten minutes so get yer fuckin skates on! I thought you would have jumped at the chance to have a chat to young Lisa!"

Bran groaned, was this just another of his Dad's schemes to throw him at Lisa Driscoll. He wondered what Pat would say when he found out that Kieran and Lisa were seeing quite a lot of each other. He wished that Kieran wouldn't be quite so secretive about it. If their Dad knew that Lisa was involved with his younger son; perhaps he would give Bran a bit of a break from all the badgering to get married!

Bran pulled up in front of the house being rented by Sean Driscoll and his family while Sean was working in Liverpool.

The two women walked out of the front door to meet him.

"Hello Mrs Driscoll, Lisa!" Bran smiled and he opened the door of the Audi and pushed forward the passenger seat, revealing the rather cramped seating in the back of the sporty little car. "Dad said you were in a hurry and I should pick you up in this," he said apologetically. "Hope you don't mind squeezing in the back Lisa?"

Lisa grinned and climbed over the back of the seat.

"Not if you don't mind my knees on your back Bran." she laughed.

It only took ten minutes to get to the big modern shopping centre down by the Albert Docks. Bran pulled up by the main entrance and jumped out to open the car door for the two ladies.

Mrs Driscoll got out first, followed by a somewhat cramped Lisa.

"I'm sorry about that." Bran apologised as Lisa stretched her stiff limbs, "but Pat insisted!"

"Don't worry." Pauline Driscoll smiled, "believe me, I've travelled in worse," she smiled ruefully at Lisa. "There was a lot more room in the front than there appeared to be in the back. Aren't you coming with us?" Pauline said, noticing that Bran was stopped in a No Parking area. Bran shook his head. "I'll have to get back to the taxi office." He said, "and pick up my cab; just ring Kieran when you're ready to go home and I'll pick you up from here. There wouldn't be enough room in the back of the Audi for you ***and*** your shopping," he grinned.

He was just about to get back into the car when Lisa placed her hand on his arm.

"Bran," she said, slipping a small envelope into his hand. "Will you give this to Kieran for me?"

Bran smiled and nodded. "Course I will Honey, haven't I always?" He was quite used to playing postman for Lisa and Kieran.

"You're a star!" she said beaming, and she threw her arms around him and hugged him.

Bran winced; his raw back complained painfully at the rough treatment.

He slid thankfully into his car and rested his back gingerly against the soft, padded upholstery and he drove away as Lisa and her mother made their way into the shopping centre.

Ten days, two weeks at the most, Rick had said, before his back would be healed enough to able to stand up to rough treatment. Bran felt the little twinges of pain from Lisa's bear hug and wondered if he would survive that long!

"Thanks bro." Kieran grinned as Bran handed him Lisa's letter. "You're not working next Friday night, are you?" he continued. Bran looked at him warily.

"You wouldn't man the radio for me for a couple of hours would you?" he said hopefully. "Lisa wants to go and see the new Robert De Niro film The Good Shepherd."

Bran arched his eyebrows cynically.

"A couple of hours? - Is that the two hours it'll take to watch a three-hour film?"

"Go on Bran." Kieran pleaded. "I'll owe you one!"

Bran snorted. "Little brother, you already owe me more than you could ever hope to pay back!"

Kieran grinned. "Then one more thing isn't going to make much difference is it?"

Bran shook his head grinning. He knew he was a soft touch as far as Kieran was concerned.

"Nice one Bran!" Kieran said slapping his brother on the back "I won't forget it! Honest!"

"Neither will I," Bran said through gritted teeth.

"Oh!" Kieran added. "You won't say anything to Dad, will you? I haven't told him about me and Lisa yet."

"Where is he anyway?" Bran asked. "I thought he was in the office with you."

"The Ferryman," Kieran said. "Where else?"

On Friday afternoon, Bran called in at The Ink Spot. It had been a couple of days since he had the tattoo done. It certainly looked a lot less inflamed than it had and as he put his shirt back on after Rick had examined the work and declared that everything was fine, just as it should be.

Rick asked him how he felt about the tattoo, now that he had had time to get used to it.

"It's good." He smiled, "and Jason likes it as well; he loves what you've done with his design."

Rick nodded.

"Well that's one ordeal you've gone through Bran, and you've made it out the other side; you know what the next ordeals got to be, don't you?" Bran nodded; that was one ordeal he was not looking forward to; Pat!

Later that night, Bran pulled into the yard at O'Donnell's Taxis. Most of the cabs were out; Friday was one of the busiest nights of the week. He made his way up to the office, taking the stairs two at a time. It was almost seven O'clock and Kieran was waiting for him.

"Hell Kieran!" Bran laughed. "You can scrub up pretty well when the mood takes you!"

Kieran grinned. "I tried on some of your designer jeans, but they're too bloody long in the leg!"

"Keep out of my wardrobe you little toerag!" Bran laughed, It's bad enough that you nick my shampoo and aftershave."

Kieran picked up the keys to his car and headed for the door.

"See you later bro and thanks again!"

"Yeah, yeah; whatever," Bran said. The phone was already flashing with waiting calls. He sat down and put on the radio headphones. It was going to be a long night!

It was nearly midnight when Kieran got back to the taxi office, having just dropped Lisa off at home. Things were quieter, but there were still quite a few of the Taxis still working.

Bran was relieved to see his brother and more than ready to head home, have something to eat and crash out in his bed. He had forgotten just how trying being in the office could be. He had had more than enough of argumentative, awkward people for one night.

Leaving Kieran to take over for the remainder of the night, Bran headed for home. He pulled into the drive; the lights were still on in the house; Pat must still be up. Bran locked his car and headed for the kitchen. Pat was waiting for him.

14

"Where the fuck have you been?" Pat swore angrily.

"Does it matter?" Bran said. "It's my night off, I can please my self where I go!

"Well don't try to tell me you've been out with Sean's lass again because I know it's a friggin' lie!"

"I wasn't going to mention Lisa at all!"

"I bet you weren't!" Pat continued, "Because I've just had Mrs Driscoll on the phone, asking me to give Lisa a message if Kieran brought her here before he took her home; seems that Kieran has been seeing quite a bit of young Lisa Driscoll!"

"Crafty little sods' been sneaking off to see her behind your effin' back!"

"Its' not like that Dad," Bran began. Pat ignored him.

"Well it can effin' stop!" he shouted!

"Dad; there's something I want to talk to you about."

"What the fuck are you doing Bran? Letting Kieran steal the bloody woman from under your nose! Sean's lass likes you, she said she likes you. You could have made a fuckin' effort!"

Bran shook his head. This was going to be harder than he thought.

"I'm not interested in women Dad."

"You could do a lot worse than marry into Sean Driscoll's family. Sean said he would be happy if you two got together. He would have given you his support; you could have a friggin' good future ahead of you!"

"Dad, I don't want you, Sean Driscoll or anyone else arranging my future; I don't need you arranging my life for me."

"Well, what are you draggin' yer effin' feet for then? I would have thought by now; you would at least have a steady girlfriend. Most Irish lads of your age are married and, on their way to building a good Catholic family!" Pat shook his head.

"And now, you dozy bastard," Pat shouted! "You let your effin' brother get in there before you. I had high hope of you two getting together; I would like to live long enough to at least see the next generation of the O'Donnell family!"

"Then you will have to pin your hopes on Kieran or Paul," Bran said, raising his voice, "kids don't figure high on the list of priorities in my relationship, and you can stop introducing me to all these bloody' women as well! I already have a partner and we are very happy together!"

"Thank Christ for that! Kieran told me you had a thing with this girl called Sarah," Pat said, "I was starting to get worried! Why haven't you brought her home, it's about time you settled down!"

"Oh, for fuck's sake!" Bran said exasperated, "Haven't you figured it out yet Dad! There is no Sarah! There never was a Sarah!" He looked Pat squarely in the eye "I've never been interested in a relationship with a woman; my partner is a MAN, and you're just going to have to get used to it!"

Pat was stunned, stunned and unable to take in what his son was saying to him. Bran was so frustrated by the look of sheer incomprehension on his father's face.

"Christ almighty Dad! Do I have to spell it out for you? I'm queer; a fag; a shirt lifter; a bum buddy; an arse pirate! I'M FUCKIN' GAY!!!

15

The backhanded blow that hit him in the mouth was vicious, thrown with all the power his father could muster.

"Don't you say that to me, Bran O'Donnell, don't you dare say that! I won't have any fuckin' perverts in this house!"

Bran staggered back, rocked by the power of the blow; he could taste blood in his mouth.

"What do you want me to say to you Dad, that I'm straight and this is all a joke! Well, I can't do that; I've been in a steady relationship with the same guy for over a year now and there's nothing you can do about it!

"We'll see about that!" Pat said. "I'll put a stop to it! I'll fuckin' knock it out of you!" He hit Bran again; the force of the blow split his lip and spun Bran round. He steadied himself by holding onto the back of a chair; he turned to face his Dad. Another backhanded blow knocked him off his feet and he fell backwards crashing into the table, Bran sat on the floor amidst the wreckage of the coffee table, he wiped the blood from the side of his mouth.

"You had better tell me this isn't true Bran O'Donnell, or so help me I'll fuckin' kill you!"

"Dad," he said as he pulled himself to his feet, "You might have been able to beat me into doing what you wanted when I was a kid, but not now, not this time."

"You've got a bloody nerve, standing there spouting this fuckin' filth at me, I won't have it, Bran. I won't have a son of mine messing with blokes." Pat shook his head as though he was unable to take in what his eldest son was saying to him. "You need… You need to see a doctor," he said. "That's it! There must be some treatment you can get!"

"Dad!" Bran said, "It's not a bloody disease, you can't be 'cured', It's just the way I am; the way I've always been!"

"I'm sick to the stomach just at the thought of it." Pat snarled; he looked at Bran as though he was something he'd just scraped off his shoe. "Christ! I never thought I would ever say that I was glad your mother was dead, but I'm glad she's not alive to hear this obscenity coming out of your mouth!"

"Well she's not here is she Dad!" Bran shouted; a lifetime of anger and pain rising to the surface. "She's not here! And when we needed a father, neither were you! You were either out working, in the pub or pissed out of your fuckin' mind!"

"I gave you a good home!" Pat shouted. "Everything I did was for you!"

"That's what I always believed Dad; I had faith in you, no matter what you did, I always believed that you thought it was the best for us; that sometimes you had to be cruel to be kind."

"After Cathleen had gone; all that was left were you three; her boys; everything I did was to make sure her boys grew up as she would have wanted them; hard-working, God-fearing Catholics; everything I did was for you!"

"God-fearing Catholics?" Bran yelled incensed. "Is that why you sent me to that fuckin' Sunday School to be raped by the fuckin' paedophile priest?"

For a second time, Pat was stunned into silence.

"You had no idea, Dad." Bran continued, "Everything you did was to keep that wall of self-pity around yourself, all you cared about was what YOU had lost, how unhappy YOU were, how angry YOU felt! You never considered me or Kieran or

Paul, you dragged us away from home, away from everything we knew, dumped us in a strange house in the middle of a strange city and then went and lost yourself in the bottom of a fuckin' bottle! Who was it that had to take the boys to school! Who was it made their tea at night? Who put them to bed 'cos their Dad was too pissed to stand up!"

Bran's eyes flashed as the memories came flooding back.

"Who was it stood in front of them when their Dad took his belt off to 'teach them a lesson'? Who was it that had made sure Father Ryan hadn't asked them to carry hymn books to the Vestry?"

"You're lying! You're fuckin' lying!" Pat yelled. "You're just an ungrateful fuckin' bastard! My Cathleen would still be alive if it wasn't for you!" He was beside himself with rage.

Something cold seemed to twist in Bran's chest; his breath was knocked out of him, the words he wanted to cry out; 'it wasn't my fault!' stuck in his throat, silencing him. His father still blamed him for his mother's death!

"I worked every hour God sent to put money in the bank and bread on the table. I worked to build a business you could be proud of!"

"I didn't want the bloody business Dad!" Bran said. "I wanted a father, Paul and Kieran just needed someone to love them, they'd lost their mum and they were losing their Dad as well. If you'd bothered to look at their school reports or talk to their teachers you would have seen how much that was affecting them; Paul was six years old for Christ's sake, Kieran was only eight! They needed someone; someone who would listen to them and help them to grow up. They didn't go to you Dad! They came to me! And if they have any problems, they still come to me! But who did I have to go to for advice? Because you weren't fuckin' there for me were you!!? You were never there. When I needed to talk to someone about how I felt when I began to realise that things were different for me when I was growing up; that I was different; there was no one I could turn to, I had to sort out all my own problems. You didn't give a fuck then and you don't give a fuck now. Nothing changes and I made excuses for you all my life. You never listened to me, never gave me the help I needed, so what makes you think I'm going to start taking your friggin' advice now!"

Bran walked to the door.

"I'm taking a couple of days off," he said, "I've things to do, I'll be back in the office on Monday either to start work or to collect my things and clear out, it's up to you; and to be quite honest, I don't give a toss either way!"

"Don't fuckin' bother!" Pat yelled, "you're no son of mine; you won't be welcome there so you can piss off now, and don't bother coming back here either. Fuck off to your bum buddies; the thought of what you're doing makes me sick! I don't want to lay eyes on you again! Do you hear!!"

"I hear you Dad," Bran said quietly, and without a backward glance, he walked out of the house.

His heart was pounding as he walked out to the car, his mouth hurt. The split lip was stinging like hell; then he realised it was because he was grinning; he felt as though a great weight had been lifted off his shoulders.

There was no turning back now. He climbed slowly into the black Audi and sat for a moment as the enormity of what had just happened washed over him. He was free; free to be himself; free to live the life he wanted to live; free to be with Jason.

Jason!

He could almost hear his mother's voice in his head,

"You're a big boy now Bran," as he turned the ignition and pulled slowly out of the drive. He didn't even look back as he headed for town and the flats at Anncolm Heights!

"Bran! What the hell's happened?" Jason said as he opened the door to a distraught Bran; he couldn't tell if he was laughing or crying, and neither could Bran.

"I told Pat! He said, "I told him and he threw me out!"

Jason ushered Bran into the flat.

"You told him what Bran."

"About us Jay! I told him I was gay and had a partner and the bastard threw me out!"

"You did what!" Jason said stunned. "You told your Dad about us?"

Bran nodded. "Yes," he said, "I told Pat I was gay."

Jason threw his arms around Bran.

"Oh, I'm so proud of you, Bran, that couldn't have been easy." Then he noticed the split lip and the bruises on his cheek; he touched Bran's face gently with his fingertips. "Yes, I can see it wasn't easy," he said softly.

Jason folded his arms around Bran and hugged him "He'll come around after he's got over the initial shock; it'll just take him a day or two to realise you're serious about this."

Bran got hold of Jason's arms and stepped away from him so that he could look into his eyes.

"No Jason, this is something that Pat will never accept; he will never forgive me for this; I will just have to get used to the idea that I am not part of his family anymore." He pulled Jason into his arms and they stood and held each other.

"I've got a new family now," Bran said quietly.

16

The house was empty. Bran unlocked the door and let himself in; it didn't look any different, the same untidy mess in the kitchen; the pots from breakfast still stacked in the sink, the swing bin in the corner crammed to overflowing. Kieran's leather jacket was draped over a kitchen chair and a pile of Paul's books sat on the kitchen unit.

Bran made his way up the stairs to his bedroom. Everything looked the same; except the cleaner must have changed the sheets and his clothes were in the neat piles on the bed. A strong emotional wave washed over him as he looked at the photos of his family that were dotted around the room; the family that had turned their backs on him. A lump formed in his throat as he picked up the photo of his mother, the only one he had. Shaking himself, he put the photo down and turning to his wardrobe, pulled out the big suitcase from the top shelf.

He flipped it open and tossed it onto the bed and began filling it with his clothes.

"Tell me this is some fucking sick joke bro!"

Bran spun round, he hadn't heard Kieran come in; turning away from the accusing look on his brother's face, he began emptying dressing table drawers.

"No joke Kieran," he said quietly.

"I don't understand." Kieran shook his head; desperately wanting Bran to deny the things Pat had said about him. "It can't be right; you're not…" The word seemed to stick in his throat. "You can't be friggin' gay?"

Bran looked up at his brother; he remained silent.

"What about Sarah? What about the night we went to the Fizz nightclub?"

"You said it yourself, Kieran," Bran said as he opened another drawer, "I was pissed out of my bloody skull."

"So, all the times you didn't come home; all the times we thought you were off shagging some bit of skirt somewhere…"

"Yeah; you've got it, bro," Bran said exasperated, "I was in bed with a man!" he slammed the lid of the suitcase down angrily.

"And nine times out of ten, I was the one being shagged! Does that paint a better picture for you!"

Kieran said nothing; his silence more painful to Bran than any angry reply could have been.

Bran grabbed the big sports bag from on top of the wardrobe.

"So where are you staying Bran?" Kieran asked as he watched his brother cram his possessions into the holdall.

"As if you give a friggin' shit where I'm staying!"

"If I didn't give a shit Bran; I wouldn't be here."

"What do you want to know for Kieran, so you can tell Paul and his friends where to find us; so he can come and finish what he started and kick the crap out of both of us?" He turned his back to Kieran; opened up the holdall and shoved a handful of his beautiful designer shirts angrily into the corner.

"Yeah, you could both have a good laugh about that over breakfast couldn't you!"

A few moments later he heard the front door slam; he turned around; the room was empty, Kieran had gone.

Bran sat down heavily on the bed. He felt like all the breath had been sucked from his body. A painful lump seemed to form in his throat, and he buried his face in the jacket he was holding as he tried to stifle the huge sobs that wracked his body.

It was a while before Bran finished packing away his belongings.

He took one last look around the room; he remembered a similar feeling so many years ago when he had looked round the room he had shared with his brothers in Belfast on the day they had left to catch the ferry to Liverpool. He remembered how the most important item in his small suitcase then, had been the battered old teddy bear his mother had given him many years before. The same battered old teddy bear had been one of the first things to go into his suitcase now.

"Time to go, Bran boy," he said to himself. Then he paused for a moment and once more flipped open the lid of the suitcase. Very carefully he slid the frames containing the family photos between the layers of clothes.

He held the last one in his hands for a long time while he gazed lovingly at that gentle face; the soft brown eyes so much like his own.

"Sorry mum," he whispered.

Bran had been to the flat many times and had slept with Jason on many occasions, but now, putting his clothes in the wardrobe next to Jason's; putting his razor and his comb in the bathroom cabinet, it seemed so strange, so foreign, as though he hadn't been here before.

Jason did his best to make him feel at ease. In the past, Bran had treated the flat like a second home; helping himself to coffee, raiding Jason's cupboards for biscuits; walking into the shower after their steamy sessions of lovemaking, but for some strange reason; now he felt like a visitor. He felt like he should ask if he could put the kettle on or use the loo or help himself to something from the fridge.

"It's bound to feel strange for a while," Jason reassured him when Bran tried to explain how he felt. "This is a bit different to a quick shag and a blow job on a Saturday night."

Bran laughed. "Do you have to be so effin' basic?" he said.

Jason grinned. "Well this is different, this is getting used to living together; so, give it time, you're still uptight, still stressed." Jason sat on the comfortable settee and patted the seat next to him.

"Come and sit down, put your feet up and relax.

Bran sighed and sat next to Jason. Jason opened his arms.

"C'mon," he said, inviting Bran to lean against him. "Put your feet up and take it easy for once."

Bran kicked off his shoes and put his feet up on the settee. Jason's arms were wrapped around him and he stroked his shoulder absent-mindedly.

"I'm sorry if my socks stink," Bran said smiling.

"Well nothing could smell as bad as that foul smelling paste your Dad put on your back that time," Jason said.

Bran was silent and Jason mentally kicked himself for mentioning his Dad.

"Look! Do you want something to eat?" Jason asked, changing the subject.

"No, I'm not that hungry," Bran said, "but if you've got a beer; I wouldn't mind one of those."

"I think I can manage a beer or two." Jason smiled and eased himself from behind Bran and disappeared into the kitchen. Just moments later he returned with two bottles; he found Bran gazing moodily out of the window as he looked out towards the river, the lights of the city a riot of colour nestled in the amber glow of the streetlights.

"Beautiful isn't it," Bran said as he took the bottle Jason offered him. "I've never really had the time just to look; always been too busy going somewhere or doing something." He took a long drink from the bottle.

"Now! – nothing to do and nowhere to go!"

17

Bran called at the Off Licence on his way to the flat; a couple of bottles of beer would go down very well with the pizza he knew Jason was making for supper. The streets around the Off Licence and Kebab Shop were, as always, crowded with students.

"Six bottles of Stella, John," Bran said as he dug deep into his pocket for the last of his money.

The manager, John, handed him the bottles and gave him his change.

"Thanks," Bran said somewhat bleakly as he pocketed the handful of loose change. He was just about to leave the shop when John called him back.

"Bran." He said, somewhat cautiously, "Are you still looking for work?"

Bran nodded. "'Fraid so," he said.

"Used to be a taxi driver, weren't you?" John asked.

Bran nodded. John pulled a page from his notebook and scribbled a telephone number on it; He pushed the note into Bran's hand.

"That's a mate of mine; Gaz. He's looking for a delivery driver, cash in hand," he said, tapping the side of his nose with his index finger, "someone who doesn't mind work and can keep his mouth shut." Bran looked at the scrap of paper, it was a mobile number.

"Nice one John." He nodded as he left the shop. "I'll give him a bell later."

Later, back at the flat, as they sat eating pizza, Bran told Jason about the possibility of a job as a delivery driver. Jason was delighted; Bran had been so quiet lately and he knew that his inability to find work had really knocked his confidence.

Later that night, as they lay together in the warm, cosy bed, Jason wrapped his arms around Bran and kissed his shoulder affectionately.

"See Bran," he said quietly. "I told you everything would turn out OK in the end." The only response he got from Bran was a long, contented, snore.

It wasn't a regular job and Bran never knew from one day to the next if he was going to be working or not, but it was cash in hand; and the money, usually seventy or eighty pounds, came in very, very useful. At least Bran felt as though he was, at last, contributing to their relationship.

It had taken Bran longer than he thought it would to drive from Bradford to Liverpool, the motorway had been crazy; one delay after another; queuing to get through road works in a clapped-out van with the engine overheating and the clutch slipping. It had been a long; long day; just to pick up a dozen boxes from Cheetham Hill in Manchester and drop them off at an off licence in Bradford.

As always, the van was left on a piece of waste ground down by the docks; the keys were to be dropped off at the off licence in town, Boozy Brothers, where he would collect the brown envelope that contained the seventy quid he had earned for the job.

As usual, there were loads of teenagers hanging round the streets close to the off licence; waiting while their older mates bought booze for them. The Kebab house on the corner was busy tonight and the Car Park opposite was hosting its' usual 'boy racer' convention. Bran walked into the off licence, it seemed busier than usual as he made his way round the stacks of beer and lager cans. John, the manager was serving a couple of guys when he spotted Bran.

"Be with you in a minute, Bran," he said as he counted out the change for his customers.

One of the men looked round and glared at Bran and as they left; deliberately barged into him on his way out.

"What the friggin' 'ell was that about?" Bran asked as he handed the van keys to John. John shrugged his shoulders and handed Bran the envelope he had for him beneath the counter.

"Dick heads," he said.

Bran tucked the envelope into his pocket. He thought about Jason and home and how good it would be just to stand in the shower and let the hot water soothe the tired muscles.

"I'll take a bottle of Grouse John," he said taking his wallet from his back pocket. "I could do with a drink tonight!"

It would only take twenty minutes or so to walk back to Anncolm Heights; back to the flat where he knew Jason would be waiting; the short cut through the industrial estate had knocked ten minutes off the usual half hour walk. He looked up at the night sky; dark angry clouds were starting to build; an ominous portent of the coming winter. He set off down the street; hopefully, he would get home before the rain began and thought longingly of his Audi TT, parked outside the flats. He hadn't left his car in town since that night he had come back from a delivery to find that some bastard had run a penknife down the entire side of the car, gouging a great scratch from one end to the other. So he pulled up the collar of his leather jacket against the cold wind and headed for home.

On the car park behind him, the two men who had been in the off licence stood watching him walk down the street; they turned and joined the group of bored young men and women who were hanging around the Kebab house. After some discussion ten or twelve of them piled into four cars and headed off in the direction Bran had taken.

It didn't take Bran long to reach the industrial estate; the big anonymous grey units clustered around un-named roads that wound their confusing ways through the labyrinth of buildings. Once he had walked through here, it would only be five minutes before he would be able to see the Flats in the distance.

At this time of night, the industrial estate was devoid of life, but it was reasonably well lit so Bran had never had any qualms about walking past the deserted units; tonight seemed no different.

He quite liked walking; walking gave him time to think, he had mulled over many problems on his walks back to the flat. Tonight, his thoughts turned to his brothers; mainly Kieran, and hoping that he was being sensible and not going off the rails. As Bran knew only too well, his younger brother could be a bit of a hothead. He had dabbled with drugs in the past and Bran desperately hoped that he was staying well away from those influences now. He was a good kid really and a hard worker when he put his mind to it. As for Paul; Bran couldn't quite weigh him up. Uni' certainly seemed to have had a big influence on him, but Bran wasn't too sure if that had been a good thing or not! He missed his brothers; he missed the laughs and the easy banter; he even missed the arguments!

So lost was he in his thoughts that he didn't notice the four cars coming up slowly behind him until they passed him and stopped on the road just ahead.

Suddenly very alert, Bran paused, and then thought, what the hell! He continued walking. As he passed the first car the door opened, and a man got out; Bran recognised him at once; it was the guy from the off licence; the one who had barged into him on his way out.

Ignoring him, he walked past.

"Hey, ass boy! Where's your boyfriend?" the man jeered as Bran walked on.

"Hey Ass fucker, I'm talking to you!"

Bran stopped, he closed his eyes as his heart seemed to drop and form a cold angry knot in the pit of his stomach; he turned slowly and looked at the man; he had a trolley jack handle in his hand.

"What the fucks' your problem dick head?" Bran said angrily.

"You are," the man said, slapping his palm with the jack handle. "You and your effin' bum buddies; you're not fit to breathe the same air as a proper man!"

Bran laughed. "Yeah! And you're a proper man are you?"

"We don't want your sort round here dick shit; you need to learn the facts of life and we're going to teach you that lesson, and it's one that you won't forget for a long time."

Bran backed into the road, giving himself room to move.

"OK you fuckin' wanker," he said beckoning the man to him. "Bring it on!"

The man stepped forward; behind him, the doors of the other three cars opened and their occupants climbed out.

Bran backed off slowly, there must have been nine or ten of them; some carried metal bars. Bran glanced at the cars and realised that a lone figure still sat in the passenger seat of one of the cars. For a second their eyes met. Bran froze in disbelief. It was Paul; it was his brother Paul.

It was at that moment that the first blow fell. He could hear the shouts of abuse and encouragement as the jack handle smashed into his arm. Bran fought back, but there were too many; far too many.

He tried to protect his head, but metal bars, and fists rained down on his arms, his ribs, and his back! Something smashed into the side of his knee and he fell to the ground. Lights danced in front of Bran's eyes and he could taste blood, the shouts and taunts continued as he was repeatedly kicked in the stomach and groin. He rolled himself into a ball trying to protect the vulnerable areas. A booted foot glanced off the side of his head. His senses swam as the blows continued to fall. There was blood in his eyes and his mouth. He gasped in pain as the metal rods continued to slash at his body, cutting his clothing and drawing blood wherever they made contact.

Lying on the cold ground, clinging to consciousness, Bran could hear laughter and he became aware of the feeling of warm liquid hitting his skin. The bastards were pissing on him.

"That's the only thing you should be using your dick for Ass fucker!" somebody laughed. The man with the jack handle picked up the bottle of Grouse Bran had dropped.

"This is a man's drink," He said, taking the top off the bottle.

"Too good for pricks like you!" and he poured the contents of the bottle over Bran. Unable to help himself, Bran cried out as the fiery alcohol ran into the cuts and open wounds on his body.

One of his attackers' a weasel-faced little man, put his foot on Bran's arm, pinning him to the floor.

"Somebody get me a blade!" He snarled, "I've always wanted to castrate one of these bastards!"

"Go on Joe!" someone shouted to the accompaniment of raucous laughter. "He can shove his balls up his friggin' arse!"

Suddenly the horn of one of the cars sounded repeatedly, it was the signal that someone was approaching. Swearing and giving Bran one last vicious kick, Joe and the gang of queer bashers returned to their cars and within seconds had disappeared down the road and away from the scene of the attack.

Bran lay in the road, barely aware that the attack had stopped. Wave after wave of nausea washed over him and the pain from broken ribs stabbed wickedly as he tried to breathe. Desperately he tried to roll over so that he could push himself to his feet, but the effort was too much, and a merciful blackness overtook him as he slipped into unconsciousness.

It was the rain falling on his face sometime later that eventually brought Bran round. He was cold and wet and everywhere hurt. For a moment he couldn't think where he was; and then he remembered the attack by the gang of homophobes; and Paul; Paul sitting in the car watching it happen. The realisation was like a physical blow. His own brother had sat and watched while his friends had almost killed him. Bran knew that these were probably the same ones who had beaten Jason; he was sure of that now and he wondered if Paul would be laughing when he told Kieran how they'd beaten up and pissed on another queer! He crawled over to the mesh fencing that surrounded one of the units and using the fence for support he slowly pulled himself to his feet. Bran put his hand down to his pocket feeling for his mobile phone. It had gone! So had his wallet; he reached up to his jacket pocket looking for the brown envelope; that was missing as well. No money; no phone. All he could do was make his way as best he could to Anncolm Heights and home where he knew Jason would be waiting.

It was the early hours of the morning when Bran finally made it. It took a supreme effort to climb the three flights of stairs.

He staggered into the hallway and leaned against the wall next to the door of the flat. He left a huge bloody smear as the rainwater and the blood had soaked into his clothes. Resting his forehead on the door, he hammered repeatedly with his fist. It seemed to be ages before at last, he heard the key being turned in the lock and the bolt being pulled back.

Jason opened the door and practically screamed as Bran collapsed into his arms.

18

"No Jay! No hospital!" Bran was adamant "I'll be fine in a couple of hours!"

"Bran, just look at the state of you!" Jason gently wiped the blood from the cuts and bruises on Bran's back and shoulders. Jason had held him in the shower while the warm water had washed the dirt, the alcohol and the piss from his battered and bloody body.

"It looks a lot worse than it is Jay," He said as he leant on the kitchen table. The fluffy white towel wrapped around his hips was stained with blood.

Bran grimaced as a wave of pain washed through his abdomen and seemed to settle in his groin.

"A couple of painkillers and a few hours sleep; I'll be fine.

"Bran you could have some broken ribs or internal injuries…"

"Yes, and at the hospital, they would tell me to take a couple of painkillers and get some sleep."

"We should ring the police Bran; they might at least be able to get your wallet and your phone back!"

"No police Jason!" Bran insisted. He gasped, doubling up in pain as he turned too quickly to face Jason.

"They could have killed you Bran; they might kill the next person they attack."

"No police Jason; promise me you won't go to the police about this." Bran shook his head. "Promise me, Jason."

"Why?" Jason asked, "why is it so important that the police

aren't involved."

Bran looked up at Jason an anguished expression on his face.

"Paul," he said. "Paul was one of the gang that did this."

Jason wasn't surprised; in fact, he had half expected it.

"Still protecting your brothers Bran," he said sadly. "Even after this?"

"You don't understand Jason…"

"You're right Bran; I don't fuckin' understand," Jason said angrily. "I don't understand how anyone can go through the crap that you've gone through over the years and still want to protect the bastards that would do this to you!"

Bran held his hands out to Jason.

"Don't Jay," he said softly. He took hold of Jason's hands and squeezed them gently. "He's my brother."

Bran slept fitfully that night, pain from his broken ribs making it difficult to find any position that was comfortable. Jason lay awake beside him, afraid to close his eyes in case he rolled over in his sleep and accidentally hurt him. Next morning Bran was sore and stiff and bruised. Jason said he was going to have a day off Uni' and stay at home to look after Bran, but Bran wouldn't hear of it.

"I'll have to go into the bank and cancel my cards and order a new cheque book," he said, "and draw some money out so that I can go and get a new mobile."

Jason tutted and clucked like a mother hen, but Bran just laughed at him.

"I'll be fine Jay," he said, "and I do need to cancel those cards; who knows what those bastards will do with them given half the chance!"

Bran picked up the lovely soft Italian leather jacket he had been wearing the night before; it was ruined. He sighed and tossed it back onto the chair.

"Get your things together Jason," he said, "I'll drop you off at the Uni on the way to the bank."

"Are you sure you can drive Bran?" Jason asked, his concern very evident in his voice.

"I'll be OK," Bran smiled. "It's only a couple of minutes into town."

By the time they got to the University, Bran was regretting his rash. "I'll be OK."

Every change of gear, every turn of the wheel, every bump in the road sent fresh stabs of pain through his battered body.

"Do you want my mobile?" Jason asked as Bran stopped the car outside the entrance to the Uni.

"No," Bran said, "I'll soon be at home and I can contact you by using the landline, but you'll be stuck without a phone; I'll pick a new one up in a couple of days."

"Take it easy today, Bran," Jason said as he left the car to make his way to the first of his classes.

It was lunchtime before Bran finally sorted out his bank and credit cards. He was eager to get back to the flat, just to take a couple of painkillers and crawl back into bed for a few hours.

Once back in the flat he decided to ring his deliveries contact, just to let them know that he wouldn't be driving for a day or two.

Sitting in the comfortable lounge at the flat, he dialled the number for his contact.

The reception he got was not what he had expected.

"O'Donnell! Where the fuck have you been! I've been ringing your mobile all morning!"

"My mobiles been stolen Gaz, I thought I had better check with you via the landline."

"Bit fuckin' late!" The voice said. "I had a job for you this morning and the customers don't like being kept waiting; I want you on the road first thing tomorrow!"

Bran shook his head.

"I can't do it for a couple of days Gaz," he said, "I got mugged last night; they kicked the crap out off me."

"I don't want to hear your fuckin' sob stories, I just want you in that fuckin van at eight o'clock tomorrow morning – comprehend?"

Bran hesitated.

"Put it this way O'Donnell," Gaz said. "If you don't pick those keys up from the shop at eight o'clock tomorrow morning, you won't be picking the keys up again; I'll find somebody else to drive for me!"

"Just a day, Gaz," Bran pleaded. "Another day and I'll be fine!"

"Fuck off," Gaz snarled. "Pick up the keys and the instructions at eight tomorrow or lose this number coz you won't be needing it again!" and the phone went dead.

"Shit!" Bran said to himself and then held his ribs trying to ease the pain as another coughing spasm wracked his body.

Shit! He thought, Jason's going to go ballistic; perhaps if he just didn't tell him; but there's no way he would get out of the flat by seven thirty without Jason wanting to know exactly where he was going. His head was spinning; he would deal with that problem later, for now; he just needed a couple of painkillers and a few hours sleep.

"Don't be bloody stupid Bran!" Jason snapped when Bran eventually told him he had a delivery to make in the morning.

"Ring him up and tell him you're not doing his bloody delivery for him; you're not fit enough to go drivin' those flamin' clapped out old vans around the country."

"Jason, if I don't do this delivery for Gaz, I'm out of a job."

"If you can call working for that tosser a job," Jason said angrily. "Bran you don't have to do those dodgy deliveries; there are other jobs and we can manage till you get something better."

"It's all right for you; you've got Daddies money going into your fuckin' account every month," he growled. "I'm still paying for the fuckin' Audi and I can't even pay my way in the flat! What sort of a fuckin' twat do you think that makes me feel?

Bran paced angrily around the room; the anger brought on yet another coughing spasm; he doubled up in agony and clung to the edge of the table till the coughing stopped and the pain from his broken ribs subsided a little.

"Stuff the job, Bran, it's not worth it," Jason pleaded.

"It's a job Jason, you know how difficult it was trying to find a driving job after Pat blew me off, none of the other taxi companies would touch me because they didn't want to get on the wrong side of Pat O'Donnell!"

"Does it have to be driving Taxis Bran?" Jason asked, "Lots of companies must want good drivers."

"And those companies want bloody good references to go with the good drivers, somehow I don't think I would get much of a reference from the O'Donnell's Taxi Company."

"Well does it have to be driving," Jason said, beginning to get a little exasperated with Bran, "There must be other jobs you could do!"

"Yeah! I could always get a job as a friggin' hairdresser!" Bran stormed. "Do you know how many friggin' unemployed there are in Liverpool? I'm a driver Jay! That's what I do, that's all I want to do!"

Jason looked away; he knew that Bran didn't mean to hurt him, he was frustrated and worried, the money he had brought with him when he moved in was all but gone. He was just about managing to meet the finance on the Audi. He had been furious when Jason had offered to help with the payments saying that he would sell the fuckin' thing first.

Jason knew just how stubborn Bran could be. Stubborn, independent and at times, unreasonable and totally 'pig-headed'.

"Please yourself, Bran," Jason said, "you always do!"

"What the fuck's that supposed to mean?"

"Do whatever you want Bran," Jason continued. "You always have in the past!"

He walked through to the lounge and sat down on the settee, his back to the door. Bran followed him.

"Yeah, that's your answer to everything isn't it; walk away and turn your back on it. Ignore it and Daddy will sort it out at the end of the month!"

"Piss off, Bran," Jason said without looking round. "Grow up and stop feeling fucking sorry for yourself!"

Bran grabbed his jacket.

"I'm going for a walk!" He said, "I'll see you later."

"Whatever," Jason said, he still hadn't turned towards Bran. His heart sank as he heard the door slam and he turned to look at the now empty room; the last thing he wanted was to have a row with Bran, he half thought about going after him, but decided it would probably be better if he just left him to calm down a bit. They could talk later when Bran had walked off some of his anger.

Bran seemed to have been walking for ages, he hadn't a clue where he was going; he just knew he needed to get out of the flat for a while before he said something that would really balls up their relationship.

Bran wandered down the quiet back streets, he didn't have any particular destination in mind; he just wanted to clear his head a little and let the anger he felt fade into the background. He knew that he wasn't angry with Jason, he was angry with himself, but that didn't make it any easier to deal with.

His ribs were hurting like hell and every cut and bruise on his body was throbbing with pain; and to top it all, it felt as though it was going to rain.

He sat on a low wall for a while, regretting, as the first big fat drops of water splashed onto his face, that he had stormed out of the flat in such a huff, he reached automatically for his wallet; of course, it wasn't there, neither was his mobile!

"Stupid bastard," he said to himself. "Now you'll have to friggin' walk back!"

He stood up and looked round to get his bearings and realised that he recognised the street he was in. It was where Sarah lived; her flat was just down the road.

The rain began to fall in earnest; Bran pulled his collar up around his ears and started down the road, his mind made up. He would call at Sarah's. Perhaps if she were at home, she would let him wait there until the rain stopped. Thunder rumbled ominously overhead as the sky grew rapidly darker. Within seconds his jacket was soaked.

The first trickle of cold water was starting to make its way through to his skin. He thought longingly about the expensive leather jacket that had been ruined when he had been attacked. He certainly wouldn't be able to afford another like that for a while.

Bran stood at the entrance to the block of flats where Sarah lived. The main door was locked and there was a panel of six intercoms by the door. Bran hesitated for a while; it had been a long time since he had last seen Sarah; he wondered if she would remember all the times he made excuses for not meeting her or going out for a drink or returning her text messages.

Another trickle of rainwater ran down his back and he punched the button marked 'S. Barnes'.

Nothing happened; he punched it again; still no response. 'Bloody typical!' he thought as he began to turn away from the door.

The intercom crackled and a soft voice said, "Hello, who's there?"

"Sarah? It's Bran O'Donnell." The silence; probably only a few seconds; seemed to go on for ages.

"What do you want Bran?"

Bran's heart sank.

"Nothing Sarah; If you want to know the truth, I was hoping you would let me come in just to get out of this bloody rain."

There was another pause; then the door lock clicked open.

"Come up, Bran," she said.

Sarah was waiting at the door; stunningly beautiful just as he remembered, her long blonde hair tied back in a ponytail. A look of shock registered on Sarah's face and Bran realised what a mess he must look. He stopped.

"I'm sorry Sarah," he said, turning to leave. "This was a stupid idea!"

Sarah's hand was on his arm.

"Bran! What on earth has happened?"

Bran just shook his head. He wouldn't know where to begin!

"Come in, Bran," Sarah said, guiding him towards the door. "At least come and get warm."

The centrally heated flat was cosy, but Sarah turned on the gas fire as she noticed Bran shivering when he sat on the settee in the lounge.

She bustled about in the kitchen, letting Bran relax a little while she made coffee.

Sitting by the warm gas fire, sipping the hot sweet coffee, Bran was thankful that Sarah wasn't bombarding him with questions.

"Look, give me your jacket," she said. "I'll put it in the tumble drier, it'll be dry in a couple of minutes."

Bran shook his head, but Sarah insisted.

Somewhat awkwardly and not without considerable discomfort, Bran eased himself out of his wet jacket. The top half of his shirt was soaked as well. Sarah threw his jacket into the dryer and came back with a big warm bath towel.

"Give me the shirt too, Bran," she said, "you may as well have both of them dry!"

Bran objected once again, but Sarah stood over him, determinedly waiting, then she realised that he was actually having trouble getting the shirt off.

"Bran, what on earth happened?" she said, dropping the towel on the settee next to him and gently easing his arm out of the wet shirt.

Bran gasped and winced as he pulled his arm out of the sleeve on the side where his ribs were broken. Sarah noticed the massive bruising and the numerous dressings taped over the angry cuts that marred his body.

"What happened Bran?" she asked.

He laughed.

"Would you believe me if I told you I tripped over the cat?"

"It must have been a very big; very angry cat!"

She made to wrap the towel around his shoulders and stopped; transfixed by the tattoo spread across his back, parts of it were hidden by gauze and tape, but the images that could still be seen were beautifully clear and very poignant.

"That's new," she commented. "You didn't have a tattoo last time I saw you."

There's a lot of things changed since then Sarah," Bran said quietly. It was practically the first time he had really said anything other than yes or no since he came into the flat.

Sarah wrapped the big warm towel around his shoulders and sat down on the settee next to him.

"Why didn't you tell me you were gay Bran? It would have made things so much easier and it would have explained a lot as well."

Bran laughed; it was a humourless laugh.

"Because I was shit scared of anyone finding out."

"When Marie told me, I wouldn't believe it at first; I told her

Kieran was winding her up; I said – what about the night we met up at the Fizz Nightclub?"

"Vodka Blues," Bran smiled.

"Drunk or not Bran," Sarah said. "You were one hell of a good snogger!"

Vague memories of that night came flooding back to Bran.

"I'm sorry Sarah," he said gently, "but I could have been snogging Kieran for all I knew!"

"And I thought your lack of interest was because of the alcohol."

Bran shook his head and smiled apologetically.

"If anything Sarah, the alcohol was responsible for the snogging in the first place!" He put the empty coffee cup down and pulled the bath towel around himself. Resting his chin on the folds of soft warm material he stared into the flames of the gas fire.

"My life has just been one friggin' disaster after another!"

Sarah was silent for a while as she sat and watched the flames as well.

"So who beat you up Bran?" she asked eventually.

"One of the gangs that hang about down by the Uni."

Sarah didn't say anything, but she put her hand gently on his arm.

He looked across at her and smiled his thanks.

"So, what are you doing wandering around here in the pouring rain?" She asked.

Bran sighed. "I've had a row with my partner; I just needed some time to cool down a bit."

"Well, the rain certainly did that for you." Sarah smiled.

"Your clothes should be dry now." She stood up and headed for the kitchen. She looked out of the window; drops of water splashed onto the glass and chased each other to the sill. "It's still raining, Bran, do you want another coffee?"

"If you don't mind me being here," he said.

Sarah walked back into the lounge, the shirt and jacket over her arm.

"If I had a problem with you being here Bran," she said. "You wouldn't have got through the door in the first place!"

19

It was after eleven when the rain stopped, and Bran eventually made his way back at Anncolm Heights. The kitchen light was on but the rest of the flat was in darkness. Bran walked through to the bedroom, Jason was asleep, or at least he was in bed and he didn't show any signs that he had heard Bran come in.

Bran stripped off his clothes and as quietly as he could, he slipped into the bed next to Jason. He put his hand gently on Jason's shoulder.

"Jay?" he whispered. "Jay?"

There was no sign that Jason had heard him.

Bran sighed, shook his head and very gingerly rolled over onto his side. He could feel the warmth of Jason's body against his back, it was a comforting warmth, he felt safe, lying here in this bed and as he drifted off to sleep, he couldn't think of anywhere he would rather be than here, with this man.

The alarm clock buzzed annoyingly. Bran groaned as he rolled over to kill the insistent drone. His whole body ached; the muscles were stiff and reluctant to move. He glanced at the clock; seven a.m. Jason was right; he was insane! What man in his right mind would leave a warm bed at this ungodly hour in the morning to drive a clapped-out van up and down the motorway? He glanced over at Jason, he was sprawled across the bed; his head on his arms, Bran could hear him gently snoring.

Bran desperately wanted to take a shower and wondered if he could risk taking off all the dressings that Jason had so carefully taped over the worst of the wounds he had sustained the other night. He peeled one of the dressings off carefully, the cut was still red and angry looking but there was no sign of any bleeding. He pulled off a couple more. Jason would put fresh dressings on tonight if they were needed. He was pleased that the cuts and bruises on his back didn't seem to have damaged his tattoo. He studied it for a while in the mirror, as always; awed by the beauty of it. He wondered for a moment what would have happened if the gang that had attacked him, had seen the tattoo; he was pretty sure that he would have been lying in a hospital bed now, if not worse!

The hot water felt good as it pelted his aching muscles. Even the stinging caused by the soap as it ran over the cuts didn't feel too bad; it felt clean; it made him feel alive!

He dressed quietly and made coffee. Jason was still sleeping. Bran stood at the bedroom door and wondered if he should wake him before he left. He glanced at the clock; seven thirty. He didn't have time for another argument and he really didn't want to fight with Jason, but he knew that if he woke him now, that was how it would end.

He lifted his jacket from the hook behind the kitchen door, where he had left it the night before; there was a handful of loose change and his keys to the flat in the pocket. He took a twenty from the pot in the kitchen, more than likely the van would need fuel.

Jason was still asleep; he would be furious when he woke and realised that Bran had already left.

Bran found an old envelope and scribbled a message on the back.

'Don't worry – I'm OK – see you tonight – B'

It was just before eight when Bran arrived at the off licence,

Boozy Brothers. The manager John was waiting for him in his BMW parked outside the shop. He slid open the driver's window as Bran walked towards the car and handed him a large brown envelope.

"Same arrangements as usual O'Donnell," he said, "you get the hundred when the deliveries made and you drop the keys off here; understood?"

Bran nodded and took the envelope. The window slid silently closed and the BMW pulled smoothly away from the kerb.

Bran ripped open the envelope, a set of keys slid out into his hand and he took out the folded sheet of paper and read the instructions printed on it.

Collect from Imam's lock up garage on the outskirts of Coventry and deliver to an auto spares shop in Kirkham.

Bran knew the Auto spares shop, but the address of the lock-up garage was something he would have to find when he got to Coventry. The directions were a little sketchy at best!

He pushed the van keys into his pocket and walked the short distance to the derelict building site where the van would have been left for him to collect. The van was an old transit that had seen better days. There was a tax disc in the window, Bran didn't look too closely, he had a good idea that the registration on the disc wouldn't match the registration on the van and if this heap of shit had an MOT it would be as bent as a nine bob note. He slid open the door and climbed up into the driver's seat. The material of the seat was torn and the foam padding; what was left of it; poked through the gap.

The inside of the van smelled like an old ashtray with cigarette ash and old dog ends all over the floor. Bran wrinkled his nose, there was another smell that he couldn't quite identify; but the odour in the van reminded him sickeningly of the smell at the back of a public toilet.

He pulled on the seatbelt; it jammed and didn't recoil.

Jason was right again, he thought; what the hell was he doing driving crap like this!

He turned the ignition. After a couple of attempts, the engine fired into life. He checked the fuel gauge; less than a quarter of a tank, hardly enough to get him to the M6 let alone Coventry.

He rammed the gear lever into reverse; it made a horrible grating sound and the van lurched forward and stalled!

Bran swore! This is the last time, he thought; Jason was right, there must be better ways of earning a living than this!

Eventually, Bran manoeuvred the van out onto the main road and headed for the M58. The sooner he got this delivery done, the sooner he could head home to Anncolm Heights and Jason. He stopped at the service station and bought diesel, cursing the fact that the van had been left with very little fuel and that had used up most of his twenty pounds. The M58 was reasonably quiet but the M6 was a different matter, he hit the heavy traffic of the morning rush hour. As Bran joined the main flow of M6 traffic, the old van jumped out of gear. Huge artics thundered past, blaring their air horns and flashing their lights' as they had to make quick lane changes to avoid the slow transit.

Bran swore under his breath and jammed the van into a lower gear in order to pick up some power. With every gear change, a fresh jolt of pain would sear his ribcage; beads of sweat appeared on his forehead as the level of pain slowly rose. The speed slowly crept up. Fifty, sixty, sixty-five, seventy. And with the speed, the engine temperature started to rise as well.

Bran contemplated pulling off at the next junction, turning around and heading back to Liverpool and telling Gaz where to stuff his friggin' van. Then he thought about the hundred pounds he had been promised; but this is the last time, he said to himself; the last time!

The old van struggled on; every time the flow of traffic slowed; the engine temperature rose alarmingly. Bran was in agony from the constant changing of gear, his breath coming in ragged gasps as the sweat rolled freely down his face and back, soaking his shirt. The salty sweat ran into the still raw wounds; an irritation that he bore stoically as it seemed irrelevant compared to the searing pain that emanated from the area of his broken ribs; but it was another factor that added to the stressful journey and the stress was responsible for the thumping headache that made him feel sick; stress, and the smell of the engine fumes that were somehow making their way into the van!

Finally, and in desperate need of a break, he pulled off the motorway onto a service area and drove to a quiet corner of the HGV parking. He turned off the engine, vaguely wondering if it would start again; but at that point, he didn't care.

He slid open the van door and stepped down into the car park; the cold air hit his lungs and brought on a bout of coughing. He staggered against the van, doubled up in agony as he wrapped his arms around his ribs, desperately trying to reduce the searing spasms of pain that wracked his body.

"You OK mate?" a passing lorry driver asked.

Bran pushed himself away from the van and forced his body into an upright position.

"Yeah, I will be," he said.

"Well you look bloody terrible," the driver said. "Are you sure you'll be alright?"

Bran nodded.

"Just need a break." He said.

The driver shrugged his shoulders and continued on his way.

Bran sat on the van steps; closed his eyes and leaned his head against the doorframe. The pain in his side slowly subsided to a dull sickening ache.

He wasn't sure how long he had been sitting there, but he became aware that someone was walking towards him. He opened his eyes, it was the lorry driver he had spoken to earlier; he had a cup of coffee in his hand.

"There you go, son!" he said, handing the plastic cup to Bran.

Bran took it gratefully, nodding his thanks as he sipped the hot sweet liquid.

"Got far to go?" The driver asked.

"Coventry," Bran said between mouthfuls of coffee.

"Not in that mate," the driver said, pointing to the trickle of brown water that was running lazily from beneath the engine. "Your radiator's shafted!"

Bran just shook his head.

"At this point; I don't really give a toss," he said resignedly.

The driver studied him for a moment.

"Pop your bonnet," he said.

Bran swivelled round to pull the bonnet release catch, gasping as the movement rekindled the embers of pain in his side.

"You look like you've had a rough time," the driver said as he lifted the transits' bonnet.

"Got mugged the other night," Bran lied. "Outside a club in Liverpool."

"Tough; loose much?"

"Wallet, mobile, dignity."

The driver smiled sympathetically.

"Bastards!" he said, as he poked around in the engine, "Yep, it's your radiator; doesn't look too bad; hold on a second, I'll be back." He walked over to his rig, a big shiny artic' and pulled out a box from a storage unit under the cab.

A minute later he was back, and he handed Bran a small silver sachet.

"Radweld," he said, "that should at least get you to Coventry.

Bran looked up, quite amazed that a stranger should be so helpful.

"Thanks mate; let me pay you for that," he said, hoping that he had enough money left.

"No Problem," the driver said shaking his head. "The firm supplies that sort of stuff." He turned to go. "Hope you get where you're going son," he said as he walked away.

"Thanks." Bran said, looking down at the sachet in his hand, "And thanks for the coffee."

There was no reply but a brief wave of the hand as the man climbed up into his cab. A few moments later the big artic roared into life and with a sharp hiss of the air brakes, it rolled slowly out towards the motorway. Bran raised his hand as the rig gained speed down the slip road. With two short blasts from the air horn, the artic disappeared into the flow of traffic heading south.

Bran climbed reluctantly back into the van. Amazingly the engine fired first time. He drove round to the service area and topped up the ailing radiator. Tearing the top from the sachet, he poured the powder into the radiator. He waited for a few minutes while the engine ticked over, hoping the Rad Weld would do its job, then very carefully, holding his ribs for support, he bent down to check beneath the engine; there didn't seem to be any water dripping onto the tarmac. He poured in a little more water then screwed on the radiator cap and, dropping the bonnet, he climbed back into the van and headed for the southbound slip road; he desperately wished that he still had his mobile, so he could phone Jason and tell him that he was right and as usual, he had been wrong. No amount of money was worth being stuck on the motorway in this friggin' heap of shit!

The motorway through Birmingham was a nightmare; one delay after another as the heavy volume of traffic crawled through the endless series of road works. Bran offered up a silent prayer of thanks to the lorry driver who stopped to help him at the services. The Rad Weld certainly seemed to have worked; the vans' engine temperature was high; but not dangerously so, as it had been earlier.

Bran glanced up at the blue motorway signs overhead; Coventry; straight on; the same sign gave directions for the National. Exhibition. Centre.

Bran remembered the first time he had gone to the N.E.C. To the Annual International Taxicab Exhibition with Pat and Kieran, walking through the vast Halls, crammed with trade stands and auto displays. His stomach seemed to flip as a wave of regret washed over him. He shook himself; no good dwelling on memories, that was in the past. He had enough to think about, just to get through today! He pulled the sheet of paper out of his pocket that had been in the envelope with the van keys.

Imam's Garage, Stoke Road, Coventry. There was a vague, hand-drawn map and a motorway junction. It was a start, but not much of one, Bran thought to himself as he continued down the M6. It was going to be a long, long day!

Bran pulled off the motorway and headed for the Stoke Road.

He struggled on; forcing the reluctant old van up and down through the gears as he negotiated the junctions', traffic lights and roundabouts; the sharp pain in his side replaced by a sickening, persistent ache. The rough-drawn map was useless and Bran angrily screwed it into a ball and threw it out of the window.

"Hey mate!" he called to a passing cyclist. "Can you tell me how to get to Stoke Road?"

After many such inquiries, Bran, at last, turned into Stoke Road. Imam's Garage was a nondescript square building set back from the main road and surrounded by high-security fences. The main gate stood open, an old-style Jag parked in the road close by.

Bran drove the old van into the garage and behind him; two young Asian men climbed out of the Jag and followed him through the gates.

"Sorry mate, we're shut!" One of them said as Bran slid open the van door.

"Gaz sent me.," he said, stepping out of the van.

The men looked shiftily up and down the road.

"You took your fucking time." One of them said as he pulled a bunch of keys out of his pocket. Bran shrugged his shoulders and followed the men over to the building.

The man with the keys removed the chunky padlock and slid back the heavy metal doors. The other one hung back, surreptitiously watching the road.

Bran knew better than to ask about the items he was collecting; Gaz had once told him very forcibly to mind his own effin' business and keep his effin' nose out!

Bran had thought on many occasions that it was better not to know; this was one of those occasions.

The young Asian man walked into the garage; towards a stack of what looked like boxes covered with an old tarpaulin.

He pulled off the tarp' to reveal a pallet stacked with various sized boxes.

Bran read the labels, Siemens, Motorcraft, Bosch, and Continental. Auto spares! It didn't take a rocket scientist to figure out that they were probably stolen.

"OK," Bran said. "It shouldn't take us long to get this lot loaded."

"What's with the 'us'" the man sneered. "That's what you're fuckin' paid for!"

"But if you helped…" Bran began.

"Fuck off!" the man swore as he rejoined his companion and they got back into their car.

Bran looked at the pile of boxes and glanced round the otherwise empty garage, there was nothing he could use to transport the boxes, he was going to have to move them all by hand. He climbed back into the van and positioned it as close as he could to the garage doors. He cast a final angry glance at the two Asians who were sitting in their car watching him. He rubbed his sore ribs gently and walked into the garage. The fuckin' boxes weren't going to move themselves!

It took Bran over an hour to load the boxes. At one point one of the men' strolled into the garage. Bran mistakenly hoped that they were going to offer to help.

"Get a fucking move on you lazy bastard!" The man snarled. "We don't want to be stuck here all fucking day!"

"Piss off if you're not going to help," Bran said. "I can do without your smart-arsed comments."

Sneering, the man turned and walked out. "Looser!" he said, as he left the garage.

At last, the boxes were loaded; Bran slammed the van doors and climbed into the driver's seat.

The two Asians didn't comment as he backed the van away from the garage, they simply walked past him and padlocked the big front door.

Bran drove the van out onto Stoke Road and headed back towards the M6. Behind him, the two Asians locked the gates and, climbing into their Jag; drove off in the opposite direction.

Bran was tired; everywhere that could ache, ached! He made his way back through Coventry and as he pulled onto the motorway slip road, he thought he had never been so glad to see the M6.

The traffic was heavy but moving quite quickly, Bran eased the van into the flow of vehicles heading north. He heaved a sigh of relief, all he had to do now was get to Kirkham as quickly as possible, offload the boxes and get home.

There had better be someone at the Auto Spares Shop in Kirkham, Bran thought, otherwise he was just going to leave the van there and get a taxi home! He had seen quite enough of auto parts, the M6 and Gaz's friggin' van!

He had only been on the motorway for a couple of minutes when Bran suddenly thought about fuel. He hadn't checked how much was left of the twenty pounds worth of diesel he had put in that morning. He looked down, looking for the fuel indicator.

In that moment he heard the screech of tyres on tarmac and looked up to see the bright red brake lights of the wagon in front of him. Bran swore and automatically slammed his foot onto the brake pedal. For a fraction of a second, he felt the resistance beneath his foot; then there was a 'crack' and the pedal dropped to the floor.

It seemed to Bran as though time itself slowed down. He had plenty of time to notice that the blue sheeting tied over the load on the lorry was torn at one corner; he could see the wooden crates underneath. He had enough time to realise that even though he was turning the steering wheel, the van wasn't going to miss the lorry in front. Then everything exploded around him. He didn't remember hitting the rear end of the lorry. There was a bang and the awful screech of tearing metal! The windscreen shattered as some of the boxes of auto parts from the back of the van flew past his head. Bran was thrown violently sideways. The last thing he saw was the radiator grill of a huge green lorry as it smashed into the van. Then there was nothing!

20

The alarm on Jason's mobile phone played its' insistent little tune and rattled across the top of the bedside table. He rolled over and stretched out his hand to feel for the snooze button. The annoying little tune stopped, and Jason sighed as he rolled back to the centre of the bed. The bed was empty; the only indication that he had shared it with someone was that the pillow next to his had an indentation the size of a head in the middle of it; Bran's head. And as he stretched his hand across the now empty space, he could still feel the slight warmth where Bran had been lying. He glanced at the clock; it was eight a.m. Bran would just be setting off to wherever it was he was going, to pick up the deliveries he was doing for this Gaz character.

Jason wished Bran wouldn't be so vague about things! The alarm started playing its' insistent little tune again. Jason reached over and turned the alarm off.

"OK, OK," he said to the mobile phone, "I hear you, I'm getting up!"

Why the hell hadn't Bran taken the mobile with him? Jason thought, at least he would have been able to ring and make sure he was OK.

He swung his legs out of the bed and reached for his dressing gown. He found the discarded dressings in the bin and swore, knowing that Bran could not have replaced them by himself.

The floor was wet and the bathroom mirror was steamed up, Bran must have had a shower before he went out.

Jason turned on the shower and wandered out to the kitchen;

he spotted the old envelope on the kitchen table. On it, Bran had written. 'Don't worry – I'm OK – see you tonight – B'.

Shaking his head, Jason went back to the bathroom. The hot water was wonderfully relaxing; he closed his eyes as he massaged the shampoo into his hair. He thought about the row they had had the night before; he really had been quite mean to Bran. He had told him to piss off and grow up! But he had been the one who pretended to be asleep when Bran had got back later that night. Bran's life had been turned upside down and all He did was criticise his attempts to deal with it. What a bastard he had been, perhaps he was the one who should learn how to 'grow up'. He turned off the shower and wrapped a towel around his waist, he would get ready and go into town and do some shopping; he would have a wonderful meal ready for Bran when he got home. A meal, a bottle of wine and a big apology. Back in the kitchen, he picked up the envelope Bran had left and smiled at the message.

"You're more than OK, Bran O'Donnell," he said, "you're bloody fantastic!"

Paul sat at the breakfast table and stared at the bacon and egg that lay untouched on the plate in front of him; he hadn't had much of an appetite this last couple of days. He couldn't eat and he didn't want to sleep, because with the sleep came the dreams and the images that kept surfacing in his mind again and again. The images of his brother, Bran, falling under a rain of blows and kicks. In his dreams he could hear the sickening thud of the metal bars as they landed; he could see the blood on his skin and his clothes. He could still hear his brother crying out as the bottle of whiskey was poured over the raw wounds. He remembered listening to their raucous laughter as they pissed on him as he lay, battered and bleeding in the road.

And he had sat there; sat there and said nothing, done nothing. He remembered the look on Bran's face when their eyes had met, the look of disbelief and for a split second, a look of such deep, deep sadness. In his dreams, Paul had watched with horror, the first blow that fell, the first iron bar that had cut through the leather jacket and slashed the skin beneath. In his dreams, Paul was the one holding that iron bar, his hands covered in blood, Bran's blood.

He had seen someone with a knife in his hand and he had brought his fist down repeatedly on the car horn. It had signalled the end of the attack and the gang had fled in their cars, leaving Bran unconscious in the road.

In the past, Paul had laughed and joked at the expense of the 'queers' they had roughed up. This time it just wasn't funny anymore.

He looked across at Kieran who was smoking a cigarette and drinking his coffee. And wondered what his brother would think of him when he found out that he had watched while Bran was beaten up; beaten up and humiliated and left lying in a dark road on a deserted industrial park and he had sat and done nothing. He looked down at the cold bacon and eggs on his plate; he felt sick.

"Kieran." He said, looking up at his brother. "Kieran; I've got to tell you something and I don't know where to start."

21

"Patrick O'Donnell," Jean said as she put the cup of coffee down on the desk in front of him. "Just how long are you going to let this ridiculous situation between you and Bran continue?"

Pat stared at the coffee cup. The bitterness inside him began to rise, boiling to the surface with an angry rush of temper.

"It's none of your effin' business," he said. "You're paid to answer the effin' phone and that's all you're paid to do!" He pushed his chair away from the desk and walked out of the office, his cup of coffee untouched. Jean sighed; she had known the O'Donnell's for many years. She had watched the boys grow from wild teenagers into young men; she smiled, in Kieran's case it had been from a wild teenager into an equally wild young man. Now it was Kieran that she worried about the most; he had become very quiet since Bran left. He had been closer to Bran than any of the family and she felt that it must have hit Kieran hard to find out that he really didn't know his brother at all.

She glanced at her watch; it was nearly time for Kieran to take over the radio for the night. She checked the diary and put the evening bookings into order and was just about to pour away the untouched cup of coffee when she heard Kieran's footsteps on the stairs.

Kieran walked into the office and dropped his leather jacket on the chair, he pulled his mobile and his cigarettes out of his jeans pocket and put them next to the radio.

"Is that coffee going spare?" He asked, pointing to the cup in Jean's hand.

Jean looked down at the cup.

"It's nearly cold Kieran; let me get you a fresh one!" Kieran shook his head.

"Don't bother Jean, as long as it's warm and wet it will do." He took the cup and drained the coffee in huge gulps. "What's got Dad in a strop?" He asked, putting the empty cup down on the desk.

"I'm afraid I did." Jean sighed.

"Oh," Kieran said, an explanation wasn't required; he had a pretty good idea how Jean had managed to get Pat so mad!

"Have you heard from Bran?" she asked.

Kieran glanced in the direction of the stairs, there was no sign of Pat returning. He shook his head. "Nothing." He said. "Dad won't talk about him at home, he goes ballistic if we even mention his name; I've tried Bran's mobile, but it's dead."

Kieran sat staring at the radio, lost in his own thoughts. He leafed absently through the diary, turning back the pages to where he had written down the jobs that Bran had done.

"I miss him, Jean," he said softly.

"Yes," she said, putting her arm around his shoulders, "so do I."

Pat O'Donnell walked into 'The Ink Spot', Rick's Tattoo studio. Melanie looked up from the desk and smiled, she remembered Pat from his many visits in the past.

"Oh, hello Mister O'Donnell," she said breezily. "We haven't seen you in a while." She smiled up at the older man. "And what can we do for you today?"

Pat looked round; he could hear the buzz of the tattoo machine in the studio at the back.

"I want to have a word with Rick about a cover-up," he said.

"I'm sure that won't be a problem, Mister O'Donnell." Melanie smiled. "Rick should be finished in a few minutes." She walked across to one of the smart coffee tables, removed the empty coffee cup and wiped the surface down with a damp cloth.

"Have a seat Mister O'Donnell," she said. "I'll get you a coffee while you wait."

A little while later, a pretty young woman wearing a strappy top walked out from the studio at the back, she was followed by Rick who was giving instructions on how to care for her new tattoo; a small red and green tree frog that perched right on the point of her shoulder. Even though it was covered in a clear protective film, the bright colours and clever shadows made it look as though it could leap off at any moment. The young woman was obviously delighted with it, moving her shoulder round in various ways while she admired the artwork.

"OK, Donna," Rick grinned. "Melanie will give you a care sheet and you can give her your card details as well." He guided her towards the receptionists' desk. "Don't forget; pop back, in a couple of days and let me check it to make sure everything is OK."

"Pat!" Rick grinned as he turned back to the older man and he sat down on the chair opposite. "Where the hell have you been hiding? We haven't seen you in quite a while."

Pat shrugged his shoulders. "Been a lot going on just lately." He said.

The young woman at the reception desk turned towards them.

"Bye Rick; and thanks!" She called waving as she walked towards the door.

"Bye Donna!" Rick said.

"Bye Miss French!" Melanie said as the young woman left.

"What is it with tattoos these days Rick?" Pat asked, nodding in the direction the young woman had gone. "When I had my first tattoo, it was bikers, villains' and servicemen; now its pop stars footballers and bits of lasses like that!"

Rick laughed. "I'm not complaining Pat; businessmen, University Dons, doctors, nurses; I've had them all in here; not had the vicars' wife yet; but I'm working on it!" He grinned.

He looked up as two fresh coffees were placed on the table in front of them. "Thanks, Mel," he smiled.

"Makes a change, not having to beg for a coffee." He said to Pat as Melanie walked away.

"I heard that!" she said without looking round.

"So, what can I do for you, Pat?" Rick asked as he sipped the hot sweet coffee. "Another tattoo?"

Pat pushed up the sleeve of his jacket. "I want you to cover one up." He said, leaning across the table to show Rick the tattoo on his forearm, it was a shamrock, and in each of the leaves was tattooed the name of one of his sons; he pointed to the central leaf and the name 'Bran'.

"I want that getting rid of." He said.

Rick looked at the tattoo; it was not one that he had done and it had obviously been there for quite a while. Rick studied the tattoo; it was in a central position in the middle of Pat's forearm. He felt quite sad, as Pat had obviously once been proud to wear his sons' names prominently on his body.

"Is this because Bran's gay?" Rick asked.

Pat was shocked and automatically looked round to see if anyone else was in the shop.

"How do you know? Who told you?" He demanded.

"Bran told me." Rick said, "When he came in for a tattoo."

"Him!" Pat sneered, "getting' a tattoo! What did he want Rick? A fuckin' fairy?"

Rick shook his head and sighed.

"Mel!" he called "Bring me the photos' of Bran's back piece will you."

Melanie placed the folder in front of Rick; he opened it and took out the A4 sized photos and spread them out on the table in front of Pat.

"A full back piece!" he said incredulously.

"The entire thing done in one session," Rick added.

Pat put on his glasses and picked up one of the photos.

"What the fuck!" He said throwing the photo' back down on the table. "What were you thinking of Rick, putting shit like that on my son's back!"

Rick leaned back in his chair.

"So, you remembered that he is your son after all." He said quietly.

"So why didn't you tell me about this Rick?"

"Because Bran wanted to tell you himself; you called him soft and a wimp because he wouldn't have a tattoo done. Believe me, Pat, you couldn't call anyone who would go through this," he pointed to the photo, "a wimp in any way, shape or form!"

Pat pushed the photos dismissively across the table towards Rick.

"It doesn't change anything!" he snarled. "I still want that!" He pointed to Bran's name, "getting rid of!"

Rick folded his arms across his chest and looked steadily at

Pat.

"Well, you'll have to go somewhere else then, Mister O'Donnell." He said. "Because I'm not doing it!"

22

Lisa Driscoll sat down on the chair in front of her fathers' office desk. She was miserable, or bored, or out of sorts; she didn't know quite which it was. All that she did know was that whatever the reason; she wasn't happy.

Sean Driscoll lifted his head from the report he was reading and peered at his daughter over his rimless glasses; Lisa had been moping around the office all day, in fact, she seemed to have been miserable for quite a while now. Sean wondered if it had been such a good idea for Lisa to take a gap year from Queens University; she got bored so quickly.

"What's the matter, hon?" He said as he heard yet another deep sigh. "Only another couple of weeks until you and mum will be flying off to Italy; you'll have plenty to keep you occupied then!"

Lisa got up from the chair and wandered over to the window. From this vantage point, high up on top of the multi-storey office block above Belfast, she could look out across the sprawl of the city and see the airport way off in the distance and watch the huge jet airliners landing and taking off, heading for destinations all over the world. Lisa's parents had agreed to her taking a year away from her studies; she was nineteen years old; she wanted to see something of the world and enjoy life a little. Sean had the money to indulge Lisa, and his wife thought it was a wonderful idea, especially as she would be accompanying their daughter on her various trips to foreign countries.

Lisa sighed again. Sean put the report down on the desk; took off his glasses and laid them on top of the paperwork. He rolled back his chair, then walked over to the window where he put his arms affectionately around his daughter.

"What's wrong?" he asked.

Lisa leant back into his arms; her head just reached his shoulder.

"Daddy, I don't want to go to Italy."

Sean said nothing; his silence was enough to prompt an explanation.

"I don't want to go to Italy; I want to go back to Liverpool."

Sean smiled; Pat would be pleased.

"You and Bran did seem to be getting on quite well."

Lisa turned to face her father; she knew that he and Pat O'Donnell had hoped she and Bran would hit it off.

"Bran is a real sweetie Dad, and we did get on well together." She looked up into her father's face; his blue-grey eyes were a startling contrast to the swarthy complexion, a legacy from his years at sea.

"But it's Kieran I love and it's Kieran I want to be with."

23

Chaos surrounded the scene that greeted the motorway police as they fought their way to the incident on the northbound carriageway just outside Birmingham. The motorway was at a complete standstill in both directions; the northbound carriageway blocked by the mangled wrecks of a number of vehicles while the southbound carriageway had been brought to a standstill by the ghoulish rubbernecking of passing motorists.

P.C. Alan Richards and P.C. Benjamin Cody were the first to arrive on the scene; amazingly motorists were moving down the hard shoulder still trying to drive through the few feet of clear road that remained past the stricken vehicles and their injured occupants.

The flashing blue lights and the deafening police siren cleared the hard shoulder and dissuaded any further impatient motorists from trying to avoid the hold-up.

Benny Cody climbed out of his Range Rover and pulled on his fluorescent yellow jacket. On the opposite side of the vehicle, his young partner, Alan, was doing the same. Benny reached into the Rover and picked up the radio mike.

"Control," he said, "this is Mike Papa Charlie six one; attending major incident northbound between junctions four and five. We are on scene.

Benny cast his practiced glance across the carnage before him; this wasn't going to be cleared up in a couple of hours, he picked up the mike again.

"Control," he said, "can you give me an ETA for the ambulance services, and we're going to need fire brigade and heavy vehicle recovery.

Benny walked down towards the nearest vehicle. A huge articulated lorry. It was sideways across the carriageway the tractor unit bent almost double as it had jack-knifed with the driver's desperate attempt to stop; its load of metal scaffolding poles had slipped and dragged the trailer almost onto its side.

The driver was sitting on the hard shoulder next to his rig. He was holding a piece of towelling against his head, the blood was seeping between his fingers, but he was conscious and answered when Benny asked if he was OK.

Benny called back to Alan.

"Alan! Find out what's holding up the bloody ambulances, will you?" and he walked down to the next Lorry that had been involved in the incident.

The driver was very badly shaken up, but uninjured, and more concerned for the occupants of the two cars that were in front of him. One of the cars, a Fiesta was almost unrecognisable, it was on its side, the front of the car crushed up against the central reservation, the back of the car was wedged beneath the front of the lorry. Two older businessmen stood by a big four by four that had obviously been involved, its front tyre shredded and the side panels caved in and twisted out of shape.

"Are you alright mate," Benny said to the driver of the lorry who was still sitting in his cab. The man didn't answer; he had a glazed expression on his face and looked very pale. "Hang on mate," Benny shouted. "Ambulance is on its way!"

In the distance, he could hear the sirens as the ambulances made their way to the scene.

Alan was making his way up past the wrecked vehicles,

checking to ensure that the ignitions were turned off. He approached the Fiesta, unsure of what he would find. Benny was watching him; about to suggest that he went to check on the driver with the head injury when suddenly, Alan recoiled; staggered away from the vehicle and threw up over the barrier of the central reservation.

Benny ran across to his partner, to the little Fiesta still on its side beneath the artic. He glanced into the body of the car, there was blood everywhere and lying against the window of the rear passenger seat he spotted what had caused Alan to lose his lunch. The head of a young male completely severed from the trunk.

"Shit!" Benny said. "Where the fuck is the fire brigade!"

Benny leaned over the Fiesta checking for any other occupants, there didn't appear to be anyone else in the car. There was only one person, the driver, still belted in his seat, his hands still gripping the steering wheel. He took off his jacket and spread it across the gap where the shattered window had been; blocking the sight of the obviously dead man from view.

"Alan!" he said, wanting to give the young constable something to think of other than the decapitated driver. "Go and check the other lorry driver, NOW!" The ambulances screeched to a halt across the motorway, having come up the now clear southbound carriageway.

The senior paramedic leapt from his vehicle and headed towards the mangled wrecks. Behind him, other crewmembers were making their way up the carriageway.

"What are we dealing with?" he asked Benny as the other Paramedics worked systematically through the wreckage.

Benny indicated the Fiesta on its side. "There's one dead in there he said and a lorry driver with a head injury. This guy looks like he's in shock." He said pointing up to the man who still sat motionless in his cab, and there's a couple of walking wounded down by the four by four." He looked down to where the four by four was standing. Alan was obviously taking statements from the driver and his passenger. One of the Paramedics was talking to the driver of the second artic checking the severity of the head wound.

Suddenly one of the Paramedics shouted "Fuckin' Hell! There's another effin' van under this wagon!"

Benny and the senior officer sprinted round the trailer Jammed between the tractor of the wagon in front and the jack-knifed trailer of the wagon behind, the remains of a transit van could be plainly seen. It was on its side, the roof caved in and the windscreen shattered. It was impossible to get to the vehicle; most of it seemed wedged beneath the side panels of the trailer and pinned by the slipped load of scaffolding poles.

"Where the friggin' hell is the fire brigade!" Benny asked, "Do we know if anyone is alive in there?

Tony, the senior paramedic tried to push his way through the twisted metal chassis of the wrecked wagon and the mess of metal poles. "I think I can see someone!" he said. He sniffed the air, trying to determine if there was any major fuel leak from the vehicles; he couldn't smell anything. He tried again to force his way into the tiny space between the van and the underside of the wagon.

"Shit!" he said, "There's not enough room!"

Benny tried to push his body between the twisted metal supports. He was just a bit too bulky to fit through the small gap.

"Alan!" he shouted. "Get your arse over here.

Alan, a lithe twenty-one-year-old was still in his probationary year, this was his first tour of duty on a major Motorway.

Tony looked at him steadily. "You're thin enough to get through that gap," he said calmly. The fire brigade is on its way but until they can get here, we need to know if we have a casualty or a corpse.

Alan looked at Benny; he looked positively green. Benny nodded calmly, "This is what you joined the force for Alan, you might be able to make a difference here. The paramedic gave him a dressings pack. Alan looked down at the dressings in his hand. "I don't know if I can do this Benny." He said, gulping air into his lungs.

Tony slapped him on the back! "'Course you can, son! Just find out if whoever is in there is alive or not, and if they're alive, do what you can."

Alan took off his bulky jacket and handed it to Benny.

"If I find another fuckin' head I'm going to fuckin' kill you!" he said, and he squeezed between the metal bars and crawled towards the van.

It was dark inside the twisted remains of the transit, dark and smelly. Alan headed for the only access point he could see, the shattered windscreen. The smell of diesel was stronger here and Alan began to wonder if this was such a good idea. Cardboard boxes hindered his progress, they were strewn across the road and wedged in the front of the van, he pushed them aside, they were full of auto parts; he breathed a sigh of relief, at least the van didn't seem to be carrying anything dangerous like chemicals or inflammable materials.

He moved a box and uncovered an arm and a hand. His heart raced and then he sighed with relief as he realised that the arm and hand were still attached to the person in the van.

Another box lay across his shoulders, Alan carefully lifted it off and checked if he could see anything else that would obviously hinder the mans' breathing. He could see the slight rise and fall of the injured mans' chest and he automatically reached across to feel for a pulse in his neck. He found one!

"He's alive!" he shouted, "But I don't know for how long; there's an awful lot of blood down here!"

"Can you find where the blood's coming from?" Tony shouted.

"It's friggin' everywhere!" Alan yelled. "There's a huge cut at the side of his head and his nose looks like its broken." Alan edged his way further into the mangled van. "I think his arms broken; Shit!" he exclaimed "Shit! The bones broken all right; it's sticking out through the top of his arm. Where's that fucking fire brigade!"

Tony could hear that the young police officer was beginning to panic.

"Alan." He said calmly. "You're doing a great job, now just tell me what his breathing is like."

Alan looked across at the man trapped in the wrecked van. He didn't look very old, probably a couple of years older than he was. "Very weak, very shallow," he called.

"OK," Tony said. "Alan, tell me if he has any chest injuries."

"I can't see anything," Alan replied. "There's a lot of blood but I think it's from his broken arm."

"What about his lower body Alan?" Tony continued, his voice calm and steady. He knew that if he could keep the young police officer focused on what was needed he would be less likely to freak out on them.

"There's a gash across his hip; Oh, friggin' hell, part of the door frame is stuck in his side and I can't see his legs, they're trapped under what's left of the dashboard! Benny! For Christ's sake! Where's the fuckin' fire brigade!"

Two fire brigade accident units and more police patrol cars arrived. All the time they were preparing to extricate Bran from the wreckage, Alan stayed with him in the van, talking to him, reassuring him that everything was going to be OK. Alan was pretty sure that the unconscious man couldn't hear what he was saying, but it made him feel calmer until at last a fireman reached into the van and touched his arm saying, "It's OK mate; you can leave it to us now."

Alan stood at the side of the motorway as the man from the transit van was moved quickly to the waiting ambulance and rushed off towards the new Birmingham University Hospital. One of the fire crews was sheeting off the Fiesta waiting for the coroner and the Accident Investigation Branch Officers to arrive. The other people involved in the incident had been taken off to accident and emergency and the heavy goods recovery vehicles were just arriving at the scene. Alan was trembling violently as though a block of ice surrounded him.

Benny handed him his fluorescent jacket. He pulled it on over his shirt; no longer white now, but covered in blood and oil. He looked down at his hands, they were shaking, and they were covered in blood as well.

"First major incident?" Benny asked as they walked back towards the land rover. Alan nodded.

"You did alright!" Benny said as they climbed wearily back into the police motorway patrol vehicle. "Now the really difficult part of the job begins." He said as they pulled away from the scene, leaving the other units to deal with the traffic.

"What's that?" Alan asked.

"The effin' paperwork!" Benny said as they headed for the hospital.

24

Jason opened the oven door; the mouth-watering aromas of rich meaty lasagne and chargrilled Mediterranean vegetables wafted out into the kitchen. He loved to prepare meals, especially for Bran who he knew really appreciated his cooking. The full-bodied fruity South African wine was open on the table. Jason wanted everything to be perfect when Bran came home; the crusty homemade garlic bread that Bran loved was ready to pop into the oven and the fresh, sweet, baby leaf salad was in the fridge.

Jason looked round the kitchen; everything was ready; all that was missing now was Bran. He looked up at the kitchen clock; it was almost six O'clock. He sighed; it might be eight O'clock or later when Bran got back, depending on where the delivery had been. All he could do now was wait. Wait and hope that the lasagne wouldn't dry out or the salad wilt before he got home.

Jason poured himself a small glass of wine and wandered through to the lounge; he could watch a little bit of television while he waited. He settled into the chair and pressed the button on the remote, flicking through the channels to see if he could find something interesting to watch. The News at Six was just starting and he leant back to watch that, wondering what was going on in the world today.

The latest scandal involving a prominent politician seemed to be the main topic of conversation; the American government's position on greenhouse gasses; the latest reports on the outbreak of Bird Flu; another serious multi-vehicle pile-up on the motorway just outside Birmingham causing massive delays while the M6 was closed. Jason listened to the reports, at the same time wondering if he should turn down the temperature of the oven in case the lasagne overcooked. He shook his head as the details of the Birmingham crash were reported; two heavy goods vehicles, a van and two cars were involved. One fatality was confirmed with two others seriously injured; one of those thought to be critical. The police were not giving any details but were appealing for witnesses to the incident. The accident had caused massive tailbacks, but the motorway was now open and the traffic beginning to get back to normal. Jason turned off the T.V. He didn't know which was the most depressing; the motorway pile-up, the bird flu or the bent politicians. He drained off the last of his wine and headed back into the kitchen to check the lasagne and put the garlic bread in the oven; He glanced at the clock, it was six forty; Bran should be home pretty soon.

Kieran O'Donnell stood watching the flight information boards in the arrivals lounge of the John Lennon International Airport. The British Airways flight BA7741 from Belfast was on time. As he watched the board, the information changed from 'on time' to 'arrived'. He breathed a sigh of relief. He never could understand why the taxi drivers liked the airport runs when they involved so much hanging around waiting and hoping that there weren't any long delays.

He moved towards the barrier as he saw the first few passengers making their way through from the baggage collection point. At last, he spotted the head of dark brown wavy hair he was looking for.

"Lisa!" he called, waving to attract her attention. A broad smile spread across Lisa's face as she hurried the last few yards to the exit gate. She let her small suitcase fall to the ground as

Kieran wrapped his arms around her and swept her into his enthusiastic embrace. He held her tight; hugging her close as though he never wanted to let her go and before he knew it, her arms were around his neck and her lips found his. Time stood still, and they kissed as though it was the first and the last.

Kieran stroked her hair as she opened her eyes and looked up into his face.

"So, what happened to Italy?" he said smiling. Lisa grinned.

"I thought Liverpool had more to offer," she said as Kieran picked up her case. She took the hand he offered her, and they walked out of the airport buildings, heading for the car park where Kieran had left his Peugeot.

Kieran opened the car door for Lisa and dropped her suitcase into the boot.

"I'll have to ring home soon," she said. "I promised to let mum know as soon as I was settled in the hotel,"

"You know you could always stay with us if you wanted to." Kieran offered, "we have a spare room now that Bran…" his sentence trailed off unfinished. Lisa fastened her seatbelt as Kieran started the engine.

"What exactly happened Kieran?" she asked as Kieran started to pull out of the parking space.

"Dad and Bran had a big row and Dad told Bran to get out."

"Was that because Bran's gay?" Lisa asked.

Kieran stamped on the brake pedal and turned to look at Lisa.

"Am I the only bugger who didn't bloody know that Bran's gay?" Lisa shrugged her shoulders.

"I didn't know; well not for sure," she said, "there was just, something about him; I suppose I guessed really," she grinned wickedly. "I suppose it was the absolute look of horror on his face one night when I tried to kiss him!"

Kieran laughed and backed the Peugeot out onto the road.

"Oh! So, I'm second best am I?" he teased.

"Second if you don't count my Ecology tutor back at Queens." She said wickedly.

Kieran pulled up in front of the big Radisson Hotel and held the door open for Lisa as she stepped out onto the busy Liverpool street. He carried her suitcase into the hotel reception and waited until she had booked in; the reservation had already been confirmed before she left Belfast.

He kissed her lightly on the lips, reluctant to leave her so soon after her arrival in Liverpool.

"I hate just leaving you here, Lisa, but I have to work tonight. I'll ring you from the office later and I'll pick you up first thing tomorrow."

"Stop worrying Kieran," Lisa smiled. "I'll be fine. A nice long soak, something to eat and an early night." She grabbed the handle of her suitcase and began wheeling it towards the lift.

Kieran watched her go with a twinge of regret that he wasn't staying the night with her.

"Don't forget to ring your mum!" He called as the lift doors closed, and she disappeared.

Kieran glance at his watch, he had better get a move on; Jean would be real pissed if he was late again!

Jason turned off the oven and slid the now cold garlic bread into the waste bin. He looked up at the kitchen clock; ten fifteen. Where the hell was Bran? He had never been this late home before, Bran knew that Jason worried about him, he would have rung somehow when he realised he wasn't going to be home till late. He poured another glass of wine, a large one this time. He wandered through the flat and out onto the small balcony that overlooked the car park below. He gazed out across the busy city; its blaze of bright lights stretched across the horizon as far as the eye could see. He looked up as he heard the drone of an aeroplane in the darkness and saw the flashing red and white lights of a jet heading for John Lennon Airport.

"Where the hell are you Bran?" he said.

P.C. Benny Cody sat in the accident and emergency department and drank coffee from a polystyrene cup. He had been glad to get away from the motorway, pleased to be able to leave the Accident Investigation Branch to get on with their job of piecing together what had happened. They would catch up with him and Alan soon enough; wanting to know what they had found when they first arrived at the scene. Benny glanced over at Alan; he was sitting nursing the cup of coffee Benny had pushed into his hands. His hands were still stained with dried blood but at least they had stopped shaking violently, as they had when they left the motorway. Benny walked across to his young partner and sat on the plastic chair next to him.

"How are you feeling?"

Alan looked down at the cup he was holding.

"What happened to the guy from the van?" he asked.

"They whisked him straight off to theatre," Benny said.

"Do you think he'll make it?" Alan asked. Benny shrugged his shoulders.

"He's got two choices." He said as he drained off the last of his coffee. He looked across at his young colleague.

"But if he does make it, he'll probably have you to thank for it."

A staff nurse; wearing a pale blue theatre gown walked over to the two policemen.

"Did you attend the incident on the M6 today?" she asked.

Benny nodded. "How's the young bloke with the broken arm?" he asked. She looked around the casualty department and drew him over to a quiet area.

"If you have any information that would help to identify him," she said quietly. "It might be a good idea to contact any next of kin."

"It's not looking good then?" Benny said.

The nurse shook her head. "The next few hours will be critical. In his favour, he's young and strong; but he's suffered severe internal injuries and, amongst others, a bad head injury."

"Did he not have any identification on him when he was brought in?" Benny asked. The nurse shook her head.

"Nothing," she said.

"I'll see what I can do," Benny said, then he looked back to where Alan was still sitting. "The young driver who was dead at the scene, has he been identified?"

The staff nurse nodded sadly.

"The hospital counsellor is talking to his wife now, they'd been married six weeks."

Benny shook his head, just thankful that he hadn't been the one who had been sent to knock on the young woman's door.

The access doors of the accident and emergency department slid silently open and two police officers walked in; one uniformed, one plain-clothes. They made their way towards the corner where Benny and Alan were sitting.

"Heads up!" Benny said, nodding towards the two approaching men. "Serious Accident Branch unless I'm very much mistaken."

"P.C. Cody?" the plain-clothes officer said, flashing his warrant card at Benny. "You were first on the scene at the M6 incident today?" Benny nodded.

"Everything's in my report." He said. "I don't suppose you have any information on the identity of the guy who was in the transit do you?" D.C. David Williams shook his head.

"We were hoping you could help us out on that one; we would like to talk to the driver; the van doesn't exist on any records and its crammed to the gunnels with knocked off auto spares.

"I think that might be a no goer," Benny said. "The staff nurse has just asked me if I can contact any next of kin."

The detective constable turned towards the younger patrolman.

"P.C. Richards, I believe you were with him before the fire brigade cut him out of the wreck?"

Alan nodded.

"Did he say anything to you?"

Alan shook his head. "He was unconscious the whole time."

"Pity," the D.C. said.

Alan looked up. "If he had been conscious, I don't think he would have been in a condition to answer any questions."

The detective looked at P.C. Cody.

"I believe constable Richards put himself at some personal

risk to help get this guy out."

Benny nodded and smiled, noting the youngsters' obvious embarrassment.

The D.C. turned to Alan.

"Well done lad! I'll let you know if I find out any further information." He turned to Benny and nodded. "Keep in touch Benny." He said and headed off to speak to the hospital staff.

Alan looked up at his older colleague.

"There was one thing I noticed Benny," he said. "The guy in the van, his shirt was torn, and he did have quite a large tattoo on his back."

Benny Cody stood up. "Hey Dave!" he called across the room. D.C. Williams paused and looked back.

"There might be something that could help identify him after all!"

25

Jason paced up and down the flat, he couldn't settle, it was two a.m. and there was still no sign of Bran. His emotions had roller-coasted through a series of changes. He had grinned, pleased with his idea to surprise Bran with a lovely meal waiting for him when he got home; looking forward to seeing the look on his face when he walked in to be greeted with a glass of wine and a plate of his favourite lasagne. He was disappointed that Bran had not arrived home while he was cooking the meal; Worried that he was later than usual then annoyed when Bran didn't ring to let him know he would be late. Sad that Bran would miss a lovely meal and furious as he threw away the ruined dinner.

Worry turned to fear as the minutes ticked into hours and now in the early hours of the morning, he was frantic. Something was wrong; Bran would never stay away overnight and not let him know where he was.

The pacing continued; all the time different reasons for Bran's absence ran through his mind. Had the van broken down somewhere? What if he had been stuck in the tailbacks from the pile-up on the M6 earlier that day? Perhaps he had to wait for whatever it was he had gone to collect? What if he had picked up a hitchhiker and had been mugged! What if he had been in an accident!

This is silly! Jason thought to himself, there's probably a perfectly good reason that Bran hadn't come home yet, he didn't have his mobile, so it wouldn't be easy for him to ring home. He turned off the lounge lights; leaving the light on in the kitchen, and he made his way to the bedroom. He put his mobile on the bedside cabinet next to the house phone and climbed into bed.

The bed seemed big and cold with only him in it. He closed his eyes and tried to sleep; but his eyes wouldn't stay closed, they kept springing open every time he imagined he heard a car outside or footsteps in the hall. Eventually, he gave up trying to sleep and just lay staring out of the bedroom window, watching the night sky slowly get lighter as daybreak approached.

"Where are you Bran?" he said quietly.

Staff nurse Gwen Owen checked the monitors on bed seven. The man on this station was a high dependency patient. Practically all of his major systems were being supported. The surgeons had sent him through from theatre with slim hope of a recovery, but Gwen was determined to give him every chance. She checked the cannula in the back of his hand; patients sometimes moved, although she knew that there was little chance of this patient moving and accidentally dislodging the intravenous needle. She checked the blood bag; that would soon need replacing. With a practiced eye, she ran through the rigorous observations that intensive care required, making notes as she went. She lifted the small watch that was pinned to her uniform; it would soon be time for the last doctors round of the day. Gwen hadn't been on duty long and the ward sister had just finished updating the night staff in preparation for the hours ahead. Gwen didn't mind night duties; at least in I.C.U. there was plenty to keep you occupied.

The downside of night duty was that critically ill patients, more often than not, seemed to choose the early hours of the morning to pass away.

Gwen looked down at the young man who balanced on that thin edge between life and death.

"Don't you dare go tonight!" she said. "You stay here and

keep me company! Do you hear?"

As Gwen prepared to replace the nearly empty blood bag, she glanced over at the ward sisters' office, there were two policemen talking to her. She wondered if they had found out who this patient was; he hadn't been carrying any identification and no one, including the police, had been able to give the hospital any information about him.

Gwen looked down at her patient. He was naked except for the small sheet draped modestly over his lower body.

He was lucky to be alive, having been trapped for some time in a multi-vehicle pile-up on the M6.

A guardian angel must have been watching over him, as there had been no fire. In these incidents, so many fatalities were the result of fires; fires and motorists trapped in their vehicles. Gwen shuddered; she had watched too many burns victims go through the long struggle to recover some semblance of normal life and was thankful that Brennan wasn't one of them.

She smiled to herself; well Brennan was as good a name as any and he did sort of remind her of the actor who played the part of a character called Brennan. The hero in one of the television programmes she sometimes liked to watch. She smiled to herself, he would probably turn out to be someone called Clive or Bob, but Brennan suited him, so for now; Brennan it would be.

Gwen had just finished replacing the blood bag when the ward sister joined her at the bedside. Gwen glanced across to the office; the two policemen had disappeared. Sister Carroll studied the observation sheets for a moment, her critical eye checking for any anomalies in the records.

"Doctors rounds in ten minutes," she said. "Make sure everything's as it should be." She started to walk away, then as an afterthought, turned to Gwen.

"Apparently this young man has a distinctive tattoo on his back; the police seem to think it may help to identify him; I've told them that I'm not flipping a critically ill patient over so they can take snapshots. But I did say that if the opportunity does arise, we will get them the photo they want; bare that in mind nurse Owen."

"Of course, Sister," Gwen said as she watched Sister Carroll make her way to the next station.

She looked down at her patient and wondered what sort of a tattoo he had on his back; she was damn sure it wouldn't be his name and address and telephone number!

"Well Brennan," she said as she continued with her observations. "You get more mysterious by the minute."

She replaced the observation sheets in the patient file and reset a couple of the highly technical monitors. At the far end of the I.C.U. the doctors had just started their rounds.

Jason put the phone down. He was so angry that he felt near to tears. He had rung the police station to see if they had any information as to Bran's whereabouts, had he been in an accident? Had he been arrested?

The police seemed less interested in Bran's whereabouts and more interested in Jason's relationship with him. When asked, Jason had told them that he was Bran's partner. The officer on the phone had asked "What? He's your business partner?"

When Jason had said that they lived together, the officers' whole attitude had changed. Jason could hear the thinly disguised sneer in his voice. Because Jason wasn't related to Bran, he didn't even bother to check the records, instead, quoting the Data Protection Act and asking lots of pointless questions. How long had they lived together? Where did they meet? Had they had an argument? Did Bran have other 'partners'? Did he take drugs?"

When Jason tried to explain that to stay away so long was totally out of character for Bran; that he wouldn't stay away from home without letting him know that he was OK, the officer had finally asked how long had Bran been missing, When Jason told him that it had been nearly thirty-six hours, the policeman had been angry and accused Jason of wasting police time and suggested that he try the gay bars in town. He wouldn't even let Jason give him Bran's description, asking him rather abruptly to clear the line for more important phone calls.

Jason flicked through the little book of telephone numbers that Bran kept in the kitchen. He eventually found the number he was looking for; it was under the simple heading 'Dad'.

He picked up the receiver and punched in the number. Before the phone even had chance to ring he put the receiver down again and walked out of the room. He walked aimlessly around the bedroom. He didn't know what to do or where to go. There must be something he could do; someone who could help. He rang the hospitals; they didn't know anything, or if they did, they weren't prepared to tell him. He even gave his name as Kieran O'Donnell; Bran's brother, but still there was no trace of Bran.

If only he knew where he had been going, if only he knew who he worked for. Bran hadn't talked about work because he knew that Jason had disapproved of the rather shady delivery job. Now Jason wished that he had taken a little more interest in what Bran was doing.

Jason knew something was terribly wrong, he just knew it!

He picked up Bran's little book of phone numbers again; if anything had happened to him his Dad might know. He took a deep breath and keyed in the number for Pat O'Donnell.

Jason's heart was racing; he didn't know which was loudest, the thumping of his heart or the ringing of the phone in the earpiece. He was almost relieved when the phone wasn't answered and was just about to hang up when a voice said.

"*Yes!*"

"Mister O'Donnell?"

"*Who's that?*"

"Mister O'Donnell, I'm a friend of Bran's."

"*He doesn't live here any more!*"

"I know that Mister O'Donnell, but have you heard from him lately; has he rung you at all?"

"*Who is this? I've told you he doesn't live here; what are you wasting my fuckin' time for?*"

"I think something's happened to him, he didn't come home last night."

There was silence on the other end of the phone for a couple of seconds.

"*You're the fuckin' puff he's shacked up with! Got himself another bum buddy has he? Ditched you has he? As though I give a fuckin toss where he is!*"

"Look, if you hear anything will you ring this number?"

"*Piss off!*"

Before Jason could give Pat O'Donnell his number, the phone went dead; he had hung up!

Jason sat down heavily on the settee, hugging the phone to his chest, his thoughts racing out of control. 'What am I going to do! What am I going to do!' He felt totally lost. He curled up into a ball in the corner of the settee. There must be someone he could turn to, someone who could help to find Bran.

"Fuckin' pervert!" Pat O'Donnell swore as he slammed the phone back down onto the receiver. "Got 'is fuckin boyfriend ringing up here looking for him!"

Kieran looked up from the kitchen table, only half interested in what Pat was raving on about now.

"What you on about Dad?"

"Yer fuckin brothers fuckin puff boyfriend ringing here because his bit of arse didn't come home last night. He'll have been off shaggin' some other fuckin queer in a public bog somewhere!"

Kieran shook his head.

"I'm going to the airport this morning Dad; do you want me to drop you off at the office on the way?"

Pat shook his head.

"No, it's a bit too early for me Kieran, I'll get one of the lads to pick me up if I decide to come in later."

Kieran finished off his coffee and crammed the last of his toast into his mouth. He reached for the soft leather jacket hung on the back of the kitchen door then he walked over to the Aga to retrieve his keys from the wall next to the big warm stove. He paused for a moment as he took his keys off the hook; the hook next to his keys was empty; that had been where Bran always hung the keys to the Audi TT. He slipped on the comfortable Italian jacket; the rich dark reddish-brown leather fitted him like a glove. He dropped his keys into his pocket and pulled up the zip; but not before he had slipped his hand into the inside pocket and checked that the little leather box was still there.

Smiling, he patted the slight bulge in his jacket and headed for the door.

"See you later Dad!" he said. There was a spring to his step as he walked across the gravel drive to his Peugeot. He checked his hair in the mirror and pulled the seatbelt across his chest. He slipped a CD into the music centre and turned up the volume. Nothing was going to spoil today! With hardcore music blasting out from the four big speakers, he pulled out of the drive and headed for the city. To the Radisson Hotel where Lisa was waiting to have breakfast with him.

Kieran pulled into the hotel car park. The impressive towers of the Radisson soared above the Liverpool city streets.

Kieran walked up the marble steps and through the glass doors into the expansive reception area. Lisa was sitting at one of the coffee tables waiting for him. She smiled broadly and got up to meet him. She squeezed his hand and kissed him lightly on the cheek.

"I've just sent a text to mum." She smiled wickedly. "Just about to go for breakfast with Kieran!"

Kieran laughed.

"I do hope you explained that I was meeting you here and not staying in the hotel with you?"

Lisa grinned. "Oh, I'm sure she'll figure it out – eventually!"

They walked through to the continental restaurant. Other guests were sitting having breakfast. Kieran pulled out a chair for Lisa then sat opposite.

"So, what do you want to do today?" He asked.

Lisa smiled. "I don't care; I'm just happy to be here." She reached across the table and touched his hand. "I couldn't think of anywhere I would rather be."

Kieran placed his hand over hers and looked round.

"Yes, It's wonderful." He said, looking round. "But you won't see much of Liverpool from here! – Eat your breakfast." He smiled as the waiter arrived "Then we'll see where the mood takes us."

Lisa spooned sugar onto her grapefruit as Kieran drank coffee and ate one of her croissants.

"So where are you taking me today?" She asked between mouthfuls.

"It's a surprise." He grinned.

"Oh, I love surprises!" she laughed.

Kieran smiled. He had planned one very big surprise for Lisa and he really hoped that she was going to love that one as well!

Staff nurse Gwen Owen was about to go off duty, she yawned, thankful that it had been an uneventful night. She recorded her final series of observations and checked the plastic tubes and wires that connected the patient in bed seven to the life support machines. Her replacement would be taking over soon and she would be able to go home and get some much-needed sleep. Brennan; as she had decided to call the mysterious patient in bed seven, had shown no signs of regaining consciousness and now remained in a drug-induced coma. Only time would tell if the injuries he had sustained were too much for his body to deal with, but at least he had made it through this night. She moistened his lips with a damp swab and absently brushed a stray lock of dark hair from his cheek. She wondered where he was from, if he lived in the Midlands, if he had a wife somewhere who was worrying because he hadn't come home.

There was another mystery; as well as the injuries he had sustained in the motorway incident, his body was covered in bruises and cuts that were at least a couple of days old and the x-rays had identified; besides the bones broken in the motorway pile-up; a couple of broken ribs that had probably happened before the crash, and now; Sister Carroll had said that he had a tattoo on his back! Gwen wondered what it could be. Maybe Skull and crossbones, a heart or perhaps a dragon? Yes! That's what she would put her money on, Gwen thought, a dragon! A big fire-breathing dragon!

The nurse who would be taking over for the next shift walked over to station seven; having just been updated by Sister Carroll before she to went off duty.

She nodded briefly in Gwen's direction and continued chatting with her friend who had just come on duty as well. Gwen frowned, she didn't know this nurse, and she was one of the younger nurses, not much experience but lots of qualifications and even more cockiness. The new nurse continued chatting with her friend.

"So apparently there's a photographer coming down this afternoon, taking a photograph of him!" She pointed to her patient, the man in station seven."

"Oh, yeah?" her friend laughed quietly. "What's that for then? Gardeners Weekly. They doin' an article for the vegetable section?" The two young nurses laughed at their own rather sick humour. Gwen didn't want to listen to any more of their childish, stupid comments! What was the health service coming to! She headed for the sisters' office to sign out, keen to get back to her flat and get something to eat and then a few hours sleep. Hopefully, Brennan would still be there when she got back on duty tonight. As she left the I.C.U she glanced back, the two young nurses were still chatting, Gwen felt like going back and slapping their silly faces. Ah well, she thought, the new Ward Sister would soon put a stop to that!

Kieran pulled onto the parking area at the Albert Docks.

"Come on." He smiled, taking Lisa's hand. "Let's go for a walk down by the river."

The river walk along the banks of the Mersey was pleasant. The cobbled walkway and ornate fencing edged the vast expanse of water and allowed a clear view across the river to Birkenhead. It was a bright morning, cold but quite sunny. A few wispy grey clouds scudded across the blue sky, propelled by the strong breeze that ruffled the surface of the water and brought the smell of the river across the land.

Lisa hooked her arm around Kieran's, enjoying the brisk walk after breakfast.

"Where are we going?" she asked, smiling up into his eager young face.

"Ah, you'll see," he said mysteriously. A few minutes later the walkway ended at the Pier Head Ferry Terminal.

"Come on," he said, pulling her towards the terminal buildings.

"We're going for a little trip." He laughed at her puzzled expression.

"We're going to take a 'ferry cross the Mersey'," he smiled.

The ferry still operated a foot passenger service across the Mersey, but most of the sailings were for the tourists and mainly consisted of circular trips.

Lisa grinned, enjoying the experience with an almost childlike pleasure as she and Kieran sat on the upper deck of the Ferry, holding hands as it made its bumpy way across the choppy water towards Birkenhead.

"This is wonderful!" She said. "I've never done anything like this!"

"It's not exactly a cruise ship," Kieran said apologetically.

Lisa turned and kissed him.

"Right now," she said, "I would rather be here than on the QE2!"

Kieran put his arm around her and she leaned against his shoulder.

"When you go back to Belfast, I'm coming with you." He said. He reached into his inside pocket and took out the little leather box he had been keeping there.

He put the box into Lisa's hand and wrapped her fingers around it.

"I'm coming with you so that I can ask Sean Driscoll if I can have the hand of his daughter in marriage." He looked into Lisa's eyes. "That's if she'll have me?" he said.

Lisa looked at Kieran. Stunned, she looked at the box in her hand then she looked up at Kieran again.

"Well, aren't you going to open it?" he smiled.

Lisa looked at the beautifully crafted little leather box in her hand, and slowly opened the lid. Nestled inside on a cushion of black velvet was an exquisite engagement ring; the beautiful clear diamond in the centre was positioned between two oblong emeralds that sat on the shoulders of the ring.

All Lisa could manage was a small gasp "Ohh!"

Kieran took the ring out of the box and gently held Lisa's hand.

"Lisa Driscoll." He said, slipping the ring onto her finger. "Will you marry me?"

She looked at the ring on her finger, and she felt as though time had stood still, she had even stopped breathing.

She looked at the ring again and took a deep breath.

"Kieran." She said slowly. "Kieran I can think of no one I would rather spend the rest of my life with; Yes I'll marry you!" she threw her arms around his neck and kissed him. "Yes! Yes! Yes!" Behind them, there was the loud pop of a champagne cork as the steward who had been waiting for Kieran's signal, poured two flutes of sparkling champagne and handed one each to the young couple. "Congratulations!" he smiled.

"You planned all this in advance?" Lisa said as she sipped champagne from the tall glass, not knowing if she wanted to laugh or cry. Kieran nodded. "Yep," he said happily.

"What would you have done if I had said no?" she asked.

He grinned. "Me and the steward would have got very drunk." He raised his glass in salute. "To us Lisa." He kissed her gently; the taste of champagne was still on her lips.

"I love you," he whispered.

Jason had spent yet another sleepless night. He had rung all the local hospitals again; no one by the name of O'Donnell had been admitted over the last couple of days. He had rung the National Missing Persons Helpline and left details; as much as he could, with their organisation, but they didn't seem to hold out much hope of a quick response.

Jason knew that something was wrong, very wrong, Bran must be in serious trouble or he would have got in touch before now, but that nasty little voice kept niggling away in the back of his mind. He kept hearing the words Bran's Dad had spat down the phone at him.

"Got himself another bum buddy, has he? Ditched you has he?"

They had been arguing quite a lot just lately; Bran had been under a lot of strain; Jason knew he had been finding it difficult to deal with his fathers' attitude.

What if he had found someone else to whom he could tell his troubles? What if right now he was in someone else's arms, in someone else's bed?

Jason sat and stared at the picture on the wall, the special picture he had painted for both of them. In his hands he held Bran's leather jacket, the one that had been ruined when he had been attacked, beaten up because he had admitted to being gay. Beaten up by his own brother! A cold hard lump seemed to form in his chest and make its way slowly up to his throat.

His eyes pricked and stung as they filled with salty tears and he cried; cried like he hadn't cried since he was a little boy.

Great sobs shook his body as he buried his face into the soft leather coat.

"Bran." He cried "Bran please come home; I don't want you to go away Bran, I want you here with me; Bran ***'please'*** don't leave me!"

26

D.C. Dave Williams pushed the photo across the desk to his colleague.

"What the hell do you make of that then?"

Sergeant Peter Lynch studied the photo for a moment, It had only just been delivered from the hospital; brought in by the patrolman who had attended the M6 incident.

Sergeant Lynch looked up at Dave Williams.

"We're dealing with a homosexual with a death wish." He said, pushing the photo over to patrolman Benny Cody. Benny picked up the photo and studied it for a moment.

"Well whoever tattooed that will certainly remember it." He commented, handing the photo back.

"I don't suppose you know how many tattooists' there are in the Birmingham area?" D.C. Williams said. Sergeant Lynch leaned back in his chair.

"That's always assuming that he's from the Birmingham area, he could be from anywhere in the country!"

Benny picked up the photo again.

"Well if I was you." He said. "I would be giving Merseyside Police a ring." He pointed to the red bird in the picture.

"My nephew supports Liverpool football club, that's the Liverpool 'Liver Bird' – it's part of their badge, I reckon there's a good chance your man comes from Merseyside!"

Jason picked up the yellow pages and leafed through till he found the Taxis and Private Hire section. He ran his finger down the columns of numbers until he found what he was looking for. O'Donnell's Taxis. He knew that Bran's brother Kieran usually manned the phones and operated the radio. He hoped that if he could speak to his brother instead of his father, he might be able to learn a little more about where Bran could be. Earlier, Jason had thought about going to find Paul, Bran's youngest brother at the Uni. But his memories of Paul and his friends laughing and joking as they dragged his jeans down around his ankles before kicking him almost unconscious, made him a little wary about approaching him again.

Paul had been among the group who had attacked Bran. Jason wondered how anyone could do what he did, to his own brother and still sleep at night and he desperately hoped that Kieran wasn't like Paul or their father.

Taking a deep breath, he rang the number for the Taxi Company. He was surprised when a female voice answered the phone.

"O'Donnell's Taxis – How can I help?"

Jason took another deep breath.

"Can I speak to Kieran please?" he said. On the other end of the phone, Jean assumed that the caller was one of Kieran's friends.

"Oh, I'm sorry, luv," she said. "But Kieran won't be in till five o'clock tonight, do you want to leave a message?"

"No, err no thanks," he said, and then as an afterthought added.

"Oh, by the way, will mister O'Donnell be in then?"

Jean smiled; Pat was always giving Kieran a hard time because his friends called him at the office.

"No." She said, "mister O'Donnell won't be in till much later tonight."

"Thanks," Jason said and put the phone down. He would speak to Kieran tonight, but he wouldn't give him the opportunity to hang up on him like his Dad had done, he would go around to the taxi office and speak to him personally. Someone had to take him seriously and believe that somewhere, Bran was in trouble!

Rick was sitting relaxing with a cup of coffee and the latest edition of 'Skin Deep'. Melanie was busy in the studio at the back, clearing up after the last client, a middle-aged businessman who had wanted a rather extensive tribal shoulder piece. They'd finished early tonight; the tattoo hadn't taken as long as Rick thought it would. Melanie already had tomorrows' appointments organised and the designs printed out as transfers ready to work with.

It would be nice to get home early for a change.

The buzzer on the door sounded as a smartly dressed man walked into the studio.

Spoke too soon! Rick thought as he got up to greet the man.

"Good evening." Rick smiled. His coffee cup was still in his hand. "What can we do for you?" he asked.

The man held out a small clear plastic wallet containing his I.D.

"D.C. Williams," he said, "West Midlands CID."

Rick frowned, it wasn't the first time the police had called at the studio, but they didn't usually come from as far away as the West Midlands. He put the coffee cup down on the desk.

"So, what can I do for you D.C. Williams?" he asked.

Dave Williams handed Rick the large envelope he was

carrying.

"A tattooist in Sefton said you would possibly recognise that. He said it looked like your work."

Rick pulled the photo from the envelope; he recognised it straight away it was part of Bran O'Donnell's back piece.

"Where did you get this?" Rick asked.

"Do you recognise it?" D.C. Williams queried.

Rick looked at the photo again.

"Why do you want to know if this is one of my tattoos?" He said.

Dave Williams started to get a little bit annoyed.

"Look!" He said. "Are we going to play twenty effin' questions; or are you going to tell me what you know about this tattoo!" Just at that point, Melanie breezed in from the studio at the back and walked up to the two men.

"Oh, you're looking at Bran's back piece!" she said, as she saw the photograph in the stranger's hand.

"Bran! Bran who?" Dave said turning towards Melanie.

"Melanie! You've said quite enough already!" Rick snapped and he turned back to the detective constable.

"We do have such a thing as client confidentiality here," he said. "Yes; I did do that back piece, but it's a very personal subject and I don't know if my client would want me to discuss it with you."

"Does this 'Bran' have any family here?"

"Why do you want to know?" Rick asked. Dave sighed; this was getting him nowhere. "OK," he said, "but you must agree to speak to no one until I have had chance to talk to the family."

Rick nodded towards one of the leather settees.

"Have a seat." He said "Melanie! Coffee!"

Dave Williams told Rick about the man with no identification who had been in a major traffic incident on the M6 in Birmingham and was now critically ill and on life support in an Intensive Care Unit. Rick was shocked.

"I need to contact the next of kin," Dave said, "because the doctors don't hold out much hope; he's in a coma and the next forty-eight hours could prove crucial. It could go either way."

Rick shook his head.

"He was only in here the other day," he looked across at the D.C. "His name is Bran O'Donnell and his father owns O'Donnell's Taxis on Allen Street."

"Thank you! At last!" Dave said, relieved to be at last getting somewhere.

Rick handed him one of the business cards that Pat had left on his last visit. Dave looked at the address and slipped the card into his pocket.

"Thanks." Dave finished off his coffee and prepared to leave. "O'Donnell.," he said, "Irish?" Rick nodded.

"So why else are you here?" Rick asked. "They don't usually send Detective Constables all the way from the West Midlands just to play messenger boy for an I.D. check! Look, I may be able to help you." Rick said. "But I need to know what you're looking for. Bran O'Donnell is a good bloke, as honest as they come; if he's in any trouble, I'd like to help if I can."

D.C. Williams looked at Rick for a moment and then sat back down.

"This guy, O'Donnell, was driving an untaxed van loaded with stolen auto spares." Rick was stunned. "No, I don't believe that!" he said. "Bran's not that sort. I don't believe he would knowingly get mixed up in that sort of thing."

Dave Williams tried to assess how much he could divulge to this Liverpool Tattooist. All sorts of villains could walk through this man's door, he might just hear something that could prove useful and if he thought it would help his friend Bran!

"We believe that a criminal organisation based in the Midlands is running a 'steal to order' operation and using casual workers driving unregistered vans to move the goods around the country. Guys like your friend Bran, who think they're doing nothing more than a bit of moonlighting for cash in hand drop, have made what deliveries we've intercepted. Of course, the phone contact and pick up points no longer exist and we've been left chasing our tails again." He picked up the photo and tucked it back in his inside pocket. "With a bit of luck, they will still be waiting for the delivery to be made, unaware that O'Donnell is out of the scene, not much to go on, but it's a start." He headed for the door. "If I can get to his contact before he does a runner it might go in O'Donnell's favour." He paused. "Thanks for the help." He said as he left the studio and climbed back into his car. He picked up his radio mike.

"Control?" he said. "Can you give me a home address for a Patrick O'Donnell, owner of O'Donnell's Taxis of Allen Street in Liverpool?"

Pat O'Donnell walked from the study to the hall.

"Alright! Alright!" he shouted. Who the hell was pounding on the front door in the middle of the afternoon!

He flung the door open.

"What yer tryin' to do? Tek it off its friggin' 'inges?"

The plain-clothes police officer held out his warrant card.

"Mister O'Donnell?" He asked. "Could I have a word with you please?"

"I don't suppose I have a friggin' choice," Pat growled. "What are you lot wasting my time with now!?"

D.C. Williams indicated the open door.

"Mind if I come in?" he asked.

Pat snorted.

"If you fuckin' must!" He said and he turned and walked back to the study. Dave Williams followed him.

Pat sat down in one of the comfortable leather armchairs.

"So, what do you want?" He said without offering the police officer a seat.

"It's about your son Mister O'Donnell."

"Kieran!" Pat snapped, "What the hell's the idiot been up to now?" Pat clenched his fist. "So, help me, if that pillock's got himself into trouble with the law again!"

"It's about your eldest son Mister O'Donnell; Brandon!"

Pat waved his hand dismissively and sneered,

"I haven't got a son called Bran." He said, "The bastard pissed off a few months ago. I don't know where he is and I don't effin' care where he is."

"Your son was involved in a serious accident, Mister O'Donnell," Dave said calmly. "He's on a life support machine in Birmingham General."

Pat was silent for a moment, he stood up and walked over to the drinks cabinet and poured himself a large Whiskey. He took a long slow drink and then topped up the glass, turning to the officer who stood watching his reactions.

"Well then," Pat said, draining the glass. "Tell them to turn the friggin' machines off and do us all a favour!"

D.C. Williams soon realised that Pat O'Donnell was not going to talk about his eldest son and the more Dave questioned him, the more he drank and the more evasive and aggressive he became. Dave gave up; he was getting nowhere here. He tore a page out of his notebook and scribbled down a phone number. He pushed the scrap of paper into Pat O'Donnell's hand.

"That's the phone number of the I.C.U.," he said. "Just in case you want to see your son while you still can."

Pat screwed up the paper and threw it onto the table.

"Good afternoon, Mister O'Donnell," Dave said. "I'll see myself out." And without a backwards glance, he left.

"And fuckin' good riddance!" he heard Pat shout as he closed the door behind him.

27

Kieran pulled into the garage on Allen Street, having dropped a very happy Lisa off at the hotel. He was only a few minutes late, but he knew Jean would be waiting to go home.

"I was beginning to worry, Kieran." She said when he finally walked into the office.

"Sorry Jean." He said, "I'll make it up to you." He couldn't stop the grin that spread across his face. "But today's been rather special." Jean looked at him quizzically.

"Jean, I asked Lisa to marry me, and she said yes!"

Jean looked at the handsome young man standing in front of her. She realised just how 'grown-up' he had become. No longer the wild teenager bunking off school or being ticked off by the police for joy riding. She looked up into his eager young face, the face that was looking for approval, the face that was beginning to look more and more like his older brother.

"Oh, Kieran, that's wonderful!" Jean said hugging him in he bony embrace. "What did Pat say? I bet he's pleased!"

"I haven't told him yet." He said, looking down into his 'auntie' Jean's face. "You won't say anything to him, will you?" He asked. "I want to speak to Lisa's Dad first."

"Of course, not honey." She smiled, looking down at her watch. "But I'll have to go or I'll miss my bus."

Kieran kissed the top of her head.

"Don't worry about the bus," he said, "Pour me a coffee and I'll order you a taxi; on the firm!"

"Alright," Jean grinned, "as long as you promise to tell me all about this secret engagement."

Jean sat sipping coffee while a very enthusiastic Kieran went over his day step by step.

"So, you had all this planned in advance." She said as he described how the steward on the ferry had appeared with glasses of champagne.

"It sounds beautiful!" Jean said as Kieran described the engagement ring. "Diamonds and Emeralds!"

"It had to be," Kieran smiled. "After all, Ireland is the 'Emerald Isle'!" Jean glanced up at the young Irishman. A fleeting look of concern crossed her face.

"It's a bit sudden Kieran; are you really sure about this?"

Kieran smiled and nodded.

"I'm sure Jean." He said. "I've never been as sure about anything in my entire life."

Jean hadn't had time to finish her coffee when they heard footsteps on the stairs to the office. It was the taxi driver Kieran had ordered to take Jean home. She put on her coat and picked up her handbag and finishing off the remains of her coffee followed the driver to the door.

"Oh, by the way," the driver said as he stepped aside to let Jean walk past him on her way out of the office.

"There's a bloke downstairs asking for you Kieran."

Kieran looked up. Who the hell could this be?

"Tell him to come up will you." He said. A few moments later a young guy with shoulder length blonde hair walked into the office. Kieran looked up.

"Can I help you?" he asked. The man looked nervous.

"I'm Jason Foster," he said. "Bran's partner."

Gwen Owen wasn't due back on duty for another two hours, but she thought she would drop into the I.C.U. and see if there had been any change in the coma patient on stations seven, the unidentified traffic accident victim whom she had temporarily given the name, 'Brennan'.

She called into the ward sisters' office; Sister Carroll was on duty already and she looked up as Gwen walked through the door.

"Hello, Gwen." She smiled, and then looked at her watch and frowned.

"You're not due on duty for another couple of hours; what on earth are you doing in here?"

Gwen looked through the window towards bed seven. "Just wondered how our mystery man was. If there had been any change."

Sister Carroll shook her head. "Still unresponsive," she said.

"But there is one bit of news; he isn't a mystery man anymore, West Mids' C.I.D. rang this afternoon, believe it or not, they managed to trace the tattooist. Apparently, his name is Bran O'Donnell and he's from Liverpool." Gwen was relieved.

"That's good," she said. "Is his family on the way?"

Sister Carroll shook her head again.

"That's the sad thing," she said. "According to the detective constable who spoke to him, there's only a father and he was a heavy drinker who wasn't the slightest bit interested in where his son was or what had happened to him; so, I guess Bran O'Donnell is on his own!"

Gwen looked out of the window towards bed seven. Poor Brennan; or Bran as she could now call him.

"Mind if I come on duty early?" Gwen asked. Sister Carroll

smiled.

"We can always use an extra pair of hands," she said. "it's the doctors round in ten minutes, you can help out with that if you will."

That will be great, Gwen thought as she prepared to join the team in I.C.U. Perhaps she would get a better idea of what the prognosis was for Brennan; she really must stop calling him Brennan and start to think of him as Bran! It was strange how the two names were so like each other.

The Neurologist walked over to the charts by bed seven and analysed the data with a practiced eye.

He turned to his colleague and pointed out something in the observations. The consultant surgeon nodded.

"Yes," he said, "any further increase and the only option would be surgery."

The Neurologist shook his head.

"I think at that point surgery would be pointless."

"Let's hope it doesn't come to that." He scribbled something in his notes. "An increase in the medication may give us a little more time, if we don't see any improvement in the next forty-eight hours; I don't think we ever will do."

"Thank you, nurse." He said, handing his notes to Gwen.

As the doctors moved on to the next station, she replaced them in the file at the bottom of the bed, pausing for a moment to check one of the catheters.

"You hang in there, Bran!" She said. "You keep fighting; do you hear me!" By the time the doctors had finished their rounds of the patients in I.C.U. it was time for Gwen to join the other night staff for sisters' update. Although Gwen listened attentively to the Ward Sisters instructions and took notes as she did so, part of her mind was on the young man on station seven. So young, with everything to live for, the rest of his life still in front of him.

Gwen sighed as she headed into the I.C.U. and to station seven. The rest of his life might only be forty-eight hours long! The young nurse who had taken over from Gwen was just finishing off her final observations when Gwen joined her by the bedside.

"Hello, Staff Nurse Owen!" she said brightly as she continued chatting away to the nurse at the next station. Oh, to be young and full of life Gwen thought; I bet these two will be off clubbing most of the night and still have plenty of energy for tomorrows duty.

"You'll be safe enough with this one Staff Nurse," she said laughing. "I've seen the tattoo on his back! - He's gay!"

Kieran stared at the man who had just walked into the office, he didn't look any different to the hundreds of other University students he saw every day. He wasn't wearing flashy clothes or carrying a handbag. He wasn't poncing about with a limp wrist. He looked normal; just like one of Paul's student mates. But he wasn't one of Paul's friends', this was the man Paul and his friends had beaten up because he was gay. This was the man who was sleeping with his brother!

"You're probably wondering what I'm doing here," Jason said, a little unnerved by Kieran's silence.

"I didn't know who else I could speak to, who else might know anything."

"Know anything about what?" Kieran asked at last.

"About Bran, where is he, what's happened to him?" Jason

bit his bottom lip nervously, hoping and praying that Bran's brother might be able to shed some light on to Bran's whereabouts.

"He hasn't been home for two nights now and I'm really worried about him; he wouldn't stay away without letting me know he was OK."

Kieran remembered the phone call Pat had received just over twenty-four hours earlier.

"You rang Dad the other morning, didn't you?"

"Look, have you any idea where Bran might be?" Jason didn't want to remember the vicious hurtful things Pat O'Donnell had said to him over the phone.

"I haven't spoken to Bran or seen him since he left home all those weeks ago. I'm sorry; I don't know where he is or even where he might be."

The news was like a physical blow to Jason. He had hoped against hope that Kieran might know something, surely, if anything had happened to Bran; someone would have informed his family.

"Look," Kieran said, noticing how tired Jason looked. "Why don't you have a coffee?" He poured Jason a cup.

"If anything had happened to Bran, someone would have contacted the family by now."

"That's the problem," Jason said. "When Bran got beaten up the other night, they took his mobile and his wallet; He has nothing on him to say who he is or where he comes from and he's driving these dodgy vans around the country and I would like to bet they're not taxed or insured!"

"Bran's pretty smart," Kieran said. "He can look after himself."

"I should never have let him go on that job." Jason shook his head. "He'd been beaten up a couple of days earlier, he hadn't had much sleep and he was in a lot of pain."

He put down his half-finished coffee.

"Look I'd better get back to the flat in case anyone tries to ring me there." He handed Kieran a card with his home and mobile phone numbers on it.

"If you hear anything; please get in touch with me, you'll be able to contact me on one of those numbers."

He walked towards the door.

"Thanks for the coffee!" he said, and he was gone.

Kieran looked down at the card Jason had left and tucked it into his inside pocket. Kieran hoped Bran was OK. He had probably just been delayed somewhere. But all the same, that niggling little seed of worry started to germinate in his mind.

Just where was Bran?

Kieran didn't have much time to think about that; already the phone was ringing. He slipped on the small headphones and pressed the headset/hands-free button on the phone.

"O'Donnell's Taxis." He said, picking up a pen and notepad.

"What can we do for you?"

"I would like a taxi," the soft Irish voice on the other end of the line said, "From the Radisson SAS Hotel to Allen Street please."

"Lisa!" Kieran recognised her voice straight away. "Lisa, what do you want to come to this dump for, you'd be bored out of your head!"

Lisa groaned.

"I'm bored here Kieran and I'd rather be bored with you."

"Lisa, I'll be stuck here till at least one in the morning. Look, why don't you take in a show or something, I've got all day tomorrow free…"

"Kieran," Lisa interrupted him. "Are you going to send me a taxi or do I have to order one from City Rides?"

Kieran caved.

"OK, Lisa," he sighed, "you win." He checked the bookings. "A taxi will be with you in about fifteen minutes, is that alright?"

Fifteen minutes later, Lisa was in the hotel reception when a man walked up to the desk.

"Taxi for Miss Driscoll?" He said to the receptionist.

"That's me!" Lisa grabbed her coat and hung her bag on her shoulder.

The driver held open the door of the cab.

"Allen Street?" he queried, "are you sure you want to go to Allen Street?"

"That's right!" Lisa smiled, "The Taxi office!" The driver shrugged his shoulders. "Right." He said. "Allen Street it is!"

It only took a few minutes to get from the Radisson to the Allen Street Garage. The driver pulled into the yard and opened the taxi door for Lisa.

"How much do I owe you?" She smiled, taking her purse out of her handbag.

"Kieran's already dealt with it." He said, nodding towards the office window.

Lisa grinned. "Thanks anyway." She said, pressing a couple of pound coins into his hand. The driver looked down at the unexpected tip.

"Cheers." He smiled and pushed the coins into his jeans' pocket. "Let me know if you want taking back to the hotel."

But Lisa was already on her way to the office.

Kieran was waiting for her at the top of the stairs, he kissed her, pleased to see her despite the fact that he had tried to persuade her not to come.

"Why on earth you want to waste your time sitting round here I don't know."

"Well, if I'm going to marry a taxi driver, I'd better find out what I'm letting myself in for." She grinned. Kieran laughed.

"I think you might be a bit disappointed." He said. "It's not exactly rocket science, sitting on your arse all night answering the phone."

Lisa looked down and patted his bum affectionately.

"But it's such a cute little arse." She laughed.

At that moment the phone rang and Kieran sat down at the desk again.

"O'Donnell's Taxis," he said. "What can we do for you?"

It was a pick up from the Railway Station to one of the Hotels in the city; Kieran radioed it through to the nearest cab, jotting the details down on the daily log.

"And that's about all there is to it Lisa, pretty boring stuff really."

"Ah, but it has its advantages," she smiled, leaning over and nibbling his ear, "Plenty of time for other things!"

But much to Kieran's disappointment, the 'other things' had to wait as the evening started to get quite busy. Lisa was quite happy just to sit and chat during the few minutes when the phone stopped ringing, or when Kieran had a break from relaying jobs to the various drivers via the radio link. It was around eight o'clock when there was a lull in the bookings, Lisa poured them both a coffee and sat on the desk beside Kieran.

"Time I was getting back to the hotel or I'll miss dinner." She said, kissing him lightly on the lips.

"What do you want to do tomorrow hon.?" He asked, putting his arm around her waist and pulling her onto his lap.

Lisa giggled as she managed to put down the coffee cup without spilling any of it. Kieran laughed and nibbled her neck.

"That tickles!" She shrieked and tried to pull away from him.

"Oh, no you don't!" he said, pulling her back down onto his lap. "You're not leaving till you decide where you want to go tomorrow!"

"Depends what the options are Kieran?" she laughed and wrapped her arms around his neck.

"Oh, I could think of one or two," Kieran said as his mouth descended on hers.

"What the fuck's going on!"

Neither of them had heard Pat enter the office.

Lisa jumped up from Kieran's lap and Kieran swung round to see who had walked in on them.

"Dad!" Kieran said, shocked to suddenly find his father in the room. "What are you doing here?"

"I could ask you the same effin' thing!" he shouted, "Is this what I effin' pay you for!"

"I'm sorry Mister O'Donnell," Lisa said, "it's all my fault, I decided I wanted to come up here, Kieran didn't really want me to…"

"Lisa?" Pat gasped. "Lisa, what are you doing here? I thought you had gone back to Belfast with your Dad."

"I did mister O'Donnell, but I decided I wanted to spend a bit more time over here, so I flew back yesterday. Kieran picked me up from the airport."

She clutched nervously at her handbag.

"But I suppose I had better be getting back to the hotel," she looked pleadingly at Kieran.

"The taxi that brought me in is still in the yard," Pat said, and he turned to Kieran.

"Go and sort it!" he ordered.

"So is Sean over here with you?" Pat asked as Kieran went to catch the taxi driver before he left the yard.

Lisa shook her head,

"No, just me, Mister O'Donnell, there are a few places I still want to see and Kieran said he would take me when he wasn't working."

Kieran walked back into the office.

"The taxi will wait for you Lisa," he said, helping her on with her coat.

"Thanks, Kieran." She smiled, "I'll see you in the morning then?"

"Course you will!" he smiled and put his arms around her waist and kissed her gently. "I'll walk you to the cab."

Pat was waiting for him when he got back into the office.

"What the fuck are you playing at!" he yelled. "What are you doin' messin' about with Sean Driscoll's lass?"

Kieran was stunned.

"I thought you of all people would be pleased that Lisa and I were spending time together."

"You and Sean Driscoll's daughter!" Pat shouted. "Don't

make me laugh, and are you friggin' blind as well as friggin' stupid? Did you not see the bloody great rock she was wearin' on her ring finger! That was an engagement ring you daft twat!"

Kieran shook his head and sighed, this wasn't how they had wanted to break the news to Pat. They had wanted to speak to Lisa's father first.

"Yes, I know it's an engagement ring, Dad, because I gave it to Lisa yesterday when I asked her to marry me!"

28

Rick turned off the lights in the studio, he had been working quite late preparing the transfers for a big tattoo job that was due in next morning. A man wanted a memorial for his son who had been killed in a motorcycle accident. Rick had some good ideas but wanted to have a few options ready for this very special piece.

He had spent quite a lot of time today; very emotional time, with a father who was still grieving for the loss of the son who had died over a year ago and as Rick climbed into his sporty little Élan he wondered about Pat O'Donnell and how he was coping with the news of his son's accident.

He had half expected another visit from the police, asking more questions', but he had heard nothing further about Bran O'Donnell. He glanced at his watch; it wasn't too late. He would call at the taxi office on his way home and find out what the latest news was on Bran. The police would have informed Pat about Bran's accident by now!

As he drove through the busy City streets, he thought about the tattoo he had done for Bran; without that tattoo, Bran might never have been identified. Tattoos' were powerful magic; they changed peoples' lives in oh, so many ways.

Everything seemed quiet as Rick pulled into the yard at the taxi office. The lights were on in the building. Rick pulled smoothly to a halt by the door and made his way up the stairs to the office. There was a young man sitting at the desk; he looked so much like Bran.

"You must be Kieran?" Rick said.

Kieran leaned back in his chair and looked at the stranger who had just walked in.

"Do I know you?" He asked. Rick smiled.

"No, not yet." He grinned, "but I know your Dad very well and your brother Bran."

At that moment Pat, hearing the familiar voice, walked in from the back room.

"Rick!" he said, puzzled. "What the fuck are you doing here?"

Rick looked at the older man, mildly surprised to see him there.

"I could ask you the same thing, Pat," he said. "I had expected you to be down in Birmingham!"

"Birmingham?" Kieran asked.

"That's none of your business, Rick!" Pat said angrily. "I think you'd better leave now, you're not wanted here!"

"Birmingham?" Kieran repeated, standing up and turning to his father. "Why the hell should you be in Birmingham?"

"Has he not told you?" Rick looked from father to son. "The police must have told you yesterday Pat!"

"Shut up Rick!" Pat said quietly.

"What have the police told you, Dad?" Kieran asked. "What have the police been here for?" Pat said nothing, all the time glaring at Rick as though defying him to speak!

"The police came to see me a couple of days ago Kieran, they had a photo of a tattoo I had done. The tattoo was on a man they couldn't identify." He looked over at Pat; he couldn't believe that he had said nothing to Bran's brother.

"I shouldn't be the one to be telling you this Kieran," Rick said, "Bran was in a big smash on the M6."

"Shut up Rick!" Pat shouted, "He doesn't need to know!"

"Shut the fuck up Dad!" Kieran snarled and turned back to Rick.

"What don't I need to know Rick?" he asked.

"Bran was in a real bad accident, he's in Birmingham General." Rick paused; he hadn't expected to be the one to have to break this news to Bran's brother.

"He's on a life support machine Kieran, and the police didn't seem to think there was much hope of recovery.

Kieran sat down heavily on the chair; all the breath seemed to have been knocked out of him.

It didn't take him long to come to a decision. He tore off the radio headset and threw it onto the desk. He grabbed his jacket pulled his car keys from the pocket and headed for the door.

"Where do you think you're going?" Pat demanded.

"Where the bloody hell do you think I'm going?" Kieran said.

"Birmingham!"

Kieran sat in the family waiting room of Birmingham General I.C.U. He had just left the unit after the nurse had suggested that he might like to sit down and have a cup of sweet tea.

He had arrived at the hospital with no idea of what he would find and had been taken through to the intensive care unit by a staff nurse who had tried to prepare him for what he was about to see.

Bran lay on a bed surrounded by monitors and computers and electronic recorders, there were wires taped to his chest and tubes everywhere. There was a plastic pipe in his mouth and tubes in his nose and things sticking in his arms.

Everything around Kieran seemed unreal. It was as though he had walked into someone else's dream.

The staff nurse with him saw the colour drain from his face.

"Come and sit down," she said. "I'll get the doctor to come and talk to you in a minute, I'm sure you will have lots of questions."

He looked up at the nurse; she was a middle-aged woman with a kind, motherly face.

"Is he going to die?" Kieran asked.

Staff Nurse Gwen Owen looked at the young man who had just driven one hundred and fifty miles, not knowing if his brother was alive or dead.

"The doctors' are doing everything possible," she said kindly,

"They'll be able to tell you a lot more than I can."

"Can I sit with him for a while?" Kieran asked.

"Of course, you can.," Gwen said, "as long as you like."

Kieran walked back into the I.C.U. and pulled a chair up to the side of the bed Bran lay on. He sat for ages, just looking at his brother, feeling so helpless and not knowing what he could do or say. The nurse was checking various monitors and making notes on a clipboard. Kieran watched her as she worked, checking, altering, and adjusting the various wires and tubes.

"Why don't you talk to him?" Gwen said when she noticed how lost Kieran looked.

"He probably won't react, but unconscious patients often know someone is with them and may even be able to hear what you say to him."

Kieran looked at Bran and then up at the staff nurse.

"What should I say to him?" he asked.

Gwen smiled.

"Just tell him you're here, and that he's not alone."

It was time for the doctors' last visit of the day and staff nurse Owen asked Kieran if he would like to sit in the family waiting room for half an hour until the doctors had finished their rounds and then she would get the consultant to come and talk to him about Bran.

Kieran sat in the boring waiting room for a few minutes, there were a few other people there, people who sat quietly, lost in their own worries about their loved ones. Like Kieran, they too were keeping vigil; patiently waiting for any news, any change or developments in their condition. After a few minutes, Kieran had had enough of the depressing little room. He walked down the long corridor and headed for the entrance to the hospital. Once outside he took out his mobile phone; he had turned it off when he had entered the hospital. Now, outside in the crisp night air, away from machines and monitors and the stifling, oppressive heat of the hospital wards, he turned his phone back on and rang Lisa.

"Where are you Kieran?" she said, worry evident in her voice.

"I tried ringing your mobile but it was switched off; I couldn't get through to you at the office, what's happening; what's going on?"

"I'm at the Birmingham General Hospital Lisa."

"Birmingham!" Lisa was shocked. "Birmingham Kieran? What are you doing in Birmingham? Are you all right? What's happened?

"It's Bran." Kieran's voice broke as the emotions overwhelmed him.

"Kieran?" Lisa whispered. "Kieran; what is it, what's happened?

For a few moments, Kieran couldn't speak. He fought to regain some control. At last, he felt composed enough to speak, at last, he found the strength to put into words the thoughts that his mind didn't want to believe.

"Bran's here, in intensive care; Lisa, I think he's going to die."

Kieran hadn't been back in the waiting room long when one of the doctors walked over to him.

"Mister O'Donnell?"

Kieran looked up at the man and nodded, he swallowed nervously.

"Would you like to come with me, Mister O'Donnell?" The doctor smiled. "And I'll try to put you in the picture as far as your brothers' condition is concerned."

He led Kieran to a small office close to the I.C.U. There was a small coffee table and a couple of comfortable chairs and a chipped glass vase with a bunch of slightly wilted flowers in it.

The doctor described Bran's injuries, the fractures to his shoulder, arm and lower leg; the internal injuries; the blood loss caused by the lacerations and massive bruising, but most serious and most worrying was the head injury he had sustained.

"Bran survived the initial injury," the doctor explained. "The first twenty-four hours is always crucial, but the problem now is that Bran is suffering from what we call Cranial Oedema, his brain is swelling. At the moment Bran is in a drug-induced coma so that we can control his breathing, his blood pressure and other functions that may hinder his body's ability to recover."

The doctor watched the young man, wishing he had more positive news to give him, and wondering just how much of this information he was taking in.

"The strain on his system is not being helped by the presence of the multiple injuries his body is having to deal with at the moment."

Kieran looked stunned.

"I wish it was better news," the doctor said. He put his hand on Kieran's shoulder.

"NO!" Kieran said. "No; don't tell me he's going to die, I don't want to hear it!"

The doctor, he was only young, Kieran thought; not much older than Bran, smiled and shook his head.

"No. I'm not going to tell you that your brother is going to die. At the moment, he's holding his own and we are doing everything possible to keep him stable. If he responds to the treatment, he should reach a turning point within the next thirty-six hours."

"And if he doesn't respond to the treatment?" Kieran asked.

The doctor looked across at him, his face sombre.

"If there are any other family members; you might like to arrange for them to be here." He said.

It was five a.m. when Kieran's Peugeot pulled onto the gravel drive at home. He had left the hospital in the early hours of the morning with Staff nurse Owens' promise that Bran would still be there when he got back.

All the lights were on in the house; Pat must still be up. Kieran sat in his car for a few seconds. He didn't really want to see his father at the moment; he didn't know what he would say to him. He killed the lights on the Peugeot and turned off the engine. He climbed wearily out of the car and headed for the kitchen door. He desperately needed a coffee; a coffee and a handful of paracetamol for the raging headache he had!

He opened the door and walked into the warm kitchen. Paul was waiting for him. At the table, his father refused to look up and sat stony-faced and silent.

"Kieran!" Paul pleaded, "for Christ's sake, will you tell me what the hell is going on?"

Kieran sat down heavily on one of the kitchen chairs.

"Ask that bastard!" he said wearily.

Paul shook his head.

"I've not been able to get a word of sense out of him all night! What's going on Kieran?"

Kieran looked up at his younger brother.

"It's Bran." He said, "Bran's in hospital; he's in Intensive Care!"

A look of shocked horror spread across Paul's face.

"Oh, no Kieran! He gasped. "No! I didn't think… I never wanted that!" his eyes were wide, terrified! "They were only supposed to rough him up a bit, frighten him!"

"Paul!" Kieran realised what Paul was thinking. "Paul, Bran was involved in an accident on the M6!" He took hold of his younger brothers' shoulders and shook him slightly to focus his attention on what he was saying.

"It was nothing to do with; …with what happened to Bran the other night! Paul, Bran was in a motorway pile-up; it's not your fault!"

Paul gave a long shuddering sigh, as though he had been holding his breath for a long time.

"What happened Kieran? Is he alright?"

Kieran glanced across at his father; he hadn't spoken or even acknowledged that Kieran was in the room.

"I don't know Paul, Bran's alive, but he has a really bad head injury; he's still unconscious."

"But he'll be OK won't he?" Paul asked.

"Get me a coffee Paul." Kieran said, "and a couple of Paracetamol. I want to get rid of this bastard headache before I have to drive back down to Birmingham."

"I'm coming with you," Paul said.

"We're all going, Paul," Kieran said looking over at his father.

Pat didn't look at Kieran, he just said "You can count me out; I wouldn't set foot in that friggin' hospital! I don't want anything to do with him!"

"Dad?" Paul was heartbroken.

"Dad! It's Bran! … Bran! He's our brother; your son!"

"He's no fucking son of mine!" Pat yelled, and he knocked his chair across the kitchen as he stood up and stormed out of the room.

"Dad?" Paul shouted as he started to follow him.

Kieran put his hand on Paul's arm.

"Let him go, Paul," he said quietly. "I'll talk to him in a few minutes' when he's calmed down; now where's that coffee?"

As Paul was making a pot of coffee, Kieran picked up the phone and rang Lisa at the Radisson Hotel.

Lisa answered the phone straight away.

"I was expecting you to call Kieran," she said. "How is he?"

"Lisa, I know I promised to come over to Belfast with you this weekend, but I can't go… Not until I know if Bran…"

"Of course, not Kieran; I wouldn't expect you to be anywhere other than at his side. Is there anything I can do?"

Kieran thought for a moment. "Would you let Jean know where we are, and there's one other thing you can do Lisa." He said quietly.

"Pray!"

Kieran walked into the study and gently closed the door behind him. Pat was standing by the drinks cabinet, a large glass of Whiskey in his hand.

"I want you to come with us to the hospital Dad."

Pat continued to gaze into space, his expression blank, as he ignored his son's pleas.

Kieran walked towards him.

"All his life, Bran has been there for you, and for me, and for Paul. After the bombing, Bran was the one who held the family together Dad; not you, you were too busy drowning your sorrows; and now, for once in his life he needs us; he needs you!"

Pat O'Donnell drained off the Whiskey and poured himself another large glass.

"He made his fuckin' choice when he crawled into bed with another man!"

Kieran's eyes flashed.

"When mum died; you made your choice, you crawled into a

friggin' bottle!" Kieran nodded towards the glass in his fathers' hand. "And you're still in there!"

Kieran sighed. "Look, you don't have to agree with how Bran's chosen to live his life, but that's his choice; it doesn't affect you!"

"You stupid fuckin' imbecile!" Pat swore, slamming the whiskey glass down on the table.

"Of course, it affects me, and you; do you think Sean Driscoll will let his lass have anything to do with you once he finds out that yer brothers a fuckin poof. Do you think the Driscoll family will want their name associated with the O'Donnell's when they find out the eldest son is a fuckin' shirt lifter?"

Kieran was stunned; was that all that his father was worried about, what other people thought of the precious family name!

"Friggin' hell Dad, that's not important now; what's important is that Bran could be dying and we're standing here arguing about what other people might think?"

"Come with us Dad," Kieran pleaded. "For once, try to be the father that Bran thought you were. For Christ's sake Dad; he's your eldest son!"

"He's no fuckin' son of mine! The dirty bastard can rot in hell for all I care!"

Kieran was stunned, he couldn't believe what he was hearing, and he felt as though he had been punched in the guts. He walked towards the door, "there's one thing for sure; he won't be on his own Dad." As he left, he turned to his father.

"I just hope you can live with what you're doing; and when your time comes, I just hope the Lord has a little more compassion than you have! And that mother; God rest her soul;

will find it in her heart to forgive you, because I certainly can't!" He walked out, leaving the door open behind him and he headed for the kitchen without a backwards glance.

"Get your coat, Paul." he said, "we're leaving."

"Kieran," Paul said as they walked towards the Peugeot, "what about Jason Foster?" Kieran paused. Jason, Bran's partner was worried sick about Bran. He remembered the desperate look on his face when he had called at the office such a short time ago and felt in his inside pocket for the card Jason had given him. He pulled it out and looked at the phone numbers. He handed the card to Paul and nodded.

"Find out where he lives, we'll pick him up on the way."

Paul climbed into the passenger seat and flipped open his mobile phone. Hey keyed in Jason's number; the phone was answered almost immediately.

"Jason? He said. "It's Paul O'Donnell. We've found out where Bran is; he's in a hospital in Birmingham; me and Kieran are just leaving to go down there now; we'll pick you up on our way to the motorway."

Jason was waiting at the entrance to the flats when Kieran pulled into the car park. Paul got out of the car to let Jason climb into the back seat. He noticed how tired and pale he looked; as though he hadn't slept in days.

There was an awkward, almost embarrassed silence as Kieran pulled out onto the main road and headed for the M58.

Jason leaned forward.

"What happened Kieran?" he asked. "Is he badly hurt?"

Kieran didn't answer for a moment; a memory of Bran lying in the hospital bed surrounded by tubes and wires flashed through his thoughts.

"He was in a crash on the motorway Jason; when I saw him he was still unconscious."

"You've seen him!" Relief rushed through Jason's body like a huge wave breaking over a rocky shore. "Oh, Thank God!" He put his hands up to his face. Paul was watching him; he could see the hands; the long, slender, artistic hands, were visibly shaking.

"I was worried that… I'd begun to think that I would never see him again." The faint ghost of a smile appeared on Jason's face.

"He's going to be alright then?"

Paul looked across at Kieran, waiting for him to answer Jason's question. Kieran didn't speak, and the smile slowly faded from Jason's face. The long journey to Birmingham continued in silence.

29

Sean Driscoll collected his overnight bag and walked through the arrivals area of the John Lennon Airport. After speaking to his daughter Lisa, he had caught the first available flight from Belfast.

Lisa was waiting for him at the other side of the barrier and as he walked into the crowded arrivals lounge, she hurried over and wrapped her arms around his neck.

"Thanks for coming Dad." She said, kissing him lightly on the cheek. "I just feel so useless stuck here on my own; I just wish there was some way I could help."

Sean Driscoll looked down at his little girl: Not a little girl anymore but a young woman.

"Kieran has gone back to the hospital," she said. "He was so disappointed that he couldn't come over to Belfast and talk to you about our engagement; he wanted everything to be just right, and now all his plans have been ruined."

Sean smiled. "Your mothers' furious!"

He grinned when he saw the momentary look of doubt flash across Lisa's face.

"She's furious because I'll get to see the ring before she does!"

Lisa smiled and raised her hand, wiggling her fingers so that the light caught the diamond and emeralds causing them to sparkle impressively.

"My little girl's all grown up." Sean kissed her forehead.

"Let's grab a cab and go to your hotel." He placed his arm

around her shoulders and guided her towards the big glass doors. "When I've booked in at the Radisson, I'll ring Pat and see if there's anything they need down at the hospital and find out what we can do to help from this end."

Once outside the airport buildings Sean raised his hand and hailed one of the black cabs. He grinned at Lisa. "Just don't tell Pat that we've used a City Rides taxi!"

The motorway was getting busier as Kieran drove the Peugeot south, towards Birmingham. The strained silence created an uneasy atmosphere amongst the three men in the car. No one knew what to talk about, how to begin a conversation. Paul gazed moodily out of the window; watching nothing in particular, aware vaguely of the green fields changing to grey buildings and then back to green fields, his mind, although he tried so hard to banish the memory, still full of the sounds of laughter the night his 'friends' had followed Bran, his brother, onto the Industrial Park. How later in the bar they had congratulated themselves on 'educating' another poof and sending a message to the other 'gays' who polluted their City.

Paul vaguely wondered what it was going to be next?

Gays; blacks; Jews; anyone who supported Everton? He looked over his shoulder at the man who sat in the back of the car.

Paul remembered another night, another dark empty lane. He had helped to pin this man against the old garage doors while others had ripped his jeans down. He could still hear the taunts.

"You like a bit of bum fun do you? Let's see how you like a size eight boot up yer arse!"

And now Bran, in hospital and Kieran, obviously worried but very tight-lipped. What if Bran was dying? What if the accident had been caused because Bran had been beaten up the night before? If Bran died, it would be his fault!

Kieran opened the car window a fraction and lit a cigarette. He was tired; it had seemed such a long time since he last slept. Snatches of conversations kept running around his head, the doctor. "If there's any family, it might be an idea to get them down here." The policeman. "The van was full of stolen auto parts." Paul, his eyes wide with fright. "They were only supposed to rough him up a bit, frighten him!" and his Dad, his Dad, angry beyond understanding. "He's no son of mine! Dirty bastard can rot in hell for all I care!"

A car horn blared as the Peugeot drifted to the edge of the lane. Kieran shook himself and opened the window a little more. He really should stop and rest for a while, have a hot drink at least. But what if something happened while he was sitting sipping coffee.

He put his foot down on the accelerator and overtook the line of lorries that were heading down the M6 towards the Midlands. There would be time for coffee once he got back to the hospital.

"For God's sake," Kieran said yawning, "will somebody talk to me before I fall asleep at the bloody wheel?"

Paul looked across at his brother.

"What the hell do you want me to say, Kieran. I'm not exactly in the mood for casual chit chat!"

Jason leaned forward a little.

"Do you know how the accident happened?" he asked.

Kieran looked at him briefly in the driver's mirror.

"Not really." He said, "Only that there were two lorries two cars and the van that Bran was driving involved. The driver of one of the cars was killed apparently."

"Do the police know what caused the accident?" Jason continued.

"The motorway police said it looked like one of the cars' blew a front tyre, clipped the other car and the two lorries ran into them; Bran was caught up in the middle somehow." Jason leaned back.

"I remember listening to the news on the telly; about a pile-up on the M6 and someone being killed, but I never thought for a second that Bran might be involved in it!" He gazed out of the window; his thoughts went back to the last time he had seen Bran.

"We argued the night before he went, I was mad at him for being so pig-headed and insisting that he was going to do this job, even though he wasn't fit to drive." He looked accusingly at Paul.

"He was covered in a mass of cuts and bruises, and he had a couple of broken ribs, I'm sure. That old van he was driving was a real wreck with no power steering; he must have been in agony."

Paul said nothing; he just bowed his head. Jason certainly hadn't made him feel any better!

"Bran always was pig-headed." Kieran said. "When we were kids' Bran was the one that told us what to do, what to wear, what to eat; there was no arguing with him then, and it sounds like he hasn't changed!"

"Oh, he changed," Jason said quietly. "He changed a lot when your Dad threw him out!"

30

Sean Driscoll threw his overnight bag down onto the bed in the hotel room. He walked across to the mini bar and poured himself a brandy.

Back in Belfast, He and his wife Pauline had expected a phone call from their daughter after she had cancelled her trip to Italy in order to go back to a cold, dreary Liverpool, so that she could spend some time with Kieran O'Donnell.

They had expected some confirmation of the relationship Lisa and Kieran had formed and were only mildly surprised, but quite delighted, to learn that Kieran had proposed to their daughter. But then, later, when Lisa had rung to say that Bran was in a Birmingham hospital on a life support machine and that Kieran had gone to be with his brother and that she was on her own in the Hotel, Sean had not hesitated. He had booked a seat on the next flight to Liverpool.

Danny could look after the business for a few days; it would be a good exercise for him before he came over to Merseyside to take over the UK based operation.

Sean knew the construction company was in good hands; Danny had a keen business sense and had shown on more than one occasion that he was quite capable of running things in his fathers' absence.

For now, Sean's main concern was for the happiness of his daughter and his future son in law, and he couldn't imagine how his old friend Pat would be feeling, knowing that his eldest son was in so critical a condition. Sean knew that if it were Danny on a life support machine instead of Bran, he would have gone completely to pieces, he couldn't imagine not having Danny by his side.

A gentle tapping at the door interrupted his thoughts. Letting his daughter into the hotel suite, he poured her a coffee and added to it, a splash of the hotels' best brandy. Nursing the cup in her hands, she settled herself into one of the comfortable leather armchairs.

"Do you think they will have reached the hospital yet Dad?" she asked as she sipped the coffee appreciatively.

Sean looked at his watch.

"You said they left for the hospital at about six forty-five? And it's nearly eight o'clock now, with luck, they might miss most of the morning rush hour. We'll ring the hospital in about three-quarters of an hour to see if they've arrived safely; hopefully, there will be some more news of Bran's condition then."

He took the empty cup from her hands and helped her to her feet. "C'mon, hon," he said. "Let's go and have breakfast, then we'll ring the hospital."

Sean tucked into a full English breakfast while Lisa, too worried to eat, pushed a few grapefruit segments around a bowl.

"It's going to be a long day Lisa." Sean smiled, "at least have a slice of toast."

"I wish I'd gone with him," she confided. "At least I would have felt as though I was doing something, it's so frustrating sitting here not knowing what's happening!"

She scraped a little butter across a piece of dry toast and nibbled half-heartedly at one corner before putting it back on the plate.

Sean, ever practical, asked about the taxi business.

"If Kieran and Pat are down in Birmingham, whose running the taxi company?"

Lisa poured herself another cup of tea.

"Kieran asked me to ring Jean, the lady who works for them during the day, to let her know where they are. I thought I would do that after we've spoken to Kieran, hopefully, we can give her some good news about Bran."

Sean reached across the table and put his hand on Lisa's.

"Don't get upset sweetheart," he smiled reassuringly. "A few weeks from now, you'll be wondering what you were so worried about."

Lisa looked up, her eyes swam with unshed tears as she remembered the haunted look on Kieran's face.

He hadn't wanted to leave her alone in a strange city. Torn between two loves he had hesitated.

"Don't be silly." Lisa had said as she kissed him softly.

"Get in your car and go! Now! I'll be here when you get back."

Lisa had waved as Kieran's car had pulled away from the hotel.

Liverpool suddenly seemed very big and very lonely.

Kieran had never been so glad to see the notorious Spaghetti Junction, junction six of the M6. He pulled off the motorway and headed for the city centre. He wasn't tired any more; his heart was racing, and he tried to fight down the feelings of frustration as he made his way slowly through the heavy traffic.

"Get out of the effin' way!" he swore under his breath as though he could make the rush hour traffic move faster by sheer will power alone. It felt as though he had to battle for every yard of road. Even the traffic lights seemed to conspire against him as at every junction he had to queue and wait for the lights to change from red to green. At last the sprawling white buildings of Birmingham General could be seen in the distance, and before long he was pulling into the huge car park.

The corridors of the hospital seemed to stretch on and on as the three young men walked in silence, purposefully following the signs that directed them to I.C.U.

Kieran paused at the big double doors that led into the I.C.U. He seemed to steel himself and take a deep breath before pushing the door and walking in, They washed their hands in the special area set aside for anyone visiting the I.C.U. Kieran led the way, unaware of what he was going to find and very afraid that his journey might have been in vain.

They walked through to the ward sisters' station; it was a different nurse, one that Kieran hadn't seen before.

The ward sister looked up and smiled at Kieran. Behind him, Paul and Jason were trying to look through the glass panels at the rear of the sisters' office to see if they could see any sign of Bran.

"I'm Kieran O'Donnell, how's Bran? Has there been any change?"

"Ah, Mister O'Donnell. staff nurse Owen said you would be back this morning." She stood up and walked round the desk towards the three young men. "Would you like to wait in the relative's room," she said. "The doctor is doing his morning rounds at the moment; as soon as he's finished, I'll get him to come and have a word with you."

Sister Johnson led them towards the family waiting room.

"The doctor won't be long," she said, and she turned to

leave, then paused and turned back to Kieran.

"Oh. Staff nurse Owen said to tell you that she kept her promise!"

Kieran breathed a sigh of relief; staff nurse Gwen Owen had promised him that Bran would still be here when he got back!

The family waiting room was warm and boring with little more than a few comfortable seats and a coffee table with a few well-read magazines scattered across it.

Kieran stretched his tired muscles and with a sigh, settled into one of the armchairs. There was a coffee machine in the corner of the room.

"Get us a coffee Paul," he said yawning.

Paul dug into his jeans pocket and pulled out a handful of loose change, which he fed into the machine. It churned out three cups of frothy coffee.

Picking up two of the cups he turned towards his brother. Kieran was fast asleep, his head resting on the back of the old armchair. He took a step forward, but Jason's voice halted him.

"Let him sleep Paul; God only knows he needs it, you can wake him when the doctor comes."

Paul handed Jason the coffee cup and sat down on the chair opposite Kieran.

"Bran's going to be alright Jason?" Paul said nervously. "He is going to be alright, isn't he?"

A lot of harsh, accusing replies flew through Jason's mind, words that he knew would cut as deeply as the vicious metal rods that Paul and his friends had used on Bran.

Jason said nothing for a while, and then he looked across at the man who was only a few years younger than he was.

"I'm sure he'll be OK, Paul," he said. "I refuse to think of anything other than him being OK."

They sat in silence for a while, sipping the hot coffee. Kieran slept soundly, exhausted by the events of the last forty-eight hours. Paul turned to Jason.

"It was wrong, what we did to you Jason, it was wrong, and I can only say I'm sorry that I had anything to do with it!"

Jason looked at Paul, the anger rising as he thought of Bran lying in a hospital bed.

"You shouldn't be apologising to me Paul," he said. "You should be down on your knees begging your brother's forgiveness."

Paul looked down at the coffee cup in his hands.

"I didn't know they were following Bran," he shook his head. He had tried many times to rid himself of the memories of that night. Every time he closed his eyes, the images of what happened on that dark, cold, industrial park would appear in his mind's eye. "I didn't know till it was too late. There was nothing I could do!" He looked up at Jason for some sort of reassurance; some form of absolution. "Do you think he will ever forgive me?" he asked. Jason looked into Paul's eyes and saw a deep, deep fear in them.

"Paul," he said quietly, "he's your brother."

There was a light tap on the door.

"You'd better wake Kieran," Jason said, as the doctor walked into the room.

Sean Driscoll picked up the phone and dialled the number for Birmingham General. After a while, the phone was answered.

"Intensive Care please!" Sean said; he was very business-like and authoritative. After a moment he was put through to the ward sister's office. It was sister Johnson who answered the phone.

"As well as can be expected." Was the frustrating reply to his enquiries about Bran O'Donnell's condition.

"Mister O'Donnell is stable but still remains in a serious condition." She said when pressed by Sean.

"Look," Sean said. "My future son-in-law Kieran O'Donnell and his father Patrick O'Donnell are both at the hospital; would it be possible to speak to one of them? My daughter, Lisa is worried sick about her fiancé, is there a phone that I can be put through to, so that I can speak to one of them?"

Sister Johnson paused for a moment.

"Well, I can put you through to the relatives waiting room." She said, "But Mister O'Donnell's father isn't here; only his brother Kieran." Sean was puzzled.

"Only Kieran?" he asked. "Are you sure Bran's father Patrick O'Donnell isn't with him?"

"I'll put you through to the waiting room." Sister Johnson said. "You can ask him yourself. Kieran O'Donnell came with two other young men and I'm sure neither of them was Bran O'Donnell's father."

Paul gently shook his brother. It took Kieran a few moments to remember where he was, and then he saw the doctor. It was the same young doctor he had spoken to on his last visit.

The doctor sat down on the coffee table; it groaned alarmingly but he was unconcerned. He had sat on this table many times to talk to worried friends and relatives who waited to hear news of their loved ones. Sometimes it was good news and he could bring hope and blessed relief from the nightmare of worry and fear that so many in this room experienced, but sometimes the news was not so good, and he would take the family through to a private room where a counsellor would be waiting to help break the news that would devastate so many lives.

He looked round at the three worried faces.

"Was Mister O'Donnell senior, not able to come?" he asked.

Kieran shook his head.

"No," he said simply, not wanting to get into a discussion as to why his father wasn't with them.

"How's Bran, has there been any change?"

"He's still in a coma, but we've started to reduce the medication slightly; Bran has had a CT. scan and an M.R.I. scan and both proved inconclusive. That means there was nothing obviously causing the Oedema; - the swelling," he said as he saw the questioning looks on their faces. "The initial head injury was caused by impact, either his head hitting the windscreen or part of the load he was carrying hitting the back of his head, it's difficult to tell, but the lacerations to the area of his Parietal and frontal bones would suggest it was the windscreen. At first, we thought there might have been some tearing of the coronal suture, that's the fixed joint between the bones but luckily, the scans didn't show anything." He paused,

"Is Bran going to be alright?" Jason asked, taking the opportunity to ask the question that had been on his lips since they arrived.

The young doctor looked at Jason,

"He's not out of the woods' yet," He said, "but it appears that the medication has begun to take down the swelling. All we can do now is wait and see; we are reducing the drugs we are giving him to keep him in a coma. All we can hope for is that there has been no lasting damage done and that he will come out of the coma on his own."

"How long could that take?" Kieran asked. The doctor shrugged his shoulders'.

"It's impossible to tell," he said gently, "it could be within a couple of hours, or it could take days, or longer, the brain is a funny thing, but it has tremendous powers of recovery; as long as nothing serious has occurred that we cant detect, he should make a pretty good recovery.

"And what if something serious has occurred?" Jason asked. The doctor paused again.

"If that were the case; and we have no reason to believe that anything serious has gone wrong; if that were the case, then the chances are that he would never regain consciousness."

"Can you not give him something to bring him out of the coma?" Paul asked.

The doctor shook his head. "No, I'm afraid not; there are no drugs that will shorten the length of a coma; it will take time, time and his own bodies ability to heal itself."

"Can we stay with him?" Kieran asked. The doctor nodded.

"There shouldn't be a problem," he said. "Just check with the Ward Sister, she may ask that you restrict the number of people when they are busy and she will ask you to leave when the doctors are doing their rounds."

"Can we go in to see him now?" Jason asked.

The doctor nodded and stood up as he prepared to leave.

"He's still heavily sedated," he said, "don't expect any sign of recognition."

Kieran and Jason walked towards the door, following the doctor. Paul hung back.

"C'mon, Paul!" Kieran said. Paul shook his head "No Kieran, you go; I don't want to see him like that, I don't want to see Bran wired up to machines and things." He sat down in the armchair. "I'll wait here; you can come and tell me when he comes round."

Kieran put his hand on his young brother's shoulder.

"He'll be OK Paul, he'll be OK!" and he followed Jason through to the I.C.U.

Sister Johnson was just about to put the call through to the waiting room when she saw Kieran and Jason walk into the I.C.U.

"Just one moment Mister Driscoll," she said. "Mister Kieran O'Donnell has just walked into the unit, I'll get him to have a quick word with you." she beckoned Kieran over to her office while Jason and the doctor walked towards bed seven where Bran lay unconscious.

Reluctantly, Kieran walked over to the Sisters' office.

"Mister O'Donnell," Sister Johnson said holding the phone in her hand, her palm over the mouthpiece. "There's a Mister Driscoll on the line, he says he would like a word with you; do you want to speak to him?"

"Sean Driscoll?" Kieran said, puzzled. "Yes, of course." He reached for the phone. Why was Sean ringing him from Belfast? Lisa must have told him what had happened.

"Please don't be too long Mister O'Donnell," Sister Johnson said. "I really should transfer this call through to the relatives' room."

Kieran took the phone, desperately hoping that Lisa was all right.

"Sean?" he said, wondering what was so important that he would call him here, in the Intensive Care Unit.

"Kieran, I was getting worried, the nurse said you were there on your own, that Pat wasn't with you. Is he alright, has something happened?"

Kieran's heart sank; of course, Sean would automatically assume that Pat was at the hospital with them.

"He's not here Sean." He said.

"What do you mean – He's not there?"

"Just that Sean, he wouldn't come with us."

The ward sister was hovering at Kieran's elbow, obviously keen for him to keep the conversation short and he was very aware that Jason and the doctor were with Bran, "Give me your phone number Sean." Kieran said. "I'll ring you back in ten minutes."

Kieran scribbled down the number.

"That's a Liverpool number Sean?" he said as it dawned on him that Sean was not in Belfast.

"Mister O'Donnell, please…" the sister reminded Kieran.

"Look, I've got to go Sean; I'll ring you back in ten." And he handed the phone back to Sister Johnson.

"Thanks." He smiled and he walked over to join Jason and the Doctor who were with Bran.

Sean Driscoll put the phone down slowly. That was strange, he thought; where could Pat O'Donnell be?

"Kieran's going to ring us back in ten minutes," he said in

reply to Lisa's questioning look. "He said Pat wasn't with them at the hospital."

"Not at the hospital?" Lisa asked. "If he's not at the hospital; I wonder if he's at the taxi office.

Sean picked up the phone again and dialled the number he had for O'Donnell's Taxis. Something wasn't right, he had been able to tell from the tone of Kieran's voice and the way he had hesitated before he had answered Sean's question.

The phone was answered almost immediately. A female voice said brightly "O'Donnell's Taxis, how can we help you?" it was Jean, the daytime radio operator and receptionist.

"Hello Jean; it's Sean Driscoll, can I speak to Pat please?"

Jean paused for a second. "Oh, hello mister Driscoll, I'm sorry, Pat's not arrived yet; he and Kieran don't usually get in till around lunchtime, do you want to leave a message?"

Sean looked at Lisa, he was a little disconcerted; Jean obviously knew nothing about Bran being in hospital or that Kieran was in Birmingham. He looked pleadingly at Lisa.

"Will you have a word with Jean?" he asked. "You can probably tell her about Bran and explain the situation much better than I can!" He handed the phone over to Lisa.

Lisa took the phone from him with a 'thanks Dad!' expression on her face.

"Jean? It's Lisa. Kieran asked me to ring you, there's been some news about his brother Bran."

A few minutes later when Lisa had explained why Kieran wouldn't be in the office that day and had given 'Auntie Jean' the number of the hospital, Lisa put the phone down and turned to Sean. She was a puzzled as her father.

"Pat isn't at the office, and Jean says she doesn't think that he's at home either because she rang there half an hour ago when she first got into work and there was no answer. She had thought that he and Kieran would probably be out together somewhere."

Lisa, Like Sean, couldn't understand why Pat O'Donnell wasn't at Birmingham General, and if he wasn't there, where was he?

Kieran sat on a chair next to bed seven. Bed seven, the bed in which his brother lay motionless, the victim of a horrific motorway crash. Bran had always said that seven was his lucky number; Kieran prayed that it proved to be lucky this time.

He looked across Bran's still form, at the other side of the bed sat Jason Foster; the man Bran lived with; his brother's partner, his brother's lover!

Jason looked shocked, his face ashen, as he nervously bit his bottom lip, his eyes glued on Bran's face, desperately looking for some flicker; some sign that Bran was climbing out of that dark place he was in.

The doctor had explained that it might be days before there was any sign of a recovery.

"Talk to him," the doctor had suggested. "Lots of patients, when they come out of the coma, say that they knew there was someone with them, even though they showed no signs of it."

Kieran had noticed that Jason hadn't said anything to Bran and realised that he probably couldn't say the things he wanted to say, while someone else was there.

"You stay with him Jason," Kieran said, "I have to go and make a phone call." He walked back into the relatives' waiting room. Paul leapt to his feet as his brother walked through the door.

"How is he, Kieran?" he asked.

"Why don't you go through and see him?"

Paul shook his head. "I can't Kieran, not yet, I want to see him smiling; telling me it's OK and that he forgives me." Paul's hands were shaking and for the first time, Kieran realised just how much Bran's accident was affecting their younger brother.

"What if he doesn't get better Kieran? People stay in comas for years." Paul looked lost, frightened. "If he doesn't get better it will be because of me. It's all my fault! I screwed up and it's Bran who's paying for it."

"Paul." Kieran put his hand on his brothers' shoulder. "Bran was in a motorway pile-up, he's here because the van he was driving was hit by a fuckin' big lorry!"

"And if he'd been one hundred per cent fit, if he hadn't been beaten unconscious the night before?"

"You couldn't have done anything. You said there were too many of them."

Paul looked up into his brothers' face, his eyes haunted by memories.

"Do you think." He said, his voice no more than a whisper, "that if it had been the other way round, and I'd been the one being beaten up, that Bran would have sat in the car and done nothing?"

"It's not your fault, Paul," Kieran sighed tiredly. "Bran would be the first one to tell you that."

He dug into his jeans pocket and pulled out a handful of coins. He unfolded the piece of paper with Sean's telephone number written on it and sat down beside the pay phone.

"Get me a coffee, Paul," he yawned. "I think the last one

went cold!" and he dialled the number on the slip of paper.

Sean answered the phone almost immediately.

"Kieran! I was starting to worry, what's happening, how's Bran?"

"Still unconscious Sean, the doctors' have told us that we just have to wait now, and hope that he comes out of it on his own. He was pretty badly knocked about and he has a couple of broken bones and some internal injuries and he lost a lot of blood, but the doctors have got that stabilised now. It's just this bloody head injury…"

"If there's anything you need Kieran." Sean offered. "Anything at all, equipment, specialists – anything! You know you only need to pick up the phone; money is no object…"

"Thanks, Sean, it's much appreciated." He paused while he took a mouthful of the hot coffee Paul had put down by his side. "Is Lisa there Sean?" he asked.

Sean smiled and handed the phone over to his daughter.

"Are you alright Kieran?"

"I'm OK Hon' I was worried about you being on your own in Liverpool; I'm glad your Dad's there with you; it's not exactly how I planned celebrating our engagement you know!"

"Don't worry," Lisa said softly, "when Bran comes home, we'll have a double celebration!"

"Of course, we will honey; biggest effin' party you've ever seen, I promise."

Kieran glanced over at Paul who was staring wide-eyed at his brother.

"Engagement?" he whispered. Kieran nodded, grinning.

"Can I talk to your Dad Lisa?" he asked and just before Lisa handed the phone to her father, she heard Kieran say "Love you, honey."

"Now tell me," Sean continued, "What were you saying about Pat? Why isn't he at the hospital with you?"

"He wouldn't come with us Sean; you know that Bran's not living at home anymore?"

"Yes; Lisa did tell me."

"Did she tell you that Bran and Dad had a blazing row and that Dad threw Bran out? And now he refuses to have anything to do with him; even when he thought that he might not make it."

"Some of it," Sean said quietly.

"Did Lisa tell you why?" Kieran asked; his heart thumping, what if Pat was right, what if Sean Driscoll felt the same way as his Dad about gays', what if he said he wasn't having a 'gay' connected to 'his' family. Sean seemed to be taking a long time to answer. Kieran wondered if he was thinking of a polite way to tell him to get the fuck out of his daughters' life.

"Lisa told me she had her suspicions," Sean said.

"Well, she wasn't wrong Sean, Bran's gay!" Kieran wondered what the reaction had been when Lisa had dropped that bombshell in Sean's lap. Was that the reason Sean Driscoll had flown over to Liverpool, to whisk his daughter back to Ireland before the family became too tainted with the stain of homosexuality!

"How do you feel about it, Kieran?" Sean's question came as quite a surprise. Kieran had to pause and take a few moments to think about that. How did he feel about Bran having a relationship with a man? Had it really made much difference to how he felt about his brother?

"I didn't want to believe it at first Sean, Bran has always been the big brother I looked up to; the big brother I wanted to be like.

"And now?" Sean asked.

"He'll always be my brother Sean, and I'll always be there for him, no matter what; I owe him that much."

"I take it Pat doesn't feel the same way?"

Kieran laughed.

"That's an understatement, Dad felt betrayed, cheated: he took it like some sort of personal insult. Like Bran was a dirty stain on the O'Donnell name; a tainted part that had to be scrubbed out; got rid of before anyone found out! He thought he would lose his friends if anyone knew, he thought you wouldn't want anything more to do with the O'Donnell family once you found out."

"So, Pat's still at home, here in Liverpool?"

"I assume so; probably working his way through the drinks cabinet. That's where he's been most of the time since mum died; in the bottom of a friggin' bottle!"

"Are you on your own down there?" Sean asked.

"No," Kieran replied. "Paul's here – and Bran's partner, Jason."

"Go back to your brother, Kieran," Sean said. "Don't worry about things here, Lisa and I will help out where we can and I'll ring again tonight."

The phone went dead and Kieran replaced the handset.

"Engagement?" Paul said again. "Friggin' 'ell Kieran, when did all this take place?"

"I'll tell you later." Kieran said yawning, "but right now I want to get back to Bran; won't you come with me, Paul?"

Paul shook his head. "Perhaps later." He said and as Kieran walked out, Paul sat down by the phone; once again lost in his own thoughts.

Sean put the phone down and turned to Lisa.

"Honey," he said. "I need to go out for a while, will you be alright here on your own?"

Lisa looked up questioningly.

"Can't I come with you Dad?" she asked. Sean smiled down at her; for once the appealing looks and beseeching tones weren't going to sway her father.

"Not this time Lisa, I'll be back later."

Sean headed down to the hotel reception. On the way he took out his mobile phone and rang O'Donnell's Taxis it was Jean who answered the phone.

"Jean, it's Sean Driscoll; can you arrange for a taxi to pick me up at the Radisson and take me round to Pat's."

"I've tried ringing him again Mister Driscoll." Jean sounded worried. "But there's no reply."

"Don't worry; I'll find him."

Sean walked out of the hotel and within a couple of minutes, the O'Donnell's Taxi had arrived. It pulled smoothly up to the big glass entrance doors.

"Are you Mister Driscoll?" the driver asked. Sean nodded and climbed into the front passenger seat of the cab.

"You want taking down to Pat O'Donnell's place?" Again, Sean nodded; his mind was turmoil. Was Pat really so hung up about what other people thought that he would sacrifice his eldest son? Was he really prepared to throw away the best part of his life because of a set of outdated values?

The taxi moved steadily through the busy afternoon traffic, like any big City, Liverpool had a pulse; the fast roads and dusty streets, the veins and arteries that carried the lifeblood that was the commerce of the city. Sean never tired of city life, and as he gazed out at the bustling crush of people going about their daily lives, he realised just how full of life he felt and how lucky he was to be living the exciting life he did, how lucky he was to have the family he had; the family that loved and supported him. Liverpool was so alive so virile; it had an energy all of its own. He knew he had made the right decision when he had decided to base his European developments in this city.

Liverpool was a new adventure, a new path and one that he would enjoy travelling with his son Danny.

His thoughts turned to Pat O'Donnell and his son Bran. What on earth was Pat thinking of!

The taxi driver interrupted Sean's thoughts.

"You're a friend of Pat's, aren't you?" he asked hesitantly.

"Yes; known Pat O'Donnell for years," he smiled.

"Is it true?" the driver said tentatively. "Is it true what they are saying about Bran?"

Sean was very wary. "It depends what they're saying about Bran." He said guardedly.

"Some of the cabbies have been talking." The driver continued. "You know how taxi drivers are real gossips. Well, they heard on the news that there had been a big pile-up just outside Birmingham and that someone had been killed." He paused. "They were saying they had heard that it was Bran who had been killed in the crash?"

Sean leant back in his seat.

"Bran was involved in that pile-up," he said. "He was badly

hurt, but he's not dead."

"Thank God for that!" The driver said, his relief obvious. "Good bloke Bran; always straight up with the other drivers. Never could understand why he jacked in taxi driving 'cos he really enjoyed it." He swung the taxi into the lane that led to the O'Donnell residence. "Must have been a good job to pull him away from the family firm." The taxi pulled into the drive, the gravel crunching beneath the tyres.

"I'll put this on your account, Mister Driscoll," the driver said as Sean got out of the taxi. "Glad to hear Bran's OK and I'm sure the other lads will be as well."

Sean took a five-pound note from his wallet and handed it to the driver.

"Thanks, Mister Driscoll!" the driver said grinning as he pocketed the unexpected tip.

Sean nodded and turned towards the house. Behind him, the taxi pulled smoothly out into the lane and disappeared towards Liverpool centre, leaving Sean standing alone in the drive. There was no sign of life from the house.

Sean squared his shoulders and walked purposefully towards the front door.

He walked up the three shallow steps and stood beneath the porch, wondering what sort of a reception he would get from his old friend.

He raised his hand and pressed the doorbell.

31

Kieran sat down on the chair next to the bed where his brother lay motionless, his life depending on the machines and equipment that surrounded them. He looked at the man who was sitting opposite. Jason looked tired; he probably hadn't had a decent sleep in days.

"Why don't you have a break, Jason?" Kieran suggested. "I'll stay here with Bran for a while if you want to get a coffee or something to eat."

Jason didn't say anything; he just shook his head and continued his vigil by Bran's side; gazing all the time at his face, praying that will power alone would somehow incite a response.

"Jason, you won't do Bran any good if you make yourself ill."

Jason looked up at Kieran.

"He needs me Kieran; where else would I be?"

How long they sat, just watching the man who meant so much to both of them, Kieran didn't know, but it was the ward sister who eventually came over and asked if they would mind leaving for a little while as the doctor was about to make his rounds.

They walked back to the relatives' room; Paul stood as they walked through the door, his face anxious for news.

"They want us out while the doctors do their rounds," he said tiredly. "I'm going out for a fag." He slipped on his leather jacket and checked the pockets for his cigarettes and lighter and without another word, he walked out of the door and headed for the hospital entrance.

Jason walked over to the coffee machine and bought himself a cup of black coffee. He eased himself into one of the cosy armchairs and sat in silence, his thoughts drifted back to the day when Bran had come home so happy, so full of bitter, sweet emotions' because he had, at last, 'come out' to his father and told him he was gay, even though it had meant that he was no longer welcome in the family home or business. Then the elation turned to depression as Bran began to realise that barriers were being put in the way of him gaining employment with any of the other taxi firms. The word had gone out that Pat O'Donnell didn't want his son working the streets for any other company. His father hadn't wanted it known that he had a 'gay' son!

At first, Bran had refused to believe what was pretty obvious to Jason. Pat O'Donnell had found yet another way to screw up his son's life. It was only when one small company who were advertising for drivers refused to employ Bran that it finally sank home.

"Nothing personal O'Donnell." The owner had said, "but I'd really rather not get on the wrong side of your old man!"

Bran's father was prepared to go to quite some lengths to ensure that no one found out about the O'Donnell families' dirty little secret!

"Is there no change Jason?" Paul asked eventually, unable to stand the long drawn out silence any longer.

Jason shook his head tiredly and then looked up at the young man who desperately wanted to hear some good news about his brother.

How old would he be? Jason thought to himself, seventeen? Eighteen?

Jason knew only too well from personal experience, just how tough University life could be if you didn't 'fit in' or 'follow the crowd'. Paul had got in with the wrong crowd, a crowd that consisted of wasters, boy racers and petty thieves. Almost as if he had read Jason's mind, Paul reached into an inside pocket and pulled out two items, Bran's mobile phone and his wallet.

"I got them back," he said, offering them to Jason, "but the money was gone."

Jason took the two familiar items and turned them over and over in his hands. How many times had he talked to Bran on this mobile, how many times had he watched Bran push this wallet into his back pocket, Jason opened the wallet, the money had indeed gone, but at least Bran's credit cards and bank cards all seemed to be accounted for.

"They were going to hurt him… really hurt him! Someone had a knife; it was like a nightmare Jason, I've never been so afraid, I didn't know what to do." Paul was wringing his hands as though subconsciously trying to clean off the memories of that night.

"I made them think someone was coming, it was the only thing I could think of, and I went with them, Jason. I went with them and left Bran lying in the road not knowing how badly hurt he was or even if he was alive or dead."

Jason looked at Paul, he felt he should say something to reassure Bran's younger brother, but the memory of Bran collapsing in his arms, following the vicious beating he had received at the hands of Paul's friends, still prevented him from offering the words of forgiveness that Paul was craving.

Instead, he turned away and picked up the cup of lukewarm coffee he had left on the table. He was just about to ask Paul if he wanted a hot drink when the door opened and Kieran walked in, followed by the doctor.

Kieran looked drained, but the doctor seemed quite relaxed.

"Has there been any change?" Jason asked.

The young doctor sat on the edge of the squeaky coffee table.

"We've taken Bran off the ventilator," he said, "and he's breathing on his own now. - But," he said as he saw the look of obvious relief spread across Jason's face, "Bran is finding it a little difficult to breathe and he will struggle for a short time until the sedative completely leaves his system, but his condition is being very carefully monitored and we will intervene if he gets into serious trouble. I just wanted you to know before you went back in as it can be a little bit distressing for relatives if you don't realise what's happening."

"But his breathing will get easier won't it?" Jason asked.

The doctor smiled.

"Yes, it should stabilise within a couple of hours, then we'll just have to hope that his level of consciousness will increase as well." The doctor looked at his watch. "You can go back in now," he said, "and if you have any questions, I'll be in the hospital for another four hours, the ward sister will know where to find me if you need me," And with a slight nod of his head, he got up and left the room.

Sean Driscoll pressed the doorbell again; he raised his fist, about to rap on the glass panel when the door swung inward.

"Who the hell...?"

Pat O'Donnell halted mid-sentence, quite shocked to see his old friend Sean Driscoll standing on his doorstep. He looked bleary-eyed and dishevelled, he hadn't shaved for a while and Sean could smell the whiskey on his breath.

"Are you going to invite me in, Pat?" Sean asked, "or are you going to keep me standing on the doorstep all day?"

"Sean? I thought you'd gone back to Belfast. What are you doing here?"

"Well if I can come in, Pat, I'll tell you?"

Pat threw open the door.

"Where are me manners?" Pat said, stepping back from the door.

"Come in Sean, come in won't you!" Pat walked down the hall, staggering slightly.

"Come in Sean; me old mate! This calls for a drink!"

Pat made his unsteady way to the kitchen and Sean followed. On the kitchen table, a half-empty bottle of whiskey stood next to a full tumbler. The kitchen was a mess, coffee mugs gathered, unwashed on every surface, half-empty packets and tins sat discarded next to the cooker hob and dirty crockery was stacked in the sink. The usually warm kitchen was quite chilly. Sean walked over to the Aga and put his hand on the now cold metal surface.

"Your Aga's gone out." He commented. Pat picked up the tumbler and drained half of it.

"Never did understand how the damn thing worked," he said. "Always left that to…" he didn't finish the sentence.

"It's warm in the study." He said, grasping the neck of the whiskey bottle "and a bit more comfortable than this shit hole!"

He led the way unsteadily through to the other room and pouring two more ample measures of whiskey, handed one to Sean, then sank gratefully into one of the big comfy leather armchairs.

"To old times." He said, raising his glass.

"Old times." Sean raised his glass and drank the toast with the friend he had known since he first set foot on the big container ship in Belfast. Sean had lost contact with Pat when he left Belfast and took his boys to Liverpool; that had been so many years ago; he looked at the man who sat in front of him now. Those years had not been kind to Pat O'Donnell. Sean remembered Pat when he had worked the container ships, and later when he had fought in the Belfast boxing tournaments, and he had won more than one bare-knuckle fight in his time as well.

Now, looking far older than his years, his grey hair was lank and unkempt, his face unshaven and he was hanging on to the nearly empty whiskey bottle as though his life depended on it! Sean wondered sadly what had happened, had the loss of his wife Cathleen really caused such a dramatic, devastating change in Patrick O'Donnell.

"I didn't think you would be back in Liverpool for a while Sean, what's brought you back so soon?" Pat asked. He reached over with the whiskey bottle and offered Sean another drink.

"A couple of reasons, Pat," he said, at the same time moving his glass out of Pat's reach. "I wanted to talk to your lad about this engagement, and I want to look for some suitable property to set up an office here in Liverpool.

"Eh Sean, I was so pleased when I heard that Kieran and your lass had hit it off; he's a fine lad Sean, a fine lad. He'll make Lisa a fine husband."

"I thought you had your heart set on Bran being the first of your boys to take a wife?"

Pat moved uncomfortably in his seat and made a disgusted huffing noise. He had been trying hard not to think about his eldest son for the last couple of days. Why couldn't he have just simply been killed in that accident, it would have solved a lot of problems.

A shiver ran through Pat O'Donnell, as though someone had walked over his grave; he automatically crossed himself; that was a terrible thing to think!

"I'd prefer not to talk about him Sean; he's gone! He's not part of this family anymore."

"Well if Kieran marries Lisa, Bran will be part of my family," Sean said quietly. "He will be Lisa's brother in law."

Pat shook his head and tipped the contents of the whiskey tumbler into his mouth.

"Believe me, Sean, it would be better if you just forget that he was ever part of this family, you don't want to be associated with the likes of him!"

Sean sat back and watched Pat; he was quite shocked at the look of loathing that crossed his face. Pat poured himself another large whiskey. It was as though he was trying to rid himself of a bad memory or to get rid of a bad taste in his mouth.

"Tell me, Pat," Sean asked, "how long is it now since Cathleen died?"

The question shook him, Sean could see that; the colour ran out of Pat's cheeks and the whiskey in the glass spilt as his hand trembled.

"Why in Gods' name would you want to bring that up? Cathleen's dead and gone," his tone was angry; what was Sean doing reminding him of Cathleen, reminding him of the wonderful woman who had been taken from him; reminding him of the daughter he never knew.

"Cathleen will never be gone Pat," Sean continued, "She'll never be gone as long as you have Bran and Kieran and Paul to remind you of her."

"Don't speak his name in the same breath as hers!" Pat snarled, "every time I hear his name, I think of her; every time I saw his face I saw Cathleen! Every time I looked into his eyes, I saw Cathleen's eyes!" Pat stood up and walked angrily around the room.

"Then why are you trying to drive him out of your life Pat, why are you trying to destroy something that is so much like his mother?"

"You wouldn't understand, you didn't know what it was like; he was there, all the time, reminding me of what I'd lost and it was his fault; he was to blame,"

Even clouded by time and befuddled by the large amounts of whiskey he had drunk, Pat could still remember clearly the last time he had seen his beloved Cathleen; he could still hear her laughing voice with its soft Irish lilt.

"I'm going into the city centre," she had said, smiling, "a bit of Christmas shopping, Bran wants me to buy something for him."

Cathleen only went to the shopping mall that afternoon because he asked her to go. He wanted her to buy him something from the mall, a Christmas present for someone. If he hadn't asked her to go to the shopping mall, she would still be alive!

"She was running around after him! Like she always did, buying his effin' Christmas presents for him!"

Sean sighed. He remembered that Christmas well. Tragedy had struck too many families that year.

"Cathleen had gone to the Mall to collect the watch she was buying you for Christmas, she had asked me if I thought you would like a gold pocket watch, one with a nice long chain that would hang across your waistcoat. Bran had been saving his pocket money all year to buy you a gold fob to go on the end of the chain. A solid gold anchor to remind you of the time you spent at sea."

A small jolt ran through Pat's mind. How many times had he seen the key fob on Bran's car keys, the gold anchor, he had often wondered where it had come from; Bran must have kept it all these years!

"How do you think Bran felt?" Sean said quietly, "thinking that his mother had died because she had gone into town to pick up the watch fob for him!"

Sean couldn't tell if his words were actually sinking in through the alcoholic fug that surrounded Pat. "Bran puts up with all the grief and the shit you give him because he thinks he deserves it; he blames himself for Cathleen's death, that's why he tried to take her place, tried to make up for Kieran and Paul not having a mother to turn to. That I.R.A. bomb too away more than Cathleen's life, it took away Bran's life as well!"

Staff nurse Gwen Owen walked out of the sisters' office into the I.C.U. The doctors had finished their rounds and the patient in bed seven was her responsibility for the night.

Bran O'Donnell had been taken off the respirator and was breathing on his own; the drugs that had been repressing his natural breathing response were almost completely out of his system now. The plastic tube that had supplied his lungs with oxygen had been removed and had been replaced by a small tube under his nose that delivered a regular flow of oxygen to support his breathing.

Gwen checked the monitors again; his breathing was a little

shallow and erratic so she increased the oxygen supply just a little.

"Come on, Bran," she said as she watched his body try to cope with the loss of the support it had relied on over the last couple of days. "You have to try a bit harder; it'll get easier in a little while."

Gwen looked up as two young men walked over to the bed in station seven. She recognised Kieran at once; Bran's brother had been the first to arrive after Bran's identity had been discovered; Gwen didn't recognise the other young man. He looked nothing like the three O'Donnell brothers and she guessed, quite rightly, that this was probably Bran's partner.

They sat on either side of the bed, keeping a silent vigil. They both looked tired and Gwen wondered how long it had been since either of them had slept.

"Have you booked yourselves into a hotel room yet?" she asked. Kieran shook his head. Jason looked up, quite startled.

"How long…" he began to ask.

"Look, I know you want to be here all the time." Gwen said, being very practical, "but it could be a little while before Bran regains consciousness. If you had a room near the hospital, you could at least go and get a couple of hours sleep and a shower and a shave," Kieran put his hand up to his chin, his two days growth of stubble must be pretty obvious by now. "You could take it in turns to have a break for a few hours, there's a good hotel less than a mile from the hospital, if there was any change, you could be back here in minutes."

Jason shook his head emphatically.

"I can get a bit of sleep in the waiting room when the doctors are doing their rounds; I'll book into the hotel when Bran's awake and I know he's going to be OK."

Gwen put her hand on his shoulder.

"You might be able to sleep here, but you certainly won't be able to shower, and I bet neither of you has a change of clothes with you?"

Kieran wondered if that was a subtle hint, and as Staff Nurse Owen walked away, he sniffed tentatively at his armpit; she had a point!

"Bran always used to complain about my smelly socks," Kieran said, he looked up at Jason and smiled. "Do you think it would bring him round if I waved one of them under his nose?"

Jason smiled; it was the first time he had smiled in days.

"I think if I took my trainers off at this moment, I would empty the hospital, let alone the intensive care unit!"

"Perhaps the nurse is right," Kieran suggested. "Perhaps a hotel room would be a good idea."

Jason shook his head,

"When Bran's conscious Kieran, when I know he's going to be alright, then I'll think about hotel rooms.

Kieran sat back, he closed his eyes for a moment and listened to the banks of machines bleeping and humming, they were almost hypnotic; in the background, Bran's shallow erratic breathing kept him focused as he listened to every breath.

The minutes ticked on and became hours and the waiting continued.

32

"When are you going to accept that Cathleen's gone, Pat?" Sean said quietly. "She would have hated to see the family broken up like this; she would have wanted you to look after them Pat, but from what I've been hearing, you expected them to run round after you, you expected Bran to look after his brothers while you wallowed in self-pity!"

"It's got fuck all to do with you, Sean," Pat said angrily. "Nobody asked you to get involved!"

"That's where you're wrong Pat." Sean's quiet voice was insistent. "Your future daughter in law asked me to get involved; and in case you've forgotten, Kieran is not only my future son in law he is also my Godson!"

Sean stood up and walked over to the chair where Pat was sitting cradling the glass of whiskey.

"When I agreed to be Kieran's Godfather, Cathleen made me promise that I would keep an eye on her boys, look out for them, make sure that they were OK. Especially Bran, because she knew he was special, she knew he wasn't the rough Irish bucko his father wanted him to be, he had a quiet, gentle side, a side that she tried so hard to hide from you because she felt you would be disappointed in him. Disappointed in the young lad who worshipped his father and tried so hard to please him, nothing he ever did was quite good enough was it Pat?"

He nodded towards the glass Pat was holding, "and now when he needs you; needs his Dad, you bury your head in the effin' whiskey bottle again!" Sean took the whiskey glass out of Pat's hand and put it down on the table.

"He's your son Pat, your eldest son, your firstborn; you should be at his side, Cathleen would want you to be there, holding the family together, not leaving all this to Kieran; leaving all this on the shoulders of a lad who's only just out of his teens!"

Pat shook his head; he couldn't look Sean in the eye.

"You wouldn't say that if you knew what I know Sean. What I'm doing is for Kieran; for his future!"

"Oh, for Christ's sake!" Sean exploded. "Now you are going to blame Kieran for your mistakes; can't you see! You're going to do to Kieran what you did to Bran, shifting the blame to someone else isn't going to change things, Pat. If it comes to the worst, are you going to tell Kieran that it was his fault that you didn't go and make peace with your dying son!"

"It's not Kieran's fault," Pat said. "It's Bran's fault, he ruined everything; it was Bran who dirtied his mother's memory and brought shame to the O'Donnell name; if you knew Sean..."

"Knew what Pat?" Sean asked, he put his hands on his hips and sighed deeply. "Knew that Bran was gay?"

The colour drained from Pat O'Donnell's face, he felt as if his old friend had just hit him. He desperately looked round for the glass of whiskey, but Sean had moved it. Sean reached across and handed Pat the glass. Pat's hands were shaking as he raised the glass to his lips.

"I suppose you'll be calling off the wedding then?" Pat threw back the remainder of the whiskey; he couldn't look at Sean, he was afraid of what he would see in his face.

"Is that what this is all about Pat?" Sean said quietly as he sat down on the chair opposite his old friend.

"Worried about what people will think if they find out you

have a son who is homosexual?"

"The O'Donnell's are an old Irish Catholic family Sean," Pat said shaking his head sadly. "Their history goes back hundreds of years!"

"History is the past Pat," Sean said. "It's gone and there's a lot of Irish history that is best forgotten."

Sean pulled out his wallet and flipped it open. He pulled out a photograph and handed it to Pat.

"That's the future Pat, our children and the grandchildren that will come after them!"

It was a family group, taken when Danny, Sean's son, graduated from University. At either end of the group of five people were Lisa and Sean's wife Pauline, next to Lisa was a very proud Sean and next to him, dressed in his graduation gown and cap was Danny, looking extremely sophisticated and very intellectual.

"Who's that?" Pat asked, pointing to the tall good-looking young man who was standing between Danny and Pauline, his arm draped affectionately around Pauline's shoulders.

"That," Sean said, "is Michael – Danny's partner!"

33

The doctors' rounds had just finished. Kieran, Jason and Paul waited expectantly in the relatives' room, sitting around the room were a few other people, and they were also waiting for news of relatives and loved ones.

The young doctor, a neurologist, who was managing Bran's case walked over to the three worried young men, he wished he had more positive news for them but all he could offer was that there had been no change and once again, all he could say was wait and see.

"Wait and see's no fuckin' good!" Kieran snapped, the stress and the lack of sleep, at last, getting to him. "This is supposed to be a fuckin' hospital! You're supposed to be fuckin doctors! Why can't you DO something?"

Jason put his arm around Kieran's shoulders and guided him back to the chair.

"This isn't going to help Kieran." He said, "They're doing their best."
"Well, their best isn't fuckin' good enough!"

Kieran threw himself down into the chair and rested his forehead on the palm of his hand. The headache he had suffered from, over the last two days was back with a vengeance.

It was Paul who came over and calmed his brother, crouching down beside him, his hand resting on Kieran's knee.

"Look, you're just about all in Kieran, why don't you try to get some sleep, you too Jason; let me sit with Bran for a while, if there's so much as a flicker, I'll come and wake you, I promise."

Kieran started to object, but it was Jason who persuaded him to take Paul's advice.

"He's right Kieran, I can't go on much longer without sleep, and I think you've had less sleep than I have; Paul can sit with Bran for a couple of hours."

Kieran nodded somewhat reluctantly and yawned, the idea of sleep suddenly seemed very, very welcome.

"OK," he yawned again. "Just for a couple of hours." He leant back in the chair and put his head in the corner, resting it on the soft padded wings. He was asleep before Paul had walked out of the room. Jason settled into a comfortable armchair and closed his eyes. Images of Bran floated across his mind's eye, Bran laughing at some silly joke Jason had heard at the Uni. Bran, waving from the window of his beloved Audi as he drove out of the car park at Anncolm Heights. Bran leaning over him in the bed they shared, his brown eyes dark with desire. Bran, lying in a hospital bed connected to machines that were keeping him alive. Bran with tubes in his mouth and needles in his hands!

Jason's eyes flew open; his heart was pounding, and his skin felt clammy. He looked across at Kieran; he was still sleeping. Jason shook his head sadly, he had always hoped that Bran would re-establish contact with his brothers, but not like this! He looked round at the dreary relatives' room, at the other people who sat waiting for news of the loved ones who hovered between life and death. 'Please, God' he thought, 'not like this'!

"It's not been easy for Danny, living in Belfast, growing up in a very Catholic community; being away from his family at University; working in the construction industry. One of the hardest and bravest things he has ever done was to tell Pauline and I that he was homosexual."

Sean noticed how Pat winced when he said the word.

"Oh, believe me, Pat, I wasn't over the moon when I found out, what father would be?" Sean continued. "But I loved my boy, and if he could only be happy with a partner who was the same sex as him; well then I would bloody well have to get used to it!"

Pat looked up at Sean as though he was seeing him for the first time.

"Does it not make you sick, you know, what they do?"

"Oh, for God's sake, Pat!" Sean said exasperated. "What do you think they do? Have sex on the dining room carpet while we're having Sunday lunch? Kiss and cuddle in the middle of the board meetings? Danny and Michael are very professional. Their private life is just that – Private. A few people know that Danny's gay and in the past some of them have given him a real hard time, but he's got where he is despite that and I'm proud of my boy Pat. Proud that I have a son who was prepared to stand up for who he is and the way of life he believes in; and Michael is an asset to the company, he's clever; quick-witted and an excellent P.R. man and as Pauline has often said. It's like having another son."

Sean watched Pat carefully, wondering if he was taking in what he was saying and wondering if he was making comparisons between Danny's life and Bran's life.

Pat was silent, his face unfathomable.

"When Cathleen was taken from you," Sean said softly, "a very special part of your life was destroyed, I understand that but then you put the blame, quite wrongly, on a fifteen-year-old's shoulders and you've been punishing him all his life; and now you've found something else to punish him for, his sexuality, so you threw him out, destroyed another big part of your life." Sean took out his mobile phone and after tapping in the number for the taxi office, spoke briefly into it.

"There will be a car here in half an hour to take us down to Birmingham." He said. "Kieran and Paul are down there on their own, not knowing if their brother is going to live or die; are you going to throw away the last piece of the life that you and Cathleen made together. You can't get Cathleen back and if you desert your boys now you'll lose them as well; the only piece of that life you will have left will be this!" and he put the empty whisky bottle down on the coffee table in front of Pat.

"Make your mind up Pat; what's it going to be?"

Pat O'Donnell said nothing; he just sat staring at the empty whisky bottle. Sean sighed and shrugged his shoulders and headed for the kitchen, he desperately needed a coffee and Pat needed some time to think. He looked at his watch; he had half an hour before the taxi arrived.

Sean sat in the cold kitchen drinking coffee, he glanced at his watch, twenty minutes had passed and he had heard no sound from Pat.

He was just about to go through to the study when the kitchen door opened, and Pat O'Donnell walked in. he had changed his clothes and was clean-shaven.

"Is there another one of those going begging?" He asked, pointing at the coffee cup.

Sean nodded.

"Just time for a coffee before the taxi arrives," he smiled. He quickly made a strong mug of coffee and put it on the table in front of Pat.

Pat looked up at his old friend.

"Thanks, Sean," he said. "Thanks for everything!"

Pat O'Donnell had plenty of time to think as he sat in the back of the taxi that was speeding down the M6 towards Birmingham. He spoke very little, and Sean thankfully was silent as well. As Pat sat with his eyes closed, listening to the hum of rubber on tarmac, his mind drifted back to the times just after the bombing, when the pain of Cathleen's loss had been at its sharpest. Odd incidents replayed themselves in his mind. He remembered how he had torn down all the Christmas decorations Cathleen had hung so lovingly around the house and on the Christmas tree. How he had taken his belt to Bran when he had caught him rescuing some from the rubbish bin to hide in his room, some of the tree ornaments that had been his mothers' favourites.

He had taken his belt to Bran the day Paul had let it slip that Bran had not gone to Sunday school, but had waited for his brothers at the church gates.

He remembered coming home to find him trying to cook a meal for his younger brothers. He had thrown the food across the table at Bran; the words he had shouted echoed in his mind now. "What's this shit? – Yer fuckin useless!"

Fuckin' useless! How many times since then had he accused Bran of being fuckin' useless?

The enormity of the hurt and distress he must have caused over the years was only vaguely beginning to sink in, and he was still doing it, he remembered backhanding Bran when the police sergeant had called because Bran had apparently been seen driving recklessly one morning. Even then, Pat had known that Bran was covering for someone, because the registration number of the car seen speeding in the early hours, was not that of the Carlton that Bran had been working on all night, fitting a new water pump. Pat had known that; but as always, Bran had been the easy target, he had given Pat another excuse to punish him.

He would make it up to him. Somehow, he would find a way to say he was sorry to the son he had all but destroyed!

Sean had given him this second chance; a chance to be the father Cathleen would have wanted him to be. He wasn't going to throw this last chance away, and he began to pray earnestly that fate wouldn't snatch Bran away from him before he could tell his son that he was sorry.

34

Kieran was vaguely aware that someone was shaking him. It had seemed like only seconds had passed since he had closed his eyes and already someone was trying to wake him!

"In a minute Paul," he said as he shrugged off the insistent hand.

"Kieran? Kieran!" the voice was as insistent as the shaking.

As Kieran surfaced slowly from the deep sleep he had been in, he began to realise that it wasn't Paul who was shaking him.

"What?" He croaked as he tried to focus on the person who was standing over him.

"Kieran, it's Sean; Sean Driscoll."

"Who?" Kieran asked, vaguely aware that he was being spoken too.

"It's Sean Kieran; I've come down with your Dad."

Kieran looked round, still groggy from sleep.

"Sean?" He shook his head, trying to clear the fog from his mind. He licked his lips; they were dry and his mouth felt like the bottom of a parrots' cage. He desperately needed a drink.

"Kieran!" he recognised Paul's voice. "Kieran wake up! Sean's here!"

"What?" Kieran stretched and looked up at the man who stood in front of him. "What the fuck are you doing here Sean?" he asked when he finally realised who had been shaking him. Then he noticed that Paul was there as well.

"I thought you were sitting with Bran?" he said suddenly worried, "How long have I been asleep? What's happened?"

"Its OK Kieran, Jason is with Bran; Sean has brought Dad down."
Kieran looked round, rubbing his chin, the heavy stubble felt rough and itchy.

"Managed to pry the bastard loose from his whiskey bottle?"

"Your Dad's waiting in the car, Kieran," Sean said sitting down next to his Godson, "I wanted to have a talk to you before he came in."

"What is there to talk about Sean?" Kieran asked, the anger rising again. "He's made it quite clear how he feels about Bran; he's not needed here;"

"Give him a chance Kieran, I think you might find he's changed."
"Give him a friggin' chance!" Kieran said angrily. "What sort of a friggin' chance did he give Bran!"

"Kieran," Paul pleaded. "If there's the slightest chance of getting the family back together again, I know Bran would want you to take it!"

Before Kieran could answer, Jason and the neurologist accompanied by the consultant walked into the waiting room, Kieran got to his feet and hurried to meet them,

Jason looked worried and the doctors were subdued.

"What's wrong?" Why aren't you with Bran?" He asked.

Jason looked across to the neurologist, waiting for him to explain to Kieran the worries that they had regarding Bran's condition.

The doctor looked over to Sean.

"Are you Bran's father?" he asked. Sean shook his head.

"I'm his Godfather?" He offered. The neurologist smiled and turned back to Kieran.

"We are worried that your brother may be slipping into what we call a vegetative state. I don't want you to worry unduly," he said when he saw the looks of horror on their faces. "What that means is that although we have stopped the drugs that were keeping Bran unconscious, he's still unresponsive and showing no signs of regaining consciousness. We had hoped, that once the drugs had cleared from his system we would see a pretty quick improvement to his levels of response to stimuli; so far we haven't had much success."

"What can we do to help," Sean asked. "If there's anything we can help you with; anything you need, just let me know."

"Everything possible is being done, mister..?"

"Driscoll," Sean said. "I'm Kieran's future father-in-law."

"Well Mister Driscoll, and the rest of the family," the doctor said, turning to Kieran and Paul, "the best thing you can do now is keep talking to him, often patients at this level of consciousness respond more to familiar voices, familiar smells. The thing is, the longer he stays in a coma; the more likely he is to have suffered some form of permanent damage or to remain long term in what we call a persistent vegetative state."

"What sort of response should we be looking for?" Sean asked.

"Coma patients quite often just open their eyes, or you might see a slight movement of the head or hands. Anything that would show some indication that you are getting through to him would be good; just don't give up." The doctor said. "There's still hope!"

The two doctors moved away to talk to the relatives and friends of other patients.

Kieran turned towards the door through to the intensive care unit. Sean stopped him briefly, his hand on his arm.

"I'm going to go and bring your Dad up."

Kieran turned and looked at Sean.

"Whatever." He said, "Just don't expect me to be enthusiastic about it."

"Just give him a chance Kieran."

Kieran didn't answer; he just walked through to the I.C.U. where he sat down, once again beside his brother.

"Come on Bran," he said quietly, "stop pissin' about and come back to us!"

35

"I don't think I can do this. I don't think I can face them, Sean." Pat stood next to the taxi and gazed at the huge sprawling hospital that lay before them. It was just going dark and the lights of the massive main building shone out, illuminating the surrounding area. Somewhere in there lay his son, the son that he had tried to deny and the two sons he had pushed away when they had come to him for help.

"You've come this far, Pat," Sean said softly.

"Do they know I'm here?" Pat asked.

"All three of them are waiting for you."

"Three?" Pat asked, suddenly confused. "Does Bran know? Is he awake?"

Sean shook his head; of course, Pat would think only Kieran and Paul were here with Bran.

"Bran's still unconscious, Pat," Sean said. He wondered how Pat would receive the news that his son's lover was at the bedside. "Bran's partner Jason is here as well."

Pat shook his head. "I can't do this, Sean; the things I've said to them, done to them…"

"Can't be undone, Pat," Sean said quietly. "But they can be forgiven if you just give them the chance." He turned to the taxi driver and slipped him a twenty tip. "Put the fare on the Driscoll account will you and tell Jean I'll be in touch." He handed the driver a leaflet. "Tell her that's the hotel we'll be staying at." Sean nodded his head towards the exit. "Go." He said quietly; wanting Pat's easy escape route back to Liverpool removed from his path. The driver understood perfectly and with a short nod of his head, he pulled smoothly away and headed back towards the motorway and home.

Pat O'Donnell looked and felt small and lost as he walked through the big entrance doors that led to the hospital reception. They walked down the long corridors, all the time, following the directions that pointed towards the Intensive Care Unit. Neither man spoke, both were lost deep in their own thoughts. At the door to the relatives' waiting room, Sean paused.

"Are you OK Pat?" He asked.

Pat looked at his old friend, probably the only real friend he had.

"Jesus. If I ever needed a drink." He smiled ruefully, "to be sure the time's now!

Sean held the door open and Pat O'Donnell walked through into the quiet family room.

"Dad!" Paul was the first to spot Pat. He left the young man he had been talking to and walked over to meet his father. "I knew you'd come. I knew you wouldn't let Bran down!"

Pat placed a shaky hand on Paul's shoulder.

"I was wrong Paul." He said, his voice full of emotion. "I've been wrong about a lot of things." He looked round the room; there was no sign of Kieran.

"Where's your brother?" He asked.

"He's sitting with Bran."

Pat nodded slowly and then he spotted the man Paul had been talking to. He was a tall, good looking young man; his long blonde hair fell in an untidy mop across his shoulders, his looks were marred by the huge black circles beneath his eyes and the haggard look on his face. He obviously hadn't slept well in days.

"You must be Bran's boyfriend?"

Jason stiffened slightly and said guardedly "I prefer 'partner' rather than boyfriend Mister O'Donnell."

Pat sighed and took a step towards Jason. Jason tensed, not sure what to expect from Bran's homophobic father.

Pat looked at Jason.

"I don't agree with what you are, or what you do," he said. "I never will do!" Pat was very aware that his son Paul was watching him in amazement. "But I had no right to treat you and Bran like I did." He stretched his hand out towards Jason, "but I hope I'm man enough to admit that I was wrong; I owe you an apology son," He said. "I owe you both an apology!"

Jason looked at the outstretched hand for a moment, and then with a tentative smile, he placed his hand in the hand that had been offered to him. The handshake was firm and honest. And Jason noted that when Pat let go of his hand, he didn't wipe it on his clothes like so many men did after touching 'a gay'.

"Can I see Bran now?" Pat asked Sean, suddenly afraid of what he would find."

"Jason, why don't you take Bran's Dad through to the I.C.U. I bet Kieran is ready for a break now, and Paul," Sean said noticing how Paul got up to follow them. "I'm desperate for a coffee, if you don't mind?"

Like everyone else who came and went from this high dependency ward, Pat carefully washed his hands in the special area beside the door.

As he walked into the intensive care unit, the first thing he noticed was just how busy it was, with nurses hurrying up and down the unit managing the individual stations for which they were responsible. Jason led the way to station seven. Kieran sat by Bran's bed, his back was to them but Pat could see that he was talking to his brother, even though Bran was unconscious. Jason put his hand on Kieran's shoulder. Kieran turned round and smiled at Jason; then he saw Pat standing behind him.

"What the hell are you doing here?" he swore, standing up to face his father, automatically placing himself between his brother and the man who had said that he wanted to see him rot in hell!

"You're a bit late, Dad!" Kieran spat the word out. "Bran's off life support now so there's no effin' plugs for you to pull!"

"Kieran don't," Jason began.

"It's alright, son." Pat said quietly, "I deserved that, and more, I'll never be able to make up for the things I've done to Bran in the past." He turned to Kieran. "The things I've done to this family." He looked past Kieran to his eldest son, who lay so motionless, so vulnerable. "I want to be here Kieran; I don't expect you to forgive me, but I want to help if I can."

The young doctor who had been managing Bran's case sat on the squeaky coffee table.

"To be quite honest," he said, "we expected some form of response long before now; all we can do is keep up the constant stimulation; That is where you all come in, talk to him; ask him questions, remind him of things that happened in the past, something might just get through and trigger off that first response, that first step. Once he decides to climb out of that dark place he is in, we can help him; but he has to make the first move."

Sean looked at the other four men who sat hanging on the doctors every word.

"We'll do everything we can doctor, and thanks."

The doctor got up to leave, "I'll check back in a couple of hours." He said.

Kieran bought himself a cup of coffee and sat down for a while to talk to Sean. He still found it difficult to speak to his father.

"Come on." Jason said to Pat as he sensed the awkward atmosphere between father and son, let's go and sit with Bran."

Pat sat opposite Jason at bed seven; he watched and listened to the man who was his son's lover, talking to Bran, reminding him of times they had shared, asking him to wake up, talking to him about the home they had built together and how it was empty without him.

Kieran joined them a little later; he talked about the taxi business and told his brother about Lisa and how he would have to get better because he was going to be Kieran's best man at the wedding.

All the time, Pat had been watching and listening and when Kieran left, finally exhausted from the constant, one-sided conversation. He turned to Jason.

"Would you mind leaving us alone for a few minutes?" He asked.

Jason looked puzzled but nodded and slowly got to his feet. "I could do with a coffee," he admitted.

Pat watched him walk out of the I.C.U. and turned to look at the son who still lay unmoving in the hospital bed. Bran had never listened to quiet, sensible conversations; since his mother died, he had heard nothing but harsh words and scathing comments. He was not familiar with polite requests and Pat knew that the gentle tones of Jason and Kieran would mean nothing to Bran.

Pat O'Donnell leaned over his son, his mouth close to Bran's ear.

"Bran O'Donnell! You open yer fuckin' eyes NOW!" he snarled. "Open yer fuckin' eyes or so help me I'll take the skin off yer back wi' mi' belt!" Pat watched his son closely. The sentiments' he had used so often in the past, now sounded so hateful, so cruel, but he was desperate to see some flicker of recognition, some spark of hope. Staff nurse Owen hurried across to station seven, horrified to hear such a tirade of hate and abuse thrown at one of her patients.

"Yer fuckin' useless you idle little shit, get off yer fuckin' arse for once!"

"Mister O'Donnell. Please!" Gwen objected. "Please control yourself or I'll have security escort you out!"

Pat realised for the first time, just how brutal the words that he had used so often in the past, really were and he hated himself, hated himself for once more lashing out at the son who had done nothing to deserve the hard life his father had imposed on him.

Pat looked at the nurse, his face stricken with remorse.

"God help me, nurse," he whispered. "It's all he's ever known since his mother died. It's the only thing he'll understand."

Staff nurse Gwen Owen stepped back, her eyes wide. Her hand flew to her mouth as she suddenly realised what Pat O'Donnell was trying to do. She nodded silently and Pat turned back to his son.

"Bran O'Donnell! You fuckin' stupid twat! You're good for nothing!" Pat shouted. "Open your fuckin eyes or I'll make you wish you'd never been fuckin' born!"

The long dark eyelashes flickered for a moment; and slowly, Bran opened his eyes.

"Pat?" he said, his voice was strange; no more than a whisper, those gentle brown eyes, so familiar to Pat, fought to focus on the source of the voice he had heard. "I didn't want to leave; it happened so quickly; I didn't get chance to say goodbye."
Pat sat down heavily on the chair, his eyes fixed on Bran's face, his thumping heart, a hundred miles away in a little house on a quiet Belfast street.

"Cathleen?" he whispered. He felt as though all the air had suddenly been sucked from his lungs.

"Dad?" Bran's voice, sounding so far away, was no more than a sigh as recognition came slowly to his mind. Staff nurse Owen hurried back to the bedside; she had seen Bran respond to his fathers' vicious words and had immediately paged the neurologist.

"The doctors on his way Mister O'Donnell, I will have to ask you to leave for a little while, the doctor will want to run some tests." She hurried around, checking monitors and ensuring all the lines and catheters and drains were in place.

"Just give me a minute nurse." Pat pleaded.

Gwen paused, she looked at the older man and recognised his need to make peace with the son he had almost lost.

"Just till the doctor arrives Mister O'Donnell." She relented, and she walked away, leaving the father alone with his son.

Pat sat down next to Bran and brushed away from his son's face, the wisp of dark hair that had escaped the dressings. The soft brown eyes looked vaguely at his father, unable yet to grasp where he was or what had happened.

Pat held his hand, rubbing it gently. Words seemed unimportant as the tears ran down his weather-beaten face.

"It wasn't your fault Bran," he whispered, "It wasn't your fault. God knows how you've put up with this shit for so many years. I was wrong, I was wrong about everything; will you forgive me?"

He felt the pressure of Bran's fingers as they gently squeezed his hand.

Pat could see the doctor hurrying towards the bed.

"Your mother's been with you Bran, she's been here in the hospital, all the time, keeping you safe; she's still with you son, protecting you like she always did."

Staff nurse Owen pulled the screens around station seven.

"Mister O'Donnell, please," she said.

Pat nodded; he bent down and kissed Bran lightly on the forehead, just as Cathleen had done a thousand times.

"We love you son." He whispered.

36

Six months later, Sean Driscoll escorted his daughter through the beautiful rooms of Belfast Castle to where Kieran O'Donnell waited to take her as his wife.

Bran O'Donnell, almost fully recovered from his near-fatal accident, leaned heavily on the stick he still needed to walk and chatted nervously to his partner Jason as he went over his best mans' speech yet again, and once more checked that the two rings were still in his top pocket.

It had been touch and go as to whether Bran would be available to act as his brothers best man, as soon as he was out of hospital the West Midlands Police had questioned him extensively, He had been as co-operative as he could be; even handing over his mobile phone for their examination. Eventually, the police decided that Bran knew no more than any of the other gullible drivers who had been conned into transporting stolen goods for what was obviously a very well organised criminal gang.

D.C. Dave Williams had left his contact details with Bran,

"If anything else turns up," he said finally, "you can get me on that number."

Bran had been relieved that no charges had been brought against him; just a few sarcastic comments about his idea of gainful employment. But that was in the past, now all Bran had to worry about was getting the speech right!

The orchestra, arranged on the balcony above the huge room, began to play as Lisa and her father made their entrance.

Later, as the afternoon sun shone across the vast gardens,

casting long shadows of the beautiful old castle grounds, Lisa O'Donnell posed for the photographs that would become the beautiful memories of a wonderful day, and amongst them would be her favourite, sitting on an old garden swing surrounded by the men in her life.

Sean Pat, Kieran and Paul. And standing beside them, Bran and Danny and their partners Michael and Jason.

Bran looked at Jason and smiled, he reached for his hand and gently squeezed it.

"It wasn't an easy journey Jay." He said. "But we made it, we got there in the end."

Jason looked across at the man who was everything to him and grinned wickedly, his blue eyes sparkling.

"The journey has only just begun, Bran. It's only just begun!"

THE END

Available worldwide from Amazon

---

http://mtp. Agency

http://facebook. com/mtp. Agency

@mtp_agency

45832553R00207

Printed in Poland
by Amazon Fulfillment
Poland Sp. z o.o., Wrocław